Things Can Only Get Better

Withdrawn from Stock
Dublin City Public Libraries

David M Barnett is an author and journalist based in West Yorkshire. After many years working for regional newspapers in the north he embarked on a freelance career and now writes features for most of the UK national press. He is the author, for Trapeze, of Calling Major Tom and The Growing Pains of Jennifer Ebert. He also writes comic books, including Punks Not Dead and Eve Stranger, for the US publisher IDW. David was born in Wigan, Lancashire and is married to Claire, also a journalist. They have two children, Charlie and Alice.

By David M Barnett

The Growing Pains of Jennifer Ebert, Aged 19 Going on 91
Calling Major Tom
Hinterland
Angelglass
The Janus House and Other Two-Faced Tales
popCULT!
Gideon Smith and the Mechanical Girl
Gideon Smith and the Brass Dragon
Gideon Smith and the Mask of the Ripper

Life has one last surprise for him

Things Can Only Get Better

Leabharlanna Poiblí Chathair Baile Átha Cliath
Dublin City Public Libraries

DAVID M. BARNETT

First published in Great Britain in 2019 by Trapeze
an imprint of The Orion Publishing Group Ltd
Carmelite House, 50 Victoria Embankment
London EC4Y 0DZ

An Hachette UK company

1 3 5 7 9 10 8 6 4 2

Copyright © David M. Barnett 2019

The moral right of David M. Barnett to be identified as
the author of this work has been asserted in accordance with
the Copyright, Designs and Patents Act of 1988.

All rights reserved. No part of this publication may be
reproduced, stored in a retrieval system, or transmitted
in any form or by any means, electronic, mechanical,
photocopying, recording, or otherwise, without the
prior permission of both the copyright owner and the
above publisher of this book.

All the characters in this book are fictitious, and any resemblance to
actual persons, living or dead, is purely coincidental.

A CIP catalogue record for this book is
available from the British Library.

ISBN (Mass Market Paperback) 978 1 4091 8516 1

Typeset by Born Group

Printed and bound in Great Britain by Clays Ltd, Elcograf S.p.A.

MIX
Paper from
responsible sources
FSC® C104740

www.orionbooks.co.uk

To the mighty Choppersquad – Paul, Tim, John, Brian and Jon.
Love and Happiness, boys.

'If you don't want to be the biggest band in the world,
you may as well pack it in.'
Noel Gallagher

'Loneliness is the ultimate poverty.'
Pauline Phillips

Pembroke Branch Tel. 6689575

I walk along the paths of the graveyard, alone in the darkness. It's been a while since I was last here, but it feels like yesterday. Cemeteries are like little oases of time, unchanging, in deference to those who have been interred there. Only the living, who haunt them regularly on Sundays, birthdays, anniversaries, notice that there's a new headstone, a length of freshly turned earth, another person who has stepped outside the passage of time and lain down to rest at last.

It's cold, but clear, the snows of earlier in the month all but thawed. Sounds seem distant and to belong to a different world; the whisper of traffic on a bypass, the gentle chugging of locomotive engines at the rail sheds, the insistent, high-pitched yap of a dog. The gravel crunches under my boots as my feet take me along paths lit by a moon that's full and round and which casts the sharp shadow of the old chapel across the silent graves.

I find the grave easily enough, without even looking for it. I know where it is. I stand for a long moment, looking at the headstone, reading the name, the dates. Then I crouch down and lay my wrapped flowers on the hard earth.

Moonflowers. Ipomoea alba to give them their proper name. They only bloom at night.

I squat until my legs start to go numb and I straighten up, ready to leave. Then I hear it, the scuff of boots on the path behind me. Not as alone in the darkness as I imagined, then. As I hoped.

'Gotcha,' says a voice.

December is no time to be old and alone, and Arthur Calderbank feels the weight of both most keenly in the dying of the year.

The chapel that sits at the centre of the graveyard has been subdivided by stud walls to provide Arthur with a bedroom and a living area. There was already a small kitchen and a washroom, which have been complemented with the addition of a microwave and a shower cubicle. Arthur did all the work himself. Always been good with his hands. It is spartan, and bare, and as far as it is possible to be in terms of comfort and cosiness from the house he shared with Molly for all those happy years. But it is, for better or worse, home. After a fashion.

Some of the old pews Arthur has arranged as storage or seating around the edges of his living space; he's made a serviceable table from the timber of three of them, with more pews along either side. The rest he's broken up and keeps in a woodstore he's built at the back of the chapel. He has electricity, but no gas, and warms the place with a wood-burning stove on which he sometimes also cooks. This morning he has a pot of porridge on the go. Through the tall windows he can see that the cemetery is carpeted in snow, luminous in the moonlight. Definitely a porridge morning. He sits by the stove, rubbing feeling into his hands. They've been muttering that he's getting too old for this, that he should be somewhere warmer, safer. And it's true, he does feel the cold more now. It takes him longer to get moving in the mornings, especially mornings like this. But while he's no spring chicken – he'll be seventy-two next birthday – neither is he ready for the knacker's yard just yet.

Giving the porridge a stir, Arthur stretches his legs and pads across the wooden floorboards, unsure if the creaking is the old timbers or his old joints. His calendar hangs from a nail by the bookshelf (made, of course, from another old pew). December the fifth already. He takes up the felt-tip pen from the bookshelf and puts a firm cross through the number 4. He never strikes out a day until he's woken up on the next one. Bit of a superstition, he supposes. Tempting fate. Strike out a day too early, and maybe you're saying your time is up, maybe you're saying *take me now*. Arthur shakes his head. Silly old sod. He never used to be superstitious, never had the time. Perhaps he has been living here, on his own, too long.

At the tall windows – the stained-glass originals had long since been broken or stolen and replaced with cheap, plain panes that rattle in the wind – Arthur looks out on the snow-covered graveyard which spreads out all around the chapel. The headstones are frosted like ornaments on a cake. He glances over his shoulder at the calendar, at the thick, felt-tip ring around the number 23. Old, he thinks, turning back to the window, there's no denying that. But never alone.

'Filthy morning, Fred,' says Arthur. He looks to the sky, and tuts. 'Don't think this snow's going to let up all day. Might be in for the week, according to Michael Fish. Then again, he told us we weren't going to have that hurricane about ten years back, and you remember how that turned out.'

With his gloved hand, Arthur absently clears the crisp snow from the top of the nearest headstone, then laughs. 'What am I talking about, Fred? You'd been in your grave for five years when that hurricane happened.'

Arthur moves along the ranks of graves, wiping snow from the stones, though there's not much point. Thick flakes dance from the grey sky, filling his footprints and piling up on the headstones again. He rights a metal pot filled with the desiccated husks of chrysanthemums at Mabel Shepherd's grave, and frowns at Don Gaskell's marble headstone, which is leaning at an angle. Arthur pushes the stone lightly and it moves another inch. That'll need resetting. He should probably call the council, but it'll be quicker to just do it himself. He'll have to wait until the ground's not so frozen, though.

Near the back wall of the cemetery, which borders the site of the old pit where he used to work what feels like a lifetime ago, Arthur sets to at a mass of dead brambles with his big secateurs, piling the thorny twigs up against the black stone. Not many folk come down to this bit of the cemetery these days, but that doesn't mean he has to let standards slip. Some of the headstones are so old that the names and dates on them have faded into indecipherable hieroglyphics. A little further down, towards the corner of the wall, there are a jumble of proper old mausoleums and walled graves, which no one ever visits at all. When he's cleared as much of the brambles back as he thinks makes the place look respectable, Arthur ties the cut pieces with twine, and wraps them in a length of hessian sack. He'll dry those out and burn them on his stove.

He pauses at the grave of Noah Jones. First resident of the cemetery, buried the day it opened on August 17, 1803. Son of one of the town's biggest cotton merchants, died of tuberculosis when he was nine. What must it have been like for his parents to lose a kiddie, Arthur wonders? What must it have been like to have children in the first place?

'Bet you loved the snow, didn't you, Noah?' murmurs Arthur. 'Bet your dad bought you a sledge, with polished runners. I bet it flew, didn't it, Noah? Bet you screamed when you went down the hills, half in terror, half in laughter.'

Nine. No age to go. But not uncommon back then, even if you had money like Noah's family. Somebody once asked Arthur if it was scary living in a cemetery, if he was worried about ghosts. Not superstitious, not Arthur Calderbank. Didn't believe in tattered shrouds and rattling chains. But he did sometimes wonder . . . what if there *were* ghosts? He thinks what it would have been like for little Noah, first person buried in the cemetery, wondering where he was and where everyone else had gone. Now, he ponders what it must be like, if they all stretch and yawn and get out of their graves just as Arthur stretches and yawns and climbs into his bed. He pictures

Don Gaskell telling Noah off for running around, Mabel Shepherd telling Gaskell not to be a nowty old sod, and Fred Ormerod asking Mabel if she'd like a dance around the mausoleums.

'Silly old bugger,' says Arthur to himself, shaking his head. The dead don't get up, and dance and scold each other. If only they would.

Before heading back into the chapel, Arthur stops at Molly's grave for the first time that day. It won't be the last time. He wipes the snow from her stone and with his gloved finger pushes the crystals of ice from the indentations of her carved name.

'Nearly Christmas, love,' he says softly. 'Nearly your birthday.'

Arthur takes a handful of the green glass chips that cover Molly's grave and squeezes the snow from them. 'Just been clearing some of the brambles back from the old bit,' he says, conversationally. 'I know nobody goes down there any more, but they've got vicious spikes on them. Could hurt a kiddie, if one wandered over.' Letting the glass chips fall from his hand, Arthur takes a rag from his coat pocket and starts to give Molly's stone a proper wipe down. 'I'm going to have to look at the wall near the top of Cemetery Road later as well. You know, where that bloody idiot boy racer smashed into it last week. Council's highways mob reckon they've made it safe but I don't like the way the capstones are sitting.' He pauses, imagining what Molly would say. 'Of course I'll be careful,' he says. 'I know I'm not as young as I was, don't worry.'

Arthur runs the cloth across the top of the gravestone again, but he knows he's fighting a losing battle against the snowfall. It feels like only five minutes since he had his porridge but his stomach's rumbling again. 'I'll look at it after my dinner. What do you think I should have? Got a bit of that ham left. Could make a sandwich.'

He knows what Molly would say. You need something warm inside you, day like this. Not a butty. 'I suppose you're right. Again. You're always right, love. But what, though?'

'How about a pie?'

'Jesus Christ!' yells Arthur, spinning around. It's that lad, the thin one with the big glasses and curly hair. Timmy Leigh. He's standing there, holding something wrapped in a carrier bag out in front of him, his eyes wide at Arthur's outburst. He takes a step back.

Arthur clutches his chest. 'Christ, lad, you nearly gave me a heart attack, creeping up on me like that.'

Timmy's Adam's apple bobs and his lips wobble. 'My mum sent me with a pie.'

Always sending stuff, was Carol Leigh. Cakes. Gloves. Books. Sent him a CD once: Glen Campbell's greatest hits. Arthur didn't know what to do with it. He didn't have a CD player and had never liked Glen Campbell. He ended up using it as a coaster.

A pie, though, that's a different matter. Arthur takes the warm plate wrapped in a tea towel out of the carrier bag and sniffs at it. His stomach rumbles more loudly. 'Tell your mum thanks, and I'll send the plate back,' says Arthur.

'She said you can keep it,' says Timmy. 'And the tea towel.' The boy blinks owlishly at him and then says, 'It's from Pwllheli.'

'The pie?' frowns Arthur. Wales was a long way to go for a pie.

'The tea towel,' says Timmy. He stares at his feet then says. 'I have to go.'

'Shouldn't you be at school?' says Arthur, suddenly realising the time.

'I've got a bug,' says Timmy. He winds his scarf – Arthur recognises it as his mother's handiwork – tighter around his neck, smiles wanly, and turns to lope with his ungainly stride back along the paths towards the big wrought-iron gates at the cemetery entrance.

Arthur wraps the tea towel tighter around the plate and has one more wipe of the snow from Molly's headstone. 'Pie it is, then,' he says to her, then heads back to the chapel. He'll do the wall in the afternoon, clear some of the paths of the worst of the snow, then think about his tea. Maybe the pie will do for both. Then a bit of radio, and bed, and another early start. He wonders what tomorrow will bring. He hopes it's another pie.

Arthur turns and inspects the graveyard. Or maybe it'll bring something else. Maybe not tomorrow, but soon. He's out there, somewhere, Arthur knows. Maybe not in the graveyard, maybe not just yet. But he's on his way. He's getting closer. Every year he's been. Every year, on Molly's birthday, 23 December. Every year since she died. Arthur doesn't know who he is, he doesn't know how he does it without being seen, and he doesn't know why he does it in the first place. All he knows is one thing.

This is the year he's going to catch the bugger.

2

Nicola has three papers to deliver on Cemetery Road. Her last three. She pauses at the top of the avenue, one foot on the pavement an inch-deep in fresh snow, her other resting on the pedal of her dad's old racer. Come on, she thinks. No time to dawdle. Need to be home before mum's awake.

Nicola hates Cemetery Road, especially on mornings like this. Her breath fogs in the still air, her fingers cold even inside her knitted gloves. Her glasses steam up. There are no lights on in the terraced houses that stretch down all along the left-hand side, dark windows looking blankly over the road and the soot-blackened stone wall of the graveyard that gives the street its name.

She glances over to where the three-quarters-full moon illuminates the cemetery, reflected by untouched, virgin snow that makes the gravel paths indistinguishable from the ordered lawns and carefully-ranked graves. White ribbons cap the headstones and the perimeter wall, and snow lies evenly on the sloping slate roof of the old chapel that crouches blackly at the centre of the graveyard. There is a light on in the old chapel.

There is always a light on in the old chapel.

Nicola tugs off her glove with her teeth and pulls back the sleeve of her coat, exposing her watch. She pushes at the button that casts a pale, weak light over the digital display. Seven-twenty-eight. She is a bit behind schedule, because the snow has made for slow going on her route. But three more papers and she can be home in twenty minutes, enough time for a bowl of Ready Brek and to get into her school uniform, get her sandwich out of the fridge and find her books, and be out of the house before her mum . . . well. Before her mum no doubt has one of her *mornings*, which will turn into one of her *days*. It'll all be there waiting for Nicola when she gets home, but she'd rather face it at the end of the day than before school.

Nicola digs into the Day-Glo yellow vinyl bag slung over her shoulder, her fingers finding the *Guardian*. On summer days, if she gets up early enough, she sometimes does her round on foot so she can read the papers before she pushes them through people's letter boxes. There never seems to be the same urgency to get home quickly in summer. Mum's never as bad when the sun's shining. It's the dark mornings when she's worst.

Nicola likes the *Guardian* best, she thinks. One time, Cliff in the paper shop had put an extra one in by mistake and Nicola had taken it home rather than going back to the shop with it. She'd read it all, the news, the features, the business pages. Some of it was a lot funnier than she'd thought it would be. It was a bit harder to understand than the *Sun* or the *Star*, but Nicola sometimes looks at them too before she posts them through. Not always for the articles. She sometimes looks critically for a long time at Page Three, at the beaming smiles but slightly empty, vacant eyes of the models, pushing their bare breasts forward. Sometimes she will try to stand like they do, chests thrust out, lips pouting. It is uncomfortable. Mostly it is uncomfortable being a girl full stop, thinks Nicola.

The *Guardian* is for number five. All the houses on Cemetery Road have small gardens at the front, and number five's is always choked with weeds, which even now poke up defiantly through the snow. The curtains are always closed, even in summer, and in the bottom left corner of the window is a sun-faded *Coal Not Dole* sticker. The letter box is loose and flaps about on windy days. Nicola glances at the front page – something about the new Labour leader, Tony Blair – then folds the newspaper twice and pushes it through the flap, listening to it slap on the mat.

The next delivery is for number nineteen, halfway down. Nicola coasts along the pavement on her bike, her thin tyres leaving a narrow groove in the snow. Propping her bike against the garden wall, she fiddles with the catch on the gate, which is always tight and freezes up in low temperatures, every time. Number nineteen takes the *Sun*. It has the same picture of Tony Blair on the front, but a story that seems to be the exact opposite of the one in the *Guardian*. Nicola can't be bothered turning the pages with her frozen fingers just to look at Page Three, so rolls up the paper and eases it through the letter box. This is a vertical one, which she has an inexplicable hatred of. There is no real reason they should be any different to a horizontal one, but they just are. Nicola can't see why you'd have a vertical letter box instead of a horizontal one. It's just wrong. Number nineteen already has a plastic Christmas wreath hanging from a nail on the door, which makes getting the *Sun* through the stupid letter box even more difficult.

One paper left. She knows without looking it is the *Daily Express*. For number forty-three. Right at the end of the street, the last house on the left. Isn't that a horror video? She's seen it on the racks in Blockbuster. Nicola shivers as she climbs onto her bike, and can't help glancing over towards the cemetery. It looks a bit eerie, the snow almost glowing under the bright moon, the blackened stumps of headstones poking through like breakwaters at the seaside.

Beyond number forty-three is darkness, a bridge over the railway line that leads to an expanse of scrubland and murky ponds, grassed slag heaps chewed up by motorbike scramblers, tangles of high bushes threaded with paths always dotted with dog muck. The site of the old colliery, filled and levelled and landscaped a decade earlier, patiently waiting for someone to come and build a housing estate or a retail park on it, but the weather-faded advertising hoardings proclaiming its suitability and prime location are all but rotted away.

Far behind her a car gingerly negotiates the slush-covered main road which Cemetery Road opens onto, and the whisper of its tyres, even as it disappears from view, gives her some kind of comfort. It is easy to imagine on these dark midwinter mornings that she is alone in the world, that the ever-present nightmares which undoubtedly haunt her mum right now, have her whimpering in the tangle of her duvet, have somehow come true. That the world has ended.

Nicola rides down to the end of the road, peering into the darkness that looms beyond the bridge. She always thinks there are ghosts in that darkness. Ghosts of the men who'd lost their lives during the frequent pit collapses, those who'd lost their pride when it closed down and took the prospects for work with it. Hurriedly, Nicola lets her racer fall into the snow and bounds up the path, hoping that this morning, this morning, this morning it will be different.

But the door, obviously on the latch, swings open even as she presses the *Express* against the letter box. The woman is there, in her dirty pink dressing gown, rollers in her wispy grey hair, toothlessly chewing her own tongue. Nicola feels her heart sink.

'Come in for a cup of tea,' demands the old woman, squinting at Nicola in the darkness. There is the smell of stale cabbage and a smoking coal fire that lingers around her like a perfume.

'I can't,' says Nicola, thrusting the newspaper into her hands. 'I have to get home for my mum. She's not well. Then I have to go to school.'

'It's Saturday!' says the woman, even as Nicola is backing down the path. 'Come in for a cup of tea. I never see anybody.'

'It's Thursday!' shouts Nicola back, picking up the bike. 'I have to go to school.'

She bumps the racer off the kerb and hurries across the road, to the graveyard wall and the iron gate, rusted open, that sits where the wall turns a sharp ninety degrees, separating the cemetery from the thorny bushes bordering the old colliery. Why does the old woman do that, wait for her every morning? It always throws her, makes her think of what her mum says when she is having her bad days. *You'll be off soon, going to university, meeting a boy, settling down at the other side of the country. I'll be all on my own.* For God's sake, mum, she'll say. I'm only fourteen.

It is only when Nicola squeezes her bike through the old iron gate that she hears the woman's door click shut. She throws her leg with difficulty over the frame, squeezing the brakes tight as she pauses at the top of the slope that leads down to the cemetery and joins the criss-crossing paths that meander between the graves. She doesn't particularly like riding home through the cemetery but it is a full ten minutes quicker than going right back up to the main road and riding through the warren of streets to where she lives, and she's already lost time talking to that daft old bat. At the centre of the sprawling cemetery the chapel sits, the harsh light burning through the tall windows. Old man Calderbank will give her hell for riding her bike through the graveyard if he catches her, and it isn't officially open to the public at this time of day anyway, but Nicola will take the chance. Besides, she finds the light in the chapel comforting, in a way. She knows when she sees it the world hasn't ended while she's been out delivering her papers.

The snow is clean and unsullied in the cemetery, like Antarctica or the surface of the moon, maybe. Nicola's racer tyres cleave slim gullies in the paths, and she freewheels along in a wide arc that takes her away from the chapel, and old Calderbank's watchful eye, and towards the older part of the cemetery, where the headstones are larger and lean against one another. In the far corner the perimeter wall is half falling down, and she can pass her bike over and then it's just a short ride across a patch of common ground to her estate.

Something catches Nicola's eye as she coasts, a sudden movement flitting between the big old gravestones that startles her and causes her to involuntarily squeeze her brakes. Her wheels fail to find purchase in the fresh snow and she feels the bike skid, then list to the side, throwing her off into a drift of white powder.

Nicola rubs at her elbow and goes to retrieve her racer, rear wheel still spinning silently where it has fetched up against a gravestone. She looks around as she rights the bike; it must have been a fox, or even a deer.

As she brushes the snow from the saddle and the gears, something else catches Nicola's eye. A series of indentations in the snow, among the graves. Footprints. She looks back at the thin track her bike has made in the path behind, and then at the jumble of imprints where she's come off. They definitely aren't her footprints. They are large, bigger than her size fives, and clear, the zig-zags of a boot or shoe sole. Their edges are sharp, they have been made recently. Old Calderbank, no doubt, come down from the chapel to give Nicola a ticking off. But the prints come from around the back of one of the old mausoleums, and weave between the headstones. Nicola looks back towards the chapel; the snow is pristine and undisturbed.

Nicola feels a chill, and shivers. It isn't Calderbank, then, unless he's flown over the graveyard from the chapel. She gets back on her bike and wishes now that she'd taken the long way round.

She pushes her sleeve back and tries to angle her watch to catch the moonlight, then jumps, startled, as a black shape rushes by on the periphery of her vision. Suddenly panicked, Nicola pushes off but her foot slips, sending her bike skidding again. She drags the bike up and stamps the pedal forward, the low-slung handlebars coming up to meet her stomach and knocking the wind out of her as the pedals spin wildly. The chain has come off. She is about to abandon the bike there and then, run for the wall, when she hears a scuffling noise behind her.

She turns to see a shape rising up behind her, blocking out the silvery light of the moon. All she can think is *Mum was right. It's not safe for me out here. It's not safe for me anywhere.*

'Don't touch me!' screams Nicola, closing her eyes tight and waiting for whatever is to come.

* 3 *

'Oh, for God's sake, I'm not going to bloody touch you,' says Arthur crossly. He knows you have to be careful when dealing with kids these days. Back when he was a lad you'd routinely get a clip round the ear, or worse, from the local bobby, or the teachers, or a shopkeeper who didn't like the look of you. You couldn't get away with that today. And you had to be especially careful with girls. That lot down at the Black Diamond who sit in the snug, always banging on about asylum seekers and illegal immigrants, they keep a special watch out for kiddie-fiddlers as well. Think they're some kind of avenging army or something. In the summer they'd painted 'peedofile', which even Arthur, with his limited education, knew wasn't right, on the wall of one of the big houses up Springfield Lane. Turned out the place belonged to some poor bloke who was a paediatrician, which was a special doctor for children, at the Albert Edward Infirmary. They are idiots, but dangerous idiots. So, no, Arthur isn't going to lay one finger on this chunky, pasty-faced girl sitting in the snow. But that doesn't mean he's not going to mark her card.

'You shouldn't be in the cemetery before it opens,' says Arthur, pulling his big old donkey jacket tight around him. 'And you shouldn't be riding a bike in the cemetery at all. It's the rules.'

The girl starts to tug at the loose chain with her stubby gloved fingers. Her doughy face is all crinkled up. Arthur realises she's going to start crying.

'See?' he shouts. 'See? This is what happens when children ride their bikes in the cemetery when it's closed. Accidents happen.

15

That's why I live here, you know. To stop trespassers. To stop silly children hurting themselves.'

The girl's bottom lip quivers. 'I have to get home for my mum,' she says, as though that's Arthur's problem. He shakes his head. 'Give it here.' He flips the chain back over the derailleur and lifts up the back wheel, spinning the pedal until it's all fixed. 'Now wheel it to the broken wall and lift it over. And don't ride it in the cemetery again.'

The girl is staring at the old chapel. Arthur says, 'It's a bit big for you anyway, this bike.'

'It was my dad's,' says the girl absently. 'He died when I was a baby.'

Arthur frowns and peers at her. Ah. She's *that* one. The one with the *mother*.

She says, 'Does it have thick walls, your house?'

Arthur raises an eyebrow. 'I suppose it does. Not thick enough to keep the cold out, though.'

The girl nods thoughtfully. 'It would be a good place to be if there's a war.'

'A war with who?' Funny thing for a girl that age to say. There was that trouble in Afghanistan he'd seen on the news, with that bunch, what were they called? The Taliban? And there'd been Bosnia, that finished last year. Used to be Yugoslavia. Led to all them asylum seekers coming over here, according to that mob in the Black Diamond. Or did she mean the IRA, who'd blown up all those folk in Manchester in the summer?

The girl shrugs and takes her bike. 'I don't know. My mum thinks there'll be a war. She read something in the papers about the millennium. All the computers are going to switch themselves off at midnight. We'll be fighting over food and water.'

Arthur has seen the girl's mother. Heard talk about her. Not right in the head. Not surprising, if what he's heard about the father is true. He feels a bit sorry for the girl now. 'Don't ride your bike in the cemetery again,' he says again. 'And don't come in when it's closed.'

The girl starts to wheel her racer off through the snow. He wonders if he should say something else, but decides he'd better leave it. He was never much good at talking to kids. Molly would have known what to say to her. It broke his heart, sometimes, when he saw her fussing over some baby in a pram or some kiddie done up in his finest at a churchwalking day or something. She'd have loved kids.

The girl has gone, swallowed by the shadows, and before Arthur knows it he's standing at Molly's grave. Seventy she'd have been on her birthday, just over two weeks away. They might have had a party or something, if she'd still been here. Maybe gone on holiday, somewhere warm. Though Molly would never have countenanced going away at Christmas. Seven years gone, she's been. And he's felt every day of it, like a burden he has to carry that feels just a little heavier every single morning when he gets up. There's been times, he admits it, that he's gone to bed and wished he wouldn't wake up again. But it's nearly her birthday, and he has to know. He has to know before it's too late. He can't die before he gets the answer.

Stirring his porridge, Arthur bangs on his chest with his fist. God knows what Carol Leigh put in that pie that Timmy brought round yesterday, but it's not half given him a bout of heartburn. Not that he's complaining; Arthur doesn't want folk feeling sorry for him, but he's not above taking a bit of charity. He takes a mouthful of his tea and puts the mug down on the Glen Campbell CD. He splutters; the tea's gone down the wrong way. Covering his mouth as he starts to cough, he turns away from the pot of porridge and casts around for a handkerchief, his hands finding the Pwllheli tea towel the pie came wrapped in, and he hacks violently into it. Grimacing, Arthur balls up the tea towel and tosses it into the flames of the wood burner. Good job she didn't want it back after all.

He's quite gone off the idea of porridge now, and goes for a sit down. His arms and shoulders are aching; probably it's just the cold getting to him, or maybe Molly was right and he shouldn't have tackled that wall down at the end of Cemetery Road. Arthur quietly chides himself. Molly didn't say any such thing. He'll have to be careful he doesn't let people catch him having his one-sided conversations with his dead wife. He doesn't want anybody to think he's doolally. Any excuse to cart him off to a home or something. Hopefully Timmy Leigh won't be telling people Arthur was chatting away to his wife's grave, bold as brass. But Arthur doesn't think he will; he's a good lad, that Timmy Leigh, if a bit of a quiet sort. In fact, Arthur feels a bit sorry for him. He doesn't think the lad has many mates. He coughs again, and remembers Timmy saying he was off school because he had a bug. Arthur hopes he hasn't given it to him.

The snow's not let up at all, but Arthur does his best to shovel it off the paths. He'll have to do it again tomorrow, no doubt, but every little helps, he supposes, even as he watches the gravel rapidly being covered up again. He doesn't have a phone in the chapel but considers whether he should walk down to the parade and use the phone box, ask the council if they'll come and put some grit or salt down. Arthur's not sure he can face the trudge through the snow, just to be told they don't have the resources or staff to do it, so in the afternoon he does his rounds up at the newer end of the cemetery. There's a little corner given over to children, where the mums and dads put teddy bears and dolls and little Lego models. Breaks his heart every time he sees a new one there or, what's worse, a bear or soft toy that's got sodden and rotten in the rain. Strictly speaking, they're not supposed to put these toys and things on the graves, but who'd be the one to take them off, or tell the parents they have to stop? Not Arthur, for sure. He doesn't talk to the kiddies' graves. Not like he talks to the graves in the older bit. There's Noah, of course, but he's different. He died so long ago. These kiddies in these new graves . . . such heartbreakingly short times between them being born and dying. No, he doesn't talk to them. He wouldn't know what to say.

Behind the big tree that hides the main road from the cemetery Arthur finds a clutch of crushed Kestrel lager cans and a few dog ends, and a sodden magazine full of pictures of naked women. Arthur tuts and pulls a crumpled up carrier bag out of his coat pocket, filling it with the detritus. Arthur doesn't class himself as much of a religious person, but he believes in respect. You've got to respect the dead, haven't you? A cemetery's not the sort of place for this behaviour. He knows who it'll be, as well; he's had to tell off a gaggle of lads more than once for hanging around the graveyard after dark.

Arthur dumps the bag in one of the black metal rubbish bins and absently wipes some snow off the nearest headstone. 'You wouldn't have put up with this, would you, Eric?' he says. Eric Batey had been a bobby, a proper, old-fashioned one who knew the value of a clip round the ear for kids, and who got respect for it. He'd died a week after retiring. Arthur couldn't remember when he'd last seen a bobby on the beat. There used to be a police station just along the road, but they'd closed that down years ago.

No, Eric would have sorted that lot out who lurk around the cemetery good and proper. Arthur wouldn't have been hanging about smoking and drinking beer and looking at girly mags at their age. He'd have been working, and then he'd joined up. He sighs as he leans on Eric's headstone. That heartburn's still giving him gip. He supposes he doesn't really blame the kids for having nothing to do; it's a different world these days. There's not a lot of work around here, and he's seen their dads drinking in the Black Diamond. What's a young lad to do when his own dad can't be a decent role model? They closed down the pit and then most of the factories. That shower who've been in government for seventeen years haven't helped matters much.

Not that all the kids are the same, though. That Nicola who he caught riding her bike in the cemetery this morning, at least she's got a paper round. At least she was doing something. But most of them, they seem content to just hang around and do nothing, and whine about there being nothing laid on for them. As far as Arthur can see, that's the entire problem. You can't just sit around waiting for someone to hand you life on a plate. You've got to go out and get it. Kids today, they've just got no ambition, he thinks, setting off back to the chapel as the snow redoubles its efforts.

* 4 *

'I want to be a rock and roll star,' says Kelly Derricott. She has no idea where that comes from. It just pops into her head, and then out of her mouth. She was just thinking what the most annoying thing she could say to rile the careers teacher might be, and there it is, out there, hanging between them.

Mr Green sits back in his chair and Kelly holds his gaze as he looks at her. He's got a smirk on his lips. He has his legs crossed, one ankle resting on his knee, the hem of the cheap fabric of his suit trousers riding up to reveal a *Simpsons* sock. He holds a Parker pen in his fist, click-click-clicking the retractable nib. She can tell from the look in his eye what he's thinking; a smart-arse girl with a sharp mouth is just about the last thing in the world he wants to be dealing with right now.

Still, Mr Green leans forward and writes *rock and roll star* on the form sitting on his desk. Kelly looks around the tiny room, the frosted windows letting in the dim light from the playground, the bookshelves piled haphazardly with titles such as *Joining The Police Force*; *First Steps to Your First Job;* a battered and ancient copy of *The British Coal Corporation – Opportunities for School Leavers*. Something patters at the window; a flurry of light snow.

'Rock . . . and . . . roll star,' says Mr Green slowly, deliberately, as he writes. He starts clicking the pen again when he's finished, and picks up another piece of paper. He frowns, a comical, theatrical thing that makes his untidy moustache droop over his mouth. 'But it says here you aren't even doing music as an option, Kelly.'

She shrugs, staring at her hands, tying themselves in knots in the lap of her school skirt. The skirt's too tight, as is the blouse, more grey than the white it's meant to be. Her mum says she might be able to have new uniform after the Christmas holidays, but Kelly knows she'll be asked to make it last until Easter, and come Easter, well, it's not that long to summer, let's just see the next few weeks out. Mum doesn't seem to have noticed how much she's filled out in the last six months. Suddenly self-conscious, she pulls the front of the shirt where it's gaping at the buttons. But even if he's inclined to glance at blooming fourteen-year-old girls, Mr Green is far too busy cultivating a self-congratulatory smugness.

'No, sir,' she mumbles. 'Not doing music.' She looks up at the teacher. 'Did Noel Gallagher do music GCSE, sir?'

He makes a derisory sort of sound, blowing air down his nose that ruffles his moustache. 'I'm sure I have no idea, and even less interest, in what Noel Gallagher did at school. I am only concerned with what Kelly Derricott is going to do *after* school.' He looks at his watch. 'Kelly Derricott and the rest of the fourth years I have to get through this afternoon. You've already had three minutes, Kelly. Two more and then I want the next child sitting on that chair.'

Five minutes, she thinks. Five minutes, that's all I'm worth. All any of us are worth. Five minutes to decide our future. She looks at the sheet in front of Mr Green, a succession of tick boxes, all blank save for the words he's already written, the ink dripping with sarcasm.

Click-click-click goes Mr Green's pen. He sighs and snatches up the form, screwing it into a ball and throwing it at the grey metal wastepaper bin. It bounces off the rim and rolls under the bookshelf.

'Let's start again, shall we?' he says testily. On a new form he writes her name, and her form, and the date – 5 December, 1996. He glances at her report. 'English, adequate. Maths, abysmal. Geography, substandard. Science, desultory. Physical Education, disengaged. Music . . .' Mr Green stares at her. 'Music, non-existent. Now, I'll ask you again. Do you have any idea what you might like to do when you leave Marigold Brook High School, Kelly?'

She fixates on her hands again. 'No, sir.'

'Well, given your projected grades in the core subjects, it seems you might have an outside chance of getting a pass, maybe even more, at English. Work really hard, you could make a secretary, a temp at least. Shall we just put down "shop assistant", for now?'

Kelly meets his glare. 'What about university, sir?'

Mr Green almost laughs, she can see that, but stops himself. Instead he takes a deep breath. 'Kelly, do you know how many Marigold Brook students have gone on to university in the past six years?' She shakes her head. He continues, 'I do. I can even name them all for you. Do you know why?' He holds up his palm, fingers splayed. 'Because there are five. Five pupils in the past six years got themselves to university. Now, do you know how many kids get themselves pregnant, in jail or addicted to drugs within a year of leaving this school?'

She shakes her head again. So does Mr Green. 'Me neither. More than I can count. More than I care to even think about.' He puts his pen down on the form. 'I've been here for twelve years. There are kids who I taught whose own children are at this school.' He shakes his head, talking mainly to himself, now. 'I could be here long enough to teach their grandchildren. Christ.'

'Did you always want to be a teacher, sir?' says Kelly softly.

Mr Green blinks, as though only just realising that she's still there. 'Yes. Yes, I did. I thought . . . I thought I could make a difference . . .'

Neither of them says anything. Even in the past minute or so the sky has darkened noticeably outside the window, and the snow is pattering against the glass. Outside in the corridor she can hear a fight breaking out and the strident tones of a teacher wading in to break it up.

Mr Green has heard it too. 'The natives are getting restless,' he mutters, turning his attention to the form, making a series of rapid ticks in the boxes. He looks at it, then nods. 'Shop assistant, then. Maybe secretary. I'll get that filed.' He looks at her. 'You know, maybe if you work hard at maths, you might be able to scrape a pass. Would open up a lot of opportunities. You could maybe even get work in an insurance office or something.' He brightens suddenly. 'And doesn't Mrs Cartwright do typing classes at lunchtimes? That would be a good thing to do, if you're going to try for secretary somewhere.'

Kelly nods. 'Thanks, sir.' She scrapes the chair's legs against the floor as she stands, and lets herself out into the corridor, nodding at the dishevelled boy with his shirt hanging out of his trousers, who's next for his five minutes of careers advice.

The door on to the break yard opens and a girl from Kelly's year rushes in out of the cold, a perfume of cigarette smoke lingering around her, snow speckling the shoulders of her threadbare blue cardigan. Her hair is dirty blonde where Kelly's is black, but they both wear it sticky with gel – bought in cheap, big tubs from the indoor market – and scraped back off their foreheads, tied in a tight, high ponytail with a bobble or, more usually, one of the elastic bands dropped on the street by the postman when delivering sheaves of bills marked *overdue* through their doors. Gemma Swarbrick. Kelly lets on to her with the briefest of nods, but then turns as there's a kerfuffle at the front of the queue for the careers sessions. Heather Wilson and her coterie of hangers on. Heather Wilson, whose sister was one of those five people in recent Marigold Brook history to go to university. Heather Wilson who will probably follow her. Heather has decided that she wants to jump the queue, and what Heather and her luscious, bright blonde curls wants, Heather gets. She'll be getting new uniform for the start of January, no doubt, even though what she's wearing now is ten, a hundred, times better than what Kelly's got on.

'What are you gawking at?' says Heather, leaning on the wall. Her friends back her up with dagger glares. Kelly is about to flip them the finger but they're looking past her at Gemma.

'Nothing,' shrugs Gemma.

Kelly stops, watching with interest. She's a funny one, Gemma Swarbrick. Her dad's a right villain, but she keeps her nose clean. If Heather Wilson talked to Kelly like that, she'd smack her a right one.

'Is it snowing or is it just your dandruff?' offers one of Heather's mob, and they all start to titter. Kelly rolls her eyes as Gemma shuffles past, brushing at the shoulders of her cardigan, heading for the back of the queue.

'I wouldn't bother,' calls Heather, nudging her friends to let them know there's a good one coming. 'Can't you just ask your dad if you can join the family business? There's plenty more houses that haven't been robbed yet.'

'Burgled,' mutters Gemma. 'Robbery is when you commit theft with violence. My dad never did that.'

Kelly watches Gemma head off. Strictly speaking she should go back to her geography class ('substandard', she hears Mr Green say. As if knowing how an oxbow lake forms will ever be any use in life) but that queue for careers consultations is long, and for all her teacher knows she was at the back, so instead she goes in the opposite direction.

She decides to go to the upper floor and see Mrs Cartwright about one of these lunchtime typing courses. Kelly wonders what life really will be like after Marigold Brook. The idea makes her stomach feel a bit funny. Will she get a job, as a secretary? Will she get pregnant? Will she end up in her own council house, on the same street as where she is now? Is that all there is? Her brother, Mick, is only a few years older than her. He's eighteen, and he's been working in the canning factory since he left school. His girlfriend, Jane, is pregnant, and she's only seventeen. As far as Kelly knows, she's never had a job since she left school. They've got a flat from the housing association. They smoke Marlboro Lights and drink Stella Artois and Mad Dog down the pub three nights a week, even though Jane's not supposed to do either. They eat takeaways, then beans on toast when the money runs out, and come round to mum's for roast chicken on Sundays. They seem happy enough.

Still, she thinks. Is that all there is?

* 5 *

Kelly stands in the corridor, looking in to Mrs Cartwright's room. There are five girls there, rhythmically jabbing with first one finger, then another, at the keyboards on a row of electric typewriters. On the blackboard Mrs Cartwright has written *the quick brown fox jumps over the lazy dog*. Kelly wonders why Mr Green never sends boys to do lunchtime typing classes. She backs away from the glass in the door as the teacher glances over, and wanders on down the corridor. Kelly's been at this school since she was eleven, she knows every inch of its shabby halls and classrooms. So why does she suddenly feel so lost?

She becomes aware of the faint, discordant noise of a trumpet, someone plinky-plonking on a piano or keyboard. She's near the music rooms. A door opens and a mousy girl with thick-lensed glasses emerges, hugging a guitar and blinking at Kelly.

Her name's Nicola Manning and she always looks like she's just seen a ghost, or maybe thinks she's about to. She's lumpy and short and her skin is pasty and peppered with zits, her hair styled by her mum with the kitchen scissors and a pudding bowl. She always has a graze on one pudgy knee, or the other, her glasses are held together with tape. Nicola lives on the next avenue from Kelly, and she always feels a bit sorry for her. Her dad died when she was a baby, committed suicide. Kelly's mum says they used to live in a nice house over by the park but had no money after the dad died and moved on to the estate. Kelly had always thought you got money, for some reason, when somebody died; maybe they didn't give it to your family if you killed yourself. A punishment, maybe. Which seems a bit unfair to Kelly, as that's probably when you need money the most.

Nicola holds the guitar tight, staring at Kelly, who shrugs. 'It's all right, I'm not going to nick it.' She leans forward to inspect the instrument. It's green and shiny, with four thick strings running along the brown neck. Is that right? 'I always thought guitars had six strings. Can you not afford to buy the others?'

'It's a bass,' says Nicola, looking around as though something bad's going to happen and someone will film it and send it to Jeremy Beadle on *You've Been Framed*. 'They only have four.'

'Why do you have a bass guitar?' presses Kelly.

Nicola looks at her tatty shoes. 'It was my dad's,' she says, so quietly that Kelly can barely hear.

'Can you play it?'

The other girl's shoulders rise and fall. 'A bit.'

Kelly nods. 'Have you seen Green? For the careers talk?'

'Secretary,' shrugs Nicola, pushing her glasses up her nose. 'If I keep on being all right at English.'

There's a whiff of stale cigarettes and the scent of cheap hair gel which Kelly recognises and she turns to see Gemma Swarbrick sloping up the corridor. She glances at Nicola and Kelly, tipping her head up briefly in acknowledgement as she walks past.

'That Heather Wilson is a bitch,' says Kelly.

Gemma looks at her and pulls a face, as if to say, *tell me something I don't know. Tell me something everybody doesn't know.*

Kelly says, 'What did Green say to you?'

'Didn't bother,' says Gemma. 'What's the point? He'd only say to me same thing he said to my sisters.'

Gemma has five sisters, Kelly thinks. Two older and three younger. Her mum's always pregnant, it seems. Kelly guesses, 'Secretary?'

Gemma nods. 'I think two of them did it, as well. Lisa worked at that factory where they make those shirts. 'Til she got pregnant. Shannon did two weeks somewhere before she got done for nicking petty cash.'

'The Secretaries,' says Kelly, looking from Gemma to Nicola. 'Sounds like a pop group or something.' She squints at the clock on the wall at the end of the corridor, and says to Nicola, 'Are you on free dinners? Shall we sit together?'

'I have packed lunch,' says Nicola. 'My mum doesn't trust school dinners. I wouldn't mind something hot on a day like this though.'

'It all tastes like shit,' says Gemma. 'But at least it's free.'

As they walk together down the corridor towards the dinner hall, Kelly says, 'So what did you actually tell Green you wanted to be?'

Nicola hugs her guitar closer. 'My mum says I should be a nursery teacher. On her good days.'

Gemma is looking in her pencil case, counting the cigarettes there. 'What does she say on her bad days?'

'That it doesn't matter,' says Nicola quietly. 'Because we're all going to die when the millennium comes.'

Gemma stares at her. 'Cheery.' She looks at Kelly as they join the queue for the canteen. 'What did you tell Green?'

Kelly grins. 'I told him I wanted to be a rock star.'

A boy in front of them, a fifth year with a battleground of a chin where the zits and random hairs fought for dominance, turns and stares at them dully. 'Girls can't be rock stars,' he says.

'They can,' says Nicola quietly as the queue shuffles forward. 'There's loads of bands with girls in them. Loads of bands with *only* girls in them.'

'Just not girls like us,' says Gemma.

No, thinks Kelly. Just not girls like us.

Straight after school, Kelly has to go into town to work on Pete's market stall. They've put on a special Christmas market on Thursdays in December, and along the cobbles on the main shopping street there are stalls selling mulled wine and candy floss and carved pieces of wood from places like Thailand and Malaysia which Kelly will never visit. There's a stall selling puppets from Prague and the smell of the German bratwurst makes Kelly's stomach rumble, though she hasn't got the money to spend on it. She'll have whatever's left over when she gets home. Pete is her dad's cousin and Kelly's worked on his market stall on Saturdays for about a year, and she's glad of the extra money from the Christmas markets, but she could do without being so cold. Pete's stall doesn't sell anything remotely

Christmassy . . . he has an eclectic selection of knitted gloves, outsize leather belts, plastic handbags, uncomfortable scatter cushions, big tubes of poster paints and, for some reason this Thursday, piles and piles of toilet rolls.

'People still need to wipe their arses at Christmas,' says Pete, a big, bald man with his belly hanging over his jeans. 'In fact, they probably need to wipe their arses more, with all them sprouts and stuff.'

Kelly wrinkles her nose and busies herself arranging another new item, fluffy ear-warmers. She picks up the least offensive pair and says, 'Can I wear these, Pete? It's perishing.'

He shrugs. 'I'll do you them at half price. I'll dock your wages at the end of the night.'

Tight bastard, she thinks and tosses them back on the velvet cloth covering the stall. 'Don't bother, I'll just freeze.'

Pete bellows his selection of wares while Kelly stands behind the stall, strapping on a money belt filled with small change and trying not to cast hungry glances towards the bratwurst seller, while vainly attempting to block out the relentless Christmas songs being pumped through a tinny speaker fixed to the nearest lamp post. She sells two pairs of earmuffs to a pair of cackling old ladies sloshing mulled wine out of their plastic cups, then Pete bursts into song. 'Oh, come, all ye faithful, wipe your arse at Christmas, my bog-roll is two-ply, it won't slide around. . .'

Kelly is so busy rolling her eyes that she doesn't realise she's got customers. She plasters on a smile, which falls abruptly when she realises who it is. Heather Wilson and her gang, all wearing definitely-not-knock-off white Timberland puffa jackets, Gap jeans and suede boots. They're all holding bratwursts in little cardboard trays, and Heather is smirking at Kelly over the poster paints and toilet rolls.

'Look who it is,' says Heather. 'All right, market girl? I see the careers talk worked a treat for you.'

'Do you want anything?' says Kelly flatly. She wants to smack her one, but she doesn't want to get in trouble with Pete.

Heather makes a production of inspecting the ear warmers and the plastic handbags while her friends giggle. 'Hmm, let's see . . .

I do want a new handbag, but I think my dad might be getting me a Louis Vuitton from his business trip next week.' Her smile drips with poison. 'Besides, as cute as these are, I don't think the Nokia mobile phone I'm also getting will fit into one.'

Kelly glares at her. 'How about some toilet roll, Heather? Or do you piss CK One and shit Ferrero Rochers?'

There's a collective intake of breath from the gang and Heather's eyes narrow. 'Only a tramp like you could think Ferrero Rochers are actually *posh*, Derricott.' She turns to her friends and says in a thick European accent, 'Ambassador, you're really spoiling us with these pound shop chocolates.'

'You fucking bitch,' says Kelly, and before she properly knows what she's doing she's picking up two of the big bottles of poster paints, one red and one green, and flicking the tops off them with her thumbs like an Old West gunfighter. The look in Heather Wilson's eyes as it dawns on her what is going to happen is almost as priceless as the expression on her face when Kelly suddenly viciously squeezes both bottles and squirts red and green splurges of paint all over Heather's blonde hair and immaculate white jacket.

'Dock two bottles of paint from my wages,' says Kelly with satisfaction as Pete lumbers over, eyes wide with horror.

'Wages?' he bellows. 'You're not getting any wages! You're sacked!'

'Good, because I quit!' screams Kelly back, taking off the money belt and throwing it at him. Heather Wilson is still standing there in mute shock, red and green paint dripping down her face, while her friends slowly back away from her.

Heather finds her voice again, and hisses, 'Don't think this is over. This hasn't even started, bitch. I am so going to get you for this.'

'Ding dong merrily on fucking high,' Kelly says in Heather's face, then gives her the fingers and stalks off into the night.

* 6 *

Arthur walks into the snug of the Black Diamond and is greeted by a fug of cigarette smoke, a hubbub of conversation, and the smell of stale beer. He stamps the snow off his boots on the sticky carpet and nods at Sarah behind the bar, who begins to pull him a pint of Theakston Traditional. So many pubs are stopping doing mild at all. It's all alcopops and whatnot these days. That's why he frequents the Black Diamond. No kids getting drunk and playing that loud bang-bang-bang music. No messing about trying to become one of them gastropubs – the only food on offer here is a packet of pork scratchings or dry-roasted peanuts, the packets hanging on a card which slowly reveals a woman in a swimsuit as each purchase is made. No telly blaring out football or soaps. Just a good, old-fashioned boozer.

Which, he imagines, is why *that lot* like it as well. They're in their usual spot at the end of the snug, gathered around two round tables, the Formica tops each filled with pint glasses and an overflowing ashtray. There are always six or seven of them, hunched over their drinks, while Keith Cardy holds court. Cardy's a stout, gammon-faced man, a good twenty-five years younger than Arthur, his meaty forearms adorned with tattoos of bulldogs and the Union Flag, a dagger wreathed with his four children's names. He spots Arthur as he turns away from the bar after paying Sarah and waves at him.

'Arthur'll know exactly what I'm talking about,' booms Cardy. 'Come here, Arthur.'

The younger men shuffle up to allow Arthur to unwind his scarf, take off his overcoat, and sit down. He takes a mouthful of his mild as Cardy taps another Park Drive from his packet of ten and lights it. 'Bloody Old Hall,' says Cardy, exhaling smoke.

Arthur waits for him to go on. The Old Hall is just up the hill from the cemetery. Used to be a good pub. Nice mild. Closed down about three years back.

'You'll never guess,' says Cardy. He takes another drag of his unfiltered cigarette. 'They've turned the Old Hall into some kind of bloody hotel. For asylum seekers.' He sits back, triumph in his eyes. 'Asylum seekers.'

'This place is going to the dogs,' says another man, with dark, unruly hair and a haunted, hangdog look. Arthur searches his memory for his name. Derricott, that's it. Brian Derricott. Used to work at the pit, he remembers now. Was a supervisor when it closed. 'Used to be a nice place, for honest, hard-working folk.'

'Don't you worry, though,' says Cardy, leaning conspiratori-ally across the table. 'We look after our own round here. Always have done, haven't we? The Old Hall's only a few minutes from you. We're going to keep an eye on you, Arthur. Make sure these thieving toerags don't bother you.'

'I don't think that'll be necessary,' says Arthur brusquely. 'Can't see what they'd want with me.'

'I heard they eat swans,' blurts out Brian Derricott. Everybody looks at him. 'They have barbecues. Killed a load in London, I think.'

Cardy stubs out his cigarette and immediately shakes another one out of the packet, peering inside to see how many are left. 'What a bloody liberty. Don't they know the Queen owns the swans?' He shakes his head. 'England for the English, that's what I say.'

Everyone murmurs agreement. Cardy's blood is up now, Arthur can see. He drags furiously on his Park Drive. 'And you know what's worse? I read the other day that they reckon immigration to this country's going to top fifty thousand next year.'

'It bloody will if Tony bloody Blair gets in,' says Brian.

'Tony bloody Blair,' says Cardy witheringly. 'Things can only get better, my arse. Labour used to be the party of the working man. This New Labour thing . . .' He gives up and drains his pint glass.

Brian clears his throat and says, 'Arthur? Did you know there's a new family living in your old house? Walked past the other day when they were moving in.'

Arthur is getting to the bottom of his pint and wonders if he'll be able to use this as an excuse to extricate himself from the conversation. He shrugs at Brian, who goes on, 'I think their surname's Patel.'

Cardy rubs his forehead as though he's in actual pain. 'Bloody hellfire,' he breathes. He points his cigarette at Arthur. 'Bloody war hero, sitting right here in front of us. He has to go and live in a broken-down chapel in the middle of the cemetery. And they give his house to . . .'

He leaves it hanging there. Arthur says, 'Well, it wasn't quite like that. Nobody made me go and live in the chapel. I—'

'That's not the point, is it?' says Cardy fiercely. 'The point is . . .' He looks at his empty glass, as though inspiration for the point might be in there. Finding none, he elbows Brian savagely. 'It's your round. Get them in. What are you having, Arthur?'

'Not for me,' says Arthur, standing up. 'Better get back.' He climbs back into his coat and wraps his scarf around his neck. Molly knitted that scarf. He looks at Cardy, at all of them. 'And I wasn't a war hero. I just did my bit. It's what everybody did.'

Cardy covers his mouth, his eyes suddenly shining and wet. 'What a bloody gent,' he says, his voice cracking with Park Drive, lager, and emotion. 'It must tear you apart, seeing what's happening to this country.'

Arthur smiles tightly and leaves, hearing the voices at the table rising as Brian says, 'Bloody hero. We should do something you know. Something for the likes of Arthur.'

'Correct!' says Cardy. 'We should organise ourselves! Do this properly! Put on a . . . a show of strength.'

Arthur is glad to get into the cold embrace of the night, and sighs as the door bangs shut, cutting off the drunken scheming of Cardy and his boys.

It's not like it was ever their house, not really. They rented it their whole married lives, moving in not long after the wedding when Arthur had come back from serving overseas. After Molly had recovered properly from what happened on that farm. The rent when they started off was 5s and 6d, he thinks, as his boots crunch on the snow and he realises his feet are taking him towards their old street. Arthur pauses at the top of the cul-de-sac, which ends in a low brick wall beyond which he can hear, even from here, the gentle chugging of the locomotives in the engineering sheds beyond. He did a couple of years working in Low Spring Branch, back in the 1950s, when he'd had his fill of the pit. He used to hop over the wall at dinner time and come back to number sixteen to eat his snap with Molly. It was steam trains back then, not the diesel and electric engines they have now.

Arthur walks carefully down the gutter of the pavements, which haven't been gritted along here. Outside their old house is a street-light, which used to throw yellow shapes through the curtains over the window of their bedroom at the front of the house. He'd lie there sometimes, Molly sleeping behind him, and listen to the trains and watch the sodium shapes shifting as the draft rippled around the curtains, and he'd wonder what life might be like if . . . but then he'd tell himself there'd be no use in *what ifs* and *maybes*, and he'd put an arm across Molly and around her belly, and she'd wriggle back into him until they were like a couple of spoons in the cutlery drawer, and eventually he'd go to sleep.

December had always been such a joyous month, before Molly passed. Christmas, of course, and her birthday just a few days before. Their little house garlanded with tinsel and lights, the sideboard in the front room reserved for her birthday cards. She always used to make a batch of gingerbread men, decorated with little white icing beards and red caps, and hang them on the artificial tree that slept in the attic the rest of the year. When the local kids hammered on the door and sang in bellowing voices one or two verses of 'We Wish You A Merry Christmas' Arthur would hold Molly tight on the settee, and they would allow themselves to think, but never talk, of the child-shaped absence in their home. They had none of their own, Molly and Arthur, never could. So Arthur made sure his love filled every corner and cranny of their little house, to make no space for the lack of children, as best as he was able.

There's a light on in the upstairs bedroom that used to be his and Molly's, but dulled behind better curtains than they had in those early days. Arthur wonders, as he looks up at it, leaning against the concrete lamp post, whether it's a kiddie's bedroom. The curtains aren't pulled closed on the bay window downstairs and he sees them, the Patels. There's a man with a moustache, sitting in a chair and picking at a dish of what looks like peanuts. He's watching the telly, stabbing at a remote control with his thumb, watching the channels cycle through, not satisfied with anything that comes up. Arthur has read that they're launching a fifth channel next year, but he's not particularly excited at the prospect. Only thing he really used to enjoy was football, but you can only get that these days if you have one of those satellite dishes. There's not many he knows got one, that's for sure, but there are one or two. Big ugly things stuck on the sides of the houses. Folk who are always crying poverty as well. They can always find the money for satellite TV. Though he did see one of Cardy's mob in the Black Diamond selling some sort of plastic cards – faked or stolen, he didn't really understand – which could let people watch the satellite for free.

The Patels don't appear to have a satellite dish, at any rate. Then Arthur sees a woman stand up and start to usher three little kids out of the room. Her dress is so colourful, silky and flowing. He wonders why Cardy's boys get so het up about people like this. They don't seem to be doing any harm, as far as he can tell. Just people trying to get on in life, like they always have done. Like they always will do.

As the three little ones troop out of the living room, and a light goes on behind the door indicating they're heading upstairs, Arthur executes a turn in the slushy gutter and begins to trudge back up the street. He pulls his scarf tighter. He can remember Molly knitting it, sitting in that chair the man, Mr Patel, was sitting in. Arthur thinks about the little kiddies, filing out of the living room, off upstairs for their bath or bed. Something gives inside his chest, like a stepped-on twig snapping, or perhaps a hole quietly and gradually getting just a little wider and deeper.

*

The first time it happened, Arthur thought it was quite a nice thought on somebody's part. A bunch of flowers, wrapped in plain paper, laid on Molly's grave. They were there when Arthur, who had just moved into the chapel, visited her plot on her birthday, December 23, that first year she died. He'd gone early, before first light, and was puzzled that someone had been there before him. Delicate white flowers, with wide petals, like a shining full moon. They were so pretty that he took them into the chapel, away from the frost, and searched among the stems for a card or note. There wasn't one. It was only after asking everyone he knew and drawing a blank that he showed the flowers to Frankie, who ran a little florist shop on the main road and who sometimes sold blooms from the back of his van at the cemetery gates.

'*Ipomoea alba*,' said Frankie, after inspecting them critically for a moment. 'They call them moonflowers, too. They bloom at night.'

'Did you sell them to anybody?' asked Arthur.

Frankie shook his head. 'I don't do them. Not much call for them. Who wants flowers that only open up after they've gone to bed? They're late bloomers, but not this late in the year. Unless they're from a nursery somewhere.'

That first year, Arthur put it down to just a well-wisher (though one who knew Molly well enough to know when it was her birthday), or perhaps even that they'd been left on Molly's grave by mistake. But the next year, before dawn had even broken on the twenty-third, when Arthur was still struggling to get used to the idea that this was the second of Molly's birthdays he would spend alone, there was another bouquet, moonflowers again. Same plain wrapping, no card or note. Left in the dead of night, white blooms shining in the darkness.

So when the third birthday since Molly's passing came around, and the fourth, and then the fifth, every time with a bunch of moonflowers wrapped up on her grave, Arthur knew there was something funny going on. Last year, the sixth year since Molly had died, Arthur resolved to find out just what the hell was going on.

* 7 *

If anything gets to Gemma at home, it's the noise. Noise, noise, noise.
All the time. Her eldest sister is back at home after splitting up with
another boyfriend. And she's got her baby in tow. Six months old.
Always bawling. Her mum says it's because she's teething, like that's
any kind of excuse. Somebody's always got the radio on or the TV
blaring or a hairdryer buzzing or the phone's ringing or— Gemma
stands there in the kitchen, looking around at the chaos, Chris Evans
on the Radio 1 breakfast show. With Lisa and the baby that makes
nine of them in one house. It's no wonder Julie, the sister one-up
from her, spends all her time at her boyfriend's. The twins are squabbling over whose school tie is whose and the youngest, Joanne, is
crawling around on the lino, grabbing handfuls of the dog's food and
squishing it between her chubby fingers. Upstairs she can hear Kyra
crying and Lisa shouting back at her. There's a sudden crash and
everybody goes quiet, staring at the broken bowl on the floor, milk
and Kwik Save's own brand of Coco Pops spilling out everywhere.

'It was her,' says Cheryl, pointing at her twin Carrie. Carrie aims
a kick at Joanne, who's trying to climb up the back of her chair.
'No it wasn't. The little turd knocked me.'

'Get the dog away from the bloody broken bowl!' bellows her
dad suddenly, appearing at the kitchen door in his vest and boxer
shorts. 'It'll eat the sodding bits!'

Gemma pulls their Staffie by its studded collar away from where
its tongue is lapping at the milk, but it's solid muscle and refuses
to budge. 'Bullseye, come away!' yells Gemma. She needs a fag.
She needs some quiet.

Her dad opens the back door, letting in a biting cold wind and causing everyone to complain, and ushers Bullseye out with his bare foot. He regards the mess on the floor. 'Carrie, clear that up.'

'It was her!' protests Carrie, pointing at Cheryl.

'I'll do it,' sighs Gemma, getting the dustpan and brush and a cloth.

While she's on her knees, her dad lights a fag and picks up the notepad from near the phone. He locates a bitten stub of pencil and announces, 'Right, given that it's the most wonderful time of the year, I'm taking orders for Father Christmas!'

'Hark at you, moneybags,' says her mum, appearing at the door. She bends down to pick up Joanne and hoists her on to her hip. 'Look at the state of you. Who let her play in the Pedigree Chum?'

Gemma tips the debris into the pedal bin and wipes Joanne's hands with the cloth. Her dad tickles the little one's tummy and she gives him a gummy smile. 'What about you, Jo-Jo? What do you want Father Christmas to bring you?'

'I want a Buzz Lightyear!' shouts Cheryl. 'One that lights up and does all the noises.'

'One Buzz Lightyear,' says her dad, making a note on his pad. 'What about you, Carrie?'

'I want a Buzz Lightyear too! A bigger one than her's. With twice as many lights.'

'Two Buzz Lightyears.'

Her mum laughs. 'You'll have a job. Rarer than hen's teeth them, aren't they? It was in the paper. People fighting over them at some toy shop down south.'

Her dad does a big wink. 'But we're not going to toy shops, are we? We're sending this list straight to Father Christmas!'

Straight to Crushing Ken, more like, thinks Gemma. Crushing Ken – so named because his swear-word of choice is 'crushing' – is her dad's man on the inside. Not the inside of Santa's grotto, but the inside of a big warehouse near the bypass that's the main storage hub for about three or four of the big catalogue companies.

'What about you, love?' says her dad to Gemma.

She shrugs. 'Get us two hundred Marlboro Lights.'

Her dad tuts. 'Not very festive, is it?'

'What about me?' says her mum, transferring Joanne to her other hip so she can fill the kettle.

Her dad grins. 'You've already had your present, haven't you, love? You told them, yet?'

Gemma can feel her heart sink as her mum rolls her eyes at her dad then bangs a spoon on the Formica work surface for attention. As if things weren't crowded and noisy enough. She feels she's going to scream even as her mum smiles and says, 'We're having another baby.'

Another baby. Gemma stands in the hall, her hand on her forehead. Well, Lisa's going to have to get her act together and find somewhere else to live with her little brat. Gemma kicks the skirting board. How can her mum even do this to her? Another bloody baby. Gemma counts off the months on her fingers. It'll be due in the summer holidays, probably. Just when she's about to go into her final GCSE year. She's got about as much chance of passing her exams as . . . she laughs, despite herself. As her mum keeping her knickers on.

Gemma pushes her face against the frosted glass of the front door to establish it's still snowing, then pulls on her wellies. As she rifles through the pile of coats hanging on the bannister she finds her dad's parka, and looking around to ensure that, mercifully and miraculously, there's nobody else about in this tiny corner of the Swarbrick household, she delves into his pockets, her hand closing on a packet of cigarettes. She's counting out five of the Regal Blue when a hand clamps on her shoulder.

'Got you now.'

'Shit, Dad!' says Gemma, putting her hand to her pounding chest.

'Little tea leaf,' he says, plucking the packet from her hands. 'Do I not give you enough, that you have to go stealing from me? I'm going to have to punish you now, aren't I?'

Gemma pulls her tongue out at him. 'What you going to do, lock me in my room? Because that would be all right with me. I've got double maths first thing.'

'Worse than that,' says her dad. 'I've got to go and see Crushing Ken. I'll give you a lift to school on my way.'

The car, an ancient Ford Escort that's mainly held together by duct tape, takes five goes of her dad waggling the key in the ignition and murmuring, 'Come on, you bastard,' a cigarette dangling from his lips, before it chugs into life. Gemma slides down as far as she can in the passenger seat as her dad noses the car gingerly along the slush-covered road.

'Anyway,' says Gemma, blowing into her hands to warm them up. 'You can talk. About thieving.'

Her dad peers through the misted-up windscreen. 'Do as I say, not as I do.'

Gemma considers. 'It's not done you any harm.'

Her dad laughs. 'Apart from that six months I did in Strangeways. You were too young to remember it now. That was no fun.'

'But you and Mum . . . you've stayed together,' presses Gemma. 'Half the kids in my class, their parents are divorced. And you and mum are still popping sprogs out.'

Her dad shakes his head. 'I've been lucky. Apart from that stretch in Strangeways, I've never been caught. I know my limits, that's why. Don't overreach myself. Play it safe. That's not really what you'd call a good career plan, though.'

Gemma wipes the passenger window with the cuff of her coat. 'Maybe I don't want a career.'

Her dad looks at Gemma seriously. 'Look, love, you've got something I never had and could never nick. Brains. You get them from your mum, but she never had opportunities. Not like you girls get now. Me and your mum, we're the way we are because we never had a choice. You . . . if you work hard at school, get your exams . . . anything could happen.'

Gemma breathes on to the window and writes her name in the condensation. 'Yeah, but it probably won't, will it? They don't give a toss about the likes of me at Marigold Brook.'

'Then don't do it for them, do it for you,' says her dad. He digs the packet of fags from his pocket, then gives them to Gemma. 'Don't tell your mum.'

Gemma leans over to give him a quick peck on the cheek and stuffs the cigarettes into her pencil case. She wipes the window again. Kelly Derricott, walking up the street. 'You can let me out here, Dad,' she says. 'I'll walk it.'

'I can give your mate a lift as well. Unless you're too embarrassed to be seen with your old dad.'

He slows the car, the bald tyres skidding in the black ice. 'I'm too embarrassed,' says Kelly.

As she opens the door, and lets in the wind and swirling snow, her dad says, 'Make sure you go to this double maths. Don't be bunking off. And think on; no nicking stuff. Do well at school. Be better than me.'

Gemma nods dutifully and pushes the door shut behind her. As he drives away, she pulls out of her packet the five pound note she'd extracted from her her dad's coat along with the fags, and grins.

* 8 *

Kelly runs her hands through her hair, slicking it with gel, and holds her ponytail up so she can twine the bobble sitting on her wrist around it, nice and tight at the top of her skull. *The Council Face-Lift*, she heard Heather Wilson and her friends say one time. Those girls who don't think twice about going to get their hair cut. If Kelly asked for money to get her hair cut her mum would just get out the kitchen scissors and do it herself.

Kelly is fed up of never having any money.

She brushes her teeth and puts her face close to the mirror, inspecting the fresh sprouting of pimples on her forehead. Downstairs she can hear her dad opening and closing cupboards in the kitchen; if he's after cornflakes then he'd better start looking down the back of the settee for coins and get himself down to Kwik Save when it opens because Kelly finished the box off last night, more out of spite than anything, because she couldn't find any bread for toast.

Kelly is fed up of never having anything decent to eat.

On the landing, still dark because the bulb's been out for God knows how long, Kelly looks through the window. It's snowed again, the few cars parked in the close looking like white jelly moulds beneath the fresh, virgin fall. There aren't any footprints at all in the snow, which is unsurprising; nobody goes out to work around here. She looks down at her shoes, lifting her leg up to see the hole in the sole. That'll be wet socks again all day, and there's no point even thinking about asking for new shoes or wellies.

Kelly is fed up the snow. In fact, Kelly Derricott is fed up of pretty much everything.

In the kitchen, her dad is standing in his slippers on the yellow and brown lino that curls up where it meets the battered cabinets and scuffed skirting boards, staring into the depths of the fridge. The yellow light paints his already sickly-looking face even paler, accentuates the stubble on his doughy cheeks, his mussed-up hair marbled with grey. He doesn't hear Kelly come in, his eyes glazed over, as though he's imagining the fridge is a bountiful treasure chest of posh food and not the supermarket's own-label cheese, half tins of beans, and margarine flecked with crumbs of burnt toast and strawberry jam.

Kelly clomps into the kitchen and her dad blinks, flips the top off the milk, and sniffs it suspiciously. He gives her a sidelong glance as she stuffs her school books into her plastic-leather bag with one handle hanging off.

'Do you want any . . .' he gestures vaguely into the fridge.

'I never have breakfast,' says Kelly.

'You should eat breakfast like a king, lunch like a prince and dinner like a pauper,' says her dad, now sniffing the margarine. 'That's what they say.'

'At least we get dinner right,' says Kelly, extracting her coat from underneath the others piled on top of the bannister post at the bottom of the stairs. Except dinner is what you have at midday and tea is what you have at five o'clock. Only on telly sitcoms about people who live in unfeasibly big houses and have important jobs do they talk about lunch or dinner. Heather Wilson probably has her dinner at night. Climbing into her coat, Kelly runs up the stairs and into where her mum is gently snoring. She's on the afternoon shift at the factory, she won't be done until nearly ten tonight. That's no way to spend your Friday nights, thinks Kelly. Won't catch her doing that.

'I'm going to school,' says Kelly, giving her sleeping mum the required peck on her cheek. She smells warm and fuzzy. Her mum mutters something and rolls over, and when Kelly gets back downstairs her dad is sitting at the tiny round table in the kitchen, staring at the *Reporter*, the free paper that gets pushed through their door every Thursday night.

'I'm going to school,' says Kelly, looking over his shoulder. He's scrutinising the first page of the jobs ads.

'Look at this,' he tuts. 'Nothing. Sod all.' He pauses. 'Did you work on Pete's stall last night? Did he pay you?'

'Where were you last night, anyway?' says Kelly, by way of changing the subject.

'Diamond,' says her dad, frowning slightly as though he can't quite remember what he was talking about.

'With that Keith Cardy?'

'He talks a lot of sense,' says her dad. 'About immigration and stuff.'

'His son's in my year,' says Kelly. 'He's a bullying little shit. Bet he gets it from his dad.'

Brian Derricott frowns again, then raises his eyebrows. 'Anyway. Pete's stall.'

'Bye,' Kelly says, giving him a quick kiss on the top of his head, which does the job of confusing him enough to throw him off his line of questioning.

'Have we got any cornflakes?' says her dad as she opens the front door. She pulls it closed behind her with a bang and doesn't bother to answer.

When Kelly gets to the end of the close, it's still dark, with no hint of sunrise in the east, the town battered down by low, snow-filled clouds. She normally walks to school on her own, or with whoever's passing at the same time, but this morning as she sets off along The Avenue, which cuts through their estate, a car shudders and judders to a halt just ahead of her, its wheels spinning in the slush.

Gemma Swarbrick gets out and gives her a little wave. Kelly walks up to her and says, 'All right?'

'All right,' agrees Gemma. She notices Kelly looking down at her wellies, and says, 'They're Hunters. Dead expensive.'

Kelly falls in beside her and they trudge along the pavement. 'Where did you get them from?'

Gemma shrugs. 'Fell off the back of a lorry. As usual.'

Kelly's stomach growls so loud that Gemma hears it. The other girl pulls a chocolate bar from her coat pocket and hands it over. 'Have you seen these? They're new. It's called a *Fuse*.'

'I can read.' Kelly plucks at the wrapping and takes a bite as they start to trudge through the snow together. 'Did these fall off the back of a lorry as well?'

Gemma laughs. 'No, they fell off Mohammed's counter into my pocket.' She pauses. 'I heard about you and Heather Wilson on the market last night.'

Kelly raises an eyebrow. News travels fast. 'What did you hear?'

'That you painted her like a Christmas elf.' Gemma breaks out into a wide grin. 'Wish I could have seen that. She'll have the knives out for you now, though, you know that.'

Kelly finishes off the *Fuse* bar and stuffs the wrapper in her pocket, and shrugs. 'I'm not scared of Heather Wilson. I could bray her with one hand tied behind my back.'

'Yeah, but then you'd get expelled. She's clever like that. She'll just keep winding you up, make your life hell, in the hope you'll just snap, then she'll be all like, *oh, poor me, the horrible council house girl assaulted me.*' Gemma stops and pulls her pencil case from her bag. 'Do you want a ciggie?'

Kelly considers, then shakes her head. 'Nah, I'm all right.'

Gemma lights her fag with a disposable lighter and starts to walk on but Kelly puts a hand on her arm, looking across The Avenue to the opposite pavement. 'Hey, look who it is. Nicola Manning.'

'So?' Gemma blows out a wonky smoke ring that weaves in and around the falling snowflakes.

'She's going the wrong way.'

'So?'

'Let's follow her,' says Kelly.

'Oh, Mum, no,' says Nicola. She has just come in from her Friday morning paper round and she hadn't expected her mum to be up yet; she only gets up early on really bad days, when her mind's turning over and over and she can't think straight about anything. And on really, *really* bad days, she watches *Threads*.

'Turn it off, Mum,' says Nicola, but Marj Manning puts her hand protectively over the remote control sitting on the arm of the sofa, never taking her eyes off the TV.

'No,' she says quietly. 'No. We need to prepare. For what's coming.'

Nicola hates *Threads*. It came out when she was tiny, about two-years-old, and her mum at some point got a VHS video of it. Nicola used to watch it like other kids watched *Postman Pat*. It was utterly horrid, about a nuclear war and a bomb attack on Sheffield, told like it was a real-life documentary. It used to make Nicola cry, but her mum fiercely insisted she watch it, like it was some kind of instruction manual for the future.

Nicola drags open the curtains in the living room, at least; letting the thin, pale daylight filter in. Her mum is staring dully at the TV screen, her lips moving silently as she mouths the dialogue and the narration. Then she seems to notice Nicola properly, and says, 'Where have you been?'

'My paper round,' says Nicola. 'Have you got your prescription? The chemist will be open and I need to go before school.'

'On the side, with some money.' Her eyes graze back to the TV. 'I put your packed lunch in the fridge last night. Tuna sandwiches.'

The kitchen sink is piled high with the dirty pots from last night. Nicola sighs. She's never known anything other than this small house on the council estate, but she's seen the photographs her mum has squirrelled away in vinyl albums and shoeboxes, the semi-detached house near the park they used to live in. Nicola's been past it on her bike, freewheeling slowly and watching the family that lives there. She wishes she could remember the happy times before . . . well, just before. There's one particular photograph, showing her mum with Nicola when she was just a baby. Her mum's sitting on the grass in the garden, her skirt splayed out around her, and she's bouncing Nicola on her knee, the camera capturing the baby laughing and the mother smiling. In the foreground of the picture there's an elongated shadow, her dad taking the picture with the summer sun behind him. That's all he is, now, a shadow. Nicola remembers reading that when the atom bomb was exploded over Hiroshima, the shadows of the people were burned into the walls of the buildings and the roads, all that was left of them.

Nicola sits in one of the chairs at the pharmacy while Mr Gower, the chemist, prepares her mum's prescription. She spins a rack displaying hair clips and scrunchies, then inspects the diet supplements on one shelf. She wonders if she should go on a diet. Nicola looks down at her legs, her socks pulled to her knees, her bulky, flat, sensible shoes. Does she wish she had legs like Heather Wilson, who wears skirts as short as she can get away with in summer, and who the boys all watch with veiled, impenetrable glances as she swishes past? Nicola pokes at her belly. She mentioned a diet to her mum, once, but she said that Nicola would be thin enough come the apocalypse, when they'd have to forage for berries and trap rabbits.

Mr Gower emerges from the back of the pharmacy with a paper package. Nicola hates the way he looks at her. He feels sorry for her. She doesn't want anybody's pity. She just wants to be normal.

Outside the chemists, there's a group of boys, fifth years in Marigold Brook uniforms. Bunking off. She shoves the paper bag in her pocket and puts her head down as she walks past them. Then she sees Gemma Swarbrick and Kelly Derricott leaning on the wall of the butchers, watching her. Nicola had left them at dinner time yesterday as they queued up for their food, and hidden herself away in the corner with her packed lunch. She had no idea why they'd even been talking to her, and didn't want to know. It couldn't be for anything good.

'I don't think they've invented a cure for being ugly yet,' says one of the boys, and they all laugh in deep, cracked voices. Gemma laughs too, but Kelly is staring at Nicola, frowning, as though she's furiously thinking about something.

Great. The last thing she needs is those two taking an interest. The lads and their stupid names she can ignore easily enough; they're just idiot boys, after all. But girls are something else. Girls are mean and vicious and never stop until they've properly hurt you. Nicola came in for some attention from Heather Wilson last summer, she used to shout names like Michelin Man and Stay-Puft Marshmallow Monster at her. Everybody would laugh. Nicola would think of songs, plucking the chords out on an imaginary guitar in her head, turning up the volume until it drowned out the names. Then she would go home and once she was alone in bed, she would stare at the ceiling and cry.

Nicola hurries on, pulling her hood up, and only stops when she rounds the corner on to the estate, and she's sure the boys and

Gemma and Kelly aren't following her. She unfurls the paper bag and glances inside; two boxes of Prozac. They're supposed to stop you being depressed, but Nicola can't see that they're helping her mum, particularly. If anything, she's seemed worse since she started taking them last year. Bad dreams all the time, always licking her lips and complaining her mouth is dry.

When Nicola lets herself into the house, she puts the pills on the sideboard with the change. Her mum is in the kitchen, washing up. Nicola watches her for a moment, staring down at the big carving knife, dripping with suds, as if she's not quite sure what it is. Quietly, Nicola goes to get her bass guitar from her room and then collects her packed lunch, gives her mum a kiss on the cheek. She gets a plastic bag from where she's hidden it among the coats, and checks her digital watch. Half an hour to school. She'll just have time.

* 9 *

'I brought you a wreath,' says the vicar. 'It's from Bobby Rigby's cremation. Seemed a shame to throw it away.'

Arthur takes the large holly ring from Revd. Brown, and looks critically at the word *Grandad* picked out in red and white flowers along the upper rim.

'He was a rugby league fan,' offers Revd. Brown, pointing to the flowers. 'Red and white.'

Arthur grunts. 'Aye, I knew Bobby Rigby well enough.' He looks at the vicar, a young, beaming, enthusiastic man with ruddy cheeks and thick glasses. Not from round here. Arthur doesn't point out that the town's rugby league colours are cherry and white, not red and white. What's the point? Instead he picks at the flowers that make the G in Grandad. 'I suppose these'll come off without too much bother.'

Revd. Brown looks around the chapel. 'Thought it might brighten the place up. With Christmas coming, and all.'

The kettle whistles on the stove and Arthur takes a dishcloth to wrap around the hot handle and pour Revd. Brown and himself a cup of tea. The vicar squints at the electric lights, still on though it's nearly nine o'clock in the morning. It's one of those days where it feels like it'll never get properly light. At least the snow's stopped, for now, though it's still so cold it's not going to thaw and melt away any time soon. Arthur has already got his shovel ready to clear the paths that snake around the graveyard; if the snow keeps off they'll hopefully stay clear for the weekend and the big Sunday visits to the graves.

'How long is it you've been living here now?' says Revd. Brown as Arthur hands him the mug of tea.

Arthur sits next to him on the pew. 'Seven years. Since my Molly died.' Revd. Brown knows this. Granted, he's only been vicar of St Mary's for three years, but Arthur's told him the story countless times. He'll have already known even before the first time Arthur told him; when you turn up to be vicar and there's an old man living in a decommissioned chapel in the oldest cemetery in your parish, it's probably something that you get brought up to speed about pretty sharpish.

Revd. Brown looks around again. 'It must get cold. And lonely.' He glances at Arthur. 'And maybe a bit . . . unsafe, for a man of your years.'

Arthur takes a sip of his tea. 'Actually, that's what I asked you to come here for. Do you think the council would put some of them film cameras up?'

Revd. Brown frowns and then says, 'You mean CCTV? Security cameras?'

'Aye, them things. Kid was riding through the cemetery on her bike yesterday morning. And there's the other thing, too. The flowers . . .'

'Ah, yes,' says the vicar. 'The flowers business.' He crosses his legs and cups his hands around the mug of tea. 'You know, Arthur, I perhaps wouldn't let that upset you. If you think about it, it's quite a nice thing, isn't it? To know that Molly was loved?'

'Molly *was* loved,' says Arthur curtly. 'By me. I was her husband for forty-three years. If anyone's going to leave flowers on her grave on her birthday, it'll be me.'

Revd. Brown stares into his tea for a moment, then says, 'You know, Arthur, for everything there is a season, and a time for every matter under heaven.'

'Yes!' says Arthur. 'That's what Frankie the Florist said! These flowers . . . *Ipomea Alba*. They flower in autumn, early winter at the very latest. These ones left on Molly's grave, they're out of season. Do you think that's a clue?'

Revd. Brown smiles sagely. 'A time to be born, and a time to die; a time to plant, and a time to pluck up what is planted.'

49

Arthur rubs his chin. 'Frankie said something about the flowers must have been grown in a nursery, or maybe a greenhouse. Do you think I should be looking for somebody with a greenhouse?' He clicks his fingers. 'Bobby Rigby used to have a big greenhouse. Used to grow chrysanths and tomatoes. Big red buggers they were. The tomatoes, not the chrysanths. But he barely knew Molly.' Arthur glances at the wreath the vicar bought. 'And he's just been burned to ashes, of course.'

'A time to kill and a time to heal; a time to break down, and a time to build up; a time to weep, and a time to laugh,' says Revd. Brown.

'Kill? I wouldn't go that far, vicar . . .' Arthur groans. 'Oh. You're bloody preaching at me, aren't you? I thought we were actually having a conversation.'

Revd. Brown's eyes shine encouragingly. 'A time to mourn, and a time to dance; a time to cast away stones, and a time to gather stones together.'

Arthur puts up a hand. 'You can leave it now. I get the message.'

'A time to embrace, and a time to refrain from embracing; a time to seek, and a time to lose.'

'For God's sake,' mutters Arthur.

Revd. Brown nods enthusiastically, putting down his tea mug on the pew and clasping Arthur's bony hands.

'A time to keep, and a time to cast away; a time to tear, and a time to sew; a time to keep silence, and a time to speak; a time to love, and a time to hate.'

'Jesus Christ,' says Arthur, pulling his hands away from the vicar's as though they've been burned. 'How bloody long does this go on?'

'A time for war, and a time for peace,' says Revd. Brown, closing his eyes and putting his palms together lightly at his breast. He opens his eyes and smiles. 'Ecclesiastes 3.'

'I never saw the first two,' grunts Arthur.

Revd. Brown drains his mug of tea and places it on the pew beside him. He beams broadly at Arthur, who scowls back. What's he hanging around for? Arthur's got things he needs to be doing. There's a funeral on at three o'clock and he'll need to go and shovel some snow away from the paths. He's running low on timber for the wood burner, and has to go and chop some from the old trees near the wall, and give it time to dry out properly. And he was thinking of making a pie for his tea.

Revd. Brown claps his hands on his knees, and says, 'Deuteronomy tells us, "If among you, one of your brothers should become poor, in any of your towns within your land that the Lord your God is giving you, you shall not harden your heart or shut your hand against your poor brother, but you shall open your hand to him and lend him sufficient for his need, whatever it may be".'

Arthur groans audibly. Hasn't he had enough sermons for one day? Revd. Brown pulls a folded piece of paper from his inside pocket and turns it over in his hands. Without looking up, he says, 'Arthur, you know that although the cemetery comes under the auspices of St Mary's, the land is actually owned by the local authority.'

Arthur shrugs. Of course he knows that. Once in a blue moon they'll send a security van round, or in spring a man will come with a big ride-on mower to crop the grass verges at the busier end of the graveyard, near the gates. They never touch the tangle of trees and bushes in the older part, though, where the ancient graves are which nobody ever visits.

'There's been an application,' says Revd. Brown. 'Which the council will consider at their next planning meeting. Which is in January.'

He unfolds the paper and hands it to Arthur, who scans it wordlessly for a moment then hands it back.

'What does it mean?'

Revd. Brown lays it on the pew. 'Arthur, you know that the Old Hall, just up the road, has been used as a temporary refuge for those fleeing war and oppression in other countries. It was never meant to be anything other than emergency accommodation, and far more of these people seeking asylum in our country are coming to the borough than these ad hoc refuges can cope with.

'What this means is that the council is considering an application to develop part of the cemetery, the older part bordering the old mine site, and create there a more organised facility with accommodation, education facilities, that sort of thing.'

Arthur frowns. 'Can they do that? But what about the folk buried there?'

Revd. Brown shrugs, and stands up. 'They can at least consider it. And the application says that the graves will be relocated to freshly-consecrated ground, a patch of council-owned land adjoining St Matthew's, over the bridge. To be honest, this area of the cemetery is rarely visited. And it's quite dangerous. A lot of the old headstones are falling down; if some child wandered over there, I shudder to think what might happen.'

And then it dawns on Arthur. 'But what about the chapel?'

Revd. Brown smiles tightly. 'I'm afraid that is part of the application as well, Arthur. You must understand, you living in the chapel . . . it's something everyone has turned a blind eye to, really. Sort of a grace-and-favour situation, you might say. But the whole idea doesn't really stand up to the sort of scrutiny the council appears to be minded to turn on it with this application. Don't worry, though, I'd do my level best to find you somewhere appropriate, and close by. A nice flat, perhaps. In sheltered accommodation.'

'But what would they do with my . . . with the chapel?' frowns Arthur.

Revd. Brown looks at him in surprise. 'Why, demolish it, I'd imagine.'

Arthur follows Revd. Brown to the chapel doors and lets him out, watching him walk away up the slush-covered paths. He stays there, ignoring the biting cold wind, until the vicar is out of sight. He looks around the graves, the lawns, the overgrown undergrowth and leaning headstones, and tries to envisage it all gone, replaced with one of those awful, squat, red-brick buildings. Full of asylum seekers.

'But this is my home,' he says, and there are only the dead to hear him.

10

With the hood on her snorkel parka zipped up all the way Nicola can hear practically nothing and see only what's in front of her through a fur-lined porthole and the lenses of her glasses. She finds it vaguely reassuring, as though if she can't see or hear people, they can't see or hear her either. She shifts the plastic carrier bag to her other hand, and continues to shuffle through the slush up The Avenue, invisible against the knots of school kids walking the other way, towards the main road.

At the top of The Avenue there's a bit of common land, the snow already pocked with gently steaming holes where the morning dog walkers have let their animals leave deposits, and beyond that a bit of old land on which there used to be a factory or industrial units, long demolished. A rough path leads through the bony branches of immature trees and then to the blackened stone wall that borders the cemetery, eventually snaking across post-industrial scrubland to the site of the long-decommissioned mine.

But it's to the cemetery wall where Nicola is heading, to the L it makes at the very corner. She would have gone earlier this morning, but after being caught in the cemetery yesterday by old Calderbank she didn't want to risk riding through there again today. So she'd decided to wait until after going to the chemist for her mum, and if she hurries she should just have time.

The wall is a little higher than Nicola is tall, and the coating of snow on the capstones is as deep as her sock-covered fingers. She hauls her carrier bag on to the top, which settles with a clanking noise, and begins to haul herself up. It's slippy, but she knows where the handholds are, the broken stones, the chipped-away mortar, that allows her to join the plastic bag on the top and gingerly let herself down the other side.

This corner of the cemetery is wild and generally deserted. People aren't supposed to go here because of the danger of injury from the unstable graves; Nicola thinks it might be something to do with the old coal mine that was on the other side of the wall, some slippage or subsidence under the surface. Besides, the graves are so old here that nobody remembers the people who are buried in them.. There are even one or two very old family mausoleums, or at least, big enclosed graves. One of them has all but collapsed, the stone roof cracked and fallen within the leaning walls. The other one is still standing, solid. This is where Nicola is going.

She likes the way the cemetery looks different throughout the year. Now it seems to glow from underneath, a blanket of white. In summer when the sky is clear the light of the moon and a million stars paint it yet differently. On black, moonless nights, the headstones themselves seem to shimmer with their own, internal light, perhaps soaked up from the long, summer days.

The entrance to the small mausoleum is overgrown with brambles, which she pushes aside with her feet. There are no coffins or anything inside, of course; they've been removed a long time ago. There was once a gate or maybe a wooden door on the mausoleum, but that's long gone. Nicola fumbles inside her carrier bag for her torch, clicking it on and shining it into the corners of the stone room. Even old Calderbank doesn't come down here much; Nicola's made sure to hide her activities as well as she can, even hauling old pieces of shattered headstone to lean against the mausoleum, making it look more unsafe than it actually is.

Stacked up against one corner are tins – soup, beans, vegetables. With a can opener, of course. Inside a Tupperware box there's an old transistor radio and a pile of batteries. She has bags of twigs and wood, which she collects when its dry, and bottles of water. Matches. An A-Z map book of the local area. A bag full of cutlery, sneaked away over the months from home and school. Matches, a couple of disposable lighters. A cardboard box of newspapers.

There's an old Peek Freans biscuit tin, as well, well hidden under the newspapers. She always takes time to look at it when she comes here. She flips the lid off and takes out a Polaroid photograph, curling at the edges, of a man with curly hair holding a baby. The baby is her and the man is her dad. She has more photos, but her absolutely most prized possession is a locket, silver gone to tarnish, on a length of thin chain. If you flip it open there are two tiny photographs, one of her dad on the left and one of her as a newborn baby on the right. She found it in the bottom of one of her mum's bedroom drawers, wrapped in tissue paper, undisturbed for years.

There's a digital watch with a metal strap. All she has left of him. Sometimes she wears the watch, puts the chain with the pendant around her neck, and tries to feel a connection with the man she can't even remember. She stares hard at the photograph, trying to dredge up something from when she was a baby, tries to recall being in his arms when that picture was taken. She squeezes the button on the digital watch. The light still comes on.

Nicola empties her carrier bag on the dry earth. A couple more tins of beans, a packet of dried fruit. Some plasters and bandages she gathered up when the St John Ambulance came into school last week to give them all a first aid lesson. And a rusty garden hand fork she found dumped in the trees the other day. She's not sure what use it would be. A weapon, perhaps.

Nicola isn't scared being in the cemetery. She doesn't believe in ghosts and things like that. If ghosts existed, it stands to reason her dad would have come back, made contact with her. The fact he never has is a pretty strong argument to Nicola that there's no afterlife. But she is a bit perturbed by yesterday morning, when she thought she saw something moving in the cemetery. She would dismiss it as a fox – she's seen enough of those, even a badger once – but for those footprints in the snow, which weren't hers and couldn't have been old man Calderbank's because there were none coming from the chapel. It's not the dead that bother Nicola, it's the living. Like her mum always says, when it comes to it, you can't trust anybody else. You can only trust yourse—

There's a crunching of undergrowth from outside of the mausoleum and Nicola falls silent, her hand to her mouth as though to keep even the sound of her breathing inside her. Then she hears a voice: 'Are you sure she came this way?'

A reply: 'I saw her. So did you.'

Nicola's heart sinks to her stomach. Gemma and Kelly.

'Hang on, I think she's in here . . .'

As the two figures peer into the mausoleum, Nicola holds out the fork and shouts, 'Why can't you just leave me alone?'

The two girls stand framed in the doorway, the thin morning light behind them. Kelly looks at Gemma, who says, 'Keep your hair on.'

Nicola stands protectively in front of her supplies, still holding out the fork. 'Did you follow me here?'

'' Course we did,' says Gemma Swarbrick. 'We wouldn't be coming here on our own, would we?'

'What are *you* doing here?' says Kelly Derricott curiously. She looks around. 'What's all this stuff?'

'Nothing,' says Nicola. She wonders if she can push past them and run away. But they're taller than her, thinner, probably faster and stronger. She wouldn't even get to the wall. She feels hot tears stinging her cold eyes. Frantically she packs the photographs and pendant back in the biscuit tin and hides it under the newspapers. 'Leave me alone.'

Kelly squats down to pick up one of the tins of beans that Nicola had kicked over in her panic. 'Seriously, though. What are you doing with all this food?'

Gemma takes a cigarette out of her pencil case and clicks her lighter, which sparks twice and dies. 'Bollocks,' she says.

'Here,' says Nicola, turning around to get one of her lighters. 'Use this. But I want it back.'

'Brilliant, ta,' says Gemma. When she's lit the cigarette she says. 'What are you doing, running a shop for the people who come to the cemetery? Have you got any Marlboro Lights? Where did you get all this stuff? Did you nick it?'

Nicola watches Gemma slide the lighter into her bag. She says, 'I haven't got any money or anything. Or fags. So you might as well go away. I'm not going to fight you.'

Kelly barks a laugh. 'Why would we want to fight you? We're not, like, ten or something.'

'Then what do you want?' shouts Nicola. Nobody ever talks to her unless they want to make her look stupid or say something cruel or tell her to walk faster or not be such a dork.

'We just wondered what our mate was doing,' says Kelly.

Nicola feels hot and uncomfortable and unzips her coat, pushing the hood back off her head. Her glasses are getting all steamed up. 'We're not mates.'

'We queued up for dinner yesterday,' says Gemma, blowing out a cloud of smoke. 'What do you want, the red carpet rolled out?' She looks around critically. 'Actually, you could do with a carpet in your den. It's a bit minging with all that dirt on the floor.'

'A carpet'll just get damp and harbour bacteria,' mutters Nicola, picking up the tins and stacking them with the others. 'Besides, it's not a den.' She looks at them, dark-haired Kelly and dirty-blonde Gemma, both with their high ponytails and thin, pinched faces. Maybe if they were going to beat her up they'd have done it by now. 'It's a bunker. In case there's a nuclear war.'

She waits for them to laugh, or worse. They glance at each other, and Kelly shrugs. 'Fair enough.'

Nicola blinks. 'What?'

Gemma flicks her cigarette end outside into the snow. 'Can we come here if there's a war? You'd need to get a carpet, though. I can ask my dad. He can get anything.'

Nicola rubs her head. She can't quite process this. 'If you haven't followed me to beat me up or take the mickey out of me, what do you want?'

Gemma looks at her digital watch. 'Yeah, what are we doing, Kelly? If we're bunking off, fine. If not, we should probably get to school.'

Nicola looks at Kelly, then Gemma, then back to Kelly, who has suddenly broken out into a wide grin. Gemma frowns, annoyed. 'What is it, Kelly? Spit it out.'

'Nothing,' says Kelly, but with a sly smile that makes Nicola wary.

Gemma pulls a face. 'Double maths. Shall we sack it off? I've got a fiver. We could go to Greggs.'

Kelly considers, then looks at Nicola. 'You coming?'

Nicola shakes her head. 'I'm going to school.'

'Then so are we,' decides Kelly.

'What fresh hell can this be?' mutters Nicola, then blinks in surprise as the other girls stare at her; she hadn't realise she'd spoken out loud. 'A woman called Dorothy Parker used to say it when the doorbell went,' she says lamely. 'I read about it in the *Guardian*.'

'The *Guardian*? That's the posh paper,' says Gemma. 'You posh, then?'

Nicola thinks about her photograph, the one with her dad's shadow, her mum sitting in a wide expanse of sunlit garden. She wishes they had a garden like that now.

'We used to be, I think.'

Kelly lightly punches her arm. 'And now you're one of us. Come on, we're going to be late.'

Nicola slows for a moment, allowing the other two to get ahead, then hurries to catch them up, wondering if Kelly really believed what she just said to be as encouraging as she made it sound.

11

'They want to knock down my home,' says Arthur to the woman on the council office reception desk. He takes off his scarf, feeling sweat bead on his forehead. Between the stifling heat on the bus, the freezing walk from the bus station to the council offices, and this dry, almost unbearable heat in the lobby, he wouldn't be surprised if he comes down with something properly.

'Oh, dear,' says the woman. 'That's not very good.'

Arthur stares at her. No, it's not *very good* at all. It's about as far from *very good* as he could possibly imagine. He says, 'I've come to see what's going on.'

'Well,' says the woman. 'That sort of depends on who wants to knock your house down.'

'Well, the council, of course.'

'Ah,' says the woman, her face hardening slightly. Here we go, thinks Arthur. Now she knows which side she's on. It's them against me. She says, 'Do you have a planning application number?'

Arthur pulls the folded paper that Revd. Brown gave him out of his inside coat pocket. The woman taps something into her computer and says, 'It's an outline planning application at the moment. There won't be a great deal more information than you already have. But the plans will be available for consultation in the planning department.'

'And where's that?' says Arthur.

She points to a door on the far side of the lobby. Arthur thanks her and makes to head there, but she says, 'Wait, you can't just go in, you need an appointment. It might be busy.'

'Who do I make an appointment with?'

'Me.'

Arthur sighs. 'All right, then? Can I have an appointment?'

She pulls a tight smile. 'I'm afraid you have to make an appointment by the phone or letter.'

Arthur takes a deep breath and rubs his hand over his sweating face. 'But I'm here, now. Is the place busy?'

She taps on her keyboard. 'At the moment . . . no.'

'So can I go in?'

'Not without an appointment.'

'Bloody hell,' mutters Arthur. He remembers what Keith Cardy said about him in the pub. 'I'm a war hero, you know. I just want to look at the plans for my house. I liberated Paris so you could sit there telling me I can't go into an empty room that's ten yards from where I'm standing because I didn't get a bloody appointment.'

'There's no need to be abusive,' says the woman primly. 'I can call security.'

'All right,' says Arthur, sighing again. 'Let's say I want to object against this plan. What do I have to do?'

'Fill in a form,' she says.

'And I suppose I need to put in a request for a form, signed in triplicate by my ward councillor and tied to the leg of a carrier pigeon?'

She glares at him. 'No need to be sarcastic.' She opens a drawer and pulls out a printed piece of green A4 paper. 'Here you go. Make sure you get it back to us at least a week before the application is discussed.'

Arthur folds the sheet, puts it in his pocket with the other papers, and leaves without thanking the woman. On his way to the door he has to stand back for a party of young people in suits and frocks, carrying a tiny baby wearing an extravagant, long white dress. The baby gives him a toothless little grin, and Arthur isn't quite sure what he's meant to do in return.

Instead he nods at a large young woman in a tight red dress. 'Christening, is it?'

'Naming ceremony,' she says. 'They wouldn't let us do a christening because we didn't go to the church.' She looks, distracted, at the man carrying the baby. 'Barry, she's eating the hem of her bloody dress.'

Arthur lets them all troop past him. Nobody holds the door open for him. He opens it and turns away from the icy blast of wind, and sees that Barry has now put the baby over his shoulder, and she's still staring at Arthur, giving him a broad, wet smile.

He'd never much been one for God, hadn't Arthur. Not after the war. How, he reasoned, could there be a God who would advocate His creations killing each other? What was the point of that? Men set against men, ripping buggery out of each other with guns and cannon, tanks and mortars, then bayonets and bare hands if it came down to it? Dropping bombs on women and children? What sort of God lets that happen? When he got back to Blighty in the October of 1945 he'd already decided that life was dictated by human beings, for good or ill, and that all you could do was try your best to be one of the good ones, and do good things, and hope there were more of you than the other sort. Of course, he kept that sort of thinking to himself on the boat back over from France, because a lot of men seemed to have done the opposite thing and found God out there on the fields of Europe. Arthur suspected that was only because they were on the winning side.

Besides, Molly had her heart set on getting married in St Mary's, and Arthur wasn't going to deny her that. So he kept his philosophical musings to himself, all the way across the Channel, on the bumpy ride to the barracks at Colchester to pick up his papers and his demob suit and wave goodbye to the British Army forever, and on the train that chugged back up north. Molly wasn't waiting for him at home, though, she was still on the farm in Yorkshire where she'd been stationed with the Women's Land Army, and the harvest had to be brought in, so he'd gone across the Pennines on a rickety bus, rain lashing at the windows, and eventually walked three miles up a sodden, muddy track to where she was sequestered.

She wasn't there. Half an hour later the farmer was taking Arthur with his dripping demob suit and his squishy cardboard case and his leather guitar case by horse and cart to the hospital, where Molly had been for a week.

It was dark and late and the matron had tutted at him but she'd let him go to Molly's room, given the circumstances. He'd stood there in the doorway for a while, just looking at her. Her hair was mussed and she was deathly pale and she was thinner than she'd been when he went away, but she was beautiful. He almost didn't want to wake her, wanted that moment to last forever. He was so filled with love he felt it spilling out of his eyes a little, mingling with the rainwater on his face. Arthur didn't want that feeling to end, and he almost didn't want Molly to wake up in case she didn't feel the same way.

He noticed an almost imperceptible change in the way she was breathing, from deep to shallow, and wondered if he should go and get the matron. And then Molly opened one eye, looked at him for a while, and said, 'Are you going to come in or are you just going to stand there making a puddle on the floor?'

It had all felt a bit unreal to Arthur, standing there sopping wet, staring at Molly in her bed, but he supposed that was what war did to men. They'd been warned they might have trouble adjusting back to Civvy Street. Arthur suspected it was just a ploy to get them to sign on for a longer stretch, but he'd had his fill of uniform, just wanted to get back and take up his job down the pit, marry Molly, and fill a little house with children. But maybe this was what they meant, when they said things might seem a bit off when they got home. But he wasn't strictly home, was he? Hadn't even stopped off at home. Came straight here.

'They said you were in hospital,' said Arthur.

'They were right,' said Molly. She tried to smile but Arthur could see it was an effort. There always used to be such a glint in her eye – a wicked glint, Arthur joked with her, though Molly Hardacre was anything but wicked – but here, even reflecting the light of the bedside lamp in this little room that smelled of disinfectant, it seemed dulled, like the edge had been taken off it.

'What happened?' He still stood in the doorway, still dripping, as though if he crossed the threshold of the room he'd make whatever was happening to Molly inside it real and unchangeable. All sorts of things had whirled through his mind. Cancer was the one that kept rolling to the surface.

Molly put her hands on her stomach, hidden under the bedsheets and blanket. She gave him that half-smile again, but the corners of her mouth were wobbling.

'There was this big barrel of stuff in one of the barns,' she said. 'It was my own fault. I'd been told not to go near it. For killing pests on the crops. You know how clumsy I am, Arthur. Knocked it over. Went all over me.'

'Was it acid?' he said. 'Are you burned?'

She shook her head tightly. 'Aren't you going to come here and give us a hug, you big, daft apeth?'

And finally he dropped his case, which hit the mopped, tiled floor with a squelch of cardboard giving way, and rushed over to embrace her, smelling her hair, putting his hands around her bony shoulders. He'd never leave her alone again.

'I thought it was something serious, way they looked at me when I knocked on the door of that farm,' he whispered into her hair.

Arthur held Molly for a long time and Molly held him back tightly. Then she gently pushed him back, and held his shoulders. She looked at him.

'It was serious, love,' she said, and at last her eyes did glint, but it was the tears reflecting the bedside lamp. 'It was the stuff in the barrel. A chemical. It didn't burn me but it did something to my insides. They say I can't have babies now.'

12

Double maths is easily as excruciating as Gemma fears. It's not that she doesn't understand the frantic chalk marks Mrs Buchanan is making on the board, it's just that she can see no possible useful application of working out the volume of the largest sphere which can fit into a cylindrical biscuit tin, if the tin has a volume V and a surface area S, and that the minimum possible surface area for a given value of V is $S=3(2piV2)1/3$. Or something. When could that possibly be of any use in your entire life, unless you were going to get a job putting spheres into biscuit tins? She looks around the class. Gemma is in the top set for maths, as she is for most things. But, to be honest, the bar isn't very high. One boy is diligently scratching his name into his desk with a compass. Another has got both hands jammed down the front of his pants. A girl with thick glasses is rhythmically snorting green snot back up her nose at – and Gemma has counted – intervals of three-and-a-half seconds.

Her dad is right. She's got brains. But what's the point of brains if nobody ever gives you a chance to use them? She could walk out of school with straight As but it wouldn't make any difference. She went to Marigold Brook, she lives on the Avenues, she's Terry Swarbrick's daughter. When you're from round here, your life is mapped out for you as soon as you plop out of your mother. And if your dad sticks around long enough to see your first birthday, then you're doing better than most.

The fiver she nicked off her dad is burning a hole in her pocket. She could have been tucking into a Greggs steak bake now. Her belly rumbles. Instead she's got whatever slop they'll be serving up in the canteen at dinner time to look forward to. She saw something on the news the other day about the 'stigma of free school dinners'. She didn't even know there was any other kind; she always wondered what was wrong with the handful of freaks who actually handed money over for that crap every day. And if your parents made enough money that you didn't have to have free school dinners, why on earth would they send you to Marigold Brook?

Mrs Buchanan's voice is droning on and on, and Gemma can feel her eyes drooping. And then she becomes aware of an expectant silence, and opens her eyes to see that everyone is looking at her. The teacher is standing at the front of the class, hands on her hips.

'Still with us, Miss Swarbrick?'

Gemma shrugs. Mrs Buchanan says, 'I asked you a question. Would you like me to repeat it?'

Gemma shrugs again. Mrs Buchanan says, 'I was wondering if you could work out, based on this value of S, how we would go about working out the volume of the largest sphere that could fit inside the tin?'

Gemma glances at the scrawl on the book in front of her, and Mrs Buchanan says, 'I didn't think so. Anyone else care to—'

'Two-thirds of V,' says Gemma.

Mrs Buchanan pauses, and looks back at her. 'What did you say?'

'You'd work out the value of the volume and it would be two-thirds of that. I think.'

Mrs Buchanan makes a harrumphing sound. 'And where did you pluck that from, Miss Swarbrick?'

'Probably your coat pocket, miss,' shouts a boy from the back of the class. Gemma turns around and sticks both fingers up at him. She turns back quickly enough to see the smirk on Mrs Buchanan's face.

'Now, now, Jameson,' says Mrs Buchanan, pretending to cough into her fist. 'That's libel. We can't go around—'

'It's slander, miss,' says Gemma levelly.

The teacher blinks at her. 'What?'

'Libel is a defamatory statement that is written down. Slander is spoken defamation.'

Suddenly emboldened, and sick to the back teeth of volume and surface area, Gemma stands up and walks calmly to the front of the class. She picks up a piece of chalk from the gutter at the bottom of the blackboard and wipes away Mrs Buchanan's equations with the sleeve of her jumper.

'So, if Karl Jameson was to say, miss, that Gemma Swarbrick is a thief because everybody knows her dad's a thief, then that would be slander.' She reaches up and writes *Gemma Swarbrick is a thief* on the blackboard. 'That, on the other hand, is libel, because it has been written down and seen by one or more third parties.'

Mrs Buchanan looks taken aback. She says, 'You . . . know the law quite well, Gemma.'

Gemma nods. 'Yeah. I know, for example, that if I went over there and kicked Karl Jameson in the balls six or seven times, and kept kicking him even when he was down on the floor, that would be Actual Bodily Harm.' There's a banging of fists on desks and monkey noises from the assembled teenagers. 'I could get five years in prison for that.'

Gemma tosses the chalk at Mrs Buchanan who catches it awkwardly. She walks slowly back to her desk, fixing Karl Jameson with a stare. He sticks two lots of two fingers up at her. She says, 'But if I was to chop Karl Jameson's balls off and shove them down his throat until he choked, that would be Grievous Bodily Harm.' She casually picks up her bag from the floor and starts to put her books into it. 'I could get life.'

Gemma glances out of the window, at the tarmac playground. She can see a knot of people at the far end. She recognises a couple of them. Gemma puts her bag over her shoulder and looks at Karl Jameson, who's suddenly gone quiet, and then at Mrs Buchanan. 'I haven't decided which one I'll do the next time that little shit bad-mouths me or my family. But I have decided I'm done with this.'

Nobody says a word as Gemma walks out of the class, just thirty seconds ahead of the bell that signals the end of the lesson.

On the way to the playground Gemma sees Kelly. She says, 'I'll ask you again, what are you up to?'

'With what?' says Kelly.

'Nicola Manning. You're up to something. What is it?'

Kelly shrugs. 'I don't know, yet. Just this idea that I've got.'

'What idea?'

'Dunno. Honestly. It'll come to me soon, though.'

Gemma sighs. 'Well, if she's going to feature in the Big Kelly Derricott Secret Plan, you'd better get outside right now, because Heather Wilson and her bitches have got her.'

Gemma lets Kelly push past her and hurries after her towards the door that's banging in the biting cold wind. She follows Kelly across the playground to where Heather is standing, holding Nicola's bass guitar, while Nicola stands in mute fury, her fists clenched, tears running down her cheeks.

'Manning the Minger, she wants to be a singer, but she's got a face like a KFC Zinger!' trills Heather, strumming the guitar tunelessly, while her cronies laugh themselves silly around her.

'Give that back, Heather, you cow,' says Kelly, marching up and shouldering two of Heather's mates out of the way. Gemma brings up the rear, wondering what she's done. She only wanted to know what Kelly's grand plan was, not get involved in a scrap. The pair of them could take this pack of bitches, easily, but like Gemma said to Kelly, there's only one side that's going to get all the blame.

'Well, look who it is,' says Heather, a sneer on her face. 'Scum and Scummer.' She raises an eyebrow at Kelly. 'Surprised you're showing your face near me after what you did last night. I'd send you a bill for the jacket but it'd probably be your family's food budget for the entire year.'

Kelly shakes her head. 'Why are you so horrible, Heather? You're no different to us.'

Gemma sees the other girl's face harden. 'Don't say that, Derricott. I'm nothing like you. I've got a dad with a job and a sister at university. We own our own house and we've got a car that starts first time you try it.'

'You still go to the same school and live in the same shithole,' offers Gemma.

Heather laughs at her, at both of them. 'It's only a shithole because they built all those council houses for scum like you. But you know what the real difference is?'

Gemma and Kelly wait for her to enlighten them. She does. 'We might be swimming in the same swamp, but I know I'm going to drag myself out of it. I'm going to go to university and get a job and probably move to London. And I'm never going to look back.' She looks Gemma and Kelly up and down. 'You lot? You're stuck here. You'll never get out. It might as well be a prison.'

Heather shoves the guitar back into Nicola's arms and with a flick of her hair indicates to her gang it's time to go. She pushes between Gemma and Kelly, hitting them both out of the way with her shoulders. Before she heads back to the school, Heather pauses, and turns back to them. 'It's a prison. And you've been given life sentences.'

✳ 13 ✳

Arthur walks around the chapel, brushing his fingers along the bookshelf, touching the kitchen worktop, putting a shovelful of coal into the burner. The things he's made, the things he's repaired, the things he's collected. All to make himself a home. And now they want to take it away from him.

Would it be so bad? Revd. Brown had said to him. A nice little flat. It would be warm, not like the chapel. There'd be people on hand, if he got ill. A warden. She could even do a bit of shopping for him. And he'd be able to come down to the cemetery, every day if he wanted. Though, hazarded Revd. Brown . . . might it be time for Arthur to . . . move on?

But he doesn't want to live in a flat. He's warm enough in here. And he doesn't get ill. Arthur exhales loudly. Apart from the bloody heartburn from Carol Leigh's pie that he can't seem to shift. Besides, it's not about being warm or safe. It's about being close to Molly, about going to bed every night knowing that he's as close as he can be to her, about waking up every morning knowing he's not left her alone, that he never would leave her alone.

Arthur decides to take a walk to mull things over. His route takes him around the top of the new estate and down the Donkey Lane, as they used to call it when he was a lad. He probably shouldn't be walking down there on his own; Cardy and his mob in the Black Diamond would be cautioning against all kinds of undesirables lurking in the trees that arch over to give the dirt track its own canopy of brittle, bony branches. The path is covered with snow and he picks his way along carefully. To one side, beyond the trees, the

69

ground gives way sharply to a sluggish brook, the Little River. On the other side, a couple of fallow fields give way to the backs of an old terrace. A dog barks from somewhere. Arthur pauses, leaning on the rough bark of one of the trees. Did he used to get so out of breath walking up the Donkey Lane back in summer? Maybe it's just the cold. Maybe those endless fags they chain-smoke in the Diamond. Arthur doesn't smoke, but that's what did for Roy Castle a couple of years back, wasn't it? Passive smoking, they call it. Great trumpet player, was Roy Castle. Not a bad voice, either. Did all those songs about it raining.

Arthur crunches up the last few feet of the track, emerging on to the quiet main road. He's just a little way uphill from the cemetery, by the bridge beneath which the railway line runs. An intercity train peeps its horn as it thunders underneath, off past the Low Spring Branch engineering sheds, from where he's just looped around, and barrelling into the darkness bound, ultimately, he supposes, for London.

The pavements are glossy and icy here, and Arthur puts a hand on the smoke-blackened wall of the railway bridge as he shuffles down. Across the road is the Old Hall. The former pub rears up darkly against the grey clouds, its snug and lounge and upstairs guest rooms divided and sub-divided to provide accommodation for God knows how many asylum seekers. Arthur sees the faces of the knot of men hanging outside the door turn to him as he passes on the other side of the road. They all have a look about them, don't they? Always seem to be wearing leather jackets. Their trousers too tight. And a vaguely haunted look. So these are the people they want to build houses for, and in the process tear down his chapel, his home.

He can imagine what Cardy and his boys would be saying now if they were walking past. But Arthur's seen that look these men have in their eyes before. It's a look that says those eyes have seen things. Arthur saw that look on too many men, back when he was overseas. And he saw it afterwards, as well, on men from all sides. The look that said you'd seen things you'd never forget, things that would keep you awake at night, things that would ferret into your dreams, make them nightmares. Things that Cardy and that lot would never understand.

Arthur wonders where they've come from, these men. What drove them to leave their homes and come here. What they've seen. He can feel their eyes still on him, but he puts his head down and concentrates on not slipping as he crosses the main road and heads for the wrought iron gates set into the perimeter wall of the cemetery.

For a moment, he thinks he sees a shape flit across the pale light issuing from the chapel windows. Arthur rubs his eyes with his fingers, their tips cold and purple. Just the wind blowing up a flurry of snow, or a bird, or his old eyes.

Arthur stops at Molly's grave, and brushes the snow from the headstone, idly wondering what she'd think about Cardy and his mob, about the Patels moving into their old house, about the men lurking outside the Old Hall. That's one of the things he misses. Molly and her opinions. Something to say about everything. What would she have to say about all this business, about them wanting to take away his home?

You had a perfectly good home, Arthur Calderbank, she'd say. *The home we shared together. Why couldn't you have just kept hold of that one? What do you have to say about that?*

Arthur doesn't have much to say about anything these days. Never really had, to be honest. Nowt to say about owt, as Molly'd have put it. There's plenty of folk likes the sound of their own voice, he thinks. Nothing Arthur Calderbank's ever got to say is going to make the slightest of difference to anything or anyone. Still, he thinks as he picks at a dead leaf sticking to the front of the stone, she's not wrong. They did have a lovely home together, and perhaps he should have kept a tighter hold of it, not just drifted away from it, let it drift away from him, after she'd died.

Arthur frowns as he catches a movement deeper in the graveyard. There's a man with a shock of dark, curly hair, and wearing a leather jacket. And he's kicking a battered little football to a small child wrapped up in a big green coat.

Arthur shakes his head and storms off towards them, waving furiously. 'Hey! It's not a play park! It's a cemetery! Show some respect.'

The man stops and picks up the ball, and drags the small child – a girl, Arthur can see now – to his side. The man looks down at his feet as Arthur approaches. He's one of that lot. From the Old

Hall. He won't meet Arthur's stare, so instead he glances at the girl. She must be three or four. Her hair is in pigtails tied up with green ribbons. She gives him a gap-toothed smile and says, 'Zdravo!'

Arthur points at the football in the man's hands. 'Not a park! Understand? A cem-e-tery. For dead people. Not for games.'

The man looks up at Arthur. He's in his thirties, maybe, the skin on his face pockmarked beneath his stubble. Their eyes meet briefly and Arthur sees a flash of something haunted there.

'I am sorry,' says the man. 'We live in the place there.' He nods his head in the direction of the Old Hall. 'It is very, how you say, cramped. I wanted some fresh air for her.'

'Where are you from' says Arthur.

The man looks at him. 'Bosnia. Sarajevo. We came three years ago, to escape the war, when Ajša had just been born.' He looks down at the girl and Arthur sees him smile fondly, sees the hollowness in his eyes replaced by something else. 'Ajša, say hello to the nice man. In English please.'

'Hello, nice man,' says Ajša shyly, burying her face in the side of her father's leather jacket.

'And you are with your wife?' says Arthur. 'You've lived in the Old Hall for three years? I didn't think they'd been using it for that long.'

The man shakes his head. 'We have been moved around. We were near London, then Birmingham, then we came here. We share a room with one other family. We are waiting for our application to be allowed to stay to be heard.'

'And do you just have one daughter?'

The man smiles, and ruffles the girl's hair. 'Ajša is not my daughter. She is my brother's girl,' he says in a low whisper. A cloud passes over his face. 'He and his wife were killed. Someone threw a landmine through their apartment window.' His shoulders rise and fall. 'We are Muslims.'

Arthur shakes his head. 'The poor mite. And you brought her over here?'

'Yes. But we treat her as if she is ours. She never knew my brother. She was too young. It is very sad what happened, but for Ajša . . .' He shrugs again. 'What is important is that she is with people

72

who love her and care for her. If we had not taken her she would have gone to an orphanage, and they are terrible places.' The man pauses, his forehead wrinkling as though he is trying to remember something. 'I hear a thing in England which people say. It is blood is thicker than water. I thought it funny the first time I heard it.'

'It means family is more important than anything else,' says Arthur.

The man nods. 'Somebody explained it to me. But I do not know if it is true. I think love is thicker than blood. I think family can be whoever you want them to be. If you just love them enough.'

Arthur says nothing. The man smiles and takes Ajša by the hand. 'Come on, let's get back.' He turns then looks back at Arthur. 'I am sorry. We will not play in the cemetery again.'

Arthur watches them go, then turns to head to the chapel.

✳ 14 ✳

When Kelly gets home from school her mum is sitting at the kitchen table in her tabard, eating a sandwich. She can see her dad in the small garden through the window, just standing there in the darkening afternoon, seemingly staring blankly at a tall patch of weeds.

'What's up with him?' says Kelly, opening the fridge and staring into its depths, her school bag dangling from her hand. There's nothing in there.

'Oh, what's always up with him?' says her mum through a mouthful of cheese and Branston pickle. 'I wish to God he could get a job, Kelly.'

'Be nice to have a bit more money,' she agrees, poking at an open packet of greying sausages.

'He can always find a few quid to go drinking with Keith Cardy in the Black Diamond,' sighs her mum.

Kelly abandons the fridge and says, 'Why are you home early, anyway? Thought you were on afternoons.'

'I am,' says her mum. 'I'm going back in a minute. And you're coming with me.'

Kelly blinks. 'What?'

'Your dad was talking to Pete. He told him what happened last night. Oh, Kelly, why do you have to be so stupid? Why don't you think before you do things? I know it wasn't much but that job brought a bit of cash in.'

Kelly sticks out her bottom lip. 'I hated it. And I hate Pete. He's a right miserable old tight-arse.' She pauses. 'Why am I coming to the factory with you, again?'

Her mum puts her plate in the sink and bangs on the window, pointing in exaggerated fashion to the front of the house and mouthing 'we're going'. She grabs her bag and just says, 'Get your coat.'

The factory is a ten-minute walk from their house, on the edge of the Avenues. It's a squat, single-storey, brick-built place, surrounded by a wire fence topped with vicious barbs. There's a reception at the front, office space above, and a distribution bay at the back where chugging vans are loaded up with big brown boxes and dispatched with goods to distant places.

Kelly realises with mild surprise that she doesn't actually know what they make there. She, like everybody else, just calls it *the factory*.

Her mum leads her into the front reception where a woman Kelly recognises as the mum of a girl from her history class nods at her. 'All right, Janice.'

'We're here to see Maureen,' says her mum, and the woman presses a button under her desk. A door to one side springs open with a beep, and her mum says, 'Come on, then.'

Kelly follows her mum along a corridor and through a set of solid doors which open out into the factory floor, a vast space dominated by a conveyor belt at which women in the same blue tabards as her mum sit and pack metallic components into cardboard boxes. It's noisy with the clatter of the machinery and a hubbub of conversation. At the far end of the space there are more machines, mainly operated by men in blue overalls, and the whine of cutting equipment, the occasional shower of sparks.

'What exactly do you do here?' says Kelly, raising her voice to be heard above the din.

Her mum points at the men. 'They make the sprockets.' She nods towards the women. 'We pack them.' Beyond the conveyor belt Kelly can see the dark blue of the darkening sky through a huge hatch, where the vans and their drivers wait. 'And they take them off to where they're needed.'

'What's a sprocket? What do they use them for?'

'They're like cogs,' says her mum, walking on past the men and through another door. 'God knows what they do with them. We

75

make bloody thousands of the things though. I suppose they go in machines somewhere.'

Up a flight of stairs is an office, lined with desks and computer monitors, and her mum waves at a big woman with red hair, wearing a pair of too-tight trousers and a blouse she's bulging out of. 'Maureen, hiya. This is Kelly.'

'Hello, love!' says Maureen with a toothy smile. 'Your mum says you'll be joining us.'

Kelly opens her mouth, then shuts it again, and looks at her mum. Maureen riffles a sheaf of papers in her hands. 'There are some forms here, just the usual stuff. Your mum can bring them back in on Monday.'

Kelly's mouth has suddenly gone dry. She glares at her mum and croaks, 'What?'

Maureen licks her finger and counts the pages in her hands. 'We won't be able to start you on Saturdays until after Christmas. We have a few students here taking up the slack over the holidays, but they'll all be gone back to university or whatever in the New Year.' She smiles at Kelly. 'Chance'd be a fine thing, wouldn't it? All that boozing and staying in bed until *Countdown* comes on. Friend of mine, her daughter goes to Liverpool. Some days she only has to go in for lectures for an hour! Imagine that! Nice work if you can get it.' She hands over the papers to her mum. 'Not for the likes of us, though, eh? Get a proper job soon as you can, that's what my old man always said.'

'It'll just be Saturdays at first,' says her mum, looking pointedly at Kelly. 'Seeing as you lost your other job.'

'When are you fifteen, love?' asks Maureen.

'February,' says Kelly. She can feel panic rising in her chest. 'But—'

'So you'll be leaving school year after next,' nods Maureen. 'You do a good job on the Saturdays, I think you'll have no trouble going full time then. We might be able to start you early, depends whether you bother doing your exams or not. We have girls leave school in March or April, come straight to us.' She sticks her tongue out and pulls a face. 'I mean, exams, urgh. Why bother if you don't need them? Money in your pocket, that's right, isn't it, love?'

'So she can start in January?' says her mum.

'I reckon so, about the middle of the month. We'd start her off on just cleaning up, bit of sweeping, wiping down the machines, that sort of thing. But we'd train her up on the packing as soon as we could.' Maureen smiles broadly. 'You could end up sitting next to your mum, Kelly. Wouldn't that be lovely?'

Her mum looks at her watch. 'Speaking of which, I'd better get back to my post. Thanks again, Maureen. I'll bring these forms back on Monday.'

Kelly numbly follows her mum back down the stairs and on to the factory floor. 'You could have said something,' she says quietly.

Her mum pulls a face at her. 'What? You'll have to get used to speaking up in here, love.'

'Nothing.' Kelly stops and watches a man with tufts of white hair taking shiny sprockets off a machine and inspecting them over his glasses.

'I'd better get back to work,' shouts her mum. 'You go straight on back through those double doors and that'll take you to the reception. I'll see you at home.'

Kelly watches her go then turns back to see what the man is doing. He tuts loudly, and tosses the sprocket into a big plastic bin. He catches her looking at him and nods. 'All right. You come for a job?'

'Apparently,' says Kelly, walking over. She points to the bin. 'Why did you throw that one away?'

The man fishes into the bin and pulls out the sprocket. It's like a star, with elaborate points. He holds it up and puts his finger on one of the spikes. 'See this? It's out a few mill.'

Kelly holds out her hand and he gives it to her. She can't see any difference between that point and the next. The man nods. 'You can't see it, but I've been inspecting sprockets for thirty years. And let me tell you, every one has to be exactly the same. Otherwise, they don't do their job, do they? You get one sprocket that's out by a fraction, and it buggers up the whole game.'

'What do they use them for?' says Kelly, scrutinising the sprocket to find the flaw.

The man shrugs. 'All sorts of things. You need lots of little cogs to keep a big machine turning. They might not look like much on

77

their own, but together they make things work. They just all have to crack on with their job. Nobody ever sees what a sprocket does, and that's the way it should be.'

Kelly glances over to where her mum has sat down at the conveyor belt and is already picking up bunches of sprockets and placing them in a cardboard box.

'Can I keep this?' says Kelly.

The man pulls a face. 'Don't see why not. But a sprocket that won't do its job is no use to anyone, is it? It can't be part of the machine, can it?'

'No, it can't,' says Kelly, putting the cog into her coat pocket and heading for the doors.

Kelly sits wrapped in her dressing gown on the sofa, watching *Live & Kicking*, and laughing at Mr Blobby as he prances around the presenters. That Jamie Theakston is well fit. But Kelly also likes that Zoe Ball. She bets she'd be loads of fun to have as a mate. Not that Kelly Derricott is ever likely to be mates with someone like Zoe Ball. Not when she's working at the factory for the rest of her life, packing bloody sprockets into cardboard boxes and sitting next to her mum. She groans and sticks a cushion over her face.

Her mum's in the kitchen making toast and her dad's half-heartedly trying to stick down a corner of the peeling wallpaper in the living room, with sugary water. He's in his pyjamas and dressing gown, too. Kelly's noticed that he sometimes doesn't even bother getting dressed some days. She remembers when he used to work at the pit. He would come home and the first thing he would do would be to pull off his tie, with a heart-felt sigh. But the mine was closed down when Kelly was about four, and he hasn't really held down a proper job ever since.

Her mum comes in and gives a plate of toast to Kelly. She watches her dad sticking down the wallpaper for a minute, then says, 'Do you think we should get the Christmas decorations down from the loft after?'

Kelly can feel her dad tense up from where she's sitting. He hates Christmas, mainly because they're always broke. He hates Saturdays, as well, because at some point today her mum's going to float the idea of going to Kwik Save, and they're going to have to address exactly how much money they've got, which is never enough. Kelly begins to wolf down her toast; she'd rather be out of the house when that inevitable row flares up. Not that she's any idea where she's going to go, especially as the snow's not let up.

The front door goes and in comes Mick, her brother. He doesn't have his girlfriend with him, but he is wearing a nice new pair of boots, Kelly notices.

'Hello, love,' says her mum warmly, kissing him on the cheek. 'Ooh, you're like a block of ice. Do you want a coffee?'

'Why not?' says Mick, plonking himself on the sofa next to Kelly. He unwinds the scarf from around his neck and holds his hands out to the one bar on the electric fire. 'Everybody happy?'

Kelly shrugs. Mick shouts over, 'Dad.'

Her dad grunts. 'Have you got any wallpaper paste?'

Mick pats his pockets and winks at Kelly. 'Not on me. Oh, your post was on the mat.' He tosses three or four envelopes on to the coffee table.

Her mum comes in from the kitchen and puts a mug of coffee on the table, picking up the post. 'Bill. Bill. Overdue bill. Oh, there's one here for you, Brian. How's Jane?'

'Still pregnant,' nods Mick, and takes a mouthful of coffee. Her dad warily circles the envelope her mum has tossed on the chair for him, inspecting it with suspicion.

Her mum picks up the envelope and pushes it into her dad's hands, sitting down on the chair and cradling her coffee. 'Have you thought about where you'll have the christening?'

Mick shrugs. 'Probably won't bother.'

Her mum tuts. 'Your nan'll be spinning in her grave.'

Kelly watches her dad as he retreats to the back of the room, staring at the envelope as though he can see what's inside with X-ray vision. Kelly turns back to *Live & Kicking*. That Jamie Theakston is *well* fit.

Her mum goes into the kitchen and there's a clatter of something falling. 'Bloody hell, Brian,' she calls. 'Have you not seen to this cupboard door yet?'

'I had a look at it,' mumbles her dad.

'You're supposed to fix it, not just look at it!' shouts her mum.

'Find me a screwdriver and I'll do it myself.'

Her dad swears under his breath and puts the letter down. 'I'm coming.'

Mick leans over and rubs Kelly's mussed up bed hair with his knuckles. 'And how's you, Smelly?'

She pushes him away. 'All right, Prick.' She pauses. 'Well, apart from the fact they've got me a job at the bloody factory.'

Mick grins. 'Yeah, I heard you got sacked from Pete's stall. Wish I could have seen you spray paint over that Wilson girl. They're a right stuck-up bunch of cocks, that family.'

Kelly grins, then her shoulders slump. 'Yeah, but Mick, now I've got every Saturday sweeping up sodding . . . sprocket dust, to look forward to. And they're going to give me a full-time job when I leave school.'

Mick punches her lightly in the arm. 'That's brilliant news, Smell.'

'No it's not!' says Kelly. She feels like she wants to cry. 'Is that it for me, then? Packing shit into cardboard boxes for the rest of my life?'

Mick considers. 'Well, maybe not the rest of your life. Just until you find somebody stupid enough to get you knocked up. Maybe you should try the blind school up town.'

'Prick,' says Kelly, punching him back.

He sips at his coffee, then says, 'Seriously, though, it's good to have something lined up. And the Saturday job means you'll be at least bringing a bit of money in.'

There's a vigorous banging then a volley of swearing from the kitchen. Kelly murmurs, 'It's *him* that should be bringing money in.'

'He's trying,' says Mick softly. 'You don't know what it's like, Kelly. There's just not the work out there. And the longer you're jobless, the harder it is to get back in the door.'

'Why doesn't *he* go and sweep up in the fucking factory then?' says Kelly sullenly.

'Because he's proud,' says Mick. 'He's got dignity. He had a good job before. You're too young to remember properly.'

Kelly stares at the TV. Zoe and Jamie are trying to talk to the camera but Mr Blobby is rolling around on them. 'So it's OK for him to be proud, but I have to work in a shithole factory until I get preggers?' She glances over as her dad shuffles into the room and stares at the curling-up wallpaper for a bit, shaking his head sadly. 'He doesn't look very proud to me.'

'What else would you do, though, Kell?' says Mick.

On the telly, Jamie has finally fought off Mr Blobby and gets to announce the next item. The camera pans quickly across the studio and a group of floppy haired boys begins to thrash their guitars.

'I don't know,' says Kelly thoughtfully.

'Mick, love,' calls her mum from the kitchen.

Kelly aims a playful kick at him as he gets up off the couch. She watches her dad trying to flatten down the wallpaper, then he gives up and goes back to look at the envelope that came for him. Another bill, probably. Another threat. Maybe they'll turn the electricity off, or the gas, or the bailiffs will come round. Except there's nothing in here worth taking, notes Kelly.

What would they do if she did get pregnant, she wonders. She couldn't live here. She'd have to get a council house, and live on her own. They put single mums up at the top of the list. The thought of having a kid makes her feel sick. She's never even done it with a boy. She wouldn't let any of the lads at Marigold Brook within ten feet of her. They're all minging. Still, it would get her out of working at the factory, she supposes. What would be worse? The rest of your life packing boxes or bringing up a baby at the age of fifteen? It's like that Indiana Jones film that was on the telly, the old knight in the cave with all the cups. *Choose wisely*. Except all the cups are filled with poison.

As her dad finally tears into the letter, Kelly glances back to the kitchen, just in time to see Mick passing her mum a wad of what looks like tenners, which she stuffs into the pocket of her dressing gown. She puts a hand on his shoulder and kisses his cheek. Then she hears her dad swear.

Her mum and Mick have heard too, and they emerge from the kitchen, to see her dad steadying himself on the wall. Her mum's face crinkles up. 'Oh, Brian, whatever is it?'

Kelly bites her lip. This is going to be bad. She's never seen her dad show any emotion at all since . . . forever. He never laughs, he never cries, he never even shouts at her any more. He just exists, drifting around the house like a ghost.

But something's knocked him off his feet, nearly. Maybe somebody's died. Maybe they're going to get kicked out of the house. Maybe, maybe, maybe . . .

Her dad looks up and blinks. 'I've got a job interview.'

✳ **16** ✳

Kelly doesn't know why she goes to the graveyard. Her feet just take her there on automatic pilot as her brain works furiously. She finds Nicola's nuclear bunker, but there's no one there. In fact, there's no one in the cemetery at all, except for a lone figure near the chapel. Old Mr Calderbank. Kelly's heard her dad talking about him. Those blokes he drinks with in the Black Diamond say Mr Calderbank is a war hero, but her mum said he wasn't to get too deep in with that Keith Cardy and his boys, that they were bad news.

Kelly watches Mr Calderbank for a while. He seems to be wiping snow from the gravestones, which is a bit of a hiding to nothing as the snow's coming down harder than ever. She's about to turn back and go home when she sees him lose his footing and disappear behind one of the headstones.

She runs over and when she gets there Mr Calderbank is picking himself up and brushing wet snow from his trousers. 'Silly old fool,' he mutters to himself.

'Are you all right?' says Kelly. 'I saw you fall.'

Mr Calderbank peers at her. 'I just slipped. Who are you?'

'Kelly Derricott. I live on the Avenues.'

The old man nods. 'Arthur Calderbank.' He pauses. 'Um, thank you. For coming over.'

Kelly says, 'I know who you are. My dad says you're a war hero.'

'That's what they say,' mutters Arthur. He looks around. 'Are you on your own? I hope you're not up to no good.'

There it is again. Everybody assumes that the estate kids are up to something. Kelly lets it go, and instead she says, 'What are you doing?'

Mr Calderbank grunts. 'Trying to keep the graves clear of snow.'

'Why?'

'Because that's my job. I'm the caretaker.'

Kelly looks around. 'It's still snowing, though. Why don't you wait until it stops?'

Mr Calderbank sighs. 'Because it's better to keep on top of things. If you wait until problems get too big, then they can be difficult to tackle.' He starts to walk off, back towards the big old chapel.

'Why do you live there?' says Kelly.

Mr Calderbank pauses and turns to her. 'Do you always ask so many questions?'

Kelly shrugs in her coat. 'Why do you live on your own?'

He looks at her for a long time, then points at her feet. 'Because my wife's dead. And you're standing right on her grave. I think you should go home, now. This cemetery's not a playground, you know.'

Kelly watches until Mr Calderbank reaches the door of his chapel and then turns around and heads back towards home, thinking furiously about the brilliant idea that's still just out of reach.

From the big window, Arthur watches the swaddled shape of Kelly Derricott working her way back through the cemetery in the snow. Perhaps if he and Molly had ever had children, he might understand them a bit more. In his day, children were seen and not heard. Young girls especially didn't stand there asking questions of their elders.

The branches he cut from the brambles have dried out and, wearing his gloves, Arthur snaps them up and feeds them into the burner. He puts the kettle on and while he's waiting for it to boil he lapses into a coughing fit. He hopes he isn't getting a chill.

When he's made a cup of tea, Arthur pulls a pew as close as he dare to the wood burner and takes another look at the letter Revd. Brown left him. He didn't even know they were allowed to build on graveyards. He inspects the red line that borders the area on which they want to build these new apartments for the refugees. Molly's grave is right on the boundary; does that mean they'll be digging her up and moving her, or not? He's not sure he could stand that. Not sure he'll let them. But the chapel's definitely within the red line, like a target in a war zone. What can an old man do in the face of all this?

It's not a done deal, of course. It has to go to the planning committee, which is on January 9. There's an address for people to send objections to. He wonders what he'll say? You can't knock down the chapel because it's my home. Revd. Brown was right; he's not even meant to be living here, not really.

Why do you live there? Kelly Derricott had said. She's too young. She wouldn't understand. He's not sure anybody understands. Plenty of people lose their loved ones and nobody ever moves into the bloody graveyard to be with them, do they? Not normal people.

If he has to move, he'll have to pack up all this stuff. Not that he has much, really. Pots and pans. Plates and cups. His medals. His guitar. He looks at it, propped up in the corner. Hasn't played it for years. Not since Molly died. Not even sure he can remember how. On a whim, Arthur picks himself up, endures a short coughing fit, and goes to get the instrument. He unzips the bag and sits down with it on his knee, head cocked as he tunes it by ear. It reminds him of the war, and of Peter Bergmann, and of Molly, and all the things he has lost.

Strumming the strings with his thumb, Arthur closes his eyes and begins to play, and sets himself adrift on a black sea of memories.

They said that, after the funeral, things would start to get better. Somebody even told Arthur that he'd be able to move on, as though his Molly was just a chapter in his life that was now closed and he was on to the next thing. But Molly wasn't a chapter, she was the whole book, and now she was gone Arthur simply closed the covers and the story was at an end.

It was all quite quick, he supposes. A mild autumn when she got the news from the doctors, and a bad winter when she died. The gravediggers had a job on to get the hole dug. Arthur had told them to make it deep enough for two, and when the mourners had gone he just stood in the rain, staring down at the hump of earth, wishing they'd just not bothered filling it in so he could just throw himself down there with Molly.

Arthur went home to their house and it was cold and empty and strange, like it was missing a room. But he walked in all of the rooms and they were all there. They just felt different, bigger, as though they were missing something. He sat for a long time on their bed, gazing into the drawer where Molly kept her tights and bras. He wondered what he was supposed to do with them. He went down to the kitchen and put the kettle on. Without thinking, he made two cups of tea. He left one to go stone cold on the side, and took the other into the living room, where he let his go cold as well. He mechanically watched all the programmes Molly used to like, the soaps and the quiz shows and the news. Then he went to bed and stared at the dark ceiling until he eventually dozed off, fully expecting that he would die in his sleep and finally be back with Molly.

When he awoke the next morning he put a hand out to Molly's cold side of the bed and for a moment wondered where she was. When the realisation hit him, it was like a hammer. He got up, absent-mindedly made two cups of tea again, then went out without breakfast, without even having a wash or a shave, to stand at the foot of Molly's grave, just staring at the mud. It was lashing down with rain again and he stood there until long after it went dark and his stomach was growling for food.

He did this for the next week. He didn't even notice that Christmas had come and gone. It was on New Year's Day that the vicar of St Mary's, the old Revd. Barker found him, sniffling, eyes rheumy, sweating hot and shivering cold all at once. He coaxed Arthur into the vicarage for a cup of tea, then called the doctor. Arthur was sent off to hospital where they treated him for pneumonia. He was in for a fortnight. It was touch and go, they said. Arthur wanted it to be go, wanted to close his eyes and never wake up. But after every fitful sleep he did wake up, and got stronger by the day. He cursed his constitution, but soon he was well enough to leave the hospital, though signed off from his job at the engineering works for a full month.

'You know,' said Revd. Barker, after Arthur had been discharged, 'you don't have to suffer in silence. God's house is always open to you.'

But Arthur already had a house, and it was there he stayed until he was strong enough to walk along the main road and visit Molly's grave, and apologise for not being there for so long. He felt guilty about being on paid sick leave when there were so many men in the town out of work after the pit had closed, but the following summer he turned sixty-five and was pensioned off.

There was a short speech on the factory floor and Arthur was given a carriage clock by a manager young enough to be his grandson. The man had to keep glancing at a card with Arthur's name on it. As he shook Arthur's hand, he said, 'Retired now, eh? The world's your oyster. You can do anything you want.'

He wasn't from round here, and had obviously no idea how much the state pension paid every week. But it was just enough to get by on, and Arthur put the carriage clock on the mantelpiece, beside the photo from his and Molly's wedding day. And he watched the hands tick round, painfully slowly, marking out the long, interminable days without Molly. They had made idle plans for their retirement, talked about maybe getting a caravan some day, of taking holidays to Scotland or the Lake District, of tea dances and gardening and other things that had sounded so normal and enticing but now seemed strange and alien to Arthur. He had promised Revd. Barker that he'd only visit Molly's grave on Sundays, more often in nicer weather, and on birthdays and anniversaries. But as each day of retirement blended seamlessly into the next, he found himself drifting towards the cemetery again, like a ghost haunting its gravel paths.

One morning, Arthur got to the cemetery to find the old chapel had been vandalised. Someone had spray-painted *THATCHER IS A BITCH* on the wall, and kicked in the door. He couldn't say he disagreed with the sentiment, but a graveyard chapel, even a derelict one, wasn't the place to air your opinions.

They'd used to use the chapel for ceremonies but it had fallen into disrepair since they decided to hold the funerals at St Mary's. Arthur surveyed the damage and pushed open the door. There were a few crushed beer cans and some dog-ends. The place was a bit of a state inside, but nothing that couldn't be fixed up. He felt his hands itching, and since it was pension day he went on the front to the shops to buy a bucket, some cleaning fluid, and some Brillo pads. Within an hour he'd scrubbed the graffiti from the soot-blackened stone. Then he considered the door. He had some lengths of timber at home that could patch that up. And a padlock. He bit his lip and ruminated for a moment, then said, 'I'll be back tomorrow, Molly.'

Over the next four weeks, as summer rolled into autumn, Arthur fixed up the chapel. To his surprise, there was still electricity and running water. He'd let himself in on rainy days, and from the windows he could see Molly's grave. He would talk to her quietly, and busy himself tidying and fixing in the old chapel. He felt at peace, though it was nothing to do with God. It was being so close to Molly, so close he could almost feel her with him. When he had to go home at night he felt bereft.

The first night he slept in the chapel, under a pile of blankets brought from home and on two pews pushed together, Revd. Barker found him, and woke him by hammering on the door. It was just after two in the morning.

'I saw a light on,' said the vicar, frowning and looking around the chapel when Arthur, bleary-eyed, let him in. 'I thought there was a fire.'

'There will be in a minute.' Arthur put a match to the scrunched up paper on the wood-burning stove he'd set up and connected to the chimney that used to lead to the crematorium furnace. He pulled an envelope from his coat pocket, glanced at it, and screwed it up, feeding the yellow flames.

'That looked important,' frowned Revd. Barker.

'I've missed some rent payments. I think they want me out of the house.'

The vicar sighed. 'You should have come to me sooner. Maybe the church can help.'

Arthur nodded. 'Maybe the church *can*.' He looked at Revd. Barker. 'Let me live here.'

Mrs Emley is a thin, bird-like woman with a downturned mouth who always wears long, pleated skirts that brush her bony ankles and high-collared blouses with a cardigan over the top. She is pale and haunted-looking, and seems too delicate a creature for the raucousness of Marigold Brook, which is probably why she's rarely seen out of the music rooms. She looks at the three girls in front of her with a look of mild horror on her face.

'Nicola? Do you want to say that again?'

Nicola stares at her feet and mumbles, 'I want my friends to sit in while I practise.'

'Please, miss,' says Kelly in a wheedling voice. 'We want to watch Nicola play her guitar.'

'Bass,' mutters Nicola.

Mrs Emley glances around, at the drum kit, at the guitars resting on their stands, at the keyboard in the corner of the room which is lined with soundproof boards, each one a matrix of tiny holes. Gemma wonders how something with holes in it can be soundproof. Stands to reason the holes would let the noise through. She should probably have taken more notice in music. Or science, maybe. Or anything, come to that.

The teacher rubs her pointed chin. 'I don't know, Nicola. I know you, and you're a wonderful student, but . . .' She takes a deep breath. 'Do you know how much trouble I had getting new music equipment last year? Nobody wants to spend budget on things like this. Tooth and nail, I had to fight. And I was told in no uncertain terms that there won't be anything in the budget next year, or the year after that, or . . . probably forever.'

'We're not going to nick anything, miss,' says Kelly.

Gemma feels Mrs Emley's gaze linger on her for a moment. That's all right. She's used to that. Comes with having a dad like she has.

Mrs Emley shakes her head, not in refusal but in resignation. 'Fine. Fine. You can sit in with Nicola this lunch hour. But any messing about, or damage, and you're all barred from the music block. Including you, Nicola.'

At the door, Mrs Emley pauses. 'Are either of you girls actually interested in music?'

Gemma looks to Kelly, and they both shrug. 'Not really, miss.'

Mrs Emley sighs and lets herself out of the room to make a rare foray into the lawless corridors of Marigold Brook.

Nicola stands in the centre of the room, staring at them. Gemma smiles encouragingly. 'Go on, then. Do your practising.'

'Why did you follow me here?'

'We told you,' says Kelly 'We're your mates.'

Gemma casts Kelly a look. *Are* they Nicola's mates? Gemma and Kelly, they've always been quite friendly, in that Marigold Brook way. Which means watching your back and not giving too much away, and navigating your way through five years of school maintaining superficial relationships but not letting anyone get too close. People make loose associations, form alliances. There's strength in numbers. In which case, maybe it wouldn't do any harm for Gemma and Kelly to be mates with Nicola Manning.

'Why don't you show us how to do music?' suggests Kelly.

'I don't know. . .'

'We won't break anything,' she says.

'Or nick anything,' says Gemma.

Nicola ponders. Then smiles. 'All right.'

Gemma slides on to the stool behind the drum kit and picks up the sticks, weighing them in her hands. She runs her palm over the taut skin of the drum to her right, picks at the metal braces on the one on the other side, and experimentally taps the pedal that thuds against the big drum in the middle. Nicola walks over and points them all out to her. 'The big one at the front is the bass. This with the wires on is the snare. This is the floor tom. And you've got a hi-hat, a splash cymbal and a crash cymbal.'

'Brilliant,' says Gemma, forgetting all the names instantly. She taps cautiously on one of the cymbals with one of the sticks.

Nicola says, 'It's all about co-ordination. You've got to be able to do different things with both hands and your foot. It's quite difficult.'

Gemma shrugs. 'My mum always says that in our house the right hand never knows what the left hand's doing, anyway.'

'Have a go,' says Nicola. 'Try to keep a regular beat on the bass, and do separate beats with your right hand on the tom and your left on the snare. I'll get Kelly set up.'

Kelly has already set herself up, strapping a guitar around her neck and standing in the middle of the room, legs set apart, wind-milling her arm and thrashing discordantly at the strings. 'I'm a rock and roll staaaaar!' she bellows tunelessly. Gemma exchanges a glance with Nicola.

Nicola takes Kelly's left hand and places it far along the neck of the guitar. 'I'm going to show you some basic chords. E, A, G and C. Then we could try to do a bit of a song.'

'Oh, I wrote a song already,' says Kelly. 'It's called 'Heather Wilson is a Fucking Bitch'. I rhymed bitch with rich in the chorus.'

Gemma laughs. 'That's brilliant.'

'What key is it in?' says Nicola.

'I've no idea,' says Kelly, strumming the strings violently and shouting, 'Heather Wilson is a fucking bitch! She thinks she's cool because she's rich! But we all know she's an evil witch! HEATHER WILSON IS A FUCKING BITCH!' She pauses and grins. 'It's in that key.'

'Hmm,' says Nicola. She goes to the battered case that holds her guitar and zips it open, and takes out a CD. There's a CD player chained to the radiator, with a big padlock on it. This is Marigold Brook, after all. After fiddling with it, Nicola keys up a track and tells them all to listen.

'I know this,' says Gemma. 'It's that guy who blew his head off.'

'Kurt Cobain,' says Kelly. 'He was well fit, too.'

They listen to 'Smells Like Teen Spirit' until the track finishes, then Nicola makes them listen to it again. She gets a sheaf of tatty papers out of her guitar case. 'I'm trying to learn it. I wrote the lyrics down, and the guitar tabs. We're just going to do the verse, with those chords I showed you, Kelly. And the drum part is fairly simple, just a two-bar repeating groove.'

Kelly grins widely. 'Two-bar repeating groove. How cool does that sound?'

Nicola looks at her digital watch. 'Let's listen to it again, then everybody practise your parts for ten minutes on your own, and we'll give it a go.'

'What you mean is,' says Kelly, 'wrinkling her forehead as she looks at the drawings Nicola has done showing her where to put her fingers on the guitar neck, 'let's make some noise!'

Two things emerge from the band practice session before they are forcibly ejected by Mrs Emley, told never to darken her door again other than to report for detention on Monday after school leaving Nicola in floods of tears.

The first is that Gemma really, really, *really* likes playing the drums. Sitting on that stool, she feels like she's hidden away from everybody, everybody and their noise. And when she starts hitting the skins with the sticks, cautiously at first, but growing in confidence and ferocity as she realises how much punishment she can inflict on them, she realises she's building a wall. A wall of sound, between her and everybody else. It's a right racket, but it's *her* racket. Gemma Swarbrick's own domain of pure sound. Her hands and feet feel like they're working independently of each other, and she sees Nicola pull a slightly impressed face as she matches perfectly the beat on the CD.

Then things get a little out of hand. Gemma isn't quite sure what happens, but she's suddenly lost in the act, she can feel sweat beading on her forehead. Her arms are aching but she can't stop. She doesn't notice that the others have stopped playing and are just staring at her.

It's like something pure, something she's never experienced before. There is just her and the drums and an incredible sound that builds and builds and builds until she stands up, not sure who or where she is, and kicks the big bass drum, thrashing her sticks down on the cymbals. The whole kit collapses and Gemma shouts a loud and triumphant, 'Fuck!'

Just as Mrs Emley lets herself back into the room to tell them lunchtime is over. The floor tom – Gemma is pleased that she remembered the name – rolls mournfully towards the teacher and spins like a penny before settling and displaying the long, ragged rip in the skin.

'Out,' says Mrs Emley, her lips quivering. 'Out and never come back.'

The second thing that has emerged from the session is that Kelly Derricott really, really, *really* cannot sing a note.

Outside the music room, as the bell rings to signal the start of lessons, Kelly grins. 'Well, that was brilliant.'

Nicola stares at her. 'Are you serious? You got me banned from the music room. You know how many things I have in my life that I enjoy?' She holds up a finger. 'One. And that's music. And now you've ruined it.'

Nicola begins to cry, and Kelly looks nonplussed at Gemma. Hefting her guitar bag, Nicola glares at her. 'This was the most stupid idea in the world. I never should have listened to you. And you know something? You can't sing a note. You sound like . . . like . . .'

'You sound like next-door's cat when it's getting shagged by the ginger tom from across the road,' offers Gemma, and she considers this a fair assessment of Kelly's performance.

Kelly scowls as Nicola storms off along the corridor, and turns to Gemma. 'I wasn't that bad, was I?'

Gemma pulls a face, trying to work out how to say it more diplomatically. 'Actually, it was worse than that.'

✳ **18** ✳

The woman pulls a face and shakes her permed head. 'What did you say they were called again?'

'Moonflowers,' says Arthur. 'The proper name for them is *Ipomoea alba*.'

'Definitely not,' says the woman decisively. She points to a display of red-leafed pot plants. 'I could do you a poinsettia. Very popular at Christmas.'

'Well, do you know where I'd get them?' says Arthur. 'The moonflowers?'

The woman shakes her head again. 'Specialist shop, I'd say. Maybe that one up by the parish church. Otherwise, a wholesaler, perhaps?'

Arthur has already tried the specialist shop up by the parish church. In fact, he's tried all the florists in town, and this is the last one. He's cold and tired and fed up of tramping around in the slush, his shoes stained with snow and salt, his toes icy cold. And as well as the tidemark rising up the uppers of his shoes, he feels a mounting sense of something approaching panic fluttering in his chest. They want to take his home away from him. That's all he can think of, the last thing he wrestles with at night, the first thing on his mind when he wakes up. They want to kick him out of the chapel.

He'll be buggered if he's going down without a fight, but it adds an extra sense of urgency to the whole flowers business. What if he can't fight them? What if one old man can't do anything against the might of the council? What if this truly is his last chance to solve the mystery?

Arthur sighs in frustration. He has to have the answers, for him and for Molly. It's just not right, is it, someone leaving flowers on her grave, never announcing themselves? Why would you do that, knowing that her husband is asleep just yards away in the chapel? Why skulk about in the darkness, unless you had a something to hide? It's not even legal, is it, being in the cemetery so late?

He pauses. That's right, though, isn't it? It's not legal. It's trespassing. Arthur stops, decides against taking the bus home, and instead turns around and heads down the sloping street towards where the concrete and glass cube of the police station sits in the middle of the ring road.

'A stake-out,' says the constable, drawing the word out, and tapping on a sheet of paper with the end of his pen.

'Yes,' nods Arthur. 'Like in the movies.'

'The movies,' says the constable, making as if to write the words down on the form, then apparently deciding against it. He's young, barely old enough to shave, and shorter than Arthur would have expected. Don't you have to be a six-footer to be in the police any more?

'Yes,' says Arthur, frowning. Is the young man hard of understanding? 'You get a team of bobbies and you put them at strategic points, hidden away. They carry out. . .' He searches for the word, the one he's heard in films and on *The Bill*. 'Surveillance!' he says at last. 'The bobbies hide and carry out surveillance, and then when the bugger comes they jump out and get him.'

The constable raises an eyebrow. 'Yes, sir, I know what a stake-out is. The thing is . . .' He puts the pen top over the ballpoint nib, suggesting to Arthur he has no bloody intention of writing any of this down on the form. 'The thing is, sir, we normally reserve *stake-outs* for when we have reliable intelligence that a criminal act is underway or about to take place.'

Arthur slaps his hand on the desk, more forcefully than he intends. He looks around the inquiry desk room; a young man with floppy hair, sitting awkwardly with his hands cuffed behind his back, gives him a blank stare. Drugs, probably. He turns back to the constable. 'A criminal act has taken place, and is going to take place again on the twenty-third of this month!'

The constable pulls a sympathetic face. 'I'm not quite sure that leaving flowers on a grave—'

'My wife's grave,' corrects Arthur.

'On your wife's grave . . . I'm not sure that constitutes a crime, sir.'

Arthur raises a finger. Aha, he has him now. 'Yes,' he says, leaning forward to the plastic grille. 'But he's doing it in the middle of the night. The cemetery closes to the public at four during winter. He's trespassing, isn't he?'

He stands back, feeling a little note of triumph, but the young constable seems unimpressed. The policeman strokes his chin for a moment. 'I think I can see a solution here, sir.'

Arthur breathes out. 'Thank God. So you're going to do the stake-out, like I said?'

'The problem is, sir, that the cemetery is owned by the local authority. So the issue of trespass is covered by their regulations, not by criminal law.' The constable puts his pen down. 'I think the best course of action is to contact the council. Perhaps they can provide some assistance.'

'The council's bloody hopeless,' sighs Arthur. 'They're the ones who want to kick me out of the chapel in the first place.'

The constable frowns. 'Yes, sir, that was something else I didn't quite understand. You're living in the cemetery grounds? Do you have the council's permission to do that?'

'Well, the church's,' says Arthur. What's he getting at?

'It's just . . . well, sir, there might actually be an argument that you yourself are in a permanent state of trespass in the cemetery. You're not actually a council employee, are you?'

Arthur feels anger rising within him. Why won't anyone ever take him seriously? Why doesn't anybody respect older folk any more? The only people who've ever talked to him the way he deserves are Keith Cardy and his lads in the Black Diamond. He remembers what Keith said about him the other night.

'Let me tell you something, laddie,' says Arthur, waggling his finger at the constable. 'I'm a war hero, you know. But for the likes of me you wouldn't even be sitting there fiddling with your pen and talking to me like I'm a child.'

The constable says impassively, 'I can assure you, sir, I've treated you with nothing but—'

'Oh, forget it,' says Arthur, casting a glance at the dopily grinning druggie and turning on his heel to march out of the police station.

Arthur decides to walk the rest of the way home, to let his anger cool in the freezing air. They can't throw him out of the chapel, they just can't. He doesn't know how long he'll survive, not having Molly so close. But who's going to help him now? Everything he's said, every plea he's made, it's just fallen on deaf ears.

He's passing the shops when a figure bustles out of the bookies, a cigarette behind his thick ear and a rolled-up newspaper tucked underneath his arm. He's only wearing a short-sleeved shirt, despite the cold, and he stops dead and gives Arthur a salute. Keith Cardy.

'Arthur! How's you?'

Arthur sighs. 'Hungry. I'm going to get a pie.'

'Me too,' nods Cardy, falling in with him. They walk for a short while and turn into the bakers, where there are two or three women waiting ahead of them. The smell of the fresh pies makes Arthur's stomach rumble.

'How you getting on in that chapel?' says Cardy. 'Not too cold for you, is it?'

'I've got my burner,' says Arthur. 'Might not be there long, though. They want me out.'

Cardy stares at him. 'Who does?'

'The council. They want to knock the chapel down. Move some of the older graves. Going to turn it into some kind of housing centre for them lot at the Old Hall. Asylum seekers.'

Cardy's eyes widen. 'You're shitting me.'

Arthur shakes his head. 'I've been to the council. They're having a meeting after Christmas. But it doesn't look like there's anything anybody can do.'

'Bollocks to that,' spits Cardy. He heaves a ragged sigh. 'Jesus H Christ on a bike.'

The women in the queue turn to look at him. Cardy shakes his head sadly. 'Bloody foreigners. Thought I'd heard everything until now.' He looks at Arthur with a frown, as though he's having trouble processing what he's been told. 'Let me get this right. They want to throw you, a bloody war hero, out on the streets so they can take your home and give it to this lot who's coming in to this country in droves when they've no rights to be here?'

The women in the queue tut and shake their heads. A rosy-faced woman in a paper hat behind the counter says, 'What would you do, Keith?'

'Send 'em bloody back!' he says. 'Send 'em all bloody back!'

There's a murmur of assent from the shop, then one woman says, 'Well, apart from them Asian lads on the market. Got some lovely material from them the other week. Made a smashing set of curtains.'

'They are lovely curtains, Deirdre,' agrees another woman.

'I'm sure there's plenty of English folk selling material,' says Cardy testily.

'Not at them prices,' says the woman who agreed with Deirdre. 'Oh, and then there's Dr Singh. You couldn't send him back. He's been at the surgery for thirty years at least. Lovely manner, he has.'

'Where's all the British doctors, that's what I want to know,' says Cardy.

Deirdre says to the woman beside her, 'Wasn't that bloke who came to fix your boiler a foreigner, Joyce? What was he?'

'Polish, I think,' says Joyce. 'Now he was a lovely fella. You'll never guess what he told me they have for Christmas dinner. Carp.'

'Bloody carp!' says Cardy with a barking laugh. 'What's wrong with a good old British turkey, eh?'

Joyce wrinkles her nose. 'I do find turkey a bit dry, to be honest. But it's only once a year. Anyway, that Polish lad was a marvel. Came out two hours after I'd called him. Very reasonable, too.'

'We're getting off the point!' says Cardy loudly. 'And that is, they want to throw Arthur here out of his home so that all these bloody illegal immigrants or whatever they are can put their feet up somewhere nice! Now that's not on, is it?'

It's Arthur's turn at the till and he asks the rosy-cheeked woman for a meat and potato pie and an iced finger. Cardy says, 'I'll have the same, love.' He leans a meaty forearm on the counter and says, 'We're not going to stand for this, Arthur, you have my word. I'm going to have a chat to some of the lads. Fancy meeting us in the Diamond tomorrow night? See what we can do? We're not having our local war hero being treated like this.'

'I'm not—' begins Arthur, then pauses. Actually, maybe he bloody is a war hero. Maybe that's what it's going to take to save his home. 'Aye, that sounds grand, Keith,' he says, handing over the money for his dinner. 'Thank you.'

'No problem,' says Cardy, scooping up his paper bags. 'Here, you couldn't stand me this pie and bun, could you, old son? Bit strapped. Lost it all on a bloody donkey that's still sodding running, I think . . .'

'Peace offering,' says Gemma, holding up the plastic carrier bag.

Nicola stares at it, standing on her doorstep, bathed in the light from the vestibule. She pulls the interior door closed behind her and says, 'What is it?'

'Tins of stuff,' says Gemma, forcing the bag into Nicola's arms. 'Fell off the back of a Heinz lorry. There's no labels on them but I don't suppose that matters when the apocalypse comes. Be a nice surprise for you and your mum when you're living in that old grave, won't it? Will it be beans or will it be tomato soup? Make the days fly by.'

'Wait here,' says Nicola. She goes into the living room to find her mum, who's sitting under the lamp, reading a book on foraging for food, while the TV burbles quietly, showing a Sunday afternoon movie. Nicola recognises it; *Beneath The Planet of the Apes*. The one where all the mutated human survivors are worshipping a nuclear bomb. Her mum says, 'Did you know rosehips are packed with Vitamin C? You need to be able to identify them. They can be used in tea. Good for fending off colds.'

'Mum, I'm going out.'

Her mum blinks and looks up from her book, then out of the window, as though surprised there's a world there where a person might want to go *out* to.

'It's dark. Out where?'

'Just out,' says Nicola. She hasn't told her about the bunker yet, and she doesn't properly know why. Part of her wants to get it fully stocked, so it can be a nice surprise when she finally unveils it. But a deeper part of her knows that this isn't right, this isn't *normal*, and showing the bunker to her mum would just . . . Nicola doesn't know. Make her worse, perhaps.

Her mum closes the book, using her finger to mark her page. 'Who are you going out with?'

'Friends.'

Her mum frowns. 'Friends? You have friends?'

Nicola glares at her. 'Why is that so weird?'

'Will there be boys there?'

Nicola snorts. 'No! It's just Kelly and Gemma from school.'

Her mum puts the book down on the sofa and folds her arms. 'You can't afford to get close to people, Nicola. You have to stay focused. When . . . when it happens, it'll just be me and you. We can't afford to be sentimental about strangers.'

'Mum—'

'Me and you, Nicola. It's a matter of survival.' She picks up her book. 'Rosehips. Remember that.'

Nicola gets her coat from the hall and pushes out past Kelly and Gemma. She takes the bag from Gemma and starts to walk up the street.

'Where are we going?' says Kelly. 'To the bunker?'

Nicola says nothing. Gemma nudges her as they tramp along the slushy pavements. 'I'm sorry for breaking the drums.'

Kelly says, 'What's up with your mum, then?'

Nicola stops and rounds on her angrily. 'There's nothing up with her. Why do you say that?'

Kelly takes a step back and holds up her hands. 'It's just what everybody says. That she's . . .'

'She's bad with her nerves,' says Nicola, walking on.

'Is it because your dad topped himself?' says Gemma.

Nicola thinks about that photograph, the one with her mum laughing and carefree, bouncing baby Nicola on her lap, the long shadow of her father on the grass, taking the picture. 'I don't want to talk about my dad,' she says.

'That must have been really shit,' offers Kelly.

'I was a baby. I don't remember anything. I don't remember him.'

Nicola leads them to the cemetery and to the falling-down mausoleum. By torchlight she carefully stacks the cans neatly at the back. Gemma stands outside, smoking, looking around the cemetery. 'Don't you get scared coming here? In the dark?'

'There's no ghosts or anything,' mutters Nicola. 'Besides, what's to be scared of? It's just dead people. Besides . . .' she nods over at the shape of the chapel. 'Old Calderbank's always around.'

Gemma takes a drag of the cigarette then says, 'I'm sorry I broke the drums at dinner time. I'm sure Mrs Emley'll let you back in the music rooms if we stay away.'

Nicola shrugs, and looks at Kelly. 'I'm sorry I said your singing was rubbish.'

Kelly sighs. 'It was though, wasn't it?' She holds out her hand and Gemma puts the half-smoked Marlboro into her fingers.

Nicola looks shrewdly at her. 'Actually . . . you were pretty good on the guitar. You picked up the chords quite well. Quicker than I did, actually.'

Kelly brightens. 'Really? Then maybe—'

She's interrupted by a volley of shouts and laughs coming from deeper in the graveyard, nearer to the chapel. There are four boys messing around the gravestones. Then one pushes another violently.

'Fight,' Kelly says. 'Let's go and have a look.'

Gemma and Kelly creep along the path and pause behind a tall headstone, just yards from the boys, and Nicola warily hurries up behind them. The boys are all from their year at Marigold Brook. Three of them have razor-short hair, surrounding a taller, skinnier boy with a mass of curls protectively holding a paper package to his chest.

'Leave me alone!' says the tall boy shrilly.

'It's Tampax,' whispers Gemma. His name's Timmy but as long as Nicola's known him he's been Tampax. He takes a briefcase to school. He doesn't live on the estate, but in the new houses near the canal.

'And that's Colin Cardy,' says Kelly, pointing to the ringleader, who gives Tampax another push. 'He thinks he's a right hard twat.'

'I hate him,' says Gemma. 'After the school disco last summer I let him kiss me. I'd had half a bottle of cider. He tried to put his hand down my jeans. When I wouldn't let him he said I was frigid. Then he told everybody I'd given him a blow job.'

'Yeah, I heard,' says Kelly. Nicola had heard it too, but decides not to say anything.

'What you got there, Tampax?' says Colin. 'Is it your gay clothes?'

'I have to deliver it to Mr Calderbank!' shouts Tampax, his voice trembling, and he casts glances towards the chapel, hoping for rescue.

'Should we do something?' whispers Nicola.

Gemma shrugs. 'Like what? It's what happens, isn't it? Saw it on a nature programme on telly once. Some hyenas stalking a gazelle or something. Tampax is the gazelle.'

'Give us a song, Tampax,' says one of the hyenas.

'Yeah,' says Colin. 'Sing that song and we'll let you go.'

'Come on,' says Kelly. 'Let's go. We don't need to see this.'

They're creeping away when Gemma casts a look over her shoulder and sees Tampax roll his eyes. 'All right. But then you have to let me go.'

'On that flat grave thing,' instructs Colin. 'You need a stage, don't you?'

Tampax climbs with his gangly limbs on to the weathered stone slab and clears his throat. Gemma tugs at Kelly's coat sleeve and she whispers, 'Hang on a sec.'

'Sing it, Tammy Girl!' laughs one of the hyenas.

'And do the dance as well!'

Nicola watches Tampax begin to sway to his own internal beat, and then he starts to sing. She blinks in surprise. They're making him sing *Saturday Night* by Whigfield..

Kelly joins her and Gemma too, and none of them are trying to hide any more. They're just standing, staring, watching the skinny boy gyrate and sing, his eyes closed.

Tampax has the voice of an angel.

20

'Little bloody devils,' mutters Arthur, peering through the window at the group of boys gathered down in the older part of the cemetery. He can't for the life of him understand the attraction of a graveyard to lads that age. When he was young he'd be off fishing in the canal or the ponds, roaming over the countryside, whittling sticks. Making stuff. Nobody seems to *make* things any more. Too many bloody distractions, that was the problem. Four channels on the telly, and talk of the BBC being on twenty-four hours a day! As far as he could see, there wasn't enough to fill the time as it was. And these video game things, and CD players. Everything designed for you to sit in front of it, doing nothing. Arthur frowns. Except, he wished this lot would be sitting down doing nothing, instead of larking about in his graveyard.

Then he notices that it's not all fun and games. There's a tall lad standing on one of the flat gravestones, and he's holding a package of some sort. One of the other boys – Keith Cardy's son, if he's not mistaken – aims a punch at the skinny kid and makes a grab for the parcel. Then Arthur recognises the boy on the slab. Timmy Leigh. He wonders vaguely if he's brought him another pie. Arthur sighs and stirs himself. He's going to have to intervene.

Arthur's just pulling the big main door closed behind him when he notices three other figures, girls, a little way off from the ruckus. Lads always act up when they've got an audience. He's just about to shout, though, tell them all to clear off, when he sees one of the girls pick up a smooth pebble, heft it in her hand, and then toss it with some force towards the gang. There's a shout and a stream of obscenities from one of the lads, and then Cardy's lad, in the melee, lands a good smack at the side of Timmy Leigh's head, and the tall boy falls from the stone platform, going down in a tangle of limbs.

Enough's enough, decides Arthur, and bellows, 'You kids! You shouldn't be here! Get out of it!'

The Cardy boy makes a signal with his hands and the boys scarper, but Arthur realises it's less to do with his presence than the fact the Timmy hasn't yet got up. The three girls are picking their way through the fallen and crooked gravestones towards him, and Arthur sets off in the same direction.

'His head's bleeding,' says one of the girls when Arthur hurries over. It's that Kelly Derricott, who was asking him all those questions yesterday. And she's right; Timmy Leigh's still on the snow-sodden ground, all knotted up like one of his mother's balls of wool, and there's a gash on his temple where he's hit the deck. The boy's crying, great, snotty, hacking sobs. Arthur shakes his head. Shouldn't do that. Those bad lads are like sharks; they sniff blood and you're done for.

'Up you get,' says Arthur brusquely. 'Let's have a look at you.'

As Timmy unwinds his ungainly legs and arms and climbs to his feet, Arthur peers at the girls. One's that Nicola Manning, who he caught riding her bike in the cemetery the other morning. He doesn't know the blonde-haired one but her dad is that Swarbrick chap, always one step ahead of the law, always up to no good. Now he's thinking of it, that Kelly's dad must be Brian Derricott, used to work at the pit before they closed it. He's seen him with Cardy's little mob in the Diamond.

Timmy wipes his nose with his coat sleeve as Arthur looks closely at the cut on his head. 'Just a scratch,' he declares. 'I could clean it up for you and put a plaster on it, if you want.'

Timmy nods solemnly and Arthur leads him off towards the chapel, turning around to see the three girls following. He frowns at them. 'What do you want?'

'We're coming with you,' says the Derricott girl.

'We're his friends,' says the other girl with the same, pulled back hairstyle. Arthur suddenly conjures the name Gemma.

Timmy Leigh forgets his wound for a moment and blinks at them, confused. 'I don't have any friends,' he says..

'You do now,' says Kelly.

Timmy Leigh winces as Arthur dabs at the gash with a corner of a flannel dipped in Dettol. His initial assessment was right; it looks worse than it is, once he's wiped away most of the blood. You have to be careful with head injuries though. He moves his forefinger from side to side in front of Timmy's eyes. 'How many fingers have I got up?'

Kelly snorts and Nicola nudges her and says quietly, 'Shush.'

Arthur peels the back off an Elastoplast and presses it firmly on the cut. Timmy says, 'Ow.'

'That'll do you,' says Arthur. 'Get your mother to look at it when you get home.'

Kelly Derricott is wandering around the chapel, touching Arthur's things, trailing her fingers over his kettle, his work top, his pews. But he keeps one eye on the Swarbrick girl; the apple probably hasn't fallen far from the tree and he doesn't want her filling her pockets with his stuff. He glances at his jacket hanging up on one of the pegs, his wallet bulging out from the inside pocket.

Timmy, upon hearing mention of his mother, looks stricken. 'Oh! I was bringing a parcel to you from my mum.'

'It's here, I picked it up,' says Gemma, producing the brown-paper package, now soaked and ripping.

'She knits stuff,' says Timmy, almost apologetically, as Arthur tears it open. It's a Fair Isle jumper, at least three sizes too big for him. Not bad workmanship, though. Come in handy, especially if it gets any colder.

'Tell her thank you,' says Arthur. He looks at Timmy. 'Why were those lads picking on you?'

'They always do,' says Timmy miserably. 'They call me Tampax.'

'*Everybody* calls you Tampax,' says Kelly. 'His name's Timmy. So that became Tammy Girl. You know, like the shop? Then Tampax.' She's looking at a dusty glass-topped wooden box Arthur's been meaning to hang on the wall but never got round to. 'Are these your medals?'

'Yes,' says Arthur, taking the box from her and putting it down on the worktop.

'I told you that you're a war hero,' says Kelly.

Arthur's about to put her right, then remembers his conversation with Cardy in the pie shop earlier. 'Aye, well.'

'My mum thinks there'll be another war,' says Nicola, the nervous-looking girl.

'That's why she's got a bunk—' begins Gemma, but Kelly elbows her in the ribs.

They all stand in an expectant silence for a moment, then Arthur says, 'You can all get off now. Don't play in the cemetery again. It's actually illegal for you to be in here after the gates have closed.'

But nobody moves. Instead, Gemma Swarbrick, looking around the vaulted ceiling of the chapel, says, 'It must be really weird, living here.'

Perhaps it does look a bit odd, him living in the chapel, he concedes. Especially to these kids. What's he supposed to say, he does it just so's he can be close to his dead wife? They could never understand. Molly was his world, his everything. If he's going to stubbornly cling on to a life without her, then he'll do it where he can at least see her grave every morning when he wakes up and every night before he goes to sleep. And maybe one night, soon, when his head hits the pillow and he closes his eyes he won't open them again, and Molly will be waiting for him, smiling like she always did, holding out her hand. And he'll stand up from the bed but his joints won't creak and his back won't hurt and there won't be any weight on his shoulders. He won't look back at the body lying still and cold on the bed, because there won't be any point. The essence of him, the real Arthur Calderbank, will be a thing as light and insubstantial as a feather, as a whisper, as a moonflower petal. And he'll put his hand in Molly's and they'll be together again at last, and nothing will ever part them again.

Arthur blinks and realises all the kids are looking at him. He coughs and says, 'It's time you lot were getting off.' He nods at Timmy. 'Get your mum to have a look at that wound, but I don't think it's anything serious.'

Kelly is still wandering around the chapel, touching his things, when she stops. She's staring at the guitar he'd left propped up against the bookcase.

'Is that a guitar?' she says.

Arthur nods.

'Can you play it?'

'A bit.'

'What's happening on the twenty-third?' says Gemma. Arthur turns to where she's staring at his calendar, the red ring around the date. He can't keep up with these kids, haring around the place.

'It's my wife's birthday.'

'She's dead,' says Kelly. 'Right, come on.'

The three girls pause at the door, and turn back to where Timmy is loitering near the kitchen. 'Come on, then,' says Gemma. 'I don't know what Kelly's up to, but if she says you're our mate, then you're our mate.'

'Oh, and by the way,' says Kelly. 'You're in detention with us tomorrow after school.'

* 21 *

Kelly walks against the flow of Marigold Brook pupils rushing towards the main doors after the final bell, the first day of the school week over, another step towards the Christmas holidays. But not quite over for her . . . detention beckons. She threads her way through the mass of kids, and is suddenly sent spinning, losing her footing, as a shoulder barges into her, hard.

Heather Wilson smirks at her, backed up, as ever, by her posse. Her puffa jacket has been cleaned, or maybe daddy has bought her a new one. Heather raises one immaculately shaped eyebrow at her and tosses back her pale blonde hair.

'Going to get you back, bitch,' she says sweetly. 'Might be tomorrow. Might be next week. But count on it.'

Kelly fixes her with her hard stare and pushes through them and on down the corridor, where she sees Gemma as the crowd thins at last. Gemma pops a mint into her mouth to cover the perfume of cigarette smoke blossoming around her and nods.

'What room is it in, again?'

'E4,' says Kelly.

'Everybody's talking about you squirting that paint over Heather Wilson.' Gemma begins to hum a song, and Kelly realises with a small shiver of pleasure that it's the one she tried to play in the music room. 'Heather Wilson is a Fucking Bitch'.

She says, 'Seen Nicola?'

'No. I'm not in her set for any classes.' Gemma cocks her head on one side. 'Are we really mates with her, then? Or are you up to something?'

'I'm always up to something. But not like that. We're really mates with her.' Kelly considers. 'She's all right.'

Nicola is waiting for them outside E4, face like thunder. Kelly guesses that she's never had detention before. She says, 'What did your mum say about being kept back?'

Nicola looks away. 'I told her I had a late music practice.'

'Not going to be too many of them any more,' booms a voice, and Mr Green, the careers teacher, pushes past them and unlocks the door to the classroom. 'Not from what I hear anyway, after what you lot did to Mrs Emley's music room.'

They troop into the room, painted in a sickly yellow, behind Mr Green, who sits at the front desk and puts his feet up on it, watching them as Gemma and Kelly slink to the back of the room and Nicola takes a desk on the front row.

'No you don't,' he says, scratching his moustache. 'Everybody at the front.' He takes a piece of paper from his jacket pocket and unfolds it. 'Hmm. I'm supposed to have Cardy, Atkins, Waterhouse. . .'

Kelly snorts. 'No chance of them turning up, sir. They got detention today for not coming to detention last week, which was for not coming to detention the week before, which was—'

'I get the picture,' sighs Mr Green.

'Nobody can even remember what they got detention for in the first place,' says Gemma.

The door goes and Mr Green looks up. 'Ah, here are the recidivists now.'

But it's not Cardy and his mob, it's Timmy Leigh. He blinks owlishly and looks at Mr Green, then at the girls. Mr Green frowns. 'Tam— I mean, Timmy? I don't have you down on my list.'

Timmy points at Kelly. 'She told me I had to come.'

Kelly feels Gemma's amused stare on her. Green shakes his head. 'You've come to detention even though you don't have to? For God's sake, lad, why?'

Timmy shuffles his rucksack off his back and goes to sit on the empty desk next to Nicola. 'Because these are my friends.'

'Are we really friends with Tampax as well, or is this part of what you're planning?' whispers Gemma, leaning over to Kelly's desk.

'Yes, and yes,' murmurs Kelly back.

'Right,' says Mr Green. He walks along the front row, putting a piece of lined A4 paper on each desk. 'We've got an hour for you to consider the error of your ways, and leave this room with the appropriate level of contrition for your misdemeanours. To that end, I propose you fill that time by filling both sides of this paper with your individual hopes and dreams for your lives after Marigold Brook, and how you plan to be productive and useful members of society.'

He sits back at the desk and pulls a copy of a big thick book called *Infinite Jest* from his briefcase. He opens it up and then looks at Kelly, eyes narrowed, as if remembering something. 'Ah, yes. Kelly Derricott. The rock and roll star.' He smirks. 'I look forward to reading how you expect to travel the world with Noel Gallagher, living the champagne lifestyle.'

Kelly pulls a face at him and glances over at the others. Nicola and Timmy are studiously writing. Gemma is drawing a big cock and balls, Kelly drums the end of her biro on the desk for a moment, then screws up her piece of paper and throws it towards the squat grey wastepaper basket near Mr Green's desk. It hits the wall and plops into the bin.

Mr Green looks down at it and then at Kelly. 'Have you changed your mind? Do you want to be a basketball player now? Come and get another sheet of paper.'

Kelly ignores him. There's been something in her head since Thursday, like a hole burning in a newspaper page, edges black and orange and widening. The thing with Kelly's big ideas is that they're slow burners. She hasn't known where she's been going with this at all, but it started with that careers talk. Then seeing Nicola with her guitar, then the factory visit with her mum. Hearing Timmy sing in the graveyard. All of it whirling round her mind, making little explosive connections against the background of the sheer lack of expectations placed on her, on Gemma, on all the kids at Marigold Brook. All the good little sprockets who are expected to sit invisibly inside the big machine and do their jobs, whether that's soul-sucking labour or popping out babies or just quietly keeping out of the way of the world. But all these things have been slowly joining the dots in her head, and now she knows why. She's had her idea.

And it's a stupid, crazy, idiotic, wonderful idea. She clears her throat and stands up, scraping back her chair. Mr Green raises his eyebrows. Everyone else looks at her expectantly.

'Fuck that shit,' says Kelly Derricott.

Gemma grins broadly. Nicola puts her head down and inspects what she's written so far. Timmy's Adam's apple bobs and he loosens his school tie. Mr Green's face clouds over. 'Sit down!' he hisses.

Kelly ignores him, and addresses the other three instead. 'You know what we are in this school? Nothing. Less than nothing. I've seen the way the teachers look at us. Like we're not even people. They just want us to come in when we're eleven and leave when we're sixteen and for most of us they don't care what we do in between so long as we don't make life difficult for them.'

'Kelly. . .' says Mr Green warningly.

She looks directly at him. 'Well, fuck that shit. We're just marks on a register. Not even that to most of them. I bet you didn't even know Nicola Manning's name before she got into trouble, did you, sir?'

Mr Green stands up. 'Now, that's enough, Derricott. Sit down and shut up.'

Kelly laughs. 'Five minutes. That's what they give us for our careers talks. Five. Minutes. And they don't even think we're worth that. Work in a shop. Be a secretary. Join the army. Go to the factory. Sign on the dole. Get pregnant. Go to jail. Buy everything on the never-never. Live in a shithole and be thankful for it.'

'Kelly!' shouts Mr Green.

'Fuck that shit!' she shouts back. 'Marry some no-hoper who can't get a job. Have kids. Sit in watching *Jerry Springer* all day. Live next door to your mum and send your kids to the same school you went to and she went to, where the same teachers ignore them and can't even remember their names and the whole thing just goes on and on and on.' She grimaces at Mr Green and shakes her head. 'Fuck that shit.'

He points his finger at her, unable to stop it shaking, and breathes in and out deeply. 'You've done it now, Kelly Derricott. You're in so much trouble.'

'The one time,' she says calmly. 'The one time someone says they want to be different, unless it's someone like Heather Wilson or one of the three or four people who have a chance at going to university, the one single time that happens, you laugh at them.'

'I didn't laugh at you,' says Mr Green uncertainly.

'You were laughing inside!' spits Kelly. 'Admit it.'

Mr Green looks at his pointing, wavering finger, and puts his arm down.

She takes a deep breath. 'Well, you can't just stick us in your boring little boxes. We're not doing what you want, just so you can forget us the minute we leave this place.' She looks at each face turned towards her. 'We're going to do something different. We're going to form a band.'

Timmy raises his hand cautiously. 'A band?'

'Gemma's on drums,' says Kelly. 'I'm guitar. Nicola's on bass. And Timmy's doing the vocals. That's what we're going to do. We're going to form a band. A proper band. And we're going to be bigger than Oasis.'

Kelly picks up her bag and walks towards Mr Green, who sits down, blinking. 'You can take that as our two sides of A4 about our hopes and dreams, sir.' She looks at the others. 'Come on. Detention's over. We've got work to do.'

Kelly walks to the door and out of it without looking back, and the others follow her. Gemma pauses at Mr Green's desk, and drops her piece of paper on it. 'Oops,' she says as he frowns at the crude genitalia inked there. 'We were supposed to write about what we wanted to be, and I went and drew a picture of what you actually *are*.'

Kelly closes the door as Gemma leaves, just in time to see Mr Green screw the paper into a tight ball and mutter to himself, 'Fuck that shit. They don't pay me enough for this.'

✳ 22 ✳

The Black Diamond is busy for a Tuesday. Arthur politely elbows his way into the snug and apologises as he jars the elbow of a man in his early fifties who frowns as his pint slops over his glass, then smiles as he recognises Arthur. It's Bill Ormerod. Arthur's about to say he was talking to Bill's dad Fred the other day, then shuts his mouth. How's that going to sound if Arthur goes around admitting that he talks to the dead people in their graves? They won't need council meetings and votes to get him out of the chapel; the men in white coats will be carting him away. Instead, as he takes off his scarf, Arthur says, 'How's Gladys?'

Bill shrugs. 'Champion.' He frowns again, as if thinking of something else to say. Not a man of many words, Bill Ormerod. Then his face lights up. 'Our Darren's getting wed. To that Julie lass.' He nods. 'Clever, that one.' Arthur can't tell if this is a good thing or a bad thing, so nods back and pushes his way to the bar. The landlord, Jonathan, is looking harassed, the bright electric lights above the bar shining off the sheen of sweat on his bald head. Arthur orders his usual.

'Not got your better half helping you out?' says Arthur.

'Sarah? Night off. She's upstairs with John Grisham.' Jon peers over his slightly steamed-up glasses. 'Wasn't expecting it to be this busy on a Tuesday, though.'

'John Grisham?' says Arthur. 'The window cleaner?'

Jon wrinkles his forehead and makes as if to say something, then waves it away. 'Anyway, they'll be glad you've turned up. They've been waiting for you.'

'Waiting for me? Who has?'

'Arthur!' booms a voice. Keith Cardy waves his big arms at him from the middle of a knot of people that's far bigger than his usual little crew. 'Over here! Arthur!'

Arthur takes his pint and heads over to the corner. Suddenly a godawful racket bursts out of the little speakers stuck to the nicotine-stained wall. Somebody – Arthur can't properly tell if it's a man or a woman – singing about 'Virtual Insanity'.

Not wrong there, thinks Arthur, with all this stuff that's going on, as all the faces spin towards a young lad pumping 50ps into the jukebox and Cardy roars, 'Turn that fucking thing off!'

'I've just put three quid into it!' protests the lad. 'How'm I supposed to turn it off?'

'Pull the plug out of the socket!' bellows Cardy. 'Or I'll pull your bloody arm out of *its* sodding socket.'

Realising who he's dealing with, the boy does as he's bid and the music cuts out. The faces turn back to Arthur, and Cardy slaps Brian Derricott across the shoulder. 'Move your arse up, let Arthur sit down.'

Arthur sits on the worn seat, wrinkling his nose at the combined odour of cigarette smoke, sweat and stale beer. He nods at Brian, and wonders if he should mention that Kelly's been round, then decides against it. He doesn't really want to get into all that here. Arthur takes a sip of beer, and suddenly he's got a meaty hand clamped on his shoulder and Cardy's half-whispering in a cracked voice. 'Arthur, old son, I've been telling this lot what they're planning for the cemetery. It's a bloody disgrace.'

Arthur isn't sure, because of all the cigarette smoke, but he thinks there are tears in the big man's eyes. 'Bloody disgrace,' says Cardy again. He looks around the faces all turned to them. 'This man, a war hero—'

Arthur looks at his pint.

'A war hero,' emphasises Cardy, massaging Arthur's shoulder, 'who selflessly works his fingers to the bone making that graveyard a lovely place for people to pay their respects to their loved ones. And what do they do? Tell him they're going to take his home, dig up graves, and for what?'

Cardy glances around, and shakes his head. They all know, of course, but nobody's going to interrupt Cardy's moment of theatre. 'I'll tell you for what. To make homes for people who have no right to be here. For freeloaders who come in from other countries to take our jobs and get our benefits.' Cardy taps out a Park Drive and lights it. 'Not satisfied with the jobs and the benefits, though, are they? Not happy with – with—' he looks around for assistance.

'With eating the Queen's swans,' offers Brian.

Cardy slaps the table, making everyone's pints jump. 'Exactly! Eating the bloody swans! No, now they want homes. And not just any homes. Brand-new houses.' He points his cigarette at a man. 'How long was your daughter trying to get a council house? Had to have three babbies with three different men before they gave her one. Bet she'd have loved a brand-new, purpose-built house, wouldn't she?'

Cardy turns back to Arthur. 'But don't you worry, Arthur old son. We're not going to take this lying down. We're going to do something.'

'There was something on the application about an address to write to, with letters of objection,' says Arthur.

Cardy slaps the table again. 'Letters? We're not writing bloody letters. We're going to take direct action.'

There's a murmur of agreement and Arthur frowns. 'Direct action? What do you mean?'

'A march!' says Cardy triumphantly, his eyes shining. 'We're going to hold a rally. Send 'em a message loud and clear that we're not having this. We're going to march from the town centre right up to the cemetery. We'll get the local paper down and everything. Maybe even the *Sun*.'

Arthur ponders this for a moment and takes a mouthful of beer. He looks around. It's a busy Tuesday night for the Black Diamond, but he imagines that when they're all on the street, it'll not look so impressive. 'Just us?'

Cardy shakes his head. 'This is only the start of it, Arthur. Tell him, Graham.'

A short, stout man with a red face and wearing a flat cap pushes his glasses up his nose and blinks rapidly at Arthur from his stool across the table. 'I play the trumpet,' he says in an unexpectedly high-pitched voice.

Arthur doesn't quite know what to say, so smiles encouragingly. 'Lovely.'

'I play the trumpet in a marching band,' says Graham tremulously, blinking rapidly. 'We do all sorts of events.' He leans forward and taps the side of his nose, causing his glasses to fall into his lap. When he's hooked them back over his ears he says, 'Lots of stuff like this. We did the EFAF march in summer.'

'E-faff?' says Arthur.

'England First and Foremost,' says Cardy. 'Bloody brilliant bunch of lads. And they're pals with Graham and his band.'

'We're all members,' says Graham proudly. 'We're getting badges made up.'

A ripple of conversation goes around the group. Brian says, 'Are we getting badges, Keith? Everybody likes badges.'

'The point is,' says Cardy, somewhat testily, thinks Arthur, 'is that the EFAF lads'll come and support the march. They won't have any truck with these asylum seekers pinching your home, Arthur. And with Graham and his band we can turn it into a proper family event, like.'

'It's not just trumpets,' says Graham. 'We've got trombones and drums and all sorts. We've got a big garage near the bulb factory where we rehearse. We've even got some CDs of us playing. I can bring you one in, Arthur. They're only £1.99.'

Arthur feels Cardy staring. 'All bloody right, Graham. It's not really about the band, though, is it?'

Graham pushes his glasses up his nose and blinks. 'Fair enough.' He winks at Arthur and whispers, 'I'll do you a CD for a quid, while it's you.'

'So,' says Cardy, 'what do you think, Arthur? We can get the wives to do some cakes or something, get some beers in. We could do the march then have the rally outside the cemetery, right where that lot can hear us in the Old Hall.'

'I could bring my home brew,' says Brian. 'I've got three tubs just about ready to go.'

'Lovely,' says Cardy.

'When are you thinking of doing it?' says Arthur.

Cardy shrugs. 'Well, we'd probably want to get Christmas out of the way. When are they discussing the application?'

'At the planning committee on January ninth.'

Cardy claps his hands. 'Then we'll do it the Saturday before. So it's fresh in their minds. So them councillors go into that planning meeting and know that we're not taking this lying down, and that they have to keep their hands off Arthur's chapel.'

'Hands off Arthur's chapel!' shouts Brian Derricott.

Cardy thumps the table with his meaty fist. 'Hands off Arthur's chapel! Come on, you wankers! Hands off Arthur's chapel!'

The call goes up, and becomes a chant. 'Hands! Off! Arthur's chapel! Hands! Off! Arthur's chapel!'

Arthur finishes off his beer, and someone puts a fresh pint in front of him, and claps him on the shoulder. He looks around at them all, punching the air and sloshing beer everywhere. Hands off Arthur's chapel. This is what he wanted, wasn't it? Someone to do something. And Keith Cardy might be a windbag, but he's right about writing letters. When did that ever make any difference? A march. A rally. That would make them have to sit up and take notice, wouldn't it? It might just mean that Arthur could stay in the chapel. Stay in his home.

He raises one fist and calls out, 'Hands! Off! Arthur's chapel!' and everybody in the snug cheers. Somebody puts another pint on the table for him.

At last, he thinks. Somebody is doing something.

So why, he wonders, does he get the faintest feeling that Molly would definitely not be impressed?

* 23 *

'So, what you after, then?' says her dad, peering at the shopping list written on the back of a brown envelope. On the front of the envelope is a plastic window and the words FINAL DEMAND written in red.

'I don't know what you mean,' says Gemma, picking up three tins of Heinz beans and putting them in the trolley. Her dad takes them out and replaces them with two tins of Kwik Save's own brand beans.

'You never offer to come and do the shopping with me,' he says, squinting at the list. He shoves it under Gemma's nose. 'Does that say *figs*?'

She laughs and punches his arm. 'It says fags. When do we ever buy figs? I don't even know what they are.'

'I am partial to a fig roll, though,' says her dad. 'Wonder if we can stretch to a packet? Anyway, what you after?'

Gemma pushes the trolley as her dad walks along the aisle, looking at his list then up at the shelves. 'Well . . . you know I said don't bother to get me anything for Christmas?'

'I think you said two hundred Marlboro Lights, if I'm not mistaken.' He puts a packet of penne pasta in the trolley, and a big jar of watery looking pasta sauce with an own-brand white label. 'Don't tell me you want a Buzz Lightyear as well.'

'I want a set of drums,' says Gemma quickly.

Her dad looks up from a box of dried peas. 'A set of drums?'

'I'm in a band. With Kelly Derricott and Nicola Manning. And Timmy Leigh.'

'Him as lives in the big houses near the canal? Mum and dad right up themselves?'

'You should hear him sing, Dad. He's amazing.'

Her dad considers. 'What sort of band?'

'I don't know, like Oasis or Blur or something.'

'And you're playing the drums? Christ, Gemma, couldn't you have gone for something cheaper? Like a penny whistle, or a triangle?'

'Forget I said anything,' mutters Gemma, snatching the list from him. 'Here, the frozen aisle's next.'

She should have known he would take the piss, just like everybody at school. Mr Green must have blabbed about the detention session to anyone who would listen, and by lunchtime it was all over everywhere. Gemma was in the dinner queue with Kelly, Nicola and Timmy when Heather Wilson cruised past with her gang, looking them up and down. She'd paused, one painted nail tapping her chin, looking at the four of them leaning against the wall.

'So . . .' she said, pointing at Kelly, Gemma, Nicola and Timmy in turn. 'We've got Scummy Spice, Thieving Spice, Ugly Spice and Poofter Spice.'

'Fuck off,' Kelly had said cheerfully, flipping Heather the finger. Heather had glared at her. 'I haven't forgotten, you know. About the paint. I'm going to get you back.'

'So you keep saying,' said Kelly. Gemma wasn't exactly what anyone would call a shrinking violet, but she was a little bit in awe of the way Kelly spoke to Heather Wilson. Heather always made Gemma clam up, feel like she just wasn't as good as the other girl, wasn't worth half of her. Hardly surprising, when the teachers at Marigold Brook fawned over Heather and her crew because their parents had money and they had the best chances of going to university, and were all on the netball and badminton teams.

'Besides,' Kelly had said. 'We're not that sort of group. We're a band. A proper band.'

Heather's pretty face had contorted in a sneer. 'Can't wait to see you on *Top of the Pops*. But I think it's more likely I'll walk past you in the dole queue.'

'Screw her,' said Kelly when Heather and her mates had walked away in a cloud of laughter and CK One. 'Screw all of them.'

Her dad picks up a big packet of fish fingers then puts it back and gets two smaller ones. 'These are on offer. You get four more fish fingers for 10p less.' He taps his temple with his finger and winks at Gemma. 'No flies on your old dad.'

They round the corner into the drinks aisle, and her dad suddenly bursts out laughing. Gemma stares at him crossly. 'What's so funny? Still thinking about me being in a band?'

'No,' says her dad, pointing to the checkouts at the end of the aisle. 'Look who it is.'

Gemma squints and laughs as well. It's Crushing Ken, wearing a tabard and sitting at one of the tills, serving an old woman. 'What's he doing here?'

'I don't know,' says her dad, putting four big bottles of cider into the trolley.

Gemma stares at him, aghast. 'Four? Mum'll go mad. She can't even drink now she's preggers.'

Her dad taps the side of his head again. 'No flies on your old dad, you'll see. Now go back and get a Victoria sponge cake. And get a Fry's Chocolate Cream for your mum. And pick me up a packet of fig rolls.' He pauses, and thinks for a minute. 'And a couple of Walnut Whips.'

When Gemma returns with her arms laden with treats her dad's already queuing at Crushing Ken's checkout. When the woman in front moves on Ken glances up then breaks out in a broad grin. He's a slight, wiry man with close-cropped grey hair and eyes that are slightly bulging with off-centre pupils. 'All right, Terry,' he says to her dad.

'All right, Ken,' nods her dad back. 'What you doing here, then?'

As Gemma puts the food from the trolley on the belt, Ken begins to sling it down into the bagging area. 'Got some casual shifts in the run up to Christmas. Have to make some crushing money somehow.'

Her dad laughs. 'The day you have no money the Queen'll have no soldiers.'

'You're off your crushing head,' says Ken, sending more food down. 'Times are hard for everybody, Terry, you know that.'

'Shouldn't you be scanning this stuff?' says Gemma as Terry flings the tins of beans into the bagging section. He winks one of his big eyes at her.

'Shush up, Gemma, love. Crushing hell.'

'Anyway, Ken, speaking of Christmas' says her dad. 'Got a bit of a list for you.'

Ken takes the piece of paper from her dad and glances down it. 'Should be doable. I'll work out some prices. I've got a couple of Buzz Lightyears put to one side. Like crushing rocking horse shit, they are, son.'

Her dad leans forward. 'Got another request as well. How might you be fixed for a drum kit?'

Gemma blinks from where she's packing the food into plastic Kwik Save bags. So he wasn't taking the piss out of her after all.

Ken sets of coughing and thumps his chest with the heel of his fist. 'Crushing hell, Terry, lad, who do you think I am? Abbey Road?'

'Have a think,' says her dad with a wink. 'Our Gemma's in a band. Proper rock band and all that.'

Ken looks impressed. 'Hey, you should get yourself to the cafe. They've got some of that new Oasis soup on.'

Gemma crinkles her brow. 'Why do they call it Oasis soup?'

'Because you get a roll with it!' Ken winks at her dad and they both burst out laughing. 'A crushing roll with it! D'you get it, Gemma, love? Crushing brilliant, that.'

Gemma rolls he eyes and her dad says, 'How much do I owe you for all this, Ken?'

Ken sucks in air and considers the five plastic bags full of food that Gemma is loading back into the trolley. 'Let's call it twenty.'

Gemma's eyes widen. Her dad hands over two tens and Ken pockets them and winks at her. 'If it doesn't go through the till they'll just write it off as shoplifted stock. Natural wastage. They factor that in. You win, I win, nobody really loses.'

Her dad moves out of the way of the next customer, and nods at her when he recognises the old woman putting three four-packs of Guinness on the conveyor belt. 'Hello, Mrs Cromwell.'

'All right, Terry. How's Janice?'

'Pregnant again.'

Mrs Cromwell shrugs, and pushes the cans along towards Ken. 'Same deal as last week, Ken?'

'Fiver should do it, Maud. Crushing hell, I am good to you, aren't I?'

Gemma pushes the trolley towards the doors as her dad puts a hand to steer it away from a display of tins of Quality Street. She says, 'He's going to get found out. They'll sack him.'

'Oh, he knows that. So long as he gets a couple of weeks in, he'll be all right.'

It hasn't snowed for the last couple of days but it's still bitterly cold, and as they push the trolley across the car park Gemma feels her fingers turning blue. 'Are we getting the bus?'

'Nah, we'll walk. It's only ten minutes. Fifteen at most.' They stop at the entrance to the car park, near a big billboard that shows the grinning visage of Tony Blair, a rip across his face that reveals a pair of demonic eyes instead of his own. Gemma starts to unload the trolley but her dad stops her. 'We'll take it. Sid the Scrappy'll give me a couple of quid for it.'

Gemma looks up at the poster. *New Labour, New Danger*, says the slogan. 'Do you think things'll be any better if Labour get in?'

Her dad lights a cigarette, sheltering it from the biting wind behind the lapel of his coat. He takes a long, thoughtful drag, and says, 'The Tories have been in power half my life, Gemma. Labour were mostly in government for the other half. The thing is, it doesn't matter who's in the driving seat in Westminster, not to the likes of us up here. You might get one lot banging on about how they represent the working man, and the other lot talking how they want folk to own their own houses and make money, but what's the point if there's no jobs anyway? The only use we were to them was to make things, to dig coal, to hammer steel, to weave cotton. Then they decided they could get those things done cheaper in other places, so they closed everything down. Now we're just an inconvenience. We still need feeding and we still need roofs over our heads, but they've taken away the means for us to earn that for ourselves. That's why I do my own thing, and always have. Self-help, I think they call it.'

'More like *help yourself*,' says Gemma, but smiles. They walk on along the main road, pushing the trolley.

After a while, her dad says, 'So, this band then . . . what do you call yourselves?'

* 24 *

'It's not a bad question, though,' says Kelly, rubbing her hands together. All four of them are squeezed into the mausoleum, lit by torches and candles. 'What *are* we going to be called?'

Gemma lights up a cigarette and Nicola says, 'If you're going to smoke can you do it outside?'

Gemma stares at her. 'It's a bloody tomb, not your mum's front room.'

Nevertheless, she stomps outside, blowing smoke into the cold, clear air as the rest of them huddle around the dozen or so candles they've lit inside the old mausoleum. She looks in and sees Nicola unzip her bass guitar case. She's also brought a big black bin-liner with her, which clanks metallically. Kelly says, 'I can't believe we're having our first rehearsal here.'

I can't believe we're doing this at all, thinks Gemma. It was a funny speech Kelly made to Mr Green, but surely she doesn't actually expect to follow this through.

'I did ask my mum if we could do it in our summer house, but she said no,' says Timmy. 'In fact, she says I should be concentrating on studying for my GCSEs, not messing about with a band.'

'We're not messing about,' says Kelly crossly. 'This is serious. You might have a chance of passing your GCSEs and getting a job, Timmy, but for the rest of us this is our only hope of getting out of this shithole.'

'What about The Graveyard Girls?' calls Gemma from the doorway.

Kelly shakes her head. 'No, sounds too goth. It has to mean something. And it has to be one word, like Oasis or Blur.'

'What does Oasis mean, though?' says Timmy, sitting cross-legged on the cold earth, folding his gangling arms and legs beneath him. 'I mean, I know what an oasis is, but what's it mean in terms of being a band?'

'It's a drink,' says Nicola.

'And a clothes shop,' offers Gemma from outside. 'Nicked a lovely top from there in summer.'

Gemma comes back in and looks at them all each in turn. 'Can I just ask, why are we doing this? Seriously? I know it was your big plan, Kelly, and your speech in detention was brilliant, but look at us. Nowhere to rehearse, no instruments. Why are we doing this?'

'I know why we're doing this,' says Kelly. 'But, yeah, Gemma's right. A band needs a reason for being together. Timmy, you go first.'

He shrugs. 'Because you told me I had to.'

Gemma laughs. 'And do you always do what you're told, Timmy?'

Timmy wraps his arms around his knees and stares into the flickering flame of a candle. Eventually he says quietly, 'Pretty much, yeah. My mum and dad. The teachers. Colin Cardy and all that lot.' He looks up and meet Gemma's eyes. 'I've always done what I've been told. But it's nice to have somebody ask me to do something nice for a change. Something fun.' His gaze falls to his feet. 'It's nice to have friends.'

Gemma sees Nicola put a hesitant hand on Timmy's arm, then move it away again quickly. She says to Nicola, 'What about you?'

'I have to practise somewhere since you got me banned from the music room,' says Nicola sullenly. Then she says, 'You don't know what it's like with my mum. She's very protective. She thinks I'm going to do my GCSEs and go to college to do A Levels then go to university and she'll never see me again.'

'I'm sure that's not true, though,' says Kelly.

Nicola turns to her. 'It bloody is. I need to escape. I need a way out. And being in a band . . . well, I sent off for some stuff from the Royal Northern College of Music in Manchester. I had to have it delivered to the newsagents where I do the paper round so my mum wouldn't see it.' Her eyes shine as she talks. 'The stuff they have there . . . and these courses they do . . . you've got a better chance of getting in if you've done your own independent projects. Maybe doing this might help.'

Gemma and Kelly look at each other. Kelly says, 'You next.'

Gemma shrugs. 'Nothing else to do, is there?'

'There must be more than that,' says Timmy.

Maybe there is, thinks Gemma. Maybe she's been thinking about what her dad said, that she's got brains, that she could make something of herself. Maybe she's allowing herself to dream, just a little bit, that her life isn't already mapped out for her, that she's not just going to be Terry Swarbrick's daughter forever, that nobody will ever trust her. But then again, she's seen what happens to dreams at Marigold Brook, on the Avenues. Somebody always comes along and takes great pleasure in grinding them under their heel. So it's best to keep your dreams to yourself, to not have brains, to not think you can make something of yourself, because you never can.

She says, 'No. There's nothing more than that.'

'Well, bullshit,' says Kelly. She stands up. 'You know why I'm doing this?' She digs into her pocket and pulls something out, something pointy that reflects the torchlight. 'Because I'm one of these.'

'A cog . . .?' says Timmy.

'It's a sprocket,' says Kelly. 'They make them at the factory. And that's where I'll be working after Christmas, sweeping up and wiping down. And after school I'll be working there every day, putting sprockets into boxes.'

'So why are you a sprocket?' says Gemma.

Kelly waves the cog. 'Because there's something wrong with this sprocket. You wouldn't know to look at it, but it doesn't work. Not the way it's supposed to. So it got chucked in the bin. Because it was slightly different.' She holds it out to Nicola, to Timmy, and to Gemma. 'I'm this sprocket. And so are you. And you. And you, Gemma. We look like everybody else but we don't want to just spend the rest of our lives stuck in some machine with hundreds of other sprockets doing the same bloody thing day in, day out, until we wear out. But you don't get a choice, do you? You either be a good little sprocket and fit in the machine, or you get tossed in the bin. Well, we're going to have a choice. We're going to do things a different way. That's why we're doing this.'

There's a long silence, then Timmy says, 'This is a metaphor, right?'

Kelly tosses the sprocket on the floor. 'Yeah, and we're a band. Let's make some noise.'

Gemma can't help but smile at Kelly's enthusiasm. 'With what, though?'

Kelly says, 'Nicola?'

Nicola reaches into the bin liner and starts passing metal boxes to Gemma, who frowns at them. 'Biscuit tins?'

'They'll do for drums for now. You can use these chopsticks.'

Each tin has a sticker on it – bass, snare, floor tom. Gemma shrugs and begins to set them up according to the plan Nicola's drawn on a piece of paper.

From the bag Nicola pulls something that makes Gemma laugh. 'You're joking, right?'

It's a shoebox with the cardboard tube from a roll of clingfilm stuck on one end, and six elastic bands stretched along its length. Nicola has drawn in felt tip guitar neck frets on the cardboard tube.

'It'll get you used to the finger placing,' says Nicola to Kelly. 'Look, if anyone's got a better idea, or a *guitar* . . .'

'What about me?' says Timmy.

Kelly takes the cardboard contraption and holds it across her body, strumming the elastic bands held taut across the shoebox. She practises putting the fingers and thumb of her left hand on the frets, going through the chords she's been trying to memorise. 'You're the lucky one, you don't need an instrument,' she says. Under her breath she recites, 'A . . . D . . . A . . . D . . . B minor . . .'

Nicola looks up from tuning her bass by candlelight. 'What are you playing?'

'*Rock 'N' Roll Star*. Oasis. I got a guitar book out of the library. I don't know if the chords are right but . . .'

Nicola strums along. 'Not far off. Give me a minute to get them right.'

'I wrote the words out for you,' says Kelly, handing a folded sheet of paper to Timmy. He angles it towards candle and reads along, his lips moving softly, his head nodding.

'What do I do?' says Gemma. She's made a little stool out of stacks of tins of beans and is tapping at the biscuit tins with the chopsticks.

Nicola considers. 'Heavy on the tom. But mainly, just go for it and keep time with my bass for now.'

'OK,' says Kelly, standing up and gripping her shoebox guitar. 'Hit it!'

Five minutes later, Gemma goes out for a cigarette and Kelly is so demoralised she accepts the offer of one. The pair of them stand in the freezing air outside the mausoleum, looking up at the stars.

'Kelly,' says Gemma gently. 'What did you expect? I'm banging biscuit tins with chopsticks and you're twanging elastic bands. In a graveyard. Is it any surprise it was such a racket?'

Kelly exhales smoke. 'I just didn't think we'd sound so . . . hopeless.'

They stand in silence for a moment, then Gemma says, 'I asked my dad for some drums. I'm not holding out much hope. I know people think my dad can nick anything but I don't know how he'd get a full kit under his coat. Any chance you can get a guitar? Even a second-hand one?'

'If I hadn't been sacked off the market, maybe.' She brightens slightly. 'Though my dad has got a job interview next week. If he gets it . . .'

Gemma throws her dog-end to the floor and grinds it under her shoe. 'If you really want us to make a go of this, we're going to have to just carry on like this then. As shit as it sounds.'

'Maybe it was just a stupid idea anyway,' says Kelly. 'We're just a bunch of kids messing about in a cemetery. Not a proper band. Let's just knock it on the head.'

From inside the mausoleum they hear the dull sound of Nicola's bass playing the intro to the song. And then Timmy begins to sing. Kelly meets Gemma's gaze.

'Maybe not so hopeless,' says Gemma.

Kelly throws her cigarette to the ground and pushes past Gemma back into the mausoleum. Timmy's voice trails off. She points at him and says, 'That was brilliant. But it's more like *sunsheee-iiiine*, right? OK, let's do it again. From the top.'

*

'I can't sing it any more,' croaks Timmy.

Nicola looks at her digital watch. 'Oh, God, it's nearly nine o'clock. My mum's going to go mad.'

Gemma's fingers are numb with cold anyway. Kelly says, 'We still sound like a mess, but I think I'm getting those chords. Can we leave this stuff here?'

Nicola bites her lip. Gemma says, 'Oh, go on. If the world ends tonight you'll at least have some biscuit tins.'

'All right,' says Nicola.

'Nic?' says Kelly. 'Honestly, what do you think?'

Nicola shrugs as she zips up her guitar bag. 'Like Gemma said outside. It sounded like somebody hitting biscuit tins with chopsticks and playing a cardboard guitar.'

'Oh,' says Kelly, crestfallen.

'But that's what we are. And we sounded less like that at the end than we did at the beginning.' Nicola nods towards Gemma. 'You've actually got good rhythm.'

'I actually really enjoyed that,' says Timmy. 'Can we learn some more songs, though?'

'When we can do this one back to front,' says Kelly. 'Which we'll be able to, by the end of the week.'

Gemma gapes at her. 'End of the week?'

'Same time tomorrow,' says Kelly firmly. 'Everybody here.' She looks around at their faces, painted yellow by the candles which have burned down to stubs. 'Any arguments?'

There aren't. The four of them blow out the candles and leave the tomb, pulling the dried brambles over the entrance to hide it. They walk along the bottom edge of the cemetery, by the wall, to where they can climb over and cut through the trees to their estate. No one is talking, which is perhaps why Kelly hears what she does.

'Shush!' she commands. 'Can you hear that?'

They all stop and cock their heads to listen. It's faint, hovering on the breeze, but unmistakeable. Gemma's eyes widen. 'That's spooky.'

Kelly starts to walk back the way they came. Gemma hisses, 'What are you doing?'

'I have to go back,' says Nicola. 'I'm in enough trouble as it is.'

'I'll walk with you,' says Timmy. 'You can't go through those trees on your own.'

And then Gemma can hear it too, the most beautiful guitar playing she's ever heard in her entire life. It makes her shiver. 'Kelly, come on,' she says.

But Kelly shakes her head. 'No. You go. I'll catch you up. I need to know where that's coming from.'

Reluctantly, Gemma hurries off after Timmy and Nicola, glancing over her shoulder to see Kelly standing there, still and rapt, as though hypnotised by the faint music.

* 25 *

Arthur sits by the wood burner, the glow from the licking flames warming him as his fingers of his left hand move unerringly along the neck of the guitar, those on his right picking out the tune on the strings. *Concierto de Aranjuez*. He's not played it for so many years, but last month that film came out, the one about the out-of-work miners and the colliery band, and suddenly it was everywhere. It's as though his hands have kept the memory of the tune, not his head. He's thinking of nothing and everything all at the same time, of Molly and of losing the chapel and of the rally and the moonflowers, but also of a great, blue emptiness, like a summer sky, while his fingers coax the music from the guitar. It's a lovely piece, but so weighted with memories. As he comes to the end, he's surprised to find his cheeks are wet with tears.

He's also surprised to see the pale orb of a face at one of the windows, looking in at him.

'Come early have you, you bugger?' mutters Arthur, laying the guitar down. 'You're not getting away this time.'

But when he wrenches open the chapel door, it isn't the mysterious visitor who lays flowers on Molly's grave standing there. Of course it's not. Her birthday's nearly two weeks away. Why would he be here now? It's that girl. Kelly. Kelly Derricott.

'What do you want?' says Arthur crossly. 'Didn't I tell you and your friends not to play in the cemetery?' Arthur looks at his wristwatch. 'It's gone nine. You should be at home.'

Kelly steps down from the pile of loose stones she's used to make a step to allow her to look into the window. 'You were playing the guitar.'

'What about it?'

'It was beautiful.'

Arthur opens his mouth to speak then closes it again. He wasn't really expecting that. Kelly says, 'Can I come in?'

'No,' says Arthur. 'Go home. Young girls shouldn't be hanging around old men.'

He turns to go back into the chapel but Kelly follows him. Arthur sighs. 'What do you want?'

'I want to hear you play. That song's off that new film, *Brassed Off*.'

'It's Rodrigo's *Concierto de Aranjuez*. It's very famous.' Arthur walks back to the fire and picks up his guitar. 'If I play it again, will you go home?'

Kelly shrugs. 'Maybe.'

Arthur plays again, watching Kelly as she scrutinises his fingers, her eyes narrowed as though she's committing to memory the chords and the finger tabs. He plays a truncated version, then quietens the vibrating strings with the palm of his hand.

'Can I play something?' says Kelly.

Arthur frowns, then hands over the guitar. Kelly sits hunched over it, carefully placing her fingers on the neck, then begins to strum along, silently making shapes with her mouth which Arthur realises are the chord she's trying to play. She's uncertain at first, and goes wrong a few times, but eventually Arthur can recognise the tune, at least vaguely.

'It's 'Rock 'N' Roll Star', by Oasis,' says Kelly.

Arthur nods. 'I think I've heard it on the jukebox in the pub. Do you take lessons?'

Kelly laughs and hands back the guitar. 'I'd never picked one up before last week. We've formed a band. I've been practising on a shoebox with toilet roll tubes stuck in it.'

Arthur laughs too, then realises she's serious. If she's not lying, if she really only has picked up a proper guitar once . . . 'You've got a talent for it,' he says.

Kelly momentarily looks suspicious, and then beams. 'Really? Do you think so?'

Arthur guesses that she doesn't get many compliments. 'Play it again,' he says, handing back the guitar.

When Kelly's finished, Arthur rubs his chin. She's rough around the edges, that's for sure. But she's better than he was when he first picked up the guitar, that's a fact as well. He takes the guitar back and says, 'Watch this, where I put my fingers.' He plays the first few bars of *Aranjuez* and hands over the instrument.

Kelly sticks her tongue out in concentration as she goes through the chords in her head, then plays a more than passable imitation of what Arthur had played. She looks up and blinks, as though she's surprised herself as much as she has Arthur.

'Hey, that was all right!'

'That was all right,' agrees Arthur, with a smile.

'I heard they want to knock down your house,' says Kelly.

Arthur nods. Her dad's one of Cardy's regulars, he remembers. 'Yes. They want to turn this part of the cemetery into flats for asylum seekers.'

Kelly gives Arthur back the guitar and stands up, wandering over to his kitchen area. 'My dad says that they're only coming over here because we're a soft touch. They want benefits and houses. He says we can't look after people from here who need help, never mind people from other countries.'

Arthur watches as she drifts through the kitchen. 'And what do you think?'

Kelly shrugs. 'I think my dad's bitter. He used to work at the mine behind the cemetery, until they closed it down. He had a few jobs after that but nothing decent. He's been out of work for a long time.'

'A lot of people have, round here,' says Arthur.

'I think he feels bad because he doesn't bring money in like he used to,' says Kelly, turning around and leaning back on the cabinets. 'It's like he feels he isn't a proper dad and husband. Thing is, I don't think he really feels like that about these asylum seekers. He just repeats what that lot in the Black Diamond say. He's not really like that.' She pauses, considering. 'I think people always need somebody else to blame, don't they? But they don't always blame the right people. I mean, it wasn't the asylum seekers who closed down the pit, was it? It was Thatcher. But then the government tells you that these foreigners are coming over and taking benefits and houses, and people start to blame them for what they haven't got, instead of the government.'

She talks a lot, this Kelly Derricott, thinks Arthur. But she talks a lot of sense. He says, 'That's very . . . astute.'

'I don't know what that means.'

'It means . . . shrewd. It means you have good observations about things.'

'I don't think they do GCSEs in being astute, though,' says Kelly. 'Besides, my dad's got a job interview next week. It's for a supervisor at an engineering company. I hope he gets it. Might stop him being so miserable.' She pauses at the wooden box with the glass top. 'What did you get these medals for?'

'For turning up, mainly.'

'What's this pointy one?'

'The 1939-1945 Star. I got that for being at the Liberation of Paris.'

Kelly moves on, and her eyes graze towards the calendar. 'Why do you put a red ring around your wife's birthday? Do you do something special? Do you miss her loads?'

Arthur looks at Kelly for a long time before replying. When he does, he speaks carefully, and haltingly. 'Every year, something . . . odd happens on Molly's birthday. Somebody leaves flowers on her grave.'

Kelly shrugs. 'Why's that odd?'

'Because she's got no family except me and it's nobody round here who's doing it – I've asked everybody. I've got nobody either.' Arthur pauses. 'Well, there's my dad's brother's son's lad. But I've not seen him since he was a nipper. I think he joined the police.'

'But they're just flowers,' presses Kelly.

Arthur says, 'But it's when they come. Always in the middle of the night. And they're always specific flowers. They're called *Ipomoea alba*. That's their Latin name. All plants have Latin names. Their common name is moonflowers. They only bloom at night.'

Kelly's interest is suddenly piqued. 'Ooh, who do you think it is? Do you think she had a secret boyfriend or something?'

'No!' says Arthur, shocked. 'Not my Molly!'

Kelly comes back to the fire and sits down, her eyes shining. 'It's a proper mystery! Like *Seven*! Have you seen that? Brad Pitt's in it. He's well fit. There's a serial killer and he's doing murders based on the seven deadly sins or something. At the end he kills Gwyneth Paltrow and puts her head in a box.' Kelly's hand flies to her mouth. 'Oh. I've spoiled it for you, now.'

'I probably won't watch it anyway,' says Arthur. He waves his hand at the chapel interior. 'I don't have a television. I just listen to the radio.'

Kelly's eyes widen. 'No telly?' she says, as if she finds this more horrific than finding Gwyneth whoever's head in a box.

'I like the radio. I listen to Radio 4 in the mornings and then Radio 3 in the afternoons.'

'I listen to Radio 1,' says Kelly. 'Chris Evans is well funny in the mornings. He's always off sick because he's been out with his mates the night before.'

Arthur frowns. 'He doesn't sound like a very good role model.'

'They don't do role models for the likes of us,' Kelly laughs. 'Nobody expects us to do anything, except get crap jobs and get pregnant.' She pauses. 'Hey, do you not have any kids?'

'No. Molly . . . had an accident. She had to work on a farm in the war. There was this barrel of chemicals. It meant she couldn't have children.'

Kelly nods, but doesn't say anything. Young people are so accepting of situations, thinks Arthur. Then she says, 'What are you going to do? Stay up all night to try to catch them?'

'Something like that. It's my last chance. If they demolish the chapel to make these houses for asylum seekers . . . I won't be here next year.'

'That sounds like you're going to die!' says Kelly.

Arthur says nothing. Because he knows that if they do make him leave here, if they put him in a flat in sheltered accommodation, if he can't be close to Molly every single day . . . then there's the distinct possibility he might just roll over and die.

Arthur stands up, and suddenly lapses into a coughing fit. Banging his chest with his fist, he takes a look at his watch. 'You should be going. Your mum and dad'll be worried about you.'

'I suppose.' Kelly stands up as well, and follows Arthur to the chapel door. He leans on the handle a moment, getting his breath, before opening it. 'You should carry on with the guitar, you know. Take lessons. You could be really good.' He pauses. The girl has a funny look on her face. 'What's the matter?'

'Nothing,' says Kelly. 'I'm just having an idea. I get ideas all the time.'

'What idea?'

'Can't say, yet.' She passes through the door. 'Thank you for letting me play your guitar.'

'It was a pleasure,' says Arthur, and is mildly surprised to realise it actually was.

'What was Paris like in the war?' says Kelly. 'Where did you learn to play the guitar? Why do you like that song you were playing?'

'No more questions,' says Arthur. 'Go home. And go along the main road, not through the cemetery and over the wall. It's late.'

She nods and gives a little wave, and walks off into the darkness. Arthur watches her go until she reaches the main gates, then closes the door. What is it with that girl and all her questions? Her last barrage has left him reeling a little, because though she might have thought they were three very different questions, they all have really the same answer.

✳ 26 ✳

Almost a decade after the war ended, there would be a popular song written by Cole Porter which contained the line 'I love Paris in the springtime'. In the first week of May of 1945, Arthur Calderbank and the City of Lights were not on such favourable terms. Paris had been liberated by Allied forces the August before, and Arthur had been there ever since. There was little to do other than wait for the day that he could finally return home to Molly. Their letters were more frequent now, thanks to the improved communications channels, and she was having a tolerable time in Yorkshire with the Women's Land Army. Paris seemed closer to Britain than it had ever done during the darkest days of the war, yet still so desperately far away for Arthur.

The city was in a state of almost delirium after so many years under occupation, and many of his comrades took advantage of the largesse demonstrated by the grateful Parisienne women – at least, those who had not had their heads shaved for consorting with the enemy. But Arthur was too true to Molly to consider such a thing, and spent his free time walking the avenues and boulevards, drinking coffee and pastis at pavement cafes, occasionally volunteering for the reconstruction work details. But even the grandeur of the Arc de Triomphe and the Eiffel Tower paled eventually in the eyes of someone who was keen to leave Paris behind forever, and Arthur took to wandering the outlying arrondissements, away from the soldiers who crowded the busier areas, where he could be alone with his thoughts.

Thoughts which tended towards the future. As soon as he was demobilised he would go to collect Molly from Yorkshire, and they would head back across the Pennines and make their home among the familiar red-brick streets. Arthur would return to work at the pit, perhaps, or find a job in one of the engineering works. Molly would take up a position at one of the cotton mills or sewing factories, but not for long. They would marry at last, and have children. Two, three, perhaps five. They would fill their house with children and love and go on Wakes weeks holidays to Blackpool or Whitby, and Arthur would never set foot in France again as long as he lived. Not after what he'd seen in the past couple of years.

One of Arthur's regular walks took him along a road that began with packed apartments and opened into small houses with well-kept gardens, eventually finishing at open countryside. There were children playing in the streets – children who were babes in arms, or not even born, when the war started. Old folk sat out in the sun, drinking in their freedom. Many of them had lived through two world wars now. Arthur wasn't one for God, but prayed nonetheless that none of them would ever see another one.

He liked this particular walk because towards the end of the road there was always a man, some kind of tramp, Arthur supposed, perhaps made homeless by the destruction, who sat in the doorway of a bombed-out property and played the guitar. He was not much older than Arthur's age, perhaps 25 or 26, but his face was lined and grimy and his blue eyes had evidently seen much. Arthur sometimes threw him a few centimes, one time had dropped at his feet a paper bag of pastries he had bought then found he had no appetite for. Beyond where the road petered out was a field churned up by a battle, the mounds of earth dry and powdery in the May heat. Right in the middle of the field was a British Challenger tank, split in two like an orange, its exposed metalwork rusting after a winter abandoned. Arthur usually turned back when he saw it, walking back towards the city centre, and his billet. This morning the tramp, wrapped in grey rags, was playing a song that Arthur didn't recognise, but which he found pleasing, and he listened to it as he looked out at the tank. It had been the scene of a battle, he supposed, the occupying forces pulling out of Paris, pursued by the Allies. He wondered why the children playing in the street some way behind him hadn't claimed the

Challenger as a makeshift fort, or den. Perhaps they'd had enough of war. Just like Arthur.

He didn't know what prompted him to head for the Challenger – a closer look, perhaps, or the thought of maybe finding some trophy or souvenir he could take back for Molly – but Arthur found himself climbing over the wooden fence that bounded the field and jumping on to the dried divots of mud. He'd barely gone a dozen steps when he heard an indistinct shouting behind him. Turning, he saw the figure of the tramp, guitar in hand, waving frantically. Arthur waved back and turned to continue.

The shouting became louder and casting a glance over his shoulder Arthur saw the tramp hurtling towards the field, still dragging his guitar. Then Arthur frowned as he heard the words.

'Nein! Nein! Nein!'

Bloody hell. He was a *German*.

Arthur took two stumbling steps backwards as the man vaulted the fence and came running along the route Arthur had taken into the field.

'Nein! Non! Halt! Stop!'

A bloody German. The man showed no signs of slowing and Arthur crouched, ready to intercept the attack. He felt his foot hit something solid and metallic in the dry earth, and then the German was on him, tackling him around the waist like a rugby player, throwing him backwards, just as the ground rumbled and trembled and exploded in a shower of dirt.

On his back, Arthur spat out mud as earth rained down on them. The German was lying across him, and looked up, meeting his eyes.

'Landmine,' said the man weakly, but Arthur could barely hear him, so deafening was the ringing in his ears. He lay back, his head swimming. Landmine. So that's why the field was fenced off. That's why the children never played here. That's why that Challenger tank was cleaved in two. The whole place must have been seeded with mines by the retreating forces.

The Germans. Arthur raised his head dizzily, looking at the man. The man who had saved his life. The German who had saved his life. He heard a fresh peal of bells, but it wasn't just in his head. The German had heard it too.

141

'Danke Gott,' whispered the man. 'Es ist vorbei.'

Then Arthur looked down and saw the bloody stump of flesh and bone beneath his saviour's right knee, and fainted.

When Arthur woke, he was in a bed on a ward with some twenty other men. A young nurse wearing a smock with a red cross on it was leaning over him, scrutinising his face.

'Ah, you're still with us. We were beginning to wonder,' she said. She was English.

'Where am I?' said Arthur. His head was still ringing and there was a fiery pain in his left thigh.

The nurse stuck a thermometer into his mouth and told him to be quiet. 'The American Hospital of Paris,' she said. 'You're in the hands of the Red Cross now, Private Calderbank.' She folded her arms and regarded him. 'You're very lucky. What were you thinking, wandering into a minefield? Didn't you see the signs?'

Arthur shook his head, then winced as the ringing started again in his ears. The nurse said, 'You've got a bad concussion. And you took some shrapnel to your leg. You'll need a couple of operations, but you'll live.'

She took the thermometer from his mouth and shook it. Arthur said, 'What about the man who saved me? He . . . he's a German. What have they done with him?'

'He's here,' said the nurse. 'He's being treated. He's not in a good way. But we'll do our best for him. I suppose we're all friends again now, aren't we?'

Arthur frowned. 'What do you mean?'

The nurse raised an eyebrow. 'Didn't you know? Didn't you hear the bells? Adolf shot himself in his bunker. The enemy has surrendered. The war's over.'

My Dearest Molly,

Thank you for your last letter, it has cheered me up no end. My recovery is progressing well but I'm going to be here for some weeks yet. They have removed most of the shrapnel from my leg but I might need another go under the knife to get a big piece out.

However, I have met the man who saved my life. His name is Peter Bergmann and he is twenty-five years old. He is from a place in Germany called the Ruhr, and before the war he was a coal miner, just like me.

Peter got separated from his unit in the final days of the Liberation of Paris and fearing that he would either be shot for desertion if he found his own side or sent to a prisoner-of-war camp if he was captured by our lot, he decided to lay low in Paris and lived in a bombed-out house.

We have become quite the pals, which I know must sound like a strange thing to say after so many years of his mob and our mob trying to kill each other. But they're not so very different than us, really. He has a sweetheart himself called Maria and he is very anxious to get back to her. Just like I am with you.

It's so very lucky that he was there on that day or I would be a goner. Peter has been teaching me how to play the guitar, which helps the days pass a bit more tolerably. We sit in the gardens of the hospital and he shows me the chords and where to put my fingers. He says I'm a quick learner. His English is excellent, which is a good job because my German is rubbish.

I hope life on the farm isn't too boring and I cannot wait until we are together again. When I am discharged from the hospital I will have to return to my unit and wait to be properly demobbed, but I am hoping that will not be too much longer now.

All my love, as always,

Arthur.

'Very good, Arthur,' said Peter, taking a drag from his hand-rolled cigarette. 'You have a gift for the guitar.'

'This is the tune I heard you playing that day,' said Arthur, looking around the grounds of the hospital. More than one nurse was pushing a wheelchair with an injured man in it; other men were sitting around playing cards in the sunshine, or smoking, or simply enjoying their own company.

'*Concierto de Aranjuez*,' said Peter. 'Now, once again, from the beginning.'

'Don't you want to sit down?' said Arthur, patting the wooden bench.

Peter shook his head, leaning on his wooden crutches. Arthur tried not to look at the bloodstained bandage wrapped around where his right leg ended at the knee. 'It is more comfortable to stand.'

'What's it like?' said Arthur softly.

Peter shrugged. 'I forget it is not there, sometimes. I think my foot is itching, but when I lean down to scratch there is nothing to see.'

'Do you think we'll stay pals, when we go home?'

'I do not see why not. You could come visit with your Molly, and meet my Maria.'

'I'd like that. When's your next op?'

'Tomorrow. And I hope it is the last. Now, enough talk! Play!'

Arthur didn't expect to see Peter the next day, nor really the one after that, given he was having another operation. If it hadn't been for Arthur's foolishness, Peter would still have his leg. The day after that, Arthur waited for him at their usual bench, enjoying the sunshine, but Peter did not come. He sought out a nurse, who said that she would find out whether Peter was well enough to receive visitors.

It was much later when Arthur, who was dozing on his bed, was woken by the nurse who he had met on his first day at the hospital. 'I have some news,' she said softly, sitting on the edge of his bed.

As Arthur struggled to sit up, she said, 'The German. Mr Bergmann. There were complications during his operation. He did not come round from the anaesthetic.'

Arthur stared at her. 'You mean he's dead?'

'He left a note in his drawer,' she said. The nurse reached down and picked something up and placed it across Arthur's lap. 'It said that if anything were to happen to him, then we were to give you this.'

It was Peter's guitar.

27

'Wow, he actually let you play his guitar?' says Gemma. 'Old Man Calderbank?'

'Yep,' says Kelly. 'And I was sodding brilliant.'

They're leaning against the wall in the arcade in town, the carpet sticky underfoot, a combination of lemon air freshener and cigarette smoke wafting around them, a barrage of bleeps and music and the clatter of coins into the one-armed bandit trays forming a relentless cacophony.

In the gloom of the arcade, Nicola and Timmy are side-by-side on *Virtua Fighter*, thrashing buttons and joysticks together. Kelly watches them for a while. What a crew she's got round herself, all of a sudden. She could see herself being mates with Gemma, because they're birds of a feather. But Timmy Leigh and Nicola Manning? Funny the turns life takes, she thinks, when you decide you're not going to be a cog in the machine any more.

'What's it like in the chapel?' says Gemma, lighting a cigarette.

'He's done it up all right. He only lives there because his wife's buried in the cemetery and he can't bear to be parted from her. It's really sad.'

Nicola and Timmy finish their game and walk up to them, their eyes shining. Nicola looks like she's been let off the leash for the first time. She says, 'I've never been anywhere like this before! My mum would kill me!'

'Tell her it's good research or something,' says Gemma. She points at another machine. 'Look, you have to shoot zombies in a graveyard on that one. Get some practice in for the end of the world.'

Timmy digs in his school trousers for more coins and he and Nicola go to the game, taking turns to wield the gun wired to the console, blowing the groaning undead into showers of pixels. Gemma shivers, and says, 'Actually, that gives me the creeps a bit. I don't like hanging round that graveyard. Plus, it's bloody freezing.'

'Yeah,' says Kelly thoughtfully. 'You know, I had one of my ideas while I was talking to Arthur.'

Gemma raises an eyebrow. 'Oh, yeah? Your ideas generally mean trouble, Kelly.'

Kelly takes the half-smoked fag off Gemma and has a drag. 'Well, Arthur's got a bit of trouble himself. The council wants to throw him out of the chapel. My dad drinks with Keith Cardy in the Diamond and they're planning some sort of protest.'

She hands the cigarette back to Gemma, who says, 'My dad says Keith Cardy's trouble. So what's your idea? We going to do a Live Aid or something in the cemetery, save the chapel?'

Kelly opens her mouth to speak to her, then blinks. 'Actually, that is a good idea. But, no, there's this other thing.'

She tells Gemma what Arthur told her, about the mystery of the flowers appearing on Molly's grave every year on her birthday, and how Arthur is desperate to find out what's going on before he has to leave his home.

Gemma seems unimpressed. 'It's probably some relative who he's forgotten exists. You know what old people are like.' She twirls her forefinger around near her temple, and stubs her cigarette out in one of the overflowing ashtrays. 'So, what's the big idea?'

'We could solve the mystery for him,' says Kelly. 'The flowers are always left during the night on the twenty-third. We could keep watch, see who it is.'

Gemma looks at her. 'And why would we bother?'

Kelly grabs her arm. 'Because, Gem, Arthur's really good at the guitar. He could teach me how to play it properly. And you should see the inside of the chapel. It's huge. It would be a brilliant place to rehearse. And it would be warm.' She looks over to where Timmy and Nicola are on the game. 'And the zombies wouldn't get us.'

Gemma scrutinises her face for a long moment. 'And what else? I know there's something else.'

Kelly shrugs and looks away. 'I like him. He's all right, for an old duffer. I mean, he's cranky and he's always telling us off for going in the cemetery, but that's because he's just protective of his wife's grave and stuff. And . . . he's like us.'

Gemma laughs, but Kelly shakes her head. 'No, really. He is. He went off to war and when he came back his wife had been working on a farm and she had this accident with some chemicals that meant she couldn't have babies. And Arthur really, really wanted kids, I could tell. But they had this lovely life together, and when she died he refused to let her go. He moved into the chapel and did it all up himself. Don't you see?'

'Not really,' says Gemma, getting out another cigarette.

'He didn't do what he was supposed to,' says Kelly fiercely. 'He was meant to just sit in his house and then retire and potter around like old people do, dragging shopping trolleys down the street and getting under your feet and telling you off. But he said screw that. He wasn't going to let his dream go. Molly was his dream, and he was never going to let her go.'

Gemma considers it for a moment, then shrugs. 'All right, then. Let's do it.'

'We'll go and see him tonight,' says Kelly, picking up her bag. 'Shall we get back? I'm starving. Wonder what's for tea?'

'Hope it's chips, it's chips, we hope it's chips, it's chips,' sings Gemma. They both turn towards the door just as a rabble of lads in Marigold Brook uniforms spills in out of the cold. Gemma rolls her eyes. 'Colin Cardy.'

'All right, Tampax!' shouts Colin as he sees Timmy. 'And look who he's with, Manning the Minger!' Colin makes a circle with the thumb and fingers of his left hand and pokes the forefinger of his right through it. 'Are you shagging?'

'His name's Timmy,' says Kelly loudly.

Gemma glances at her, and looks down. 'Kell, don't wind them up,' she mutters.

Kelly looks at her. 'You've got to stop trying to melt into the bloody background, Gem. We're wonky sprockets, remember.'

Colin plucks a cigarette from behind his ear and swaggers to them, looking Kelly up and down. 'Say something?'

'I said, his name's Timmy, and hers is Nicola,' Kelly says defiantly, staring him down. 'Don't call them those names.'

Colin's gang jostles around him. He stares at Kelly's chest for so long she pulls her coat defensively tighter. He says, 'Oh, yeah, heard you lot was in a band. You need any groupies?'

The boys laugh raucously. Timmy and Nicola move hesitantly to stand behind Gemma and Kelly. Colin lights his cigarette and says, 'Seriously though, Derricott, we should go out.'

She can't stop herself laughing. 'You joking, Cardy?'

He shrugs. 'Why not? Our dads go drinking in the Diamond together. They're planning this march against the immigrants.'

'I thought it was to save Arthur's chapel,' says Kelly.

'Same thing. That's why we should go out. My dad's going to the pub tonight and my mum's at bingo. You could come round. There'll be nobody in.'

One of the boys whistles and they all start to laugh and giggle. Colin winks at Gemma. 'Ask her. She'll tell you what a good time you'll have.'

There's more whistling and cat-calling. Gemma's face reddens and she looks away. Kelly can feel anger, hot and hard, inside her chest. 'You're a lying little shit, Cardy,' she spits.

He raises his eyebrows then puts his hand in front of his crotch, as though it's on top of an invisible head, and begins to thrust his hips. Kelly pushes him hard in the shoulder. 'She wouldn't let you touch her and you made that up.'

Colin staggers back, his face clouding. He stares at Gemma. 'You did it and you loved it.'

Gemma looks away, then back at Cardy. 'No, I didn't.'

There's a low chorus of *oooohs* from Colin's gang. 'Yes you did. And you let me finger you.'

Kelly sees Gemma's face harden. Go on, girl, she thinks. Stop trying to fit in. You're better than this.

'No, I didn't,' says Gemma, more forcefully, pushing Colin hard in the shoulder, just like Kelly had. He takes a step back, his feet getting tangled with those of the boys behind him, and ends up on his backside on the sticky carpet.

'Slag,' he says, picking himself up. But his conditioning from his dad won't let him hit a girl, Kelly realises, though treating them like objects to be abused is obviously fair game. So instead he elbows Gemma out of the way and grabs hold of Timmy's tie. 'What you say, Tammy Girl? You say something to me?'

Timmy is trying to put his hands up in surrender and stammer out an apology or an excuse. The boys have started to form a circle, sensing that a fight – though an inevitably one-sided one – is imminent.

'Oh, fuck off,' says Kelly, and swings a punch at Colin, connecting not this time with his shoulder but his jaw. He sprawls backwards, smacking his head against one of the video games. She goes to stand over him, and glares at each of his mates until they back off. Then she realises that Gemma's at her shoulder, and Nicola and Timmy at her side. She looks down at Colin.

He glares back at her. 'You're hanging about with a bunch of fucking losers, Derricott.'

Kelly kicks him hard in the ribs, and he rolls over, groaning. She marches to the door, Timmy, Gemma and Nicola beside her, and turns back to where Colin is glowering and climbing to his feet. 'Yeah, maybe,' she says. 'But they're *my* fucking losers.'

28

'So we're all agreed, then,' says Keith Cardy, cigarette hanging out of his mouth, in the Black Diamond snug. 'The march will take place on Saturday the fourth of January. We'll start about three-ish, finish up near the Old Hall, where they can all see us. I've been in touch with the *Observer* and they're going to send a reporter and a photographer. It's the last weekend of the Christmas holidays so I expect all you bastards to turn out, and bring your bloody kids as well. We want a show of force. That sound all right to you, Arthur?'

'Hmm?' Arthur hasn't been listening, but he imagines that he's expected to agree with whatever Cardy has just said. 'Aye, that sounds grand,' he says hopefully.

Cardy smiles and points his ballpoint pen at Graham. 'Now, the EFAF lads . . . are they on board?'

Graham nods. 'They are. They'll send a good contingent down. They'll want to do a quick speech, if that's all right?'

Cardy ticks something off on a sheet of beer-stained paper on the table in front of him. 'Sounds fair enough.' He looks around. 'Talking of speeches . . . anybody any ideas who else should make one?'

'Well, Arthur, of course,' says Brian Derricott.

Cardy looks at him testily. 'Goes without saying. Anybody else, I mean. Anybody to represent the community. A figurehead, so to speak, for the movement.'

There's a collective murmuring and looking at hands and Cardy says pointedly, 'Brian? Any bright ideas?'

Brian's eyes widen. 'Oh! Yes! Sorry, Keith. What about you?'

Cardy smiles benevolently and holds up his hands. 'Oh, no, I'm sure I—'

'Go on, Keith!' shouts somebody else. 'Do it for Arthur!'

'Well, if you insist . . .' says Cardy. 'So long as Arthur's all right with that?'

'Hmm?' says Arthur. 'Oh, aye, sounds grand.' Ever since he spoke to Brian's daughter, that Kelly, he's been feeling a bit odd about all this. The things she was saying about folk always needing someone to blame.

'That's settled then,' says Cardy, making another note on his piece of paper. 'Next item . . . bad news from Graham.'

Graham takes off his flat cap and wrings it in his hands. Who's died? wonders Arthur. Graham says mournfully, 'It is my sad duty to tell you that we've been the victims of a criminal act. Somebody broke into our lock-up and stole a number of musical instruments.'

'Bloody disgrace,' says Cardy, nudging Brian to go and get him another pint. 'Can't trust anybody, these days. What did they take, Graham?'

'Funny, really,' muses Graham. 'They only took a set of drums. Ignored the brass instruments, which would have fetched 'em a lot more. And we've got spare drums as well.'

'So we still get our marching band?' says Cardy.

'Well, it's our second-best set of drums, but we should be all right.'

Cardy nods. 'Item five. Booze. I'm thinking we have a kitty, all put in a fiver, and get down to Kwik Save on the Saturday morning. We can get a table set up near the cemetery. Get a few of the wives to look after it. All agreed?'

And on it goes, in the same vein, until Arthur feels he's been there long enough to excuse himself without seeming rude. He gets a volley of cheers and applause as he puts his scarf on and heads out into the cold. It's not as if he's not grateful for all they're doing – he's quite moved, really – but he's increasingly of the suspicion that his plight is rapidly becoming secondary to the opportunity to down some beers and push their own agendas.

Besides, the closer it gets to the twenty-third, the more anxious he feels. What if Keith's grand march doesn't make any difference, and he's out on his ear? What if he's not solved the mystery of the flowers? He won't get another opportunity, he can feel it in his gut. This is the last chance saloon.

The walk back seems to take it out of him more than usual. He hopes he's not coming down with something. It would be just his luck to be laid up in bed on Molly's birthday and not have a hope of catching the bugger red-handed. He wonders what he's going to say to him when they finally come face to face. He hasn't even thought about that, he just knows that he has to have answers, and this might be the last chance to get them.

He's just let himself into the cemetery and is planning to stop at Molly's grave to say goodnight when he sees them, four figures lurking about the entrance to the chapel. Arthur dithers; should he go back and get someone from the pub? Then a raucous laugh rings out, and peering into the darkness he recognises the shapes. Those girls again, and Timmy Leigh.

'What now?' says Arthur, digging in his overcoat pocket for his keys. 'Don't you lot have homes to go to? How many times do I have to tell you not to play in the graveyard? You're trespassing. I'll get the council on you.'

'That's the thing,' says Kelly Derricott. 'We *have* been playing in the graveyard. But not, like, hide-and-seek or something. We rehearse here. Our band.'

Arthur pauses, his key in the lock, and turns to her. 'You practise in the *cemetery*?'

'It's not ideal,' admits Kelly. 'Which is why we've got a proposal for you.'

Arthur looks at them all, from Kelly to Gemma Swarbrick to Nicola Manning to Timmy Leigh. Common sense tells him he should get them to sling their collective hooks. But he doesn't, for some reason, think they're here to rob him or cause trouble. Not after that Kelly was round the other night. If she'd wanted, she could have taken anything she fancied and he wouldn't have been able to do anything. He glances at Gemma again. On the other hand, her dad's Terry Swarbrick, and everybody knows what he's like . . .

As if reading his mind, Gemma says, 'We're not here to nick anything, you know.'

'All right,' grumbles Arthur. 'I suppose you'd better come in, then. But only for five minutes. And no guitar playing.'

After the requisite five minutes is over, Arthur stands up stiffly from where he's been feeding kindling into the fire and says, 'No. Absolutely not.'

'But it's perfect!' pleads Kerry. 'You teach me to play the guitar and let us rehearse in here, and we help you solve the Moonflower Mystery.'

'You make it sound like something off *Hetty Wainthropp Investigates,*' laughs Gemma. 'The Moonflower Murders. That would make an ace film.'

'Mystery, not murders,' says Arthur crossly. 'Nobody's been murdered.'

'As far as you know,' says Timmy. 'Maybe he's a serial killer who leaves these flowers on his victims' graves.'

Everybody looks at him. 'Timmy,' says Nicola quietly. 'It's his wife's grave . . .'

Timmy blinks. 'Sorry. I didn't mean . . .' He smiles wanly. 'I like the *X-Files*. Does anybody else like the *X-Files*?'

'Arthur doesn't have a telly,' says Kelly.

There's a hubbub of disbelieving shouts as everyone looks around to find Arthur's non-existent television set. Kelly holds her hands up to calm them down. 'He likes the radio, all right? Radio 4 in the morning and Radio 3 in the afternoons.'

'Wow,' says Gemma. 'I didn't even know there was a Radio 3.'

Arthur rubs his temples. 'It's still no. Can you all go, now? I feel a bit under the weather.'

'That's my point!' says Kelly, her eyes shining. 'You can't be sitting outside all night waiting for this guy to turn up. Not in the middle of winter. But we can.'

'Can we?' says Nicola doubtfully.

Kelly turns to her. 'You tell your mum you're staying at mine, I'll tell mine I'm staying at Gemma's.'

Gemma laughs. 'Have you seen how many people are in our house?'

'Where do I say I'm staying?' says Timmy.

This time it's Kelly's turn to rub her head. 'This is just details. It doesn't matter. We'll sort that out. We're trying to convince Arthur, all right, not organise the bloody . . .' She glances over at his kitchen, where his medals sit, then at Arthur. 'Not organise the bloody Liberation of Paris.'

And suddenly Arthur is not in the wintry chapel but in the sun-drenched gardens of the American Hospital of Paris, where Peter Bergmann is patiently showing him where to put his fingers on the neck of the guitar, and which strings to pluck to bring forth the beautiful sound of *Aranjuez*. Peter Bergmann who saved Arthur's life, and who enhanced Arthur's life, and who died too young while doing both. And what did Arthur do with the gift that Peter bestowed on him, the gift of music? Serenaded Molly, on occasion. Played at Christmas, and on her birthday. And nothing else. But now . . . is this a chance to take Peter's gift and pass it on? Pay it forward? The girl has talent, he's already seen that. Arthur is passable at best, but he could share what little knowledge he has.

And what they're offering in return . . . their help in catching the mystery man. Molly's birthday is fast approaching. Arthur knows he's sickening for something, he can feel it tightening his chest. Even if it's just a cold, if it laid him out on the twenty-third, he'd never forgive himself.

Arthur throws some dried brambles on the fire and stokes it with the metal poker. He goes to fill the kettle for his bedtime drink, and while he's there brushes some dust off his little box with his medals in it. He really should put that up somewhere. He isn't a war hero, not like Cardy keeps saying. Arthur only met one war hero in his entire life, and he was the man who saved him, and who, by rights, should have been trying to kill him. That's what makes a hero, he thinks. Doing the thing that's least expected of you. Like Peter Bergmann.

Like, he thinks, turning around to look at them, these kids. It was just as Kelly said, nobody expects anything of them except to lead unremarkable lives. He can't claim to like, or even understand, this music they want to play. It just sounds like a racket to him. But imagine if it could be their way to a better life? Imagine if Arthur was the one to throw them off the landmine of low expectations and miserable prospects?

'All right,' says Arthur eventually, as the four faces turn expectantly towards him. 'All right. Let's do it.'

29

'You're doing all right, you know,' says Arthur, standing up stiffly from the pew and stretching. 'Do you want a cup of tea?'

Kelly shakes her head. 'Have you got any Coke?'

'Tea or coffee. Or corporation pop.'

'What flavour's that pop?'

Arthur laughs and goes to fill the kettle. 'Corporation pop only comes in one flavour, and that's the one that comes out of the tap.'

'Har har,' says Kelly, and lays the guitar down on the pew. 'Do you really think I'm good?'

'I didn't say good,' says Arthur, putting the kettle on the stove. Seeing her face fall, he smiles. 'But you could be. Probably better than good. But only if you practise. Nothing comes easy, you know. You have to work hard.'

'Things come easy for some people,' grumbles Kelly. 'Just not for the likes of us.'

It's the third or fourth night that Arthur's been giving Kelly guitar lessons. Any minute now the rest of them will turn up, and they'll make a racket for an hour, all shouting and talking at the same time and going on about things Arthur's never heard of.

Kelly really is coming on, they all are. That Timmy's got a beautiful voice. Effortless. He could probably be a proper singer, with a bit of training, though Arthur's no expert in these things. Terribly nervous, though. First band practice they had, he could barely sing, even though he'd apparently been doing it fine in the old mausoleum.

'What's *up* with you?' Kelly had asked, exasperated.

'It's just different here,' Timmy had muttered. 'It was all right when it was just us, but . . .'

'I'm not bloody leaving,' Arthur had said.

'Christ, Timmy, you've got to learn how to play in front of other people!' Gemma had shouted. 'Like, an audience? What goes to watch bands?'

'Here,' Arthur had said. 'Focus on me. A friendly face. Keep looking at me when you sing, don't think about anything else.'

And it had worked. That first night, Timmy kept his gaze firmly fixed on Arthur, and for every practice after, and he sang enough to make your heart break.

The funny thing is, Arthur's sort of beginning to enjoy having them here. Maybe Molly wouldn't have died so soon, if they'd had kids and, by now, maybe even grandkids to keep them both busy. But he doesn't suppose cancer takes notice of things like that, doesn't really worry about whether you're busy or not, if you've got kids. If you've got a loving husband and you're his entire world and after you've gone life for him just becomes a big, gaping black hole, like the old pit shafts and tunnels that marble the old mine site over the wall. He doesn't suppose cancer cares about anything at all.

The door bangs open, letting in a biting wind and Gemma. And not just Gemma. Two men, who he recognises as Gemma's dad, who everybody says is a thief, and the little wiry chap they call Crushing Ken. Arthur takes the kettle off the stove and stands up straight.

Gemma is smiling as her dad and Ken drag in clanking black bin bags. Ken says, 'Crushing hell, I can't feel me fingers. It's bitter out there.'

'Hello, Mr Calderbank,' says Terry genially, looking around the chapel. 'Got it done up quite nice, haven't you?'

'Thank you,' says Arthur uncertainly, frowning. What do they want? What's in the bags?

'You will never guess what I've got,' says Gemma as Kelly rushes over. They start to rip open the first bin liner and Gemma lifts out a small drum, and flicks its tight skin with her finger.

'A set of drums!' squeals Kelly.

'Early Christmas present,' says Terry, rubbing his hands together and blowing into them.

'Yeah, t'crushing elves have been working overtime,' says Ken with a wink. He nods at Arthur. 'Don't suppose there's a chance of a cuppa, is there, Mr C? I'm nithered.'

While Arthur makes the drinks, Gemma and Kelly get the drums out. 'Only thing is there's no stands,' says Gemma.

'Crushing hell,' mutters Ken, taking the cup of tea from Arthur with a little salute. 'I'll have a word with Santa's crushing elves, shall I?'

Arthur inspects the drums. 'I could probably make you some stands. I've got lots of timber and bits of wire around here. You'd have to show me how high they need to go and everything.' He glances around the chapel. 'There's an old stool somewhere that might do, as well.'

'That's brilliant, Arthur!' says Gemma, throwing her arms around his neck.

Terry laughs. 'Get off him, our Gemma. He doesn't want your nits.'

She gives her dad a withering look. 'I haven't had nits since I was, like, seven or something.'

'There's a sticker on this big drum,' says Kelly. 'What does this mean? *England First and Foremost*?'

'Don't you worry your head about that, love,' says Ken. 'It'll peel off nicely with a bit of vinegar. Come on, Terry, drink up. I'm due at the grotto in an hour and you wouldn't want to miss out on those Buzz Lightyears, would you?'

When they've gone, Arthur sets about finding some bits of wood to start making stands for the drums, while Gemma arranges them on a pew and starts to bash hell out of them with a pair of weathered drumsticks. He winces, but at least it's better than those biscuit tins she's been hammering away at all week. It's a raw, raucous noise, but he can pick out a beat in it, at least, a measure of timing. He wonders were Nicola and Timmy Leigh are. They've usually arrived by now.

Right on cue, the door goes again, and in they come, together. Arthur is about to shout to them if they want a cup of tea but even at a distance he can tell something's wrong. Timmy is wide-eyed and gingerly shutting the door while Nicola, tearing at her scarf, stomps towards Kelly and Gemma, face like thunder.

'Where is it?' she screams.

'We've got drums . . .' Kelly falters. 'Nicola?'

The girl stops at Gemma, who pauses with the sticks in her hand. 'Where is it?' says Nicola again, her voice quieter but cracking.

Gemma gives her a stare, and a shrug. 'What you on about?'

'You know what I'm on about, Gemma Swarbrick. My necklace. The one with the picture of me and my dad in it. It's gone missing from the bunker and you took it.'

Everybody goes quiet. Gemma stands up, almost a head taller than Nicola, and looks down at her coolly. 'What did you say?'

'You took my pendant. It has to have been you.'

All eyes are on Gemma, who says, 'Why? Why does it have to be me?'

The wind seems to go out of Nicola, and she slumps so she's even shorter. 'Because you knew it was there. Because you . . .' She trails off.

'Because I'm Terry Swarbrick's daughter,' says Gemma, her face hard. She jabs Nicola in the collarbone with her middle finger. 'Because, like father, like daughter.'

Nicola takes a step back but Gemma moves forward, jabbing her again. 'Because the apple doesn't fall far from the tree.'

Jab. 'A chip off the old block. Don't worry, Nicola, I've heard them all before. That's what happens when you're surname's Swarbrick. Everybody looks at you when something's gone missing. I've had it since I was at nursery.' Gemma picks up her coat. 'And you know what, yeah, maybe I have used the five-fingered discount sometimes. But that doesn't mean everything that gets nicked is down to me.'

'Where are you going?' says Kelly as Gemma drags her coat on. 'For a fag?'

'I'm going home,' says Gemma, walking to the door. She stops and turns. 'One thing my dad taught me, is you don't shit in your own backyard.' She cocks her head on one side, considering. 'Well, Bullseye does, but he's a Staffie. The point is, you don't nick from your mates.'

Gemma opens the door and looks at Nicola. 'And I thought we were mates. I thought you knew me better.'

Gemma slams the door behind her. Kelly picks up the drumsticks and throws them back on the floor, glaring at Nicola. 'That's great. That's just bloody great. We got drums!'

'Where did they come from?' says Nicola helplessly.

'Gemma's dad nicked them, I think,' says Kelly. 'But that's not the point! Why did you accuse her of taking your pendant?'

'Because it was in the bunker and she saw it that first time and somebody's been in there and there's other stuff gone,' says Nicola, the words tumbling out, tears filling her eyes.

Arthur clears his throat. 'Excuse me,' he says. 'What do you mean by *bunker*?'

Ten minutes later they are all standing in the cold night at the doorway of the mausoleum while Nicola lights candles inside. Arthur shakes his head. 'No. No, no, no. You can't do this. A cemetery is consecrated ground. You can't have a . . . a *den* in here.'

'It's not a den, it's a bunker,' says Timmy, speaking for the first time since the argument in the chapel. 'In case there's a war.'

Arthur remembers when he caught Nicola riding her bike through the graveyard that snowy morning, her peering at the chapel, asking how thick the walls were, whether they'd withstand a bomb blast. The girl's obsessed by war. He wonders if it was anything to do with her dad dying when she was a baby?

'Look,' says Nicola, as they squeeze inside. She points to her neatly stacked tins at the back, in disarray. Some of the water bottles have been drained and left crumpled on the damp earth. 'Somebody's been in here.'

'What's missing? Apart from the pendant?' says Kelly, squatting down and thoughtfully touching the earth near the supplies.

'Some beans. Some water. I don't know, maybe other stuff. We just found it.'

Kelly looks up sharply. 'We?'

'I came with Nicola to . . . to put some more supplies here,' says Timmy. 'Before band practice.'

'What size shoes do you wear, Timmy?' says Kelly. 'And was anyone else with you?'

'Just us,' says Nicola. 'Why are you asking what size—?'

'Eights,' says Timmy, lifting up his leg and leaning back to look at the sole of his boot. Arthur raises an eyebrow. Fourteen-years-old and has to check what his shoe size is?

'Look at this,' says Kelly. 'Don't come too close. Bring me that torch.'

She shines the beam into the earth. Arthur leans over to look too. It's a footprint in the earth, deep into some soft loam. There are others nearby, but they've been scuffed up by Nicola and Timmy, presumes Arthur. This is clear and sharp. And big.

'At least a size ten, maybe eleven,' says Kelly. She looks at Arthur. 'What's the date?'

He knows, of course, knows because he crosses them off every day. 'Friday. The thirteenth.'

Timmy's eyes widen. 'Whoah. That's unlucky!'

Arthur keeps his eyes locked with Kelly. She says, 'Nobody else knows about this place. It's too well-hidden. What if . . . what if it's him?'

'Too early,' says Arthur. 'Why would he be here ten days before Molly's birthday?'

'He might have even been here longer,' says Nicola, looking around nervously. 'When I fell off my bike in the cemetery and Arthur helped me . . . I thought I'd seen someone moving between the gravestones.'

'We should call the police,' says Timmy tremulously.

Arthur is about to agree but Kelly scoffs. 'And what good would that do? Other than drive him away and then we'd never solve the mystery.'

'So what do we do?' says Nicola.

Kelly stands up, brushing dirt off her hands. 'We pretend we don't know he's been here. But we keep watch on this place. And we carry on as normal. But first we need to speak to Gemma.'

'What for?' says Nicola, screwing up her face.

'So you can apologise. And we don't ruin our only chance of getting out of this shithole.'

30

'One week left at school, thank God,' says Kelly as they lean on the wall of the parish church. It's only two o'clock in the afternoon but the clouds are low and black and some of the streetlights are already fizzing into dull orange embers. She takes a bite into her steak bake, the heat from it mingling with her breath and pluming out into the cold air in feathers of condensation. 'Does anybody else have this stupid geography field trip on Monday?'

'I don't do geography,' says Gemma. She's rooting through the over-flowing rubbish bin, plucking out pieces of paper and smoothing them out on the lid. 'Are you going on a trip to a field? In this weather?'

'No, we have to come into town and count empty shops or something.' Kelly pauses. 'I've no idea why they call it a field trip.' She pauses. 'What are you doing?'

Gemma holds up half a dozen pieces of paper. 'Receipts. People are so stupid. They just screw them up and throw them away.'

Nicola frowns. 'What are you doing with them?'

'I collect them, like stamps,' she says, sticking her tongue out. 'They can actually come in useful. See, this one is for Dorothy Perkins for twenty quid. I go in, pick up a top for the same price, and go and get a refund for it from the service desk.' She snaps her fingers. 'Ker-ching.'

'What are you getting for Christmas?' says Timmy, absently picking carrots out of his pasty and throwing them on the floor. 'I've put a PlayStation on my list.'

The others stare at him. 'You write a list?' says Kelly. 'What, like a letter? To Father Christmas?'

Timmy mumbles something and takes a bite of his pastie. Gemma says, 'Have you been a nice boy, though, Timmy? Because he knows if you've been bad or good . . .' She casts a narrow-eyed glare at Nicola. 'And he knows if you've been trying to get off with the bass player.'

Timmy chokes on his mouthful of pastry and Nicola stomps off to put her pie wrapper in the bin. Kelly rubs a hand over her mouth to hide her smirk then says, 'Leave it, yeah?'

'You lot wanted to meet me here,' says Gemma, leaning against the wall. 'So, come on, then, what do you want?'

'Nicola's got something to say to you,' says Kelly.

Gemma raises an eyebrow and folds her arms. Nicola kicks her shoes against the wall and says, 'I'm sorry. I shouldn't have accused you of stealing my locket.'

Gemma shrugs. 'I'm used to it, believe me. Is that it? Because I want to go home.'

Kelly says, 'We want you back in the band.'

Gemma sighs and rolls her eyes. 'We don't have a band, Kelly. We're just a bunch of kids messing about. What's even the point? Are we going to go on *Top of the Pops*? Make a record? Do a bloody tour?'

'Yes!' says Kelly. 'We're going to do all those things! But only if we practise. You've got the drums—'

'I'm going to sell them,' says Gemma shortly. Her shoulders slump and she looks at Kelly. 'Look, I'm not trying to be an arse. But what have we managed to achieve? Getting Nicola banned from music. Getting in detention. Picking a fight with Colin Cardy and his gang. He was right in the arcade, you know. We're just losers. And that's all we'll ever be.'

'We're not!' says Kelly. 'We're wonky sprockets, remember!'

Gemma closes her eyes and waves her away. 'Maybe I don't want to be a wonky sodding sprocket, Kelly. My dad's not exactly knuckled down to life, has he? I don't want to end up like him. I just want to have a normal life.'

'You don't have to be like your dad! And normal's boring! We've got a chance to do something better for ourselves!'

'But do we, really? What's our chance? It's not like we know anybody in the music business or anything like that? We're just having a laugh, except it's not much of a laugh any more.'

They stand there in silence for a bit. A knot of lads in Christmas hats, getting started early for a works party, jumps boisterously through the little gardens at the back of the parish church, chanting, *It's coming home! It's coming home! It's coming!* Only nearly six months after the Euros. Gemma says, 'I'm going home. Anybody coming to the bus station?'

'I need a new bass string from the music shop. Rimmer's,' says Nicola. 'It's on the way.'

'We'll all go,' says Kelly firmly. She falls in with Gemma, behind the other two.

Gemma lights a fag. She takes a long drag and says, 'Admit it, when she stormed in like the Incredible Sulk you thought I'd done it too, didn't you? Nicked her necklace. If you hadn't been playing at *A Touch of Frost* or something and finding footprints, you'd still think I'd done it.'

Kelly takes the fag off Gemma and has a drag before handing it back. 'You do nick stuff, though. You can't deny it.'

'Only from shops. Not from people. And never from mates. It's what my dad calls victimless crime. You go into Top Shop, see, and nick some leggings. That's cool because they factor in wastage for shoplifting. Nobody gets hurt.' She lights another cigarette. 'You nick from a big warehouse like Crushing Ken does, that's the same. It's all insured. But I wouldn't, like, con my way into an old lady's house and nick her purse.' She nods her head at where Nicola and Timmy are talking together as they walk on ahead. 'I wouldn't nick a mate's necklace. That's just low.'

Kelly considers. 'It's still wrong, though. Nicking.'

'I suppose.' Gemma's eyes shine. 'You know what I'd really like to do, though? A bank job.'

Kelly blinks at her. 'What, like a robbery?'

Gemma nods enthusiastically. 'There was this guy called John Dillinger. Back in the olden times in America. He's sort of my hero. He used to go round robbing banks and he'd shout *Everybody lie down and keep calm, this is a robbery* or something. There was this one time him and his gang were robbing a bank and there was a farmer paying in his money and he held it out for Dillinger to take it but Dillinger said no, he didn't want the guy's money, he only wanted the bank's.' Gemma kicks at an empty Coke can on the pavement. 'That's class, that is. Victimless crime.'

'Hey, look,' says Kelly, pointing across the street. 'It's Arthur!' She waves frantically and shouts, 'Arthur!'

He peers at them and they cross the road. 'Where have you been?' says Kelly.

'To the market,' says Arthur, wrapped in his coat and scarf. 'There are some stalls selling flowers there. I thought I'd ask if anybody has ever bought these moonflowers. No luck. I'm going for the bus now.' He looks at Gemma. 'The group back together, then?'

'No,' says Gemma. 'I'll come for my drums tomorrow. Sorry I dumped them there.'

They walk on with Arthur, ducking down a side street towards the bus station where the music shop sits in the middle of the row. Kelly's walked past Rimmer's dozens of times, hundreds probably, but she's never taken much notice of it. Until now.

She stands at the big window, eyes wide, staring at the guitars lined up in the window of the music shop. At one particular guitar, in the middle of the display, emblazoned with a union jack design.

'Noel Gallagher's guitar,' she breathes.

Nicola joins her at the window, but Kelly barely notices her reflection in the glass until she says, 'An Epiphone Sheraton. Paul McCartney played an Epiphone. They're basically what you play if you can't afford a Gibson.'

Kelly cranes her neck to see the price tag dangling from the neck. 'And what do you play if you can't afford an Epiphone?'

Gemma nudges them aside and puts her face to the glass, peering through a shade made by her fingers. 'Whoah! Look at that drum kit they've got set up!'

Kelly looks over her shoulder at Arthur, who raises an eyebrow in Gemma's direction, but neither of them say anything.

'I come here a lot,' says Nicola nervously. 'Don't get me banned like you did from the music room at school.'

But Gemma is already pushing through the glass door and the rest of of them bundle into the warmth of the shop, Arthur bringing up the rear. Kelly looks around in awe. There are keyboards and drums and big black boxes and guitars . . . so many guitars. Behind the till there's a thin, craggy-faced man with long hair that curls around his shoulders. He wears jeans and a black T-shirt with *Zildjan* written on it. He scowls at them as Gemma says, 'Can I have a go on your drums?'

'It's not bloody Toys R Us, you know,' he says, then brightens up. 'Nic! You all right? Didn't see you with this rabble. What you after?'

'Hiya, Des,' says Nicola. 'My G string is on its way out.'

Gemma snorts with laughter but Kelly gives her a warning glare, and looks back to Nicola. She seems to be . . . different, in the shop, somehow. Less . . . Nicola. More confident. Timmy has noticed too. Kelly sees him casting shy glances at her.

'So who's this mob, then?' says Des.

'Well . . .' says Nicola. 'We were in a band. But I don't think we are any more.'

Des tosses his hair back. 'Personal or musical differences?' He nods at Arthur. 'Hello. Who's this, your manager?'

Kelly laughs. 'Sort of.'

Des inspects them all in turn. 'What sort of stuff did you do?'

'We've been doing nothing but 'Rock 'N' Roll Star,' says Gemma, rolling her eyes and pointing at Kelly. 'Because she says so.'

Des peers at Kelly. 'You the boss, then? Going to be the next Oasis?'

'We would be if I could afford that Epiphone in the window,' says Kelly.

'You going to let me have a go on your drums, or what?' says Gemma.

'I thought you'd left the band,' says Kelly slowly.

Gemma looks at her. 'I have. Because there's no point, is there? But I still want a go on them drums.'

Des looks at each of them, then smiles. 'All right, then. Let's see what you've got.'

*

This. Now this is more like it. Des has got the actual Union Jack Noel Gallagher Epiphone from the window display and plugged it into one of the black boxes – they're called amps, apparently. It feels alive in her hands, like an animal that's straining to get off a leash. She's got it strapped around her neck and can feel the hum of electricity in the neck, the tension of the strings. Arthur's guitar is made for coaxing beauty from; this is something to be reined in and channelled and controlled. She looks around at Nicola, who's plugging a bass guitar she's selected from the wall into another amp with a burst of squalling noise. Gemma has already seated herself at the drum kit, running her hands over the chrome rims. As Des stands Timmy in front of a mic stand and taps the head to make sure it's turned on, Kelly can't stop grinning. They look like an actual band.

Des stands back, arms folded, considering them. He tilts Kelly's amp away a little more from Timmy's, and nods to himself. 'All right, Nic, you're good to go.'

They all look to Kelly. She gets her fingers in position, and nods at Gemma, who does a quick roll on the rims of the drums then launches into the tune, Nicola and Kelly coming in with the bass and lead guitar for the short intro. And when Timmy starts to sing . . .

Kelly gets a shiver that starts at the back of her neck and runs down her arms. It's like four distinct parts coming together to make something that is far bigger than just the four of them playing and singing. It's like a chemical reaction. Timmy is singing staring at Arth, up against the mic. He's rocking from side to side, not quite in time with the music but that makes it look even cooler, for some reason, like he's off in another dimension. Nicola seems taller, rocking with the music, assured. Gemma keeps going wrong but in the mix of it all, it doesn't feel like it matters because she's in her element, as if the drum sound is a lion and she's doing her best to tame it. And Kelly . . . she feels like this is what she was born for.

When the song ends Kelly realises she doesn't know if they've been playing for four minutes or four hours. She feels exhausted and exhilarated, her heart is thumping and her fingers are tingling. She looks down at the guitar, and it's like she's looking at a wild stallion that's been broken in by a cowboy.

Yes. This is what she wants to do. This is what she *has* to do.

The electric silence is suddenly punctuated by a clap, and another, and another. It's Des, standing by his desk, watching them, and Arthur, who's applauding furiously beside him.

'That's not half a racket, but it's a good racket,' says Arthur.

'All right, fun's over,' Des says. 'It's not the Kids from fucking *Fame*, you know. Pardon my French, Arthur. I'm trying to earn a living here.'

'Well?' says Gemma, sweat beading on her forehead, her cheeks red. 'Were we ace, or what?'

Des shrugs. 'She's got potential,' he says, nodding at Kelly. 'Nic's a workhorse, but is afraid to experiment. The lad can carry a tune. You, love, you need a bit of discipline. Playing the drums isn't just about thrashing the bastards half to death.'

Kelly's mood deflates instantly. Des turns to his desk and gets a sheet of paper, and walks back over to them.

He's smiling. 'But, you know what? Yeah, you were pretty ace.'

Kelly punches the air and Timmy blinks rapidly, then breaks into a grin. Gemma high-fives Nicola over the drum kit. Des says, 'But I thought you weren't a band any more.' He nods at Gemma. 'No point, she said.'

Des hands the piece of paper to Kelly. 'Maybe this'll give you a reason. I'll give this to you, seeing as you're the boss. You should enter.'

She looks down at it. It's a flyer for an event at Maxine's nightclub in town. She looks up at Des. 'Battle of the Bands competition?'

'January fourth,' nods Des. 'Got a thousand quid prize.'

'And you think we could do this?'

Des pulls a face. 'Practise your arses off between now and then and I don't see why you couldn't at least put on a good show. There'll be rougher sounding bands than you there. Not saying you'll win, like. Want me to put your names down? I know the organisers.'

'Shit, yes!' shouts Gemma. She walks from around the drum kit and points at the mic, and says to Timmy. 'And fuck the PlayStation, this is what Father Christmas is putting in your stocking this year.'

Kelly gapes at Gemma. 'You're back in the band, then?'

Gemma grins. 'I don't remember ever saying I wasn't, did I?'

Des grabs a pen and a notebook from the till and says, 'So, what are you called, then?'

* 31 *

On Sunday, Arthur goes up to St Mary's to see Revd. Brown. The vicar had pushed a note through his door saying he'd call round when he'd got the afternoon service out of the way, but Arthur had fancied the short walk up to the vicarage, where Revd. Brown greets him with a cup of tea and a plateful of home-made biscuits that bear the perfectionist hallmarks of the work of Timmy Leigh's mother.

'I had some more information delivered to me yesterday,' says Revd. Brown conversationally as he pours the tea from a pot cocooned in a knitted cosy in the shape of a smiling cat. Probably also Mrs Leigh's handiwork. 'About the planning application.'

Arthur perks up in the wooden chair. 'Oh? They've not decided to scrap it, have they?'

The vicar pulls a face. 'I wish, for your sake, I could say they had. Though I am, of course, sympathetic to the needs of those who require this housing.'

Arthur frowns at him. 'Whose side are you on in all this, vicar?'

'It's not exactly a question of taking sides,' says Revd. Brown hesitantly. 'More about . . . doing the right thing.'

Arthur nods, and accepts the mug of tea. 'That's all right, then. Because you know that the right thing is for me to stay in the chapel.'

The vicar grunts and goes to the kitchen worktop to retrieve a manila envelope. 'I'd imagine you'll be getting a copy of this yourself, perhaps Monday now,' he says, withdrawing a sheaf of papers. 'The application as it stands has been amended slightly and . . .'

He places the document in front of Arthur on the table, flipping over a few pages until he comes to a plan of the cemetery with a red rhombus in thick lines marking out the section that will be affected. Arthur studies it. The vicar says, 'As you can see they've—'

'They've moved the boundary,' says Arthur, brusquely, jabbing his finger at the plan. 'They've made it bigger.' He traces the line, locating the chapel, and looks up at Revd. Brown. 'This covers Molly's plot, now.'

'You'll keep an eye out for me, won't you, Fred?' murmurs Arthur as he pauses to lean on the headstone. 'He's here, that bugger. He's been here. You'll keep watch, won't you?'

The cold air knifes into Arthur's lungs. He stops at Mabel's grave to right the flowerpot. Did *he* kick that over, skulking around in the graveyard? 'A week tomorrow, Molly's birthday, Mabel. That's when he'll do it. That's when he'll lay the flowers.'

'What about you, Mr Gaskell?' calls Arthur. 'Have you seen anything?'

He realises how crazy he must sound. Maybe he is just feet away, hiding, listening. If anybody else could hear him, they'd cart him off to the funny farm straight away, there wouldn't be any need for rallies and marches and chants of *Hands! Off! Arthur's chapel!* But Arthur doesn't mind if *he* hears him. Do him good to know that Arthur's not scared, and if he thinks Arthur's a bit off his rocker, well, nothing lost there. Mad folk are known to do mad stuff. Might show him that Arthur's not to be trifled with.

Since leaving the vicarage he's just been pottering about the cemetery, avoiding doing the one thing he knows he has to. He has to go to Molly's grave and tell her what will happen if he loses his fight. They'll dig her up and move her to another graveyard, and though Revd. Brown insisted it will be done with dignity and respect, Arthur is sure that this might well kill him.

When it's cold like this, his leg aches from the old shrapnel wound, and that makes him think of Peter Bergmann. He wonders what might have been if Peter had survived, if Arthur had got home from the war earlier and had collected Molly, and she'd never had her accident. He imagines going to visit Peter and Maria, him and Molly with their children, and sitting in Peter's garden in the Ruhr valley, comparing notes of what coal mining was like there with back home. They would have drunk sweet white wine while the children played together in the garden, and one or the other of the little ones would have come shyly up to the two men and asked how they were friends.

Peter and Arthur would have looked at each other, and tried to explain that in a different time, their job was to kill each other. But instead, Peter saved Arthur's life, when he didn't have to. And that, Arthur would tell the gathered children wisely, was what made people special. That sometimes they didn't do what they were supposed to, or thought they were supposed to, or had been told it was what they were supposed to, and that could, in a funny little way, make the world a better place.

Peter and Maria and Molly and Arthur would smile and Molly would have said, yes, but that doesn't mean these children don't have to do what they are told, especially at school, and *especially* when it is bedtime and the grown-ups want to sit and drink wine and talk and watch the sun go down over the hills of the Ruhr valley.

Arthur has never been to the Ruhr, has never seen pictures, so he has no idea if there are hills or if the sun goes down over them. But that's what he likes to believe.

There's a sluggish tear on Arthur's cheek, warm and salty against his freezing skin. 'Silly old fool,' he mutters to himself. Silly old fool. Talking to the dead and dreaming of things that never were.

He pats Mabel's headstone and tiptoes past young Noah's grave, thinking that he doesn't want to wake the boy, then summons the courage to go to Molly.

'It's been a funny old week, Molly, love,' says Arthur, taking a rag from his coat pocket and wiping her stone down. 'A funny old week, that's for sure. The chapel's been filled with kids. Playing music.' He pauses and looks up at the lights burning in the chapel. 'I think you'd love it. The old place is full of life.'

He stars for a long moment at her name carved into the stone, at the dates that bookend her life. He stares until the words and numbers just become grooves, the mason's chiseled lines and curves, and become detached from their meaning. This is what we all become in the end, he thinks. Just lines hammered out of a piece of polished stone. And when there's nobody left to read those words, what happens then? When Arthur's gone, and Molly's been dug up and reburied God knows where, who will there be to remember either of them? They only ever had each other.

Arthur sniffs the cold air, and lapses into a coughing fit so violent it leaves him seeing winking lights on the periphery of his vision. He steadies himself on Molly's stone. But if he died here, tonight, right now, there would still be someone to keep Molly's memory alive, wouldn't there? He'll be here, in a week, laying his moonflowers and disappearing into the night. He's out there, somewhere, in the night. Arthur wipes his mouth with his handkerchief. 'No, I'm not going anywhere, love,' he says. 'Not until I've seen this through. And after that . . . well, it doesn't matter who remembers us, or not. Because we'll be together.'

When Arthur gets back to the chapel Kelly is waiting for him, arms around her body, stamping her feet on the stone step. 'Bloody hell, Arthur, it's freezing. Open up.'

He looks at his watch. 'It's too late for a guitar lesson. I'm tired. I think I've got a bit of a cold coming on.'

She follows him into the chapel. 'It's all right. I'll just have a cup of tea.'

He feeds the wood burner and puts the kettle on. Kelly sits as close as she can to the burner, rubbing her hands in front of it as the flames start to lick up. 'I even sort of missed you lot today,' says Arthur, surprised at himself as the words come out. He hands Kelly a packet of Hobnobs.

'S'all right,' she says through a mouthful of biscuit. 'We know we can't rehearse on Sundays when people are coming to put flowers on graves and stuff. Besides, you saw us at the music shop. Weren't we brilliant?'

'You weren't half bad,' agrees Arthur.

'Only thing is, everybody keeps asking us what the name of the band is and we have no idea.'

Arthur sits down creakily on the pew, banging his chest gently. That cold air feels like it's still stuck in there. 'You need something memorable. Like Kelly Derricott and the Somethings.'

'Gemma would never go for that. It's got to be short and snappy. One word, like Oasis or James, or The Something, like The Charlatans or The Verve.'

'I'll have a think,' says Arthur. 'That's lovely news, though, about the concert. Are you sure you're ready to play to an audience, though?'

She shrugs. 'How different can it be to playing in front of you and that Des in the shop?' Her face falls. 'Only problem is, I'm going to need a guitar.'

'You can borrow mine. If you take care of it.'

She smiles. 'Thanks, Arthur. But I think I'm going to need an electric one. With a box. An amp.'

'And how much is this Neil Gallagher guitar?'

She tells him and he whistles. 'And it's Noel, not Neil.' Kelly leans forward conspiratorially. 'But I've got a plan. My dad's got that job interview tomorrow. It's the first one for years. He might be in the mood to treat me for Christmas if he gets it.'

Arthur winks. 'That's a good plan. And speaking of plans … .'

'The Moonflower Mystery!' says Kelly. 'Don't worry, we haven't forgotten. Next Monday night. I've been working on it. We're going to do a proper stake-out. Have you seen that film?'

'What film?'

'*Stakeout*. It's well old, like from the eighties or something. Emilio Estevez is in it. He's well fit.'

Arthur starts to say that no, he's not seen it, but he knows a bit about stake-outs and that the police aren't very interested in doing them, but Kelly's off again. 'Nicola is saying she's sleeping at mine and I'm saying I'm sleeping at Gemma's and Gemma's saying she's sleeping at Nicola's.'

'Where's Timmy saying he's sleeping?'

Kelly laughs. 'Timmy Leigh's mum wouldn't let him sleep at any of our houses. We're too common.' She cocks her head, considering. 'Except maybe Nicola. She lives on the estate but not because they're proper poor, like us, because her dad died and they couldn't afford their other house.' Kelly taps the side of her nose. 'Gemma reckons there's something going on there.'

'Timmy and Nicola?'

Kelly nods. 'Yeah. All them lads say he's gay. I don't know if he is. Not that it would matter if he was.' She frowns. 'Besides, Tampax is a stupid nickname for somebody who might be gay. I mean, a tampon is the one thing that does go inside a—'

Arthur coughs loudly, to cut her off. 'Well, quite.'

Kelly pauses thoughtfully. 'Did they have gays and lesbians when you were young?'

Now it's Arthur's turn to laugh. 'I think they've had 'em forever, love. Me and Molly used to have this joke, because back in Victorian times they had these places called molly-houses where the qu—' He pauses. The girls had already told him off once for using that word. 'Where . . . gay people . . . used to go in secret.'

'I saw this thing on telly, I think it was Brighton or somewhere, where they call poor kids mollies.'

'And I was *Molly's*,' smiles Arthur. 'I suppose that makes us all mollies of one sort or another.'

There's a long silence and then Kelly looks at Arthur. Her mouth drops open and she says slowly, 'That's it.'

Arthur frowns. 'What's what?'

She grabs his arm, her eyes shining. '*The Mollies*. That's the name of our band. Arthur, you're a genius.'

Kelly jumps up and kisses him on the top of his head. He pushes her away, but can't stop himself laughing. 'Get off, you daft bugger.'

Then Kelly's hand flies to her mouth. 'Do you think she'd mind, though? Do *you* mind?'

Arthur considers this for a moment, then says solemnly. 'I think Molly would be very honoured indeed that you've named your group after her.'

'Sorted!' says Kelly. 'I need to go and tell the others!'

Arthur walks with her so he can let her out and lock the gates again afterwards, and pauses at Molly's grave on the way back. 'You don't mind, do you, love? I said you wouldn't.' He pats the cold gravestone. 'Maybe when I'm gone, people will remember you after all, if those kids are as good as they think they are.'

✳ 32 ✳

'I'm setting off,' says Kelly while her dad stands still in the living room and her mum brushes the shoulders of his blue suit.

Dad looks down at himself and tuts. 'Do they still wear double-breasted? I've had this about ten years. More.'

'You look very smart, Brian,' says her mum. 'Very professional. Just what Oldfield Engineering is looking for in a supervisor.'

'Well, it'll have to do. It's the only suit I've got. They buried my dad in my best one.' He glances at Kelly. 'Did you say something, love?'

Her mum starts to fuss with a handkerchief, folding it and refolding it and putting it in the breast pocket of his jacket. 'They're not going to be employing you for your suit. They're going to be looking at your experience and at you. Make sure you make a good impression.'

'I said, I'm setting off. We've got this geography thing in town this morning. Counting empty shops.'

Her dad looks through the window, at the sliver of blue in the east. 'It seems dry. I might walk. Clear my head a bit. It's been such a long time since I had an interview. I don't want to be rushing. I'd rather get there early.' He pats his coat for his wallet. 'Counting empty shops. There's enough of them, that's for sure. I'll walk with you.'

Kelly rolls her eyes. 'You don't have to.'

But her dad insists, and they walk briskly through the Avenues and towards the main road. It'll take them about twenty minutes to get to the town centre. Her dad says, 'God, Kelly, I'm nervous. What if I mess it up?'

'Job interviews are easy,' says Kelly. 'You just turn up and say you'll throw sprockets in boxes until you die and they sign you up.'

'There's nothing wrong with working hard, Kelly,' says her dad sternly. 'I thought I had a job for life at the pit. Nobody could believe that woman just went and closed them down.'

That woman being Margaret Thatcher, of course. All through Kelly's early childhood she remembers a volley of shouts and disdain every time that face came on the telly. Sometimes her dad or mum would even get up and turn the telly over if she was on the news. Kelly began to think of her as some kind of wicked witch.

'Half of the other kids at my school, their dads are out of work,' says Kelly. They're coming up to the factory in the cold, brightening morning. 'The ones who know who their dads are, at any rate. Most of them aren't bothered.'

'I'm bothered,' says her dad. She knows he is. She's seen the way he drifts around the house in his dressing gown, not able to concentrate on anything, frowning as though he's forgotten what he walked into a room to do. She can't remember the last time she saw him get dressed properly, never mind in a suit, and never mind to actually go outside.

As they walk past the brick building, Kelly says, 'I wish Thatcher would come and close down this place.'

'Kelly!' says her dad, shocked. 'Your mum works there! You're going there!'

'That's the bloody point! I don't want to!'

'You have to do *something*,' he says, helplessly. 'You'll enjoy it when you get there. Meet some friends. Get a bit of money in.'

'I've got friends, Dad. Do you know anything about me at all? If you'd think this is what I want to do? Do you even know what I'm into?'

They cross over the road and under the railway bridge. Kelly can tell her dad is thinking furiously. If he says *My Little Pony* she's going to scream. Instead, she puts him out of his misery.

'I'm in a band, Dad.'

'A band? What, like a pop band?'

'Me and Gemma Swarbrick and Nicola Manning and Timmy Leigh. We're called The Mollies. We're really good.'

He says nothing as they hit the edge of the town centre. Kelly says, 'We rehearse at Arthur's chapel.'

Her dad looks at her. 'Arthur? Arthur Calderbank? The one whose home we're trying to save?'

Kelly nods. 'Yeah, you and Keith Cardy and that lot. Except Arthur thinks you're not that bothered about his chapel really, I can tell. He thinks you're just wanting to have a go at those asylum seekers.'

Her dad goes quiet as they walk through the centre. Eventually he says, 'It's not that I'm, you know . . .'

'Racist?' offers Kelly.

'No,' he says. 'I'm not that. But . . . well, Keith, he's the only person who seems to understand, really. The only person who's given me a proper reason for what's happened.'

'And what's the reason, Dad?'

'Well,' he says, but doubtfully. 'They're coming over, aren't they, and there's no jobs, and they're taking all the housing and benefits and . . .' He trails off. Even Kelly, fourteen-year-old Kelly Derricott, can see that he hasn't thought this through. That he's been looking for somebody to blame and Keith Cardy has served somebody up, and that's good enough for him.

'Dad,' says Kelly. 'I want to show you something.'

They stand at the darkened window of Rimmer's, which is still yet to open. Her dad whistles. 'And that's Noel Gallagher's guitar, is it?'

'Well, it's the same as the one he uses. We're going to do a competition and if I win I'm going to buy it.'

Her dad has a weird look on his face. Like he's going to cry or something. He says softly, 'Kelly, love, why didn't you tell us about the band?'

'I thought you'd think it was stupid. Everybody else does.'

'Why would I think it's stupid?'

'Dad, everybody thinks we're scum. That we can't do anything. That we're going to be nothing for the rest of our lives. And it's ten times worse for the girls.'

Somewhat unexpectedly, her dad enfolds Kelly in his arms. 'Don't let anybody tell you that,' he says into her hair. 'Things are going to change, love. I promise. I'm going to go and do my best at this interview and get this job and things will be on the up for us. I won't feel so useless and I won't let anybody ever tell you you're useless.'

Kelly lets him hug her for a moment, then says, 'All right, Dad, get off. My mates might see us.' When he's let go she sings that song. 'Things Can Only Get Better'. He looks at her oddly for a moment, then laughs and joins in. 'Yes,' he says. 'Maybe they can.'

Her dad scrutinises the guitar in the window again and says, 'Where are you meeting your class?'

'Bus station entrance,' says Kelly, pointing to the end of the side street Rimmer's is on. 'We can get down there.'

Her dad looks up at the pale blue sky. 'Actually quite a nice day, after all that snow we had. Good to see the sun. Still cold, though. Don't get frozen doing your geography thing.'

They walk towards the end of the street. Her dad says, 'I'll cut across the bus station. Oldfield's have their office up on King Street. Don't worry, I won't let your mates see you with your old dad.'

'You should go and get a coffee from Maccie D's or something,' says Kelly. She digs into her bag and hands over a fluff-covered packet of chewing gum. 'But don't spill it down you and don't go in with coffee breath.'

Dad smiles. 'You sound like your mum.'

Kelly stops him and straightens his tie. 'You can do it, Dad. I know you can.'

'Right,' says her dad as they get to the end of the street. 'I'll head off this way and—'

Everything suddenly goes into slow motion for Kelly. She can't process what she's seeing at first, as three figures step out from the corner of the street and block their way. It's Heather Wilson and two of her cronies. They're holding something and Kelly can see what it is but she can't work out why.

Heather fixes Kelly with a hard, steely stare.

'I told you I'd get you back,' she says.

Then Kelly realises what's going to happen. 'No,' she says. 'No, Heather, don't. I don't care about me but—'

But it's too late. Heather is holding a tin of paint with the lid already off, a bright, sky blue. Her friends have pink and yellow paint. And with one movement they step back and heave the tins forward. Kelly instinctively ducks behind her dad and sees the multicoloured tide momentarily blot out the low sun. She hears hysterical laughter and the clatter of the abandoned tins thrown to the floor, and the slap of feet on the cold pavement as Heather and her gang scarper.

The worst of the paint, apart from a couple of splatters on her coat, has missed Kelly. Because her dad was shielding her. She takes a step back as he slowly turns to face her. She puts her hand to her mouth, she feels like she's going to throw up, or faint.

Her dad is standing in the street, covered head to toe in blue, yellow and pink paint. The blue and yellow are running down his chest, merging into green. Pink coats his hair like a swimming cap. His suit his ruined. His only suit.

He looks at her and his eyes are dead.

'Kelly,' he says, helplessly.

'Dad.'

He turns around. 'I'm going home.'

'But Dad!' she shouts. 'The interview! What about the job?'

Her dad keeps walking. She sees him pause outside Rimmer's, look at the Epiphone then look back at her. Kelly wants the ground to open up and swallow her, wants to go and find Heather Wilson and batter her within an inch of her life, but she's frozen to the spot, and can't do anything but watch her dad as his shoulders slump and he walks away, leaving a trail of pink and yellow footprints behind him.

✳ 33 ✳

'Your move,' says Heather Wilson smugly in the corridor the next morning.

Kelly opens her mouth to retort but Gemma, Nicola and Timmy drag her away. Her coat is still spattered with paint. As soon as they're out of earshot she says, 'Right, we need to plan what I do next.'

'You leave it,' says Gemma.

Kelly stares at her. 'What? Whose side are you on?'

'Yours,' says Gemma. 'And that's why I'm telling you to leave it.'

'She's right,' says Nicola. 'Escalation is just going to make things worse for everybody.'

'And we've got to rehearse,' adds Timmy. 'And catch the Moonflower Murderer.'

'He's not a fucking murderer!' shouts Kelly. 'He leaves flowers on an old woman's grave! Jesus.'

But she knows they're right. She hasn't got the time or energy to get into an ongoing war with Heather Wilson. And, after all, Kelly started it, as her mum and dad were at pains to point out last night.

'It's all your fault,' said her dad. He'd had a bath but his hair was still full of stringy pink paint. Her mum had said she could try to get his suit dry-cleaned but in a fury he'd stuffed it into the wheelie bin.

'What were you thinking?' said her mum exasperatedly. 'Spraying paint on that girl?'

'She's a bitch,' said Kelly. 'She deserved it.'

'And I suppose I deserved this?' said her dad, shouting. 'I deserved to have the one chance I had to make things better for us ripped out of my hands, because of your childish little spat with another girl?'

Kelly sighs and leans on the corridor wall. 'OK. Forget Heather Wilson. We're rehearsing tonight after tea. And we should go through the plan with Arthur for next Monday night.'

'What if we don't catch him?' says Nicola. 'Have you thought about that? What happens then?'

'We will catch him,' says Kelly. 'We have to.' As the four of them drift off to their separate classes, she thinks, we *have* to. I can't fuck up something else.

After school, Kelly goes into town and to the offices of Oldfield Engineering on King Street. She pushes from the cold street into a foyer where the walls are lined with photographs of cranes and diggers and half-constructed steel buildings. There's a big map on the wall with red rings showing the Oldfield Engineering works around the country. In the middle of the foyer there's a reception desk where a woman wearing a cardigan and pearls pulls her glasses slightly down her nose and peers coldly over the rims at Kelly.

'Yes? Can I help you?'

Kelly marches up to her. 'I want to see the boss. Mr Oldfield. Or whatever he's called.'

The receptionist looks up and down Kelly's battered shoes and grimy uniform and paint-flecked coat, and smirks. 'Mr Oldfield is a very busy man and out on appointments for the rest of the day. Can I ask what it's regarding? Is it for work experience? Because we have a formal process of application through schools. Though we don't take many girls on the engineering side.'

And not girls like me, thinks Kelly. Why don't you just say it?

She says, 'Will he be in tomorrow?'

The woman doesn't even check a diary or anything. 'No, no I don't think so. What did you say it was about?'

A door opens behind the reception desk and a man in a three-piece pinstriped suit pops his head around. He's bald and in his fifties and looks dripping with money. He has a folder in his hand and Kelly can see a gold watch glinting on his wrist.

'Brenda? I've got these letters to send out which need typing up, and Margaret is on a day off tomorrow. Do you think you could—?'

'Are you Mr Oldfield?' blurts out Kelly.

The man blinks and frowns. 'Yes, yes I am. To whom do I have the pleasure?'

'This girl was just leaving,' says Brenda.

'I'm Kelly Derricott. My dad was supposed to come for an interview yesterday. Brian Derricott.'

Mr Oldfield steps fully through the door and puts the folder on the desk, appraising Kelly. 'Ah, yes. A promising candidate, we thought. He didn't show up.'

'It was my fault,' says Kelly quickly. 'I sprayed some paint on Heather Wilson because she's a right bitch. She said she'd get me back and she did and three of her friends jumped out on us yesterday when my dad was on his way here and he got covered in paint and had to go home. He only has one suit. They buried my grandad in dad's best suit. It wasn't his fault.'

'Hmm,' says Mr Oldfield. 'Quite unfortunate.'

'He should have phoned but he was too angry. And upset. He's been out of work for a long time but he's a good worker. He'd be brilliant for the job. You have to give him another chance.'

Brenda looks up at Mr Oldfield. 'Do you want me to call Trevor to get rid of her?'

Mr Oldfield waves her away. 'And he sent you in, did he?' he says to Kelly.

'God, no!' she says. 'He'd flip if he knew I'd come in. I just wanted to say it wasn't his fault and you have to give him another interview.'

Mr Oldfield rubs his chin. 'We did about seven interviews yesterday. Your dad was a very good candidate on paper, like I said. But we need a new supervisor at our main works as soon as possible. I'm sorry, but we've already offered the position to someone else.'

Kelly feels herself deflate, her shoulders slump. 'Is there not another job he can do?'

'Not a position that would suit his skills, I'm afraid.'

'Right,' says Kelly. She glares at Brenda. 'I'll go now and stop cluttering up your office.' At the door she turns round to where Mr Oldfield is still watching her. 'If he'd turned up, would he have got the job?'

He raises an eyebrow. 'Would it make it better or worse if I told you?'

'I just want the truth.'

Mr Oldfield nods. 'Based on his CV and his covering letter . . . if he'd given a good interview . . .' He shrugs. 'Yes, he'd probably have got the job.'

'Right,' says Kelly. 'We're doing a new song.'

Arthur has made some stands for Gemma's drums and is reading the paper at the far end of the chapel while they rehearse. She has run the name The Mollies past everyone else and there have been no objections – not that Kelly would have allowed any.

'Thank God,' says Timmy. 'I'm getting a bit fed up of 'Rock 'N' Roll Star.'

'We're still doing it,' says Kelly crossly. 'We need a second song for the competition, though.' She pulls a tape recorder from her bag, adjusts the volume, and presses play. Everyone listens to it. 'Things Can Only Get Better', by D:Ream,' announces Kelly.

Everybody stares at her. Eventually Nicola says, 'We can't play that, Kelly. They've got samplers and synths and keyboards.'

'We need a keyboard player,' says Timmy.

'Not like D:Ream's, though,' adds Gemma. 'He looks like he should be a science teacher or something, not in a pop band.'

'We don't need a keyboard player,' says Kelly. 'We're going to do it with the guitars and drums.'

'Yeah, dance bands normally remix old guitar tunes, not the other way round,' says Gemma. 'How are we going to do that?'

Kelly shrugs and points at Nicola. 'You're the music genius. Sort it out.'

Nicola grabs a pencil and some paper. 'Give me that tape and let me have another listen. We could probably do it with simple guitar melodies, I suppose. I'll need a bit of time, though.'

'Why are we doing that song?' says Timmy.

Kelly doesn't know for sure. Just that when she was walking into town with her dad, and they were both singing it out of nowhere, that for one tiny moment – before Heather Wilson went and ruined it all – she really, truly believed it. But then things go and get worse, not better. But it stands to reason, things can only get worse for so long, right? At some point you have to hit the bottom. And then you can start climbing up again. And that's why The Mollies are going to do it. Because things are going to get better for them.

'We just are,' she says. 'We're The Mollies, and we're going to show them. We're going to show them all.'

34

Arthur rises late on Saturday, shocking himself. He never sleeps beyond six thirty. He peers at his watch. Gone nine. His eyes are bleary and hot and his chest is tight. He's definitely coming down with something, has been for days. He just has to see it through until Monday night. He just has to have answers. Then he doesn't care what happens.

He's barely dressed and had his porridge when there's a hammering at the door. It's Keith Cardy and a couple of his mates. Arthur invites them in and they all throw their cigarette butts on his step, grinding them into the frost with their boot heels.

'Thought we'd come round to see you, haven't seen you in the Diamond for a couple of nights,' says Cardy, almost accusingly.

Arthur bangs his chest with his fist. 'Coming down with something, I think.'

'There's a lot of it about,' says one of the men. 'The missus has been off it all week.'

Cardy chuckles. 'How would you know the difference with your missus?' He winks at Arthur. 'Sour-faced old cow.'

Arthur makes a round of teas and Cardy pulls a rolled up newspaper out of his jacket pocket. 'Brought this round for you. Weren't sure if you got the *Post*.'

Arthur unfurls the paper and Cardy directs him to page ten. There's a big picture of Arthur's chapel, and a smaller one of Cardy and his lot standing outside the Black Diamond, raising their pints and giving thumbs up. The headline reads: BATTLE IS ON TO SAVE WAR HERO'S HOME.

'I'm not really what you'd call a hero,' says Arthur.

Cardy nudges one of the lads. 'Modest as they come.'

Arthur reads the story and looks up. 'Why didn't they speak to me?'

'Ah, well, we didn't think you'd want to be bothered,' says Cardy. 'Especially as you're under the weather.'

I've only just told you that, thinks Arthur. He reads the piece again. It's mainly Cardy who is quoted. He's talking a lot about foreigners and how they shouldn't be taking homes that belong to war heroes. At the end there's a small quote from somebody at a place called the Asylum and Refugee Network North, saying that the people who the new homes will be for have seen terrible things and suffered greatly.

'Just send 'em back,' says Cardy.

Arthur looks at him. 'This lady says some of them could be killed if they have to go home.'

Cardy shrugs.

'I don't know about all this war hero stuff.'

Cardy leans forward and taps a cigarette out of his packet, which he puts behind his ear. He says, 'Arthur, did you ever kill a man in the war? One of the enemy?'

Arthur stares at him for a long time. 'Yes.'

'Then you're a bloody hero,' says Cardy. He stands up and the other two follow suit. 'You can keep the paper. Hope you're feeling better soon. See you in the Diamond before Christmas, yeah?'

Arthur nods absently, reading the article again, as Cardy and his boys let themselves out.

'I'm sorry I never told you about what happened, about why they say I'm a hero,' says Arthur. He has brought a small stool from the chapel and is sitting by Molly's grave. 'Cardy's right. I did kill a man. I didn't want to put it in a letter and by the time I'd got home you'd had the accident and it was more important to look after you than talk about the war.'

Arthur sighs a long, ragged breath. 'Funny thing, though. Next German I saw after that was Peter Bergmann. And he went and saved my life. Doesn't seem right that, does it? Especially after he died because he'd done it. Seems to me that I should have been the one saving Peter's life. Maybe that would have balanced things out a bit for what I did.'

Arthur traces Molly's name on the headstone with his fingers. 'I hope there's never another war. I can't imagine what the likes of young Timmy would do if he got called up. Or if those girls had to work the land like you did.' He pauses, and considers. 'Actually, come to think of it, I don't think I'd want to be on the wrong side of those lasses. They're a formidable bunch, Molly. Tough as nails. But good kids. I think you'd like them if you met them.'

Arthur stays silent for a bit, because he's talked a lot, and though he can't hear anything, he likes to give Molly a chance to talk, if she wants. Sometimes he tries to guess what she might say back to him, other times, like now, he just stays quiet, and doesn't think about anything, and hopes that somehow, somewhere, she's listening and talking and their words might just connect and brush together like leaves falling from a tree.

The thing about a cemetery is that you get used to a certain sort of silence. It's as though it's in a bubble, as though when you step through the gates you're walking into another world, one that's just slightly off-kilter from the rest of it. You can still hear the sounds of traffic, distant sirens, dogs barking, snatches of music. But it's as though the cemetery is insulated, protected, shielded from the world. Which is why Arthur has become attuned to the slightest disturbance in the graveyard, why unfamiliar sounds seem to ripple towards him on the air. And he feels one such disturbance now, though not wholly unfamiliar. He twists around on the stool but he already knows who he'll see, the four of them walking along the path, chatting and laughing and scuffing their feet. The Mollies.

'All right?' says Kelly. 'Thought we'd come to do an hour's rehearsing and then talk about Monday night.'

'We have a cunning plan,' says Timmy. 'You ever see that, Arthur? *Blackadder*? Well funny. I like the one set in the First World War.'

'I don't really watch war programmes,' mutters Arthur, standing stiffly.

'You were in the paper today,' says Gemma as they walk back towards the chapel.

'Well, Keith Cardy was,' says Arthur.

'That big march thing they're organising is on the same day as our Battle of the Bands competition,' says Kelly. 'We were hoping you might like to come. It's at night so the rally should be finished.'

Arthur feels strangely touched that they've asked him to go. 'I'll see how I'm feeling,' he says. Inside he puts the kettle on and grabs four cans of cola from the fridge. 'I got these in for you. And some crisps.'

He watches them while they set up and start to tune their guitars. They look more natural with their instruments now, like they're extensions of their bodies. Kelly, especially, has come on so far, he thinks, as he looks at her hunched over his guitar, strumming it and listening intently as she twists the tuning keys. He wonders if they really have a chance to do what they want to do, to make it as pop stars. He wonders if it's a good thing or a bad thing that they're even trying. What if they get close, but fail? Would that be better or worse than never dreaming at all, than just doing what's expected of you? Arthur never did anything in his life that was out of the ordinary, and he doesn't think he's suffered from it.

While they play their new song, which seems to be called 'Things Can Only Get Better', Arthur flicks through the rest of the paper that Keith Cardy left him. There's a story about the library getting a computer that can connect to the world wide web. Arthur has no idea what it means, or expects that it is something that will ever trouble him. He'll stick with the radio and newspapers; he doesn't expect they're going anywhere anytime soon. After that he reads the sport. The football's having a good run, everyone saying they might get promotion out of the Third Division if they carry on like they are. All down to those Spanish lads they brought in, who they call the Three Amigos. Arthur wonders if Keith Cardy would like to send them home, too, or if they're all right because they score goals.

Then he peruses the death notices, to see who's gone, and the small ads. He's about to close the paper when something catches his eye in the items for sale column. He casts around for a pencil and puts a big ring around it, then stands up and goes to get his coat.

'Can I trust you on your own for a bit?' says Arthur when there's a break in the music.

Gemma glares at him. "Course you can. What do you mean by that?'

'Nothing personal,' Arthur assures her. 'I just need to go out and make a phone call from the box on the main road.'

'Fine, Arthur,' says Kelly.

'Don't touch the wood burner,' he cautions, but The Mollies have already struck up again, and are so lost in the music they're making that they barely notice him slip out through the door.

* 35 *

The morning of Monday, 23 December dawns and finds Arthur brooding by his woodburner, where he's been for a good three hours. The winter equinox has just turned; the solstice, which Arthur always thinks of a very Christmassy sort of word. The days are as short as they ever get. Which is fine by Arthur, because the night-time is when *he* will come. And this year Arthur will finally have answers.

'I'm scared,' says Arthur, out loud and to nobody in particular, and he surprises himself with his words. *I'm scared.* Scared of what? Scared of losing his home. Scared of losing his home without answers to who's leaving the flowers. Scared of losing Molly.

But you lost her seven years ago, he tells himself. You lost her when the cancer took her. He looks around the chapel, looks at the navy blue sky filtering in through the windows. It's like she moved to leave, but Arthur grabbed her hand at the last moment, and he can't let go. Molly's gone, but not quite; not as long as he grips her hand for all he's worth. But if they make him leave the chapel, and move Molly's grave, how long can he hold on?

The kettle whistles on the stove and Arthur makes himself another cup of tea, then sits back down by the burner. Nobody understands. The vicar doesn't understand, the council didn't understand, the police couldn't care less. Even The Mollies don't understand, God bless 'em. They just want a place to play their music. But it's lovely of them to help, because Arthur doesn't know what he'd have done if he was on his own tonight, if he missed him or scared him away. At least now he's got a chance.

Still, nobody understands. They can't for the life of them see why Arthur would get so wound up by a stranger leaving flowers on his wife's grave. He can tell what they're thinking: Well, isn't that actually a *nice* thing? Isn't it *good* that someone remembers Molly in this way? Shouldn't he be *glad* that she meant so much to someone?

But it isn't nice, it isn't good, it doesn't make Arthur glad. It makes him burn with anger, and shame, and regret.

Because while Molly was alive, Arthur never bought her flowers.

Not on her birthday, or for Valentine's Day. Not at Christmas, or their wedding anniversary. Not just because he felt like it, bursting through the door, covered in coal dust from the pit or engine oil from the train sheds, a bouquet in his arms. Not roses nor chrysanthemums, lilies or orchids. Never moonflowers. Not to say sorry, or just that he loved her. It never occurred to him, he never thought. They had each other, through good times and bad, and that was enough, he had supposed.

But maybe it wasn't. Molly is lying there in her grave and somebody is bringing her flowers. What do they know that he never learned through all those years of marriage? That Molly loved flowers? How can that be? How can someone presume to know her better than Arthur did?

And that's why he's angry, and that's why he feels shame, and that's why he regrets. Perhaps if he had bought her flowers, then she wouldn't need these blooms dropped on her grave in the dead of night. Perhaps – and the thought makes his heart feel as though it's shriveling inside his chest – she died in sadness, having never had her husband push a red rose into her hand and tell her that he loved her.

'You know I loved you, don't you, Molly?' he says to the still air, untroubled this morning by the radio. 'You know I *love* you?'

Arthur walks over to the calendar on the wall and stares at the number 23, a big red ring around it. 'Happy birthday, love,' he says, and thinks about all the birthdays she had when she was here. No flowers, perhaps, but not unhappy. Or so he presumed. Nights out, at the Labour Club or the Rock Ferry Inn, sometimes a meal, when times were good, maybe at Roberto's Italian restaurant in town. When life wasn't so good to them, a special tea around their little kitchen table, steak from the butchers, well done, like Molly liked it. And then the next day was Christmas Eve, and work would finish, and they would maybe go out again, if they were flush, for a couple of drinks, or they'd drink sherry in front of the telly. And if either of them felt the absence of children in their lives, then nobody would say anything about it.

Arthur pulls on his boots and opens the door. The day's shaping up to be bright and cold. The last traces of the snow are gathered in the lee of the stone walls that surround the cemetery, and he wraps himself in his coat and scarf and walks the short distance to Molly's grave.

He stands in front of the stone, feeling curiously distant from her. Today of all days. But it's as though Molly's birthday is no longer for him. It's for the other person, whoever's coming in the dead of night. It's as though *he's* claimed her, stolen her from Arthur, at least just for this one day.

During one of the band rehearsals, one of the girls asked Arthur why he was so sure it was a man who was coming every year. He didn't have an answer, not a real one. He just knows, deep down in his bones, that it's a man. A woman would not do this, would not employ such subterfuge, would not creep around under cover of darkness. It's a man, all right, a man with a secret.

And Arthur's not just scared of not finding out the truth tonight; he's perhaps just as scared of what that truth will be.

He walks up to unlock the gates, then does his rounds, up and down the paths. He's in no mood to talk to the dead, today. His route takes him over to the far wall, that borders Cemetery Road, and beyond that the Old Hall, its windows blank and dirty. He wonders if the people inside are looking out, at him, at his graveyard, excited about what's to come in there, new flats and a community centre for them, and all the others who will follow them from foreign parts. He wonders if they know that his world has been shattered and is falling apart, just for them.

Get Christmas out of the way, and it'll be the march. He hopes it does some good. He's under no illusions that Keith has his own agenda to push, but if they're all pulling in the same direction, then what's the harm? If Keith Cardy wants Arthur to be a war hero, and that saves his home and Molly's grave, then why not? What's a hero, anyway? It's just somebody who comes home alive.

In the afternoon, Arthur has a little doze, the radio gently burbling on in his ear. His dream is like an old film, a really old film, all jerky and scratchy. He sees himself, as a younger man, running through the cemetery at night, the Mollies haring about, all holding their musical instruments. In his dream he feels himself getting annoyed at the kids, telling them they'll never catch the intruder if they're banging drums and strumming guitars. But they do catch him, and he's like an old villain, with a top hat and a cloak he's pulled over his face, brandishing a huge bunch of moonflowers. Arthur grabs at the cape to reveal his identity, and Gemma is standing by him, repeatedly banging one of her drums. Just as the cloak falls away, Arthur wakes up.

Gemma is still banging her drum. Arthur shakes the cobwebs away. No, not a drum. It's the door. Someone knocking at the door.

There's a woman there, a little younger than Arthur, but not by much. She's got dyed blonde hair and her face is lined and deeply tanned, and she holds a wrapped bunch of flowers. She apologises for disturbing Arthur, but she is looking for a grave. It's her cousin's; she died seven years ago but the woman has been living abroad. Arthur has a sudden desire to feel the sun on his skin. It seems like this winter will never end.

'What's her name?' asks Arthur, getting his coat. And for one mad moment he imagines she's going to say Molly Calderbank, and just like that the mystery will be solved. But instead she says, 'Winnie Houghton. Winifred.'

Arthur recognises the name, just as he recognises all of the names etched into the gravestones. She's buried just a couple of rows back from Molly – must have died earlier the same year. He leads the woman to the grave.

'Thank you,' she says. 'I haven't been back since before she died so I thought I'd pay my respects while I'm visiting.'

Arthur nods, and makes to leave, but pauses and asks the woman, 'Where do you live, then? Abroad?'

'Spain,' she says.

'And what do you do?'

She laughs. 'Eat and drink, mainly. We're retired now. We get our pensions paid to us over there. My husband gets his disability benefit, too. It goes a damn sight further there than it would here.'

'Why did you go there?' asks Arthur.

She frowns and looks at him as though he's crazy. 'I just told you,' she says. 'For a better quality of life.'

Arthur smiles and walks away, back to the chapel. Far beyond, he can see the roof of the Old Hall. Full of asylum seekers and refugees. He glances back at the woman, arranging the flowers in a pot at her cousin's grave, drawing her pension and living it up in Spain.

There's obviously a difference, he thinks. Keith Cardy would be able to explain it to him. It's just that, right now, he can't for the life of him see what it is.

36

'I'm sleeping at Gemma's,' says Kelly, hauling her bag into the living room.

Her mum looks at the holdall. 'How long for? A month?'

'Just tonight. But their central heating is broken so I'm taking my big coat. And my gloves. And warm clothes.'

Her mum narrows her eyes, but shrugs and her eyes graze back to *Emmerdale*. Her dad is sitting on the sofa, staring into the middle distance. He's barely spoken to Kelly since the paint incident, barely spoken to anybody. He hasn't shaved for three days.

'We're doing some band practice on the new songs,' says Kelly. She sits down next to her dad. 'If we win this competition we get £250 each.'

'Pity it couldn't have been before Christmas,' murmurs her mum.

Her dad glares sharply at her. 'What are you saying?'

Her mum keeps her eyes on the telly. Her dad frowns. 'You're saying it's my fault, that this bloody girl threw a tin of paint over me and I missed my interview? You're saying I could have done something about it?' He stares at Kelly. 'If anybody's to blame it's her. She started this stupid fight with that Wilson girl.'

Kelly stands up and grabs her bag. 'What I was going to say, was if we win and I get two hundred and fifty quid I'll buy you a new suit!' she yells. 'Then maybe you can get another interview somewhere! But if you're not interested, then fuck you!'

'Kelly,' says her mum warningly. 'Language.'

Her dad looks at Kelly, his face crinkling weirdly. Then he slumps back into the sofa, staring at his hands, knotting his fingers over and over again. Kelly sighs loudly and drags her bag to the door. 'See you tomorrow.'

She puts the bag awkwardly on her shoulder and slams the door behind her, heading off into the cold night. When she gets to Nicola's she dumps her bag on the pavement, out of sight, and rings the doorbell. Nicola's mum answers, staring at Kelly through narrowed eyes.

'My mum sent me over to walk Nic to ours, while it's dark,' says Kelly cheerfully. Behind Mrs Manning she can see Nicola wrapped in her big coat, a bobble hat on her head, her bag hanging from a mittened hand.

'Can I have your phone number in case I need to speak to Nicola?'

'Our phone's broke,' smiles Kelly. 'But we'll be in all night. We've got some frozen pizza from Iceland.'

'Lovely,' says Mrs Manning, as though she thinks it's anything but. Nicola edges past her but her mum grabs her and plants a kiss on her cheek. 'Don't stay up too late. You still need to do your paper round tomorrow.'

Nicola sighs and wriggles out of her mum's grasp. When she's shut the door Kelly says, 'God, your mum doesn't half worry. She needs to chill out a bit.'

'She's just troubled,' says Nicola, walking ahead as Kelly hefts her bag up on her shoulder again. 'She's just worried about me. All the time.' She glances back to their house. 'And I'm a bit worried about leaving her on her own, to be honest.'

Kelly overtakes her on the pavement. 'She'll be fine. You're going to have to cut the apron strings sometime. Come on, we're meeting Gemma at Timmy's.'

Gemma is smoking under a street lamp at the corner of Timmy's street, near the bridge which goes over the canal. 'Thank God,' she says as they walk up and drop their bags near hers. 'I'm freezing my tits off here.'

'Which is Timmy's house?' says Kelly.

'That one,' says Nicola, then stares at her feet. Kelly gives Gemma a raised eyebrow glance. Nicola mutters, 'I rode past on my bike once and saw him in the window.'

The three of them look at the detached house. It's massive, at least compared to theirs, thinks Kelly. And clean. The houses on the street all have big, tidy gardens, none of them filled with junk or old cars on bricks. There's no graffiti, no boarded-up windows, no scruffy dogs crapping on the pavements. When she's a famous rock star, Kelly is going to buy a house like this. It has a gated drive and a security light over the garage next to the front door.

'So how we going to spring Tampax from Alcatraz?' says Gemma, taking a drag on her cigarette.

'Don't call him that. Timmy's told them he's gone to bed early with a cold,' says Kelly. 'He says his mum won't bother him until the morning. He should be packed and ready to go. He's going to slip out of the back door, over the garden fence, and we'll meet him round the back.'

'So why aren't we meeting him round the back?' frowns Nicola.

Kelly winks at her. 'Because we have to create a diversion.'

A light goes on behind the frosted glass of the door and it's opened by a woman with a pinched face and blow-dried hair, who looks down her nose at them. Got to be Timmy's mum, thinks Kelly. Behind her she can see a wide hall and a staircase, and a thick, floral carpet. There's a Christmas tree in the hall, a real one, festooned with co-ordinated silver and gold baubles and warm lights.

'Yes?' says Timmy's mum.

Kelly nudges Gemma and the three of them burst into loud song. 'We wish you a Merry Christmas! We wish you a Merry Christmas! We wish you a Merry Christmas! And a happy New Year!'

Timmy's mum touches a painted fingernail to her forehead and grimaces. 'Oh,' she says.

'Good tidings we bring!' bellows Kelly. 'To you and your king!'

'It's *kin*, not king,' says Timmy's mum. 'As in family. Speaking of which, my son is unwell in his room. I'd rather you didn't—'

'We wish you a Merry Christmas! And a happy New Year!'

A man appears behind Timmy's mum, his dark hair flecked with grey, wearing a shirt and slacks. He frowns and Timmy's mum turns and says, 'Carol singers. Avenues girls, by the looks of them. Have you got a pound?'

197

Kelly launches into the same verse again as Timmy's dad searches his pockets.

'Please,' says Timmy's mum. 'My son . . .'

Timmy's dad hands over a pound coin to Gemma, who pockets it, and Kelly leads them into the chorus with gusto and increased volume. Timmy's mum closes her eyes and says, 'Oh, dear, I feel one of my heads coming on. I think I might need a lie-down as well.'

Timmy's dad hands over another pound coin, smiles politely at them, and pushes the door shut, steering his wife away across the hall. Their song trails off.

'Think we gave him enough time?' says Gemma.

'Only one way to find out,' says Kelly.

Timmy's house backs on to the canal and they find him crouched down behind his garden fence, holding his bag. Gemma begins to whistle the theme tune to *The Great Escape*.

'Shush!' hisses Timmy. 'They might hear you.'

'Jesus, Timmy,' says Kelly. 'Your mum is a right witch.'

Timmy scuttles off along the towpath by the black waters of the canal and it's only when they're a hundred yards away that he speaks. 'She's all right. She's just . . .'

'She's just a snob,' says Gemma.

Kelly says, 'Did you ask them to get you a mic for Christmas?'

They get to the main road and turn down to walk to the cemetery. 'Yes,' says Timmy. 'But I had to tell them it was so I could enter a public speaking competition.'

Kelly and Gemma share a glance, and Gemma shakes her head in disgust. She says, 'Why can't you just tell her you're in a band? What's she going to do? Christ, people have a pop at the likes of us but at least we tell stuff like it is and don't fanny about.'

'She'd probably take to her bed for a week,' says Timmy morosely. 'I don't think she could handle the shame. She wants me to be a doctor.'

'Why do you even go to Marigold Brook?' says Kelly. 'It's a shit school. You could be at Park Fold or somewhere like that.'

Timmy sighs. 'That's my dad. He runs his own business and he dragged himself up with nothing. He went to Marigold Brook. He says if it was good enough for him to make a success of himself, it's good enough for me. He thinks it's character building. My mum nearly had to go to hospital when he insisted on it.'

'Anyway,' says Kelly. 'She's going to have to get used to you being in a band. Because I've had a brilliant idea.'

'Uh-oh,' says Gemma.

'What is it?' says Nicola.

Kelly stops as they reach the cemetery gates. 'I was thinking about what Arthur said. About us doing the competition and playing live in front of an audience for the first time. That's why I think we should do a practice gig first.'

The others consider and then Nicola nods. 'That makes sense, I suppose.'

'I'd be up for that,' says Gemma. 'And Timmy's getting his mic when Father Christmas comes down the chimney tomorrow night.'

'I'm glad you said that,' says Kelly. Arthur has left the gate unlocked, as agreed, and Kelly pushes it open. 'Because we're playing on Friday night at the Black Diamond. I've already sorted it.'

Gemma, Nicola and Timmy stop and stare at her in the darkness.

'What did you say?' says Timmy.

Kelly grins at them, framed by the tall cemetery gates. 'You heard. But first we've got a mystery to solve.'

* 37 *

So, this is it, thinks Arthur, 23 December. Molly's birthday. The day he's going to catch the bastard who's been leaving flowers on her grave since she died. He feels anxious and excited and angry and, most strangely, as though there's a dull weight in his stomach. What if he doesn't come? What if they've missed him already? What if they scare him away? He looks at The Mollies, all wrapped up in their coats and scarves and warming themselves by the wood burner. What is he doing, dragging kids into this?

Arthur coughs violently, and holds his chest. His cold is getting worse. But all he has to do is get through tonight, then tomorrow he can relax. Tomorrow he can let it all go. He closes his eyes. Wouldn't it be a thing to just . . . let go? To see Molly again? But what if . . . what if what the church people say is all wrong? What if when he closes his eyes for the last time there's just . . . nothing? No Molly. Just infinite, endless blackness. Is it better to hang on as long as he can, to at least be able to talk to her, even though she can't listen? Or is he just condemning himself to more empty years without her?

His mind whirls around in circles and he takes a deep breath. When he opens his eyes Timmy is holding out a glass of water to him. 'For the cough,' he says.

'Thanks, lad,' says Arthur, taking it gratefully from him. Good kids, all of them. He looks at Kelly. Should he tell her now, or after . . .? He decides now and goes off to the back of the chapel to get the two big black bin liners.

'We haven't time to take the rubbish out, Arthur,' says Gemma, rubbing her hands together in front of the fire.

'We're just going through the plan,' says Kelly. 'We think it's better if you stay in the chapel, because that's what he'll expect. You need to keep walking past the windows every now and again to show you're inside. We're going to split up and patrol the cemetery.'

Timmy raises a hand. 'For the record, I think that's the worst idea ever. Have you never seen a single horror film? You want us to creep around a cemetery on our own in the middle of the night? We'll get picked off one by one.'

'Jesus, Timmy,' says Kelly. 'For the hundredth time he's not a killer. He's leaving flowers on a grave.'

'As far as you know!' yells Timmy. 'He might do serial killing on the side! As a hobby!'

Kelly mulls it over. 'All right. We can do pairs. Like Scooby-Doo.'

'I'll go with Timmy,' says Nicola quietly.

Arthur coughs, to distract Gemma and her big grin from whatever she's about to say next. Even Arthur can see there's something flowering between Timmy and Nicola. They're both odd kids, but maybe that's what they needed. To find each other.

Kelly looks up at him and frowns. 'What's in the bags, Arthur?'

'The other day, when I went out to the phone box,' he says. 'I'd seen this ad in the paper.' He starts to tear open the bin liner. 'It's not a posh one and it's not that Neil Corrigan one, it's just a second-hand thing. I've only got my pension, you know. But it works. The fella I bought it off showed me when he brought it round.'

'Oh. My. God,' squeals Kelly when Arthur reveals the electric guitar and the tiny little amplifier.

'It's my Christmas present to the band. To The Mollies. For everything you're doing tonight,' says Arthur. He thinks for a moment. 'For everything you've done so far. Molly would have really liked having you round here, I think, filling the place up with your music and laughter.' He pauses. 'Even if it is a godawful racket.'

Then Kelly is throwing her arms around him and the others are too, even Timmy, and they're all saying thank you, thank you, and Arthur is trying to push them off, calling them daft apeths and silly sausages and he's an old man and he doesn't want to give them his cold but as he's enfolded in their arms he feels happy and wanted and – dare he even think it? – *loved*, in a way that he never has since Molly died and never thought he would again.

Arthur knows from previous years that the flowers are never put on Molly's grave before eleven at night and never after six in the morning, when he always finds them. He guesses it's before midnight, because otherwise it would be the next day, Christmas Eve, and not Molly's birthday any more. He's kept watch from the chapel before, but never seen anything. He wonders if they'll really see anything tonight?

He looks at his watch. Eleven thirty. The Mollies are out, doing their patrols. They're being pretty good, he has to admit; he's been passing by the window regularly, as instructed, but he's never seen hide nor hair of them out there. Unless they've got bored and gone home, of course. But he doesn't think they'd do that.

Who is it? Who is it? He turns over possibilities in his mind. They have no family, no friends who would do that and not tell him. There was no one before Arthur for Molly. They were childhood sweethearts, they gave themselves, trembling and nervous, to each other on their wedding night. Apart from the war, they were never apart, until the day she died. Who would do this? Why would they do this?

Arthur makes himself another coffee, determined to stay awake all night if needs be. But he couldn't go to sleep now if his life depended on it. He has a sudden flash of guilt, or fear. What if the man *is* dangerous, like Timmy keeps saying? What if Arthur's put those children in trouble? He dithers over making his coffee, wondering if he should go out and get them and just call it all off.

But somehow Arthur knows this isn't one of Timmy's serial killers, or anything like that. It's a mystery, that's all it is, a mystery that's been burning for seven years and is going to be solved tonight. Arthur checks his watch again. Only five minutes since he last looked. He's going to drive himself mad at this rate.

Arthur walks past the window again with his coffee, peering out at the dark graveyard. The moon is a slim crescent, not giving much light. He squints in the direction of Molly's grave, but can't see anything beyond the ranks of gravestones. Maybe he should just go out for a moment . . .

Instead he sits by the wood burner and feeds more kindling into it, and sips at his coffee. He grabs a couple of cushions to make himself more comfortable, and stares into the fire, trying to think of nothing at all, trying not to check his watch. The flames lick high and are warm on his face. If only Molly were here with him. He'd put his arm around her and they'd drink cocoa, not coffee, and he'd put Christmas carols on the radio. He closes his eyes for a moment, savouring the idea, composed of fragments of memory and half-dared wishes. Arthur opens his eyes and blinks, then decides to just rest them again for a second.

* 38 *

'One thing about Scooby fucking Doo was that it never showed them standing around freezing their arses off,' says Gemma, puffing hard on a cigarette under a tree close to the older corner of the cemetery.

'Shush,' says Kelly. 'We don't want to scare him off.'

She squats down, back against the tree, peering into the darkness. Then she checks her watch; just after half eleven. If Arthur's right, he'll show up in the next thirty minutes. She says, 'We should maybe get closer to Molly's grave. There's a couple of bushes, just nearer to the gate, do you see them?'

'Has anybody thought that all this might be complete bollocks?' says Gemma.

'Shush!' commands Kelly, then whispers, 'What do you mean?'

Gemma slides down the tree to squat besides Kelly. 'I mean, we've only got Arthur's word that all this is even happening. He's an old man. He might be going a bit doolally. What if there's never been anybody leaving flowers? What if he's done it himself, and just forgot? And I mean, moonflowers. What's that all about? Sounds like something out of one of those bloody fantasy books that Timmy reads. Are they even real?'

'I don't know,' mutters Kelly. 'I mean, yeah, course they are. Arthur's not soft in the head. He's not made this up.'

'You're only saying that because he bought you a guitar,' says Gemma. She stubs her fag out in the damp grass. 'Come on then, let's go and hide in the bushes. At least that's nearer the main road. Gives me the creeps being down in this old bit of the cemetery.'

As they tiptoe between the graves, Kelly whispers, 'Do you think we can do it, really?'

'What, catch the bad guy?' says Gemma. 'Rip his mask off so he can say, I woulda got away with it if it hadn't been for you meddling kids?'

'No,' says Kelly. 'The band. The contest. Do you think we can do it?'

Gemma shrugs. 'I don't know. We sound pretty good. I've no idea what the other bands are like, though.' She pauses. 'Do you?'

'Yeah,' says Kelly after a bit. 'We have to. I can't . . . Gem, I can't do it. The factory, all that shit. Just be another Marigold Brook cast-off. I don't want to spend the rest of my life on the Avenues.'

Gemma's about to say something when Kelly grabs her arm, and pulls her behind a tall headstone. She clamps her hand over Gemma's mouth and puts a finger to her own lips. They're not far from Nicola's bunker, and she can hear scuffling, things moving, the scrape of boxes on the earth. She slowly moves her hand from Gemma's mouth and points in the direction of the mausoleum.

'Dirty bastards,' mouths Gemma, stifling a laugh.

Kelly frowns at her. 'What?'

'Nic and Timmy,' whispers Gemma. 'He's sexing her up in the bloody bunker.'

'They're supposed to be on patrol!' hisses Kelly. 'I'm going to get them.'

Gemma pulls her coat. 'Nah, leave it. Let's get over the bushes, catch the Hooded sodding Claw, and then we can all go home.'

'I've got a good view of Molly's grave from here,' says Timmy, peering over the top of a headstone. Nicola looks up at him from where she's sitting cross-legged behind him. Her bum's getting wet. Timmy says, 'What time is it?'

Nicola consults her watch. 'Eleven forty-eight. We should see something in the next twelve minutes, if Arthur's right.'

He stays where he is, his coat hood up, staring over the edge of the gravestone like a sniper. Nicola shifts a bit on her bum and says, 'Timmy, have you ever had a girlfriend?'

He doesn't turn round, but whispers, 'What do you think? With a nickname like mine?'

She says, 'Are you? Gay? It doesn't matter if you are.'

'No. I don't think so. I like girls,' says Timmy. 'I think I do, anyway. I mean, how do you even know if you are one?'

'Why does everybody call you those names then?'

'Because my mum makes me take a briefcase to school,' he says, turning round to look down at her. 'Because I can't play football and I don't get into fights and I've never had a girlfriend and I do my homework and I always have tissues.'

There's silence for a moment, then Timmy asks, 'What about you? Have you ever had a boyfriend?'

'Look at me, Timmy,' she says quietly.

His bony shoulders rise and fill inside his coat. 'You're all right.'

As compliments go, thinks Nicola, it's not exactly a line from *Four Weddings and a Funeral*. But then, she never gets compliments, and this one makes her tummy feel all funny. She brushes it away, though, and says, 'My mum wouldn't allow it anyway. She says things like *You can't afford to be weak, and boys make you weak.*'

'Does she really believe all that stuff? About the end of the world and society collapsing and things?'

'Mmm,' says Nicola. 'She thinks it's—'

Timmy holds up a hand, and she can see his eyes widen behind his glasses in the shadow of his hood. 'What's that?' he mouths.

She listens, suddenly alert, and hears it, a distant, plaintive cry on the still night air. She smiles. 'It's an owl.'

Timmy breathes out. 'I wish we'd never played that zombie game in the arcade. I keep thinking they're going to come for us. I don't like it here in the dark.'

Nicola's about to say, *not even with me?* but then she sees a dark shape out of the corner of her eye and Timmy suddenly whimpers, 'Don't eat my brain! It's the only thing I've got!' and pitches forward, crashing into her and pushing her back on to the grass. She sees the shape of the owl gliding past and then lifting up, flapping away silently into the night.

Timmy is lying on top of her. She feels his weight on her chest, and her legs. He's just staring at her, like he's forgotten how to speak or move. Nicola takes a deep breath and then something catches her eye. She looks over the graveyard and her eyes widen.

This time it's definitely not an owl.

'What time is it?' says Gemma. 'This is bollocks. Shall we just knock it on the head?'

'Nearly five to,' says Kelly. She's beginning to think that Gemma is right. Nobody's going to show now. Maybe Arthur has imagined it all. They've pushed right into the middle of a thorny bush, just a dozen or so yards from Molly's grave. Kelly's leg has gone to sleep.

'Any sign of the dirty shaggers?' says Gemma.

Kelly peers across the graveyard. 'No.'

'Who'd have thought Timmy had so much stamina,' grins Gemma in the dark.

'Oh, hang on,' says Kelly. 'Is this them?'

Gemma leans over her shoulder and pushes a handful of leaves out of the way. 'No, it's just one of them. Must be Timmy . . .'

She goes quiet and Kelly meets her eye, before looking back at the figure loping across the graves. It's too tall for even Timmy, too broad in the shoulder, and they're wearing a jacket over a hooded top, which is pulled over their head.

In their hands is a bunch of flowers.

'Oh, Jesus fucking shit, it's him,' squeaks Gemma.

Kelly can't breathe. It is as well. She reaches down and her hand finds a slimy, broken branch. She whispers, 'He's coming from right where we were standing before.'

'I bet he caught Timmy and Nicola in the bunker,' hisses Gemma. 'Timmy was right, he *is* a serial killer! I bet he's done them in!'

'When he gets to the grave, we rush him,' says Kelly. She looks down and finds another stick, and pushes it into Gemma's hands.

'Fuck that,' says Gemma. 'I'm making a run for it.'

'No!' whispers Kelly. 'We have to do this. For Arthur.'

Gemma blinks and nods. Kelly peers through the leaves; the man is standing at Molly's grave, with his back to them, just looking down at it, the flowers in his hand.

'On three,' mouths Kelly. 'One . . . two . . .'

Before she can get to three, she sees the man look up, startled, as two figures leap out from behind a headstone twenty yards in the opposite direction. It's Timmy and Nicola, screaming and yelling and waving their arms like idiots. The man starts to back away.

'Bollocks,' says Kelly. 'Come on.'

She pushes out of the thicket and brandishes the stick high, yelling, 'Now we've got you!'

The figure spins round, is face still hidden by his hood, and Kelly holds up the stick like a one of those Japanese warriors, yells, 'Charge!' and runs towards him, just as Timmy throws himself in a tangle of arms and legs at the intruder.

39

When Arthur opens his eyes again the coffee cup is cool in his hands. He looks at his watch. Five minutes to twelve. He curses himself for dropping off, then he hears something. A shout. He realises he's been woken by a shout, and there it goes again, a volley of voices, calling his name.

Arthur is at the door quicker than he can credit, yanking it open and stepping out into the sobering cold night, not even bothering with his coat. He can see Molly's grave from the step and there's a commotion there, a huddle of bodies. Then he hears Kelly's voice, distinct and clear in the night.

'Arthur! Arthur! We've got him!'

We've got him.

The years seem to drop off him as he sets off for the grave, and by the time he gets there he's almost running. The four Mollies are piled on the ground, swaddled like Michelin Men in their coats, wriggling around. There's someone underneath them.

There's someone underneath them.

He's underneath them.

On Molly's grave is a bunch of flowers. Moonflowers. Stems snapped and heads crushed in the scuffle.

'Get off! Get off!' shouts Arthur. 'Get off him! Let me see the bugger!'

One by one they get up and form a circle around Molly's grave, arms spread wide to stop him escaping. There's a figure on the ground, half on Molly's plot, face down, his arms over his head. He seems to be shaking and making tiny, mewling noises. He's wearing a rough donkey jacket and shapeless jeans, his feet in thick-soled boots with no laces. He's wearing some kind of hooded top under his coat, the hood up, hiding his face.

'Up, you bugger!' shouts Arthur. 'Get up!'

The man stops making the noises and pauses, taking a ragged breath. Arthur looks at the Mollies, all of them wide-eyed and breathless. Timmy has a streak of wet earth down his coat.

'We got him, Arthur!' says Kelly triumphantly. 'The plan worked. We saw him creeping through the graves and we closed in on him from different directions. Then we just jumped him. We got him!'

'Aye, you got him,' says Arthur. 'Now get up! Who are you? Show me your face.'

The man is whispering something, which sounds like *sorry sorry sorry sorry* over and over again. Arthur suddenly feels a pang of something, that punctures his anger and adrenaline. More calmly, he says, 'Get up. We're not going to hurt you. I just want answers.'

Slowly, the man removes his hands from his head. Curious position, thinks Arthur absently. He's seen that before. In the war. Captured or surrendered men, lying face down, hands locked behind their heads. The man slowly pushes himself up on to all fours, then deliberately reaches up with one hand to push the hood off his head.

His dark hair is close-cropped, and he turns to look at Arthur, his eyes wide and white and fearful in his face. His nostrils are flaring with his laboured breathing, and he bares his teeth in a grimace, spitting out a mouthful of soil.

Arthur doesn't know any black people.

'Who are you?' says Arthur.

'Leon,' whispers the man, wiping his jacket sleeve across his mouth.

The man straightens up, kneeling in front of Arthur. The four Mollies close in. Two of them are holding sticks, gnarled tree branches.

'Don't you hurt him,' warns Gemma. 'We'll do you, you bastard.'

Arthur waves at her to stand down. 'Why are you leaving flowers on my wife's grave? What is she to you?'

The man – Leon – looks at the headstone for a moment, his eyes following the lines of Molly's name. Arthur gets a proper look at him. How old is he? Fifty, maybe? His clothes are patched and ragged. He looks thin. He looks tired. His face is carved with lines.

'I'll ask you again, then I'm calling the police,' says Arthur. 'Why are you here? What's my Molly to you?'

Leon sighs and rubs his head, then looks Arthur dead in the eye. 'She was my mum,' he says.

✳ **40** ✳

'You're a lying bastard,' says Arthur.

He is sitting on one of the pews, facing Leon, the Mollies ranked behind him, glaring over his shoulder at the man. Leon looks down at his feet, his shabby boots. He isn't just unkempt, he smells odd, like cold air and mustiness. In the light of the chapel, Arthur sees that his chin is covered in scrubby, uneven beard, his hair flecked with grey.

'I'm not lying,' mumbles Leon.

'Molly couldn't have children,' says Kelly over Arthur's shoulder. 'She had an accident on a farm.'

Arthur sits back, staring narrow-eyed at Leon. 'That's right. And I think I'd know if she'd ever had a baby. Especially a . . .'

He leaves it hanging there. Gemma leans forward over the pew. 'It's a con trick. He's trying to say he's due an inheritance.'

'It's not a con trick,' says Leon quietly.

Arthur laughs, but without a trace of humour. 'It's a bloody misguided one if it is. I don't have two ha'pennies to rub together. We didn't even own a house. Molly didn't leave anything.'

And then Leon looks up, and meets Arthur's hard stare, and holds it. 'She left *me*,' he says.

Arthur shakes his head. 'What are you hoping to gain by this? It's ridiculous nonsense.' He taps the side of his temple. 'You're not right in the head, is that it?'

'How old is he?' says Nicola quietly.

Arthur nods vigorously. 'Aye, tell us that. When's your birthday? And I'll tell you what me and Molly was doing when she was supposed to be giving birth to you.'

212

Leon rubs his hands together. The palms are ingrained with grime. He stares at the floor again. 'Thirteenth October, 1945.'

'Ha!' says Arthur in triumph. 'That was about a week before . . .'

He stops.

He stares at Leon.

Timmy taps his shoulder. 'Arthur? Tell him. What were you doing in October 1945?'

'I'd just got back. From Europe. From the war. It was the twenty-first when I went over to Yorkshire to see Molly.'

No, he thinks.

'She'd been in hospital. After the accident on the farm.'

No. No, I'm not having this.

Arthur looks at Leon. 'The accident with the chemicals in the barrels. The stuff that meant she couldn't have children any more.'

The Mollies have gone quiet behind him.

'That would have been about the thirteenth.'

Suddenly, Arthur feels very, very tired. The adrenaline of the night has suddenly departed, like a flock of crows rising up on a misty morning. He just wants to put his head down and sleep.

'You're a lying bastard,' says Arthur again, but more weakly.

'She was my mum,' says Leon.

There's a low rumbling sound, which at first Arthur thinks is thunder, but then he realises it's coming from Leon's stomach. He frowns. 'Have you not had any tea?'

'I had something to eat,' says Leon uncertainly. 'Yesterday, I think.'

Arthur's frown deepens. 'Yesterday? Where do you live?'

Leon shrugs. 'Nowhere, really. I wander about a bit. I come up here in the winter. Ever since my m— ever since your wife died.'

'You mean you're homeless?' says Kelly.

Leon nods. Arthur turns to the Mollies. 'There's a couple of tins of tomato soup in the back. Do you want to warm them up with some bread and butter for him?'

When they are alone and the kids are clanking and messing in the kitchen area, Arthur leans forward and says quietly, 'I don't know what game you're playing, sunshine, but I don't believe a word of this. I won't see a man starve, God knows I've not been too proud to accept charity myself. But as soon as you've had your soup and bread you're out of here, right? And you never come back. Not on her birthday, not ever again.'

Leon looks Arthur in the eye. There's something unnerving about that look, thinks Arthur. Leon says, 'I'm telling the truth. Why would I lie?'

Timmy appears, carefully cradling a big bowl of soup, with Nicola at his side carrying a plate of buttered bread. Arthur says, 'Sit over here by the fire. But take your coat off, or you'll not feel the benefit when you go out.' He raises an eyebrow at Leon. 'And you are going out straight after it. Back where you came from.'

Leon stands and takes off his jacket. The sleeves of his hooded top are rolled up and on the inside of his forearm Arthur can see a tattoo, what looks like a leafless tree or plant. There's a motto in Latin beneath it and a word above that Arthur can't quite read. Leon sees him looking and quickly pulls down his sleeves. He takes a pew a little closer to the fire.

'Get closer,' commands Arthur. You must be freezing.'

'I don't like open fires,' mutters Leon.

'You were in my bunker,' says Nicola as Leon wolfs down the bread. 'You took my locket. With my picture of my dad in it.'

Something passes across Leon's lined face and he reaches for his coat, digging into the pocket. He pulls out the pendant and hands it over.

'I'm sorry,' he says. 'I found the food and I was hungry. I took some beans. And water.'

Arthur watches Nicola flip open the locket and look at the tiny picture there. 'It's all right. I just wanted this back.'

'Why are you homeless?' says Timmy.

Leon glances away. He absently rubs his arm. Right where the tattoo is that Arthur saw. 'I had troubles. Never got back from them.' He looks around the chapel. 'You live here. Why?'

Arthur keeps his gaze on Leon. 'Because I wanted to be close to Molly when she died. My Molly. My Molly who never had any children.'

Leon sighs and puts down his empty dish on the pew. 'I don't know what to say, Arthur.'

'Mr Calderbank,' says Arthur sharply. 'To you.'

Leon smiles for the first time, a sad smile. 'I'm sorry. I almost feel like I know you.'

'Know me!' scoffs Arthur. 'How can you possibly know me? You don't know anything about me.'

'I feel like I do,' says Leon quietly. 'From Mum's letters.'

There's a long silence in the chapel. Arthur feels the eyes of The Mollies on him. His mouth feels dry and he licks his lips, but his tongue is like sandpaper. He takes a drink of tea and eventually says, 'Molly sent you letters?'

'I got in touch with her. Through the adoption agency. Ten years ago.'

Arthur stares at him. 'You've been corresponding with my Molly for ten years? And she didn't say a word about it to me?' He shakes his head. 'Ridiculous. Lies, lies, lies.'

Leon shrugs. 'It's not lies.'

Then Arthur feels the lethargy displaced by anger, again. He stands up and waves his finger in Leon's face. 'Lies! Because if what you're saying is true then my Molly must have . . . must have done that thing with another man! While I was at war. And it would mean she lied to me, that she never had an accident on the farm, that the reason she couldn't have children . . . that we could never have children . . .' Arthur's hand flies to his mouth, and he stares wide-eyed. 'It would mean it's your fault.'

Arthur sits down, heavily. 'It would mean she had a baby that wasn't mine and couldn't have any more and she spun me a web of lies. It would mean that all our life was a lie.' He looks up. 'And I don't believe that. Go. Just go.'

Leon stands and puts on his jacket. He pauses, and says, 'Thank you for the soup. I'm very grateful.' He reaches into his pocket. 'I can leave these with you. But I'd like them back. I can come for them tomorrow. They're all I have left of her.'

Arthur frowns as Leon pulls from his inside pocket a ragged stack of envelopes bound by an elastic band. Leon holds them out and Arthur stares at the curly writing on the envelopes. Molly's handwriting, unmistakably.

'Everything you need to know is in there,' says Leon.

Arthur, his hand shaking, takes the letters and just stares at them.

'Can I come back tomorrow?'

Arthur nods wordlessly, unable to take his eyes from the letters. He looks up when Leon is at the door, then turns to The Mollies. 'And you lot can bugger off as well.'

He sees them frown at each other. Kelly says, 'Hang on, Arthur, we caught—'

'You bloody stuck your noses in, is what you did!' shouts Arthur. 'You had to keep coming round here, didn't you? Couldn't leave me alone. Now you've gone and brought this on me.' He waves the letters in his hand at Leon, standing by the door. 'Brought that bugger in here.'

'Christ, Arthur,' says Gemma. 'This is what you wanted!'

'Oh, just go, the lot of you. Go and never come back.'

Kelly's face crinkles. 'Arthur? You don't mean that?'

'Go!' he roars, and they do.

The Mollies stand in the quiet, dark graveyard, looking at Leon. He stares back at them, then looks away. Nicola instinctively moves closer to Timmy; there's something in Leon's eye, something a little unusual, maybe a little wild. Maybe Timmy was right all along, perhaps he really is a killer.

Gemma lights up a fag and Leon looks at it greedily. She takes a drag then offers it to him and he gives a small smile and takes it.

'Sorry about jumping on you,' says Kelly, taking charge as ever. 'Hope we didn't hurt you.'

Leon stares at his boots, smoking Gemma's cigarette. Kelly says, 'Is it true? Was Molly really your mum?'

He nods sadly. 'I got in touch with her through an adoption agency. I wrote her a letter and she wrote me one back. Then we sent more letters. I never met her though. She didn't want Arthur to get upset.'

'Job's buggered there,' says Gemma, lighting up another fag.

'Sometimes it's better not to know,' says Timmy sagely.

Nicola nods agreement, but Kelly and Gemma stare at them. Kelly says, 'You mad? It's always better to know everything. Get it all out in the open. It's easier to deal with stuff when it's not a secret.'

Nicola looks away, careful not to catch Timmy's eye. What do they know? What is there to know anyway? Timmy fell on top of her, that's all. She feels a quiet thrill at the thought of it. Maybe there's a lot to know, after all. But for the moment, it's for her and Timmy.

'Where are you going to sleep?' says Gemma to Leon.

He shrugs. 'There's a hostel in town but it's too late to go now. I was just going to put the flowers on and then head off, maybe try to hitch somewhere. There's a lorry park a few miles away, somebody might still be about to set off.'

'Why don't you sleep in the bunker?' says Kelly.

Nicola blinks at her. 'What?'

Gemma nods. 'Better than sleeping on the street. You'll die in this cold. Isn't there a little gas stove in there, one of them camping things?'

Everyone looks at Nicola and she says, 'Fine. But don't steal anything.' She sees his downcast eyes and relents. 'You can have food. And water.'

'Timmy, give him your coat,' says Kelly.

'Why me?' says Timmy.

'Because you're the tallest. You might be a long streak of piss but you're closest to Leon in size.'

Grumbling, Timmy gets out of his coat and hands it over to Leon. They've wandered towards Molly's grave, and Nicola sees the broken stalks and flattened flowers on the scuffed earth.

'Oh,' she says. 'The moonflowers. We ruined them.'

Leon looks sadly at them and Kelly says curiously, 'Why moon-flowers? Were they Molly's favourites?'

Leon squats and tries vainly to rescue them, but they're beyond help. 'I don't think so. They're a tropical flower. *Ipomea alba*. They grow in Argentina. And other places.'

'Have you been to Argentina, then?'

He shakes his head. 'No, but not far away. Someone had them in a garden in Port Stanley.' He looks up at the girls. 'The Falkland Islands.'

'There was a war there,' says Timmy knowledgeably. 'We were all babies.'

'Hmm,' nods Leon, abandoning the flowers. 'These . . . they only bloom at night. I was . . . attracted to that. As though they're a secret from the real world.' Nicola sees his eyes fall to the battered flowers. 'Just like me, really.'

'Where did you get them from?' says Gemma. 'Arthur's been all over and can't find anybody who sells them.'

Leon stands up, still staring at the flowers. 'I do a bit of casual work at a plant nursery, near here. Always before Christmas, when they're getting orders ready. Just for a couple of weeks. They have them there and they always give me a bunch to bring up.'

'It's Christmas Eve tomorrow,' points out Timmy. 'What will you do?'

'Go and see Arthur again, get my letters back. Then see if I can get a ride out of here.' He pinches his nose in his broad fingers. 'What a disaster.' He gives a ragged sigh and smiles. 'I'll leave your coat with Arthur. Thank you for your kindness. It's a rare and wonderful thing.'

Kelly laughs. 'Mate, when you've got nothing, it's easy to share it around.'

Nicola watches Leon pick his way through the gravestones towards the bunker, then looks at her watch. It's nearly two. 'What are we supposed to do now?'

'Well, we can't stay out all night,' says Timmy, crossing his arms over his chest and thrusting his hands into his armpits. 'Especially those of us with no coats.'

'I can't go home,' says Kelly. 'They'll have locked up.' She looks at Gemma. 'Can I bunk in with you?'

'I suppose. But you know what it's like at our place. My mum's preggers again and you can't move for people. I don't think we could all go. Sorry.'

'That's all right,' says Nicola. She can't stop thinking about what Kelly said, about secrets and lies. She's fed up with skulking around, trying to be invisible to everybody, putting her head down and walking past in the hope the world won't notice her. She feels strangely bold. 'I'm going to stay at Timmy's.'

Timmy stares at her. 'What?'

Nicola sighs. 'I can't go home at this time. I'll never hear the end of it from my mum. So it's either walk the streets all night or go to Timmy's.' She looks at him, not a typical Nicola Manning look, but a strong, uncompromising, no-more-secrets look. 'Well?'

Timmy twitches awkwardly in the gaze of the three girls. Then he brightens up. 'We could stay in our summer house! It's at the bottom of the garden. It's warm and dry, and there's loads of rugs, and—'

'Hey, we could all stay there!' says Gemma.

Nicola and Timmy look at their feet, and eventually Kelly coughs. 'Nah, Gem, I think we'll go back to yours.'

'But—'

'Gem,' says Kelly quietly but forcefully.

'Ah, right,' she says, twigging at last. 'Fine. Come on then. We'll have to top and tail. I hope you've washed your feet.'

They stand around for a moment longer, then Gemma says, 'Do you think Arthur was serious? Do you think he'll stop us rehearsing there now?'

Kelly shrugs. 'We're knackered if he does. We only just got the guitar as well. And the gig's on Friday night at the Diamond.'

'We could just not do it,' says Timmy. Nicola winces.

'We are bloody doing it,' says Kelly. 'One way or another.'

They walk to the gate together then Gemma and Kelly hive off down towards the Avenues, and Timmy and Nicola off to the canal bridge. They walk not so close together that their bodies are touching, but close enough that their arms and sometimes their hands brush with a spark of static as they come off the main road and on to the canal towpath, to lead them to the back of the houses.

'Ssssh!' he hisses, pointing at the darkened windows at the rear of his house. He makes a pantomime of silently lifting the latch on the gate and easing it open at a glacial pace, then ushers Nicola into his garden. He points at the angular shape of the summer house on the lawn, what looks to Nicola like a glorified shed, then he does a comedy tiptoe stride across the grass. Nicola rolls her eyes and follows him, and it takes another three minutes for him to retrieve a key from under a garden gnome and unlock the door and let them both inside.

'Can I speak now or have they got it wired up with microphones?' says Nicola, looking round. There's a small wicker table and two chairs, and a wooden box overflowing with cushions, rugs and ethnic woven blankets.

'You don't have to be so sarcastic,' says Timmy in a normal voice. He starts to get the rugs and blankets out and fashion two neat beds on the parquet floor.

'Just make one bed,' says Nicola. Timmy frowns at her. She says softly, 'Do you want to give me a kiss?'

Timmy presses his lips against hers again and puts his cold hand on the side of her face. Nicola is hot, and needs to get out of her coat, but she doesn't want to interrupt the moment.

Someone else, however, saves her the trouble, as the door to the summer house is wrenched open, a blinding light shines on them, and the voice of Timmy's dad bellows, 'What the bloody hell is going on here?'

✳ 42 ✳

December 31, 1944

'But you have to come, Molly! It's New Year's Eve!'

Liz pouted at herself in the cracked mirror and applied another layer of bright red lipstick. Rita gave her a stricken look. 'Liz! Don't use it all! It's almost at the end as it is.'

Molly tried to concentrate on her book, sitting on the bed in the attic room of the farmhouse, which she shared with the two others. A pair of stockings suddenly landed on her open page.

'There'll be more of that tonight. And these. Come on, Molly, get your glad rags on.'

Molly sighed. Liz was from London and seemed to have spent all her life going to parties. She'd been like a dog straining at a leash when she joined the Women's Land Army and had been sent to North Yorkshire with the rest of them.

'She's right, Molly,' said Rita, inspecting the remnants of the lipstick. 'Old Norman's given us the next few days off. You're not wasting them with your nose in a book.'

There would be enough hard work for them on the farm for the rest of January, Molly had to admit. Silage to be spread on the frost-hardened crop fields, the calves would have to be weaned on to sugar beet. Norman was a tolerable boss, but worked them hard. She looked at Liz, all coolly blonde and London sophisticated, and Rita, fiery and Mancunian and red-headed. They were both in their underwear and their stockings, and any minute now they would start to fight over whose turn it was to wear the black dress they both adored.

'I'm not in the mood for dancing,' said Molly, placing the

stockings to one side of her on her bed. 'Besides, you just want to dance with Americans.'

Rita and Liz looked at her as though she'd just stated the obvious. 'Don't you?'

Molly turned the page. 'Well, I'm not sure what my Arthur would say about that.'

Liz laughed, a sound that tinkled like a breaking champagne glass. 'I'm sure your Arthur, being in Paris and all, is having an absolute whale of a time.'

Molly felt her cheeks burning. She couldn't deny she'd been worried about that. Paris had been liberated in August; as far as she could tell from Arthur's letters home, which took a painfully long time to be forwarded to her at the farm, he was doing very little other than waiting for the war to be over. She'd heard about those French girls and what they were like. Arthur loved her, she was sure of it, and they'd faithfully promised to each other that they would be wed as soon as the war was finished. And now they were saying it could be any time now, that the enemy was on the run.

As if reading her mind, Rita perched on the corner of Molly's bunk. The attic was dry but it was cold, and there was no electricity up here. Liz had put their entire collection of oil lamps at the dressing table so she could put her face on, save one that Molly had fiercely protected so she could read.

'Molly,' said Liz, arching one eyebrow. 'The war might be over soon. Arthur will be back. You'll have the rest of your life together. Come out tonight; have fun. It's New Year's Eve. Let's say goodbye to 1944 and hope next year is a little brighter.'

Rita held out the lipstick. Molly hesitated, then laid her book face down on the bed, and took it from Rita's fingers. She sighed.

'Fine. But I'm not staying out late. And I'm not dancing with any GIs.'

'Overpaid, oversexed and over here,' trilled Liz. She tossed the coveted black dress on Molly's bed. 'And it's your turn for this.'

As Rita and Liz fell into a half-serious catfight about the ownership of the frock, Molly held it up, wide-eyed at its soft satin sheen and scandalous tightness.

Much later, she would say it was all because the dress. She had to put the blame somewhere, after all.

The New Year's dance was in Skipton, and Norman had taken them there in his wagon, dropping them on High Street where Christmas lights still gaily blazed and soft snow whirled in eddies in the moonlight. 'Tha'll have to make thi' own way back,' he'd cautioned. 'A'll be cracking into't whisky soon as a'hm home.' They all kissed Norman on his bald head, leaving bright red lipstick marks there. 'Daft buggers,' he'd muttered, though his cheeks were rosy and a smile played on his lips as he rammed the wagon into gear and chugged back along the road.

The dance was in the town hall and the cold of the night gave way to heat and chatter and the sound of a band swinging like everything was all right with the world. The three of them checked their coats and pushed into the hall. It was full of men in uniform, Americans stationed just a few miles to the north. Around the edges of the dance floor there were the few local boys who hadn't gone to war, through health problems or having reserved occupations, or who were home on leave themselves, glowering as the GIs took all the attention of the land girls and the local women.

'Brad!' shrieked Liz, waving frantically at a tall man with a square jaw and twinkling blue eyes. She said conspiratorially to Molly, 'He's the one who gets me the nylons and the lipstick. Isn't he an absolute dreamboat?'

As Brad whisked Liz away on to the dance-floor, Rita appeared at Molly's elbow with two glasses of punch. Molly looked at it doubtfully. Rita sighed. 'Molly. Look. Please try to just enjoy yourself, eh? We're here to just make memories. Nice, happy memories in a world that's dreadful. Nothing more.'

Molly took the glass and sniffed at it. It was fruity. She took a sip, then downed it in one. Rita laughed, wide-eyed. 'Bloody hell, Moll. Go easy! It's not pop!'

Then a GI with slick hair was there, holding his hands out at Rita. 'Baby, baby, baby!' he said, in that thrilling American accident. 'Where have you been all my life?'

'Chorlton-cum-Hardy,' said Rita, pushing her glass into Molly's hands. 'But now I'm right here. You going to ask me to dance, or what?'

As they whirled away and the band struck up 'Swinging On A Star', Molly stood there for a moment, feeling a little stupid. Nobody had asked her to dance. But she didn't want to, did she? She wondered what Arthur was doing. Was he at a dance, too? Was he asking some French girl with thick black eye make-up and a cigarette where she had been all his life? Molly drank the rest of Rita's punch. It was nice, and it warmed her up from the inside. She watched the dancers for a while, catching flashes of Rita's red hair and Liz's platinum blonde, then went to get herself another glass.

Molly wasn't sure how many glasses of punch she'd had when she became aware of a man looking at her. He was standing with three others, leaning on the wall at the back of the hall. He wore a pale khaki uniform and his eyes shone in his dark face. Molly averted her eyes, then stole another glance. She had never really seen a black man before. They didn't have any back home and she'd only glimpsed the black GIs stationed near Skipton from a distance. Their eyes met briefly and he looked away.

Molly scanned the dance floor for Liz and Rita, and wondered how long it was until they went home. She wasn't quite sure how long they'd actually been there. She looked back towards the GI, but he'd gone. She felt unaccountably crestfallen. She should just go home, go and get a taxi. Molly whirled round to go and immediately crashed into a solid figure, her glass flying to the floor.

'Oh, my, ma'am, I am so sorry,' said the GI, bending down to pick up the pieces of glass. 'Let me get you another drink.'

It was him. Molly watched him straighten up, a head and a half taller than her. 'I was just leaving,' she said.

The man nodded and looked down at his feet. 'Sorry again, ma'am.'

Molly felt strangely annoyed. Was she so terrible compared to Liz and Rita? Shouldn't he have made a little more effort to get her another drink? Surprising – shocking – herself, she said, 'Actually, you can get me another one.'

When he came back he had one drink. Puzzled, she said, 'Do you not like punch?'

'I wouldn't want to presume to drink with you, ma'am,' he said.

'Stop calling me ma'am,' she said. 'My name's Molly. What's yours?'

'George, ma— Molly,' he said, smiling. He had wonderful white teeth. 'Delighted to make your acquaintance.'

'I thought you might have asked me to dance,' said Molly. Inside she screamed at herself. What are you saying? What are you doing?

George smiled ruefully. 'Not sure it's my place to ask a fine-looking lady like yourself to dance. Why, back home . . .' he trailed off.

'Where's back home?'

'Montgomery, Alabama,' said George.

'Don't you have fine-looking ladies like me in Montgomery, Alabama?' she said boldly. She was simultaneously appalled and proud; it was something Liz might have said.

George smiled. 'We sure do, Molly. Maybe not quite as pretty as you. But they're not for the likes of me to dance with.'

Molly was confused. Perhaps it was the punch. 'Soldiers, you mean? GIs? Are you not allowed to dance in Montgomery, Alabama?'

George looked at her curiously, as though he wasn't quite sure whether she was making fun of him or not. His eyes seemed to harden slightly. 'Blacks, ma'am. Why, if I even talked to a lady like you . . .'

Molly didn't ask him to continue. She suddenly thought she knew what he meant. Alabama was in the south, wasn't it? She'd seen in the newspapers about some of the things that went on there. Instead, she said, 'But they don't mind you going to war for them. Where have you seen action?'

George looked her in the eye, and held her gaze this time. 'I was at Omaha Beach,' he said quietly. 'Normandy. In the summer.'

'Was it terrible?' she said quietly.

George nodded. 'It was hell, Molly. Hell on Earth. I took a bullet to my thigh. I didn't think I'd get out.'

Molly bit her lip and then said, 'Would it be all right if I asked you to dance, George?'

226

He glanced around. For the first time, Molly noticed some of the other GIs, the white ones, casting looks at the pair of them talking. Some of them weren't friendly looks. Maybe the Americans had brought more than lipsticks and nylon stockings over with them. Maybe they'd brought some not-so nice things too.

Before George could speak, Molly said, 'I've changed my mind. Would you like to get some air? You can perhaps walk me to a find a taxi to' take me home.'

George smiled broadly. 'I'd be honoured, Molly.'

She thought the cold air might have had a sobering effect, but it seemed to do the opposite, causing her to stagger as they stepped outside. She instinctively put a hand out and grabbed George's arm; it was solid and strong. After a moment's hesitation she kept her hand there, and linked him as they walked on the frost-sheened pavements.

They walked in silence for while, up towards the ancient castle. They passed a number of taxis, but Molly didn't pause. She felt George looking at her and returned his stare. He said, 'That's a beautiful dress, Molly.'

'I have a sweetheart,' she blurted out. 'His name is Arthur. He's in Paris.'

She shivered and George pulled her closer to him. She didn't pull away, or complain. He said after a moment, 'I do, too. She's in Montgomery. Her name is Recy.'

'That's a pretty name,' said Molly. They turned at the top of the lane, around the castle walls, where it was dark and quiet. The moon was high in the night sky. 'What would she think, George, to see you walking with me like this?'

George was silent for a long moment. Eventually, he said, 'The way I see it, Molly, Recy is in Alabama and I am here. I'll always love Recy and she'll always love me; at least, she says so, and I believe her. But I don't like to think of her being alone and scared while I'm over here. So maybe there's somebody walking her around town like this right now. And maybe that makes her feel safe and happy. And, so long as I don't think about that too much, maybe it should make me feel happy as well. Recy and me, we're forever. That's just for tonight, or tomorrow, or the day after.'

'You make me feel safe and happy,' whispered Molly. 'Just for tonight.'

George nodded. 'That's the way it goes, I think. If we can't look after our loved ones because we're so far away, maybe we have to look after someone else. For a little while. So we don't forget how to love.'

Molly stopped. She leaned against the rough stone walls of the castle, which rose darkly up above them, blotting out the stars. She said, 'George, I would have danced with you. Happily. Proudly.'

He smiled sadly. 'I should have danced with you. I'm sorry we didn't, Molly.'

'Then you can do something else to make up for it.'

George raised a quizzical eyebrow.

Molly put her hands on his elbows, and pulled him towards her. 'Will you kiss me, George?'

* 43 *

Arthur reads the letters, then reads them again. And from them he manages to put together a picture of what happened, a film running in his head, one that makes his heart break right in two.

By the time he's finished he realises he's been up all night, and that the slightest paling of the sky in the east heralds a fine, bright dawn to come. He is up against the wood burner, has been absently feeding kindling and logs into it as he reads the letters that Molly had sent to Leon over the past ten years. Letters that had answered Leon's questions. Where did I come from? Who was my father? Where was I born?

Why did you give me away?

From a completely detached point of view, he is surprised at the way Molly wrote, how good she was with words, how her letters painted a vivid portrait of those hidden, secret, shadowed corners of her life of which he had been blissfully ignorant for so many long years. *You could have been a writer,* he thinks to himself, and the very idea of it almost makes him weep. How had he not known this about her, that she had this ability to put words down on paper with such heart-wrenching beauty? Molly had saved the letters he'd sent to her during the war, and when he brought her letters home from France she put them together in an old shoebox. He stands stiffly and goes to dig it out now, taking out the yellowing sheets of paper and reading them again, marvelling at the sheer poetry in her language. He'd always just accepted it, that Molly had a nicer way of putting things down than his clunky, stuttering phrases. But now the beauty and rhythm of her words does indeed bring tears to his eyes.

Why had he never seen this? Why had he never encouraged it, celebrated it, feted this talent?

Why had he never sent her flowers?

In one letter, Molly replied to something Leon had obviously said along the same lines. *Thank you for your kinds words*, she'd written. *I do enjoy writing. But I don't think books and such are the sort of thing people like me do.*

It's just like with The Mollies, thinks Arthur. Kelly and the rest. Nobody thinks anybody from round here is worth a damn. Nobody gives them the chance to do anything. And that goes double if you're a girl. Everybody's born equal, or so they say. Unless you're born right on to the scrapheap.

'I never knew,' says Arthur, out loud. 'How did I never know?' And he feels a stab of guilt that he didn't know, that he never took the time to find out. Molly was happy, he'd always thought. Their lives were full enough. The only thing that was ever missing was children, and they got by well enough.

Or so he'd thought.

And from a completely undetached point of view – because how can he be detached from what he's just read, this tapestry of lies and secrets that has taken the unshakeable foundations of the trust his decades with Molly were built upon, and wrecked them, bringing down his whole life in a shower of dust? – he is angry. He is furious. He is heartbroken and numb.

It's true. It's all true. Everything Leon said was the truth.

Leon is Molly's son.

Arthur is tired and jittery and cold. He looks at the fire. He looks at the letters. Then, his mouth set in a straight, loveless line, he touches the corner of the sheaf of handwritten papers to the licking flames of the wood burner.

Around noon, there is a knock at the door of the chapel. Arthur had managed to have a couple of hours' sleep, tossing and turning and going through everything in his mind in the tiniest detail. Even when he had slept, he'd dreamed of Molly in the arms of George. He is just boiling the kettle; he hopes it isn't the girls – he can't even bring himself to think of them as The Mollies any more. He knows he spoke harshly to them but he's still raw and does not want to talk to them. But it isn't the girls.

It's Leon.

'I said I'd come back for the letters,' he says, staring at his feet. He looks starved and freezing on the step.

Arthur nods his head towards the kitchen. 'I've just put the kettle on.'

While making the drinks, Arthur says, 'How was your night?'

'I've had worse,' says Leon.

'Do you want something to eat? I've got bacon and eggs. Black pudding. Do you a few mushrooms and a sausage.'

He hears Leon sigh raggedly. 'That would be very kind of you.'

While the bacon is sizzling and spitting in the pan Arthur brings over the letters. Leon looks at the corners of them, singed and brown. Arthur says, 'It's only the edge. It doesn't affect the writing. I'm sorry. I was angry. I nearly did it, but I didn't.'

'I understand,' says Leon, folding the letters and putting them in the inside pocket of his jacket.

Arthur watches Leon wolf down the fry-up. He can't face food himself. When he's finished, Leon takes the plate over to the sink and washes it himself. Then he stands awkwardly and says, 'I suppose I should go now.'

'Yes,' says Arthur. 'I suppose you should. You did what you came to do.'

Leon nods. 'Thank you for the food. You didn't have to.'

'Sit down,' sighs Arthur. 'I'll make another cup of tea. There are still things I need to understand.'

Leon does as he's bid. Arthur makes the drinks then thinks for a bit, and says, 'I got back to Molly about a week after you'd been born. I was told there'd been an accident and that's why she couldn't have babies with me.'

'There were complications with my birth,' says Leon slowly. 'She told me in her earlier letters. I don't have them. They were stolen from me in a hostel with some other things.' He pauses. 'They got me out alive and saved mum's life, but it damaged her inside.'

'And what happened to you?'

Leon closes his eyes. 'It had been agreed I would go for adoption as soon as I was born. Mum – Molly – didn't even look at me. She said she kept her eyes tight closed until they'd taken me away. She said . . .' he looks at Arthur, and there are tears in his eyes. 'She said if she'd seen me then she might not have been able to give me up and that would have been wrong because you had to be the most important person in her life.'

'Did she name you?' says Arthur.

'No. She told me in her letters that she couldn't bear to.'

'And did you ever meet up?' Arthur tries to wrack his brains, thinking of times when Molly could have stolen away to meet Leon in the years before she died, perhaps claiming she was going to bingo, or shopping, or—

'Never,' says Leon. 'I would have loved to have done, though. But she said it wouldn't have been right. That I'd grown up without her, and I didn't need her now.'

Arthur feels tears prickling at his own eyes. He says softly, 'Did you get adopted by a nice family?'

Leon smiles crookedly. 'It was 1945. Nobody wanted a mixed race bastard. That's what we say now, isn't it? Mixed race. Back then it was half-caste, or worse. I ended up being sent to an orphanage for babies in London. Then I grew up in kids' homes. When people came round looking for babies or children to adopt, they never gave me a second glance.'

Arthur stares at him. 'You never had a family? At all?'

'I had a family, eventually,' says Leon. 'Just the wrong sort. When I was a teenager I got involved with some gangs in East London. I got into trouble a lot. I did time in Borstal, and then Wormwood Scrubs.' Arthur feels himself shy away and Leon says, 'Nothing violent. I never did anything violent. I never hurt people.' He goes quiet for a long time, and says, 'Not until I joined the army.'

Arthur sips at his tea. It's gone cold already. He says, 'I saw your tattoo yesterday. Welsh Guards, am I right?'

Leon rolls up his sleeve again and Arthur can see the crest properly on the paler skin on his forearm, what he recognises now as a leek. And the motto beneath it: *Cymru am Byth*. Wales Forever. Above the crest is tattooed: *Galahad*.

'You were in the Falklands,' says Arthur. 'On the *Sir Galahad*.'

A faraway look appears in Leon's eyes. Arthur has seen that look before, many times. During the war, in Paris. In the hospital, on the men who just sat in the gardens and never spoke, and who flinched at the sound of a car backfiring or a door slamming. In the eyes of the men who hang around the asylum seeker hotel at the Old Hall, just up the road. The look that says *I have seen things. Things you wouldn't understand if you haven't seen them yourself.*

The look that Arthur saw in his own eyes in the cracked shaving mirror in the final days of the war.

'It was 8 June, 1982' says Leon eventually. 'They were putting us off in Port Pleasant. I was thirty-six. Was going to leave the Guards, but then the Falklands happened. It had been a good life. Turned me around. I was happy, even over there. I made proper friends. Then these three Skyhawks came out of nowhere.'

Arthur waits for him to go on. He knows he's reliving every moment, hearing the bombs hit the ship, seeing the flashes and the roaring walls of fire and the plumes of thick black smoke.

'We were just about to get off the boat,' says Leon softly, almost to himself. 'My mate Carl was standing at the side of me. I just heard him scream. And then nothing. He was on fire. Right at the side of me. On fire. I grabbed him and dragged him to the edge and we went over into the water and I could just see bubbles around me and that was it, I thought, I was going to die.'

Leon stares at his hands for a long time, and Arthur notices the smooth patches there, skin grafts on his palms. From where he grabbed his mate and tried to drag him into the sea to put out the fire that was killing him. Leon looks up.

'I heard later they'd winched me out of the sea, on to a Navy helicopter. There was no sign of my mate. I always wondered whether I should have just left him, whether he'd still be alive if I hadn't done that.'

'Did you leave the Guards after the Falklands?'

Leon nods. 'But the Guards didn't leave me. Nor did the Falklands.' His mouth quivers and there are tears in his eyes. 'I don't think I've ever had a night's sleep where I didn't see Carl on fire at the side of me.' He blows out a long sigh. 'After the Guards, I tried to get work, but I couldn't hold a job down. I spent some time in a hospital.'

He touches his temple. 'A mental hospital. I thought I should have died instead of Carl. I thought it was wrong I was still in the world. And that's when I started to wonder where I came from, and I got in touch with an adoption service, and eventually found the right people who said they would pass on a letter to my mother.'

Arthur says, 'And what have you done since then?'

Leon shrugs. 'Drift. Do a bit of work here and there, casual labour. Stay in hostels sometimes, at winter. Walk. Nothing.'

Arthur makes another cup of tea while he thinks about things. Then he says, 'Did you ever get in touch with this other feller, this George? Your father?'

'One letter. He replied and said I wasn't to contact him again. He married Recy and they had six children. I don't know if he's still alive.'

Arthur stares at the boiling kettle. 'Did . . . did Molly keep in touch with him?' Well, why not? She's spent ten years secretly corresponding with the son Arthur never knew she had. Why not with her lover. The word is like a punch to his gut. Her *lover*.

'Mr Calderbank . . .' says Leon softly. 'Arthur. Molly and George . . . they were just two lives who brushed together. A glancing blow. A temporary thing. As short-lived as a butterfly. It was never meant to be anything more. It was never meant to be real.'

Arthur turns to look at him. 'You're real. You're what came out of it. You make it all real.'

'She loved you, with all her heart. She told me that, but I could tell from her letters anyway. She said you were a lovely man. Generous. Warm. Big-hearted. She was right. I've seen what you did for those girls.'

They drink their tea in silence, and eventually Arthur says, 'Where will you go now?'

'Probably try to find a hostel for tonight. It should be fine. There are more places open on Christmas Eve.' He smiles. 'People like to help us at this time of year, even if they'd rather we didn't exist the rest of the time.'

Arthur blinks. 'It's Christmas Eve. I'd totally forgot.'

Leon stands up. 'Well, I should get into town to sort something. Thank you for not burning the letters. I understand why you nearly did. But they're very precious to me. They're all I have of her.'

Arthur walks him to the door. 'Were you planning to come back next year? On her birthday?'

Leon shakes his head. 'No. I've caused enough trouble. It's time to let it go.'

Arthur says nothing, just watches Leon walk away from the chapel. He feels the weight of stares upon him, and can only imagine it's the ghosts of Fred and Mabel and Mr Gaskell and young Noah. Staring at him. Willing him to do something, to say something. And the heaviest stare of all is Molly's. And, somewhere, somehow, though Arthur can't imagine why, he feels Peter Bergmann, looking at him down the long tunnel of years.

Christmas Eve, thinks Arthur, watching the figure of Leon dwindle in the distance. He shakes his head, and closes the door on the lot of them.

* 44 *

Nicola's mum is waiting for her in the living room when she gets home. The plastic Christmas tree has been put up in the corner, at last, but her mum hasn't bothered with baubles or even lights. It just looks like a dead thing in the gloom. Nicola stands in the doorway, staring at her mum, still in her dressing gown.

'You didn't go for your paper round,' says her mum dully. 'Cliff phoned for you. I said you were ill.'

Nicola stays nothing, just continues to look at her mum.

'Where have you been, Nicola?'

'I stayed at my friend's,' says Nicola levelly. 'Then I went to the library.'

Her mum stands up at last. Her hair is unbrushed. Her eyes are lifeless. She's having one of her bad days. Nicola steels herself inside. It's about to get worse.

'You're lying. You've been with a boy. What have I told you? How many times have I said it? You don't get involved. You stay with me. When the End Times come—'

'Shut up shut up shut up!' screams Nicola, shocking a flash into her mum's eyes. 'Stop it! Stop talking like this! It's not normal.'

Her mum's face hardens. 'Normal? You don't want to be normal. The *normal* won't survive. When the time comes—'

'Please,' says Nicola quietly. 'Shut up.' They glare at each other for a moment. Then Nicola says, 'Why didn't you tell me?'

'Tell you what?'

Nicola can feel tears coming, but blinks them away. 'That when dad killed himself, he tried to kill me too.'

Her mum's eyes widen, then her shoulders slump. She sits down heavily on the sofa and stares at her hands. 'Who told you?'

When Timmy's dad had shone the flashlight at them, his mum hovering behind, touching her head and saying this was bringing on one of her funny turns, Nicola had pulled her coat tighter around her and sat up. Timmy's Adam's apple bobbed and he blinked rapidly, like he wanted to run away.

'Timothy?' said his dad, almost incredulous. 'Are you with a girl?'

Timmy's mum slumped against her husband, which was a tad dramatic, thought Nicola. His dad took a step into the summer house. 'Get up. Get inside.'

He shone the light into Nicola's face. 'Who the hell is this? What are you doing with my son?'

'I know her,' said Timmy's mum.

'She's one of those carol singers,' said his dad. He frowned. 'That was all some sort of scam, wasn't it? To get Timothy out of the house.'

'No,' said his mum. 'I know who she is. She's the Manning girl. They used to live up by the park. He killed himself.'

'Mum,' said Timmy, breaking his silence at last.

His dad gave a little self-satisfied smile. 'No wonder she's leading Timothy into bad ways. After what happened to her.' He shone the light at her again. 'Stay away from him, right? It's no surprise you're bonkers, given what happened to you, but I don't want you turning my lad weird as well.'

Nicola got to her feet. 'What do you mean, what happened to me?'

'Trevor,' said Timmy's mum quietly. 'She might not know . . .'

'Know what?' said Nicola, her voice cracking.

Timmy's dad grabbed his son roughly by the shoulder and pushed him out of the summer house. 'It was in all the papers. He killed himself and he tried to take you with him. It's no wonder your mother went over the edge.'

'It took me a while to find the articles in the library,' says Nicola, putting down a small sheaf of photocopies on the sofa. She sits down next to her mum. 'In the inquest report his name is down as Kevin Simpson.'

'That was his name,' says her mum. 'Manning is my maiden name.'

Nicola says nothing for a moment, and then, 'I read these. I know I was one when he died, so I went through all the papers for 1983 until I found these. But I want you to tell me what happened.'

Her mum takes a deep breath. 'Do you know that photograph you like? You're on my knee in the garden of our old house. Your dad took the photograph. You can see his shadow on the lawn, from the sun behind him.'

Nicola nods. 'It's my favourite. We look so happy.'

'It was a lie,' says her mum quietly. 'That was taken the day he tried to kill you.'

They say nothing for a long moment, then her mum looks into the middle distance, as if seeing down the long years to that summer's day. She begins haltingly, 'When I first found out I was pregnant with you, your dad didn't take it very well. He had just been made unemployed. He was drinking a lot. We were worried that we'd lose the house. Then I found out he was seeing another woman.'

Her mum looks down, and Nicola can see tears on her face. 'Go on,' says Nicola.

Her mum nods and composes herself. 'And then he started to hit me. Said it was all my fault. Said I should have been more careful. Said I was dowdy and fat and that's why he went with other women.' She looks at Nicola. 'I started divorce proceedings before you were born. I went back to my maiden name. I didn't want you to be a Simpson. I didn't want you to have anything to do with him.'

'But the photos,' presses Nicola. 'There's more than one.' She thinks of the photograph of her and dad in the locket.

Her mum nods. 'After you were born, he kept pushing to see you. He said he was sorry, he was a reformed character. He got a job. He said he didn't want these other women. He only wanted me and you. He wanted to be a family.'

'So why didn't you let him?' says Nicola sharply.

Her mum looks her in the eye. 'I tried, Nicola. I allowed him to come round. I let him see you. But when a man has done what he's done . . . when he's *hit* you . . .' She shakes her head. 'I couldn't be sure. Couldn't be sure he'd changed. And I could never trust him again.'

'So what happened on that day?'

Her mum gathers her thoughts. 'I'd sent a letter to him from a solicitor saying I didn't want to reconcile and I'd prefer it if he didn't come round again. He begged for one last chance to say goodbye to you, and then he'd leave us.' She smiles, without humour. 'I didn't realise he meant it literally. It was a hot day, and we were in the garden. I didn't really want him in the house. We chatted, and it was quite amicable and friendly. He promised he was a better person, and said he hoped I would change my mind in a year, or two years, or however long it took. He was actually quite sweet.'

Nicola runs her hands over the photocopies. 'These say he stabbed himself with a kitchen knife. Is that what he was going to do to me?'

Tears are flowing freely down her mum's face now. 'You needed changing. He asked if he could do it, one last time. He'd been so nice, I thought there was no harm in it.' Her mum lets out a strangled sob. 'He took you inside. I waited. And waited. And started to get worried. I came into the house in case he needed help. He'd taken you upstairs to your nursery. I don't think he heard me coming up the stairs, because when I opened the door he jumped and looked shocked.' Her mum closes her eyes. 'You were lying in your cot and he had a pillow over your face.'

Nicola's hand flies to her mouth. She thinks she is going to be sick.

Her mum says, 'I just picked up the nearest thing. It was a vase from a shelf. I threw it at him and screamed. It hit him on the head and he fell away, taking the pillow with him. I just ran and grabbed you and you started crying and I've never been so glad to hear that sound in my entire life.'

'What did he do?' whispers Nicola.

Her mum takes a deep breath. 'Then I saw he was holding a knife. A big carving knife from the kitchen. My blood ran cold. It was only then that I realised what he was doing. He said to me, *if I can't have a family, then you aren't going to have a family either.*'

Nicola says nothing, just stares wide-eyed, willing her mum to go on. Eventually she does. 'I just turned and ran, ran down the stairs holding you, screaming, out of the door, into the garden and into the street. I turned round but he hadn't come after us. The neighbours came out and I just screamed and screamed at them, told them to get the police and an ambulance for you. It felt like an hour before the sirens sounded; they said later it was three minutes.'

'And Dad?'

Her mum closes her eyes. 'They found him in your nursery. He'd cut his own throat with the knife.'

They sit there in silence. Nicola stares at the Christmas tree. It seems weird and alien and wrong. Everything is quietly falling down around her, everything she thought she knew, everything she believed.

Her mum starts talking again. 'You suffered no ill effects. But I did. Not long after, I had a nervous breakdown. You had to live with my mum. She was still alive then. She died not long after herself. You don't really remember her. I went into hospital for three months.'

'Is that why . . . is that why you're . . .?' Nicola can't find the words to finish the sentence.

'Not long after I came out that film was on the TV. *Threads*. It was a bad time, Nicola, everyone thought we were going to be at war with Russia any day. Nuclear war. You've seen *Threads* often enough; you know what it's about. Something chimed with me, especially with the mother and daughter trying to survive.' She rubs her face with her hands. 'I'd seen how close I'd come to losing you. I'd seen what men were capable of. I wasn't going to let that happen again. I had to be ready. Had to prepare you.' She looks squarely at Nicola. 'It will happen. It will come. And nobody will ever separate us.'

Nicola sighs and stands up. 'Where are you going?' says her mum.

She goes out into the yard and wheels the bike in. Her dad's old bike. She dumps it on the living-room carpet. Then she goes upstairs and gets her bass guitar, and puts that with the racer. Finally, she takes the necklace out of her coat pocket, flips open the locket, and looks for a moment at the photograph of her dad and her, before dropping it on to the guitar case.

'This was all his stuff. I don't want it any more.'

Her mum looks at her. 'Nicola, what have you been doing? Where have you been going every night? Is it a boy?'

'Yes,' says Nicola. 'And no. I've got friends. We're in a band.'

Her mum frowns. 'A band?'

'We're called The Mollies. We're really good. I've been having fun, Mum. I've been having a life.' She looks down at the bike, at the bass. 'Now I find out that I nearly died when I was a baby. And I wonder why you would spend all these years not letting me have a life. I thought it would have been the other way round.'

'I just wanted to protect you,' says her mum hoarsely.

Nicola looks at her for a long time. 'You practically locked me away. Cut me off from everything. Filled my head with horror. You're no better than Dad, really.'

Then she turns around and walks away.

45

Kelly is watching *Emmerdale at Christmas* with her mum when her brother Mick bundles his way into the house, wearing a Santa hat and laden with Kwik Save bags and bellows, 'Merry Christmas! Ho ho ho!'

Her mum jumps up and helps him with the bags. Kelly can see they're stuffed with food, a turkey, potatoes, Christmas pudding, bottles of wine. Her dad looks at them, then quietly takes himself off upstairs.

'Ignore your dad,' says her mum, carrying two of the groaning plastic bags to the kitchen. 'He's a bit down.'

'I heard,' says Mick, rubbing Kelly on the head as he passes. 'Ugh, how much shit do you put on your hair, Smelly?' He wipes his hand on his jeans.

'Fuck off, Prick,' says Kelly, staring at the TV. Her dad has still barely spoken to her. She glances over at the bags. 'How come you're Mr Moneybags all of a sudden?'

Mick tips her a wink as he carries the last of the bags through. 'Been doing a bit of extra work. And don't swear like that in front of Mum.'

Her brother shrugs off his coat and throws it over the sofa. 'Any chance of a brew, Mum?'

'Kettle's going on, love,' she calls from the kitchen.

Mick sits down and rubs his hands together. 'That was a shitty move, you know. Making dad miss his interview.'

Kelly rolls her eyes. 'It wasn't my fault. It was Heather Wilson. Why's nobody going round hers to whine at her?'

'Because you started it, from what I heard,' says Mick. 'And got yourself sacked from Pete's stall in the process.' He shakes his head. 'Kelly, we all do stuff we're not meant to, but you have to be clever, right? Don't get caught and don't let somebody else have the last word.'

Her mum brings him in a cup of tea then heads back to the kitchen to finish putting the shopping away. Mick says, 'I also heard you're playing a gig at the Black Diamond on Friday.'

'You hear a lot.'

He taps the side of his nose. 'Keep my ear to the ground. No, I think it's dead cool.'

Kelly looks at him. 'Are you taking the piss?'

Mick puts up his hands. 'Honest, no. I do think it's great. Have you told Mum and Dad?'

She shakes her head. 'Don't really want them there. It's just a practice, in front of a few people. It should be quiet on Friday, everybody's skint from Christmas and saving their money for New Year's Eve.' She glances at him. 'We're doing Battle of the Bands the week after, though.'

Mick looks impressed. 'You're really going for it, aren't you?'

'Well, what am I supposed to do? Pack sprockets for the rest of my life?'

'Kell, we've been through this . . .'

'Mick? Can you give us a hand with this turkey?' shouts her mum.

'Do the band, yeah, but keep one foot in the real world,' says Mick, getting up to go see Mum.

Kelly stands up as well. Mick says, 'You going out?'

'Yeah,' she says. 'See a bit of the real world.'

Kelly lies on Gemma's bed, sorting through a pile of CDs. 'You can have them,' says Gemma carelessly. 'They're nicked.'

'I wish my dad nicked stuff,' says Kelly.

'No, you don't. It's shit. That's why you're right, Kelly. We have to make The Mollies work. We have to get away from here.'

'We should go and see Arthur,' says Kelly.

'Yeah, we should,' says Gemma. She looks towards the window at the sound of two car doors slamming. 'Hang on.'

'Shit,' she says, as Kelly joins her and sees the two uniformed officers walking up to the door from their police car.

Kelly feels her insides turn to water. 'Oh, God. Are they after us? Maybe that Leon said we assaulted him or something.'

'Don't be stupid,' says Gemma. 'Remember whose house you're in; the pigs don't even bother knocking any more. Come on, let's see what's happening.'

In the living room Gemma's dad and mum are sitting on the sofa while the twins, Cheryl and Carrie, are sitting on one of the moth-eaten chairs, crying in unison. The two coppers are standing by the TV, and on the coffee table are two Buzz Lightyears in their boxes.

'Come on, Terry, lad, let's not play silly buggers,' says one of the officers. 'It's Christmas Eve. Let's just get this sorted out and we can go to our Christmas do and you can get yourself a lawyer for a nice little court appearance in the New Year.'

'I've no idea what you're talking about,' says Gemma's dad.

The other officer sighs. 'Terry. We know that the warehouse was done over. We know that it was probably somebody on the inside. We know that Buzz Lightyears are on the top of everybody's Christmas list and, hey, presto, we come knocking and you're wrapping a couple up in front of *A Question of Sport*. How about you turn out your pockets and let us have a look round your gaff?'

'Is that all you've got?' says Gemma. Kelly glances at her in surprise, as do the coppers.

'The grown-ups are talking, love,' says the first officer.

Gemma holds his gaze. 'Have you got a warrant?'

The two officers look at each other. 'We're just making inquiries. Your dad's been good enough to let us in.'

'We're allowed to search people if we believe a crime has been committed,' says the other.

Gemma smiles. 'According to Section 60 of the Police and Criminal Justice Act 1994, yeah, you are. But only in an area authorised by a senior police officer if they've reasonable belief criminal activity has or is going to occur.'

Kelly stares at Gemma. How does she know all this stuff? Emboldened, her dad pipes up, 'That's right! You tell them, love.'

The first copper glares at Gemma. 'This is the Swarbrick house-hold. We have reasonable belief that criminal activity is or is going to occur here on a daily bloody basis.'

'That's not reasonable grounds to come into the house,' counters Gemma. 'You're going to have to leave, and come back with a warrant. But I can save you the time. Wait here.' She goes to her coat hanging on the stairs and comes back with a receipt that she hands to the first officer.

He scrutinises it and hands it to the other. 'And you purport that this receipt for £75 from Debenhams for goods obtained on 13 December is for these two items on the table?'

'Along with a couple of other things,' says Gemma. 'Christmas presents.' She looks at the twins. 'For my sisters. Christmas presents that you've just ruined for them by coming in here and making my dad come in from the kitchen with them while my pregnant mum was wrapping them up in the living room. God knows what the stress is doing to her.' She smiles. 'Don't worry, it'll all be in our formal complaint.'

The two officers look at each other, and the first sighs and points at Gemma's dad. 'We're watching you, Terry. We're always watching you. One of these days you'll make a balls-up, either you or Crushing Ken. And we'll be back.' He puts on his helmet and glares at Gemma. 'And you've got a smart mouth, girl. You should learn not to be so bloody uppity.'

When the police car has pulled away, Kelly remembers to breathe. 'That was amazing. So that's why you collect other people's receipts.'

Gemma shrugs. 'You just have to know how to handle them. And yeah.' She taps her head with her finger. 'Always thinking, right?'

'Bloody well done, lass!' says her dad, clapping her on the back. 'We live to fight another day, eh?'

The twins have already started squabbling over which Buzz Lightyear is best.

Gemma gives Kelly a pained look. 'Fancy getting out for an hour?'

Kelly nods. 'Yeah. I was thinking we could maybe go over to Arthur's? Even if he was serious about kicking us out, we at least need to get our kit back.'

Gemma grabs her coat. 'And we need to get all the dirt on Nicola and Timmy as well . . .'

✳ 46 ✳

Arthur is listening to carols on the radio when the first knock comes. It's Nicola, on her own. She looks upset, and angry. He looks beyond her to the dark graveyard.

'It's late,' he says. 'And it's Christmas Eve. I'm not sure I'm in the mood, to be honest.'

'I just needed to get out of my house,' says Nicola. 'I'm sorry. I know you don't want to see us any more. I went to the bunker but I just wanted to talk to someone.

Arthur grunts. 'What's the matter, love? You look like someone died.'

Nicola looks at him, tears rolling down her face. 'Somebody did. And I nearly did as well. And apparently it was common knowledge to everybody but me.'

Then it all comes flooding out. Arthur listens to it all, and doesn't have the faintest idea what to say. He'd heard about her dad, he remembers now, but wasn't sure he'd had all these details.

'That's awful,' he says eventually, realising how inadequate it sounds.

Nicola looks up at him, tears magnified by her glasses. 'You'd never have done that if you and Molly had children, would you, Arthur? Nobody would ever do that.'

Then she buries her face in his woolly jumper and begins to sob. Not quite knowing what to do, he awkwardly enfolds her in his arms. No, he thinks, I would never have done that. Not in a million years. Not if I'd had children.

They're still standing there like that when the next knock comes. Arthur carefully extricates himself from Nicola, who says, 'It might be Leon.'

'I'll be sending for the police if it is,' mutters Arthur, flinging open the door. But it's not Leon, it's a woman, pale with dark rings under her eyes, her hair messy.

'Is Nicola Manning here?' she says. 'I'm her mother.'

Arthur sighs and asks her to come in. Nicola groans and puts her head in her hands. Mrs Manning looks around the chapel.

'Is my daughter bothering you, Mr Calderbank?'

'No, no she's not,' says Arthur. He thinks carefully how to phrase his next words. You have to be careful with mothers. Especially mothers like this. 'She's been a tremendous help to me.'

'Mum, what are you doing here?' says Nicola. 'How did you find me?'

Mrs Manning pulls her coat tighter around her. 'I went asking for you at Kelly Derricott's house. I spoke to her mum.' Her face hardens. 'You didn't stay there last night, did you?'

Nicola is about to speak but her mum puts up a hand. 'It doesn't matter. Not right now. Mrs Derricott told me you'd probably be rehearsing. With your band.' She looks at the drum kit in the corner, and Kelly's guitar leaning against the wall.

'I told you, Mum,' says Nicola. 'I don't want to talk about it. About any of it. I'm not coming home just yet. Can't you just leave me alone for a bit?'

Mrs Manning nods thoughtfully, then goes to the door. She opens it but doesn't leave, instead reaching around to the outside wall. When she comes back in she's carrying what Arthur recognises as Nicola's bass guitar case.

'If you're going to be doing band practice you'll need this,' she says.

Nicola looks away. 'I told you. I don't want it.'

'Mrs Derricott told me you have a gig or something next week. How are you going to do it without your bass?'

Nicola frowns at her mother, but says nothing. Mrs Manning begins to unzip the case. She takes out the bass and walks over and holds it out by its neck at Nicola.

'I don't want anything of his.'

'Nicola,' she says. 'I was wrong not to tell you. But I never thought it was the right time. I always thought that I would wait until you were old enough. But when was that going to be? How old do you have to be to be told something like that?'

'It's not just that,' mutters Nicola. 'It's everything. It's how you are with me.'

Mrs Manning smiles sadly. 'I was wrong about that, too. I can't stop how I am, Nicola, I can't help what I feel or think. But maybe I can try. I'm going to get help again. Straight after Christmas. I don't want to feel like this. I want to look forward to the future, not dread it.'

Nicola looks at her mum, and she's crying, and Arthur can feel something in his eyes as well. He turns away and surreptitiously rubs them. When he glances back, Mrs Manning has crouched down in front of Nicola, steadying herself on the bass.

'This was his, Nicola, but it's not *him*. It's yours. It's *you*. You've made it your own. And you can do good things with it. The rest of it . . . it's just history. History's only good for one thing, and that's making sure we don't make the same mistakes twice.' She pushes the guitar towards Nicola. 'This is who you are, not who he was.'

Cautiously, uncertainly, Nicola puts out a hand and takes the bass.

Mrs Manning stands up and looks at Arthur. 'It's quite late, Mr Calderbank. Would you like me to take Nicola home?'

'Can I stay for a bit, Mum?' says Nicola. 'I just want to do a bit of practice.'

'Well, if Mr Calderbank doesn't mind . . .'

And suddenly he doesn't. He feels bad for what he said to the Mollies. He walks Mrs Manning to the door, and says quietly, 'Did you mean what you said, about history being of no use?'

Mrs Manning smiles. 'We can't change history, Mr Calderbank. But we can learn from it. And we can move on from it. That's what I've realised today. What's done is done; it's what happens to us next that's important. And that's the thing we can have a say in.'

Arthur opens the door, and jumps a little; Timmy is standing on the step, carrying a plate covered with a tea towel. 'It's a yule log,' he says, apologetically. 'My mum made it for you.'

Arthur lets him in as Mrs Manning heads off into the darkness, and Nicola and Timmy look at each other, but don't speak. Arthur frowns. What's going on between these two? Lover's tiff? He hovers on the edge of them, and says, 'Piece of yule log? And a cup of tea?'

Before he can even put the kettle on the door goes again. It's like *A Christmas Carol* round here today. But no ghosts, just Kelly and Gemma, together. 'The gang's all here,' says Arthur.

He makes them all tea and cuts up the yule log. They're all sitting quietly on the pews, staring into the fire. 'It's Christmas Eve,' he says with forced jollity. 'What's up with you lot?'

'Well, you told us to bugger off, if I remember rightly,' says Gemma. 'We just came back for our things.'

'Where are you going to rehearse?' says Arthur.

'We'll find somewhere,' says Kelly. She looks around. 'Where's Leon? Did he come back?'

Arthur frowns. 'He came back for his letters. Why would you think he would still be here?'

They all look at each other, as though the answer's obvious. Gemma says, 'Um, because he has nowhere to go? And it's Christmas Eve?'

Arthur shrugs. 'And what's that to do with me?'

Even Nicola is looking curiously at him. 'He's Molly's son.'

'And doesn't that make him sort of your stepson?' says Timmy.

Arthur can feel his anger rising again. 'No it does not!' he says. 'He's nothing to do with me. Nothing.'

Gemma stares at him. 'My two older sisters both have different dads than me,' she says. 'My dad took them both on. He loves them as much as me or the twins.'

'That's different,' says Arthur.

'Family's family,' says Kelly.

'Leon's not my family!'

'He's Molly's family,' points out Nicola.

'And Molly was your family,' says Timmy.

'You don't understand!' says Arthur. His chest feels tight. 'You're too young. You can't know what it means to find out that . . . that . . .'

He sits down heavily. 'Look, you can stay. For as long as I live here, which isn't long. I miss having you around. I like the music. Can you play that song for me?'

'Which one?' says Kelly, picking up her guitar.

"Things Can Only Get Better," says Arthur, feeling tears beginning to trickle down his cheeks.

'Everybody have a good Christmas?' says Timmy as they stand outside the Black Diamond. The weather has warmed up slightly, and the roads are wet and shining, reflecting the orange light of the lamp posts. On the pavement near the main door is a blackboard on which is written in rain-streaked chalk, *Tonite – local band The Mollies*.

Gemma leans on the pebble-dashed wall of the pub, smoking. 'Yeah. Every man and his dog squeezed round a tiny table. Everybody pissed by the Queen's Speech. Bullseye chewed up one of the Buzz Lightyears.' She shrugs. 'The usual.'

'I watched *The Wizard of Oz*, which was better than what we watched last year,' says Nicola.

'What was that?' says Gemma.

'*Panic in Year Zero*.'

'Sounds festive,' sniffs Gemma.

They've already been in earlier in the afternoon to set up their instruments in the little back room where they're playing. Kelly had a thrill as she saw the drum kit, and the guitars and their tiny amps leaning on chairs on the little wooden platform. It was really happening. The Mollies were playing live to complete strangers. Timmy had been true to his word and asked for a mic and amp, and even got a little box with twiddly knobs on that could do special effects. There's a tarnished mirror in the room, and Kelly had posed in front of it, in her new Adidas tracksuit top that Mick had thrust into her hands on Christmas Day, holding her guitar slung low.

'Did you get your PlayStation as well?' asks Nicola. 'Even after . . . after what happened?'

Timmy nods. 'They'd already bought it by that point.' He kicks his feet at the wet pavement and stares at his trainers. 'I think they just want to forget about . . . me being caught in the summer house, and the band . . .'

Kelly's dad was still giving her the silent treatment, but he'd thawed a bit by Christmas morning. He'd bought her a book. She thinks he's been labouring under the misapprehension it's about being in a band, because it's called *On The Road*, by some old dead guy with a French-sounding name that Kelly can't remember properly. It's about hitchhiking across America, as far as she can gather. When she was flicking through it, her eyes lit upon a passage that she kept re-reading and has almost got off by heart. All about mad people and roman candles, which she thinks are like fireworks.

Even though it's not, as her dad thought, about bands, there's something weird about the rhythm of the writing in the book that makes her think of music. She didn't know books could be like this – the ones they read at school are usually dull. Kelly wants to be one of the mad ones, the ones who want everything all at the same time and explode like fireworks.

'Are we just going to play the two songs?' says Nicola, breaking into Kelly's daydreaming.

'We only know two songs,' says Kelly. 'We'll just do them twice.'

'We could do "*Rock 'N' Roll Star*" three times,' suggests Gemma, lighting another fag. 'We're good at that.'

They are good at it, as well. It's like it's in the blood. 'We'll do it again for an encore, if they like us enough,' decides Kelly. 'What time is it?'

Nicola looks at her digital watch. 'Nearly seven.'

Kelly feels something yawn in her stomach, like she needs to go to the toilet really, really badly. 'Oh, God, we're on at half past.'

They've all been home for their teas and extracted promises from their parents that they will not come along – except for Timmy, who has not told his mum and dad that he's playing the gig. 'They already think I'm flushing my future down the toilet,' sighs Timmy.

They are about to go in when a crowd of men appears around the corner, laughing and talking about the football. Kelly gapes as she recognises one of them.

'Prick! What are you doing here?'

Her brother grins and pats her head. 'Still too much shite on your hair, Smelly.'

She pushes him away. 'What are you doing?'

'Told Mum I'd come and keep an eye on you. You're still kids, you shouldn't be in a pub on your own.'

'Y'all right, Mick?' says Gemma.

'Get you a pint in,' says one of Mick's mates to him, peering at The Mollies. 'You the band, then?'

"Course we're the band,' pouts Kelly. 'Best one you've seen this year.'

He laughs. 'I saw Oasis at Maine Road in April. But no pressure, eh?'

Mick pauses before following his mates into the pub. 'Seriously, though, Kel. Knock 'em dead. I'm proud of you.'

'Oh, shit,' whimpers Timmy when they've gone.

Kelly frowns at him. He looks terribly pale, all of a sudden. 'What's up with you?'

'I feel sick,' says Timmy.

'Don't be such a wimp,' says Gemma, throwing her fag butt on the floor.

'It's all right for you,' he sulks. 'You can hide behind the drums. I have to stand at the front.'

'It'll be fine,' says Kelly. 'Me and Nicola will be standing there, too.'

'But I have to sing,' whines Timmy.

'Yeah, that's your job!' says Kelly.

Timmy closes his eyes and takes a deep breath. 'All right. Let's go in.'

They push into the snug and Jon, the landlord, points towards the back room where their kit is. It's a lot busier in the pub than Kelly was expecting, then she sees Keith Cardy and his gang taking up one half of the snug, making their plans for the rally next week. She looks round hopefully for Arthur; he'd said he would try to come but had been coming down with a bad cold for days. She can't see him; she hopes he's all right.

When they get into the back room, Mick and his mates are already there, taking up two tables. One of them shouts, 'Do you do requests?'

'Yeah, can you all please fuck off home?' yells Kelly back and they all collapse into laughter.

Nicola helps Kelly tune her guitar then hunches over her bass, while Gemma gets behind the drums. Timmy adjusts his microphone stand and taps the head; it thuds dully from the amp and he turns it off, then takes off his coat.

The three of them stare at Timmy, and Kelly says, 'Have you brought something to change into?'

He blinks and looks down at his neatly ironed white shirt, top button fastened and shoved into a pair of beige slacks, at his well-polished brogues. 'No. Why?'

'Because you look like you're going to the bloody Women's Institute or something,' says Gemma.

'That's exactly where I did say I was going!' says Timmy. 'Mum's made a load of cakes but she's having one of her headaches so I said I'd drop them off.' He points to a big carrier bag in the corner. 'I'll go after the gig.'

'Rock and roll,' sighs Kelly, then gets a roll of gaffer tape and begins to stick setlists on the wooden platform in front of each of the band.

'Do we really need this?' says Nicola. 'We're only doing two songs.'

'It's our first gig,' says Kelly, biting off a piece of tape. 'Yes, we do need this. We're doing it proper.'

A chant of *Why are we waiting?* goes up from Mick's mates. Kelly taps her wrist and looks at Nicola.

'Nearly half past.'

Kelly's insides feel like water. She strums the guitar experimentally, trying to picture in her head the chord changes, letting her fingers find the fret placings by instinct and practice. Attracted by the noise from Mick's mates, more people begin to file into the room, followed by Keith Cardy and his mob.

'What's all this? What's all this?' booms Cardy, peering through at the stage. 'Girls? In a band?'

'Oh, Jesus,' Kelly hears Timmy mutter in a quavering voice.

'Ignore them,' she says quietly. 'Pretend they're not there.'

The room is half-full now. Kelly jumps as the lights suddenly dim and red and yellow spotlights shine on to the stage. At the back of the room she can see the shining bald head of Jon the landlord, and his two thumbs raised in encouragement.

Nicola looks at her, and Kelly glances back at Gemma. 'I suppose this is it, then,' she says. She looks at Timmy and hisses, 'Announce us.'

'What do I say?' His face is stuck in a toothy, terrified grin.

'Never mind,' says Kelly, pushing him to one side. She clears her throat and says, 'Good evening, Black Diamond!'

There's a smatter of applause and a volley of shouts from Mick's table. Kelly's heart is beating ten to the dozen. Her mouth has gone dry. She suddenly feels for Timmy, having to sing to this lot. 'We are The Mollies!' she cries. There's a murmur of conversation and one or two claps. Kelly pushes on. 'And this is . . . "*Rock 'N' Roll Star*"!'

Kelly rushes back to her spot and Timmy takes his position in front of the mic. There's a moment's silence, and Kelly looks at the other three, waggling her eyebrows and counting them in with nods of her head. Come on, she wills them. Just like in Rimmer's music shop. We nailed it then and we can nail it now. Kelly hits the first, prolonged note. Gemma grins and does a roll on the drums and launches into the beat, and Nicola and Kelly stare at each other, wide-eyed, and then start to play together, and it's like the biggest rush that Kelly has ever had in her life. She's suddenly connected to everyone in the room, can hear the rhythm of their breathing, can feel the beating of their hearts, can feel their eyes on them. On The Mollies. Drums, guitar and bass, coming together to make a noise that is instantly, undeniably recognisable. That is music.

The intro is coming up to its end and Kelly looks up at Timmy, standing with his hand gripping the mic on its stand so tightly she can see the whiteness of his knuckles. She begins to see the lyrics in her mind, waiting for him to come in.

Which he doesn't. Kelly glares at him then at the others, and by some unspoken mutual agreement they almost seamlessly go into the intro again. It's all right, she thinks furiously. He just missed his cue. It happens. Then: I'm going to kill the skinny bastard as soon as this is over. At last she can see him almost shaking himself, as though he's waking up. They're coming up to the critical point, and at last she can see Timmy open his mouth.

Nothing comes out.

Kelly keeps playing but Gemma's all over the place on the drums and Nicola has taken her hands off her bass. Kelly stops and hisses, 'Timmy? What the fuck?'

He turns to her, his face drained of blood, that stupid grin stuck to his face, his lips peeled back off his teeth. 'I can't do it.'

'From the top,' commands Kelly, but Timmy shakes his head furiously.

'I can't. Not in front of all these people. I'm sorry.'

'Remember what Arthur said,' she whispers urgently. 'Pick out a friendly face.'

'There are none,' he whines.

A chorus of booing starts up from the crowd. Kelly elbows Timmy to one side and says in the mic, 'Sorry about this. Slight technical hitch. We're starting again now.'

They're now stamping their feet along with the booing. Kelly can hear laughter. Her cheeks start to burn. This is not what was supposed to happen. She can almost see Heather Wilson and Mr Green and every single one of them at school who thought she'd amount to nothing laughing at her, knowing they were right all along. She glares at Timmy and whispers, 'I swear to God, you get your arse here and start singing or I'll—'

And then a short, stout man wearing a flat cap pushes to the front, peers through his glasses at the stage, and shrieks in an unexpectedly high-pitched voice, 'Oi! Those are our fucking drums!'

Keith Cardy elbows his way into view as well. 'What's that, Graham? The drums?'

Graham is pointing with a quivering hand at the kit. 'The drums! The drums that were nicked! Them's 'em! You can still see the EFAF sticker on that bass one!'

Then Kelly notices that there are an inordinate number of young men in shaved heads and wearing Harrington jackets among the crowd. One of them puts up his fist and shouts, 'England First and Foremost!'

The chant is taken up and Cardy takes a step forward and says, 'Graham, are you saying these kids nicked your drums? The drums the band were going to play for the Hands Off Arthur's Chapel march?'

'The exact same drums!' squeaks Graham.

Kelly glances at Gemma. The blood has drained from her face. 'Oh, shit,' Kelly breathes. She looks around. There's a fire escape directly behind the stage. But what about all their gear?

The idiots in the pub are chanting, 'England First and Foremost! England First and Foremost! Hands off Arthur's chapel!'

'Well, let's take the drums back from the little bitches!' declares Cardy. 'Let's show them what we do to thieves around here.'

Cardy and Graham move forward, the chanting EFAF meatheads behind them. Kelly is rooted to the spot. Then a shout goes up and she sees Mick vaulting over the table from the corner, knocking over everyone's pints.

'Hey!' bellows Mick. 'Don't you lay a finger on those girls! That's my sister.'

And then everything goes to shit. Almost as though she's watching a film that's been slowed down, Kelly sees one of the skinheads take a swing at Mick, who ducks out of the way and rugby tackles him. Mick's mates jump up, knocking their tables over, and wade in. Cardy and Graham stagger back, pointing at the drums and shouting.

'Let's get the shit out of here!' shouts Kelly. She unplugs her guitar and her amp, picks one up in each hand and kicks open the fire door.

'What about the drums?' yells Kelly. Nicola is dragging the plug from her amp from the wall. Timmy is just standing there like a statue.

'Sod the drums, we've lost them,' says Kelly. Cardy and Graham are almost at the stage. 'Grab Timmy's mic and amp.'

'What about the cakes?' says Timmy dumbly.

Gemma grabs the carrier bag, reaches in and pulls out a Victoria sponge. She looks at it then hauls it across the pub, hitting Keith Cardy smack in the face. Kelly hears a crack and Mick is thrown on to the stage, rubbing his jaw. He looks up at her and grins.

'Get the hell out of here, sis.'

She winks at him and nods towards the door, Gemma propelling Timmy out and Nicola, whimpering like a dog, hurrying behind her with her bass. Kelly takes one last look at the chaos before following them, and can't help herself grinning. 'Now that's what you call rock 'n' roll,' she says to herself, as the wail of sirens sounds distantly on the night air.

They run all the way to Arthur's chapel, and collapse on a heap on the doorstep, laughing and panting and crying and swearing all at once. Arthur opens the door and stares down at them, nonplussed. He's wearing a thick jumper and a bobble hat, and coughs into a gloved hand.

'How did your concert go?'

'Amazing!' says Kelly.

'Are you insane?' says Nicola. 'It was the most terrifying experience of my life.'

'We lost the drums,' says Gemma. She picks herself up from the damp stone. 'Oh shit, we lost the drums.'

'And Timmy lost his balls,' says Kelly, wiping her mouth with the back of her hand. 'It was a complete disaster.'

Arthur sighs. 'I suppose you'd better come in, then.'

When Arthur's made them all a cup of tea and sliced up what's left of Timmy's mum's yule log, he says, 'And you knew the drums were stolen, Gemma?'

She shrugs. 'Well, they came from Crushing Ken. So there's every chance.' She taps the side of her nose. 'Ask no questions and get told no lies.'

Arthur doesn't approve, Kelly can tell. Well, of course he wouldn't. She doesn't approve either, but a set of drums was too good to pass up. And the fact they were stolen from a bunch of knobheads like EFAF somehow makes it . . . less bad. Like what Gemma was saying about robbing banks and victimless crimes. She's seen plenty of these EFAF types and people like them. Blame everybody else but themselves for what they haven't got, and the easiest people to blame are foreigners or those that are different.

'I don't know why you bother with Keith Cardy and that lot, Arthur,' she says. 'They're not interested in you, really. They just want to have a pop at those asylum seekers.'

Arthur looks at her for a long time, the way he did when they first met near Molly's grave. When he called her . . . what was it? Shrewd. Eventually he says, 'Aye, I'm not as green as I'm cabbage-looking. But I suppose it's what you'd call a means to an end for both of us, isn't it? He gets to have his little protest, I get to have people listen to me about keeping my home. I don't think anybody would be taking notice of me without the march.'

Kelly sits back on the pew. She feels exhausted now the adrenaline has left her. The enormity of what happened sinks in. 'Oh, God. We've got no drums. We're stuffed for the competition.'

Nicola is inspecting her bass for damage, and satisfied that it seems all right, zips up the carrying case. 'We've still got the guitars. I bet one of the other bands will let us use their drum kit. I can have a word with Des if you want.'

Gemma wipes chocolate from her chin and points at Timmy. 'Yeah, we've got a bigger problem though, haven't we?'

Timmy has stared at his feet since they got there and not spoken. Kelly sees Nicola put a hand on his, but he shrugs her off and stands up, and walks to stare out of the window. Arthur says quietly, 'What happened?'

'He can't sing,' says Gemma loudly.

Arthur frowns. 'But he's got a beautiful voice.'

'Yeah, but he can't use it in front of a crowd, apparently,' says Kelly. 'Which, when you're in a band, is a little bit of a problem for gigs.'

'It was just first-time nerves,' says Nicola defensively.

Timmy turns from the window. 'I can do it. It was just . . . it was just all a bit too much. I can do it.'

'You'd better do it,' says Kelly. 'One week tomorrow. At the Battle of the Bands contest. Provided Nicola can get someone to let us use their drums.'

Timmy goes to the door. 'I'm going home. I'm going to be in enough trouble about the cakes anyway.'

When he's gone, Gemma says, 'Do you think he can do it? Because I don't. This competition's going to have ten times as many people at it. He's got no chance.'

'He can do it,' says Nicola again.

'All right, Juliet,' sneers Gemma. 'Just make sure you do what you have to so that Romeo performs, yeah? Because I'm not getting up on a stage at Maxine's and making myself look as much of a tit as I did tonight.'

Nicola stands up. 'I'm going home. Are you coming?'

'Thanks for the tea and cake,' says Kelly, taking the plates to the kitchen. 'Did you see Leon over Christmas?'

'No!' says Arthur. 'Why would I?' He lapses into a coughing fit, banging his chest. 'Why would I? Besides, I've not been well.'

'Take care of yourself,' instructs Kelly, grabbing her guitar to practise with over the weekend.

She walks with Gemma to the road, Nicola marching off ahead. She says, 'You don't think he can do it, do you?'

Gemma shakes her head tightly. 'He froze. Like a deer in the headlights of a car. We're going to look like idiots.'

Kelly says goodnight to Gemma and walks slowly to her house. She still believes. Believes in The Mollies. She knows they can do this. After tonight, they *have* to do this. Because word will get out, it always does. They have to prove that they're not failures. She has to prove that she's not a failure. Otherwise, they'll be in a worse position than they were before they started all this.

Kelly frowns as she gets to her house. All the lights are off. It's too early for everyone to have gone to bed. She feels a flash of hope; maybe her mum and dad have gone out for a drink. Maybe things are getting better at home. She fishes in her pocket for her key, lets herself in, and climbs the stairs to collapse on her bed.

* 49 *

Arthur casts a critical eye over the room. There's a sofa and a chair, and a place for a television in the corner. The walls are white and clinical-looking, but softened at the window by floral curtains. At the back, near the door to the kitchen, there's a table, its sides dropped. 'Aye,' he says after a while. 'It's all right, I suppose.'

The Revd. Brown waggles an orange cord that dangles from the ceiling near the door almost to the beige carpet. 'There's one of these in every room. Don't mistake it for a light switch though, ha ha. Pull this and it sends a message straight to the warden's bungalow that you need assistance. Just a bit of peace of mind.'

Revd. Brown takes Arthur into the kitchen, which is tiny but looks out on to a postage-stamp size of garden. 'That's all yours, too. Let me show you the bedroom. It's all on one level, so no stairs to climb.'

'I've no stairs to climb at the chapel,' says Arthur, looking out at the little garden. You could probably just about get a bench out there, at the bottom. He can imagine himself sitting on it, with Molly, in summer. What he can't imagine is sitting on it alone.

'You're only five minutes from the shops,' says Revd. Brown, looking hopefully at Arthur. 'And you can be at the church where they're moving the graves to in ten, fifteen at the most. I could even come to pick you up if the weather's bad.'

Arthur makes a show of considering it, then smiles and shakes his head. 'I appreciate you bringing me here for a look, but I think I'll pass. I like it in the chapel. I'm near my Molly.'

Revd. Brown sighs. 'I know, Arthur, but with the planning application and everything . . . isn't it time to perhaps accept that you need to move on? This flat is available now, but it won't be for long. They've put a hold on it for today, as a favour to me. You could be in by next weekend.'

'No, I don't think so. I wouldn't want to miss the rally.' Arthur looks at Revd. Brown pointedly. 'You know, the one to save the chapel. The one organised by the people who know what's best for me, and that's to stay where I am.'

Defeated, Revd. Brown offers to drive Arthur back to the grave-yard but he says he'll walk. He needs to pick up a few bits from the front and fancies a swift half in the Black Diamond. When he's filled his little string bag with bread, milk, eggs and some more Coke for the kids, he calls in the pub to find the snug empty.

'If you're looking for Cardy and his crew, they're not here,' says Jon the landlord, frowning from behind the pumps. 'I had to bar the lot of them after last night. I'm not having brawls in my pub. The police were called, Arthur! Sarah was furious and told them they weren't to come back.' He looks round the gloomy snug. 'Bit quiet now, though, for a Saturday. If you want them, I think they've moved to the Rock Ferry.'

The Rock Ferry Inn is back along the main road, towards town, and the opposite direction to which Arthur is going. Besides, he's not really in any great rush to see Cardy again. 'I'll just have a pint of best,' he tells Jon, then sits in the corner, savouring the quiet and warmth.

Bereft of any more customers, Jon takes to wiping tables and replenishing beer mats. Arthur watches him for a moment, then says, 'What do you think about all this march business?'

Jon shrugs, wiping his hand over his bald head. 'I sympathise, Arthur. You've lived there a long time. It's your home.'

Arthur takes a sip of beer. 'But?'

Jon pulls a face. 'I just think you might have better people on your side than Keith Cardy. Those lads who were in here last night . . . England First and Foremost. I don't like 'em. I don't know if they've really got your best interests at heart.'

'Hmm. Somebody else said that to me.'

Arthur finishes his drink and walks back to the chapel; thinking. He knows he's just an excuse for Cardy and his boys to have a little jolly, but like he told Kelly, it's a means to an end, isn't it? He scratches their back, they scratch his. And maybe he gets to keep his home.

But then, he thinks, do I even want to keep my home? He stares at Molly's grave like it's a strange, alien thing he's never seen before. He doesn't know Molly at all, he thinks. Never really knew her. And if their entire life together was a lie . . . he looks at the chapel. What's the point of even living here any more?

Across in the old part of the cemetery he can see a lone figure trudging along the line of the wall. He recognises the waddling gait. Nicola.

By the time he gets there she's in the old broken-down mausoleum, the one they call the bunker. She jumps as he coughs in the entrance.

'Arthur! You scared me to death.'

He looks at the pile of plastic bags she's got. She's loading the stuff stacked against the stone walls into it, the tins of beans, the bottles of water, the candles. 'What are you doing?'

'Packing up. Taking all this stuff away.'

'Have you got a new bunker, then?'

She looks around at him. 'No.'

'Is there not going to be a war any more?'

'Probably. There's always a war.' Nicola stands up and hefts one full bag to the doorway.

Arthur says, 'So, why?'

Nicola takes her glasses off and rubs the lens on the hem of her coat. 'Because I want my mum to get better. And this isn't making her better. I was doing this because I wanted to help, wanted her to think I was doing something for her. But I was just making things worse.' She pauses, and thinks. 'Or at least, not helping her to get better.'

'You love your mum, don't you?' says Arthur thoughtfully.

Nicola frowns. 'Of course I do.'

'Do you have any other family?'

Nicola goes back and gets another bag, and starts loading candles into it. 'No, there's just me and my mum.' She looks at Arthur again. 'At least, that's what I'd have said a few weeks ago.'

'And now?'

Nicola thinks about it. 'Now I'd say The Mollies are my family. And I'd say you were my family. But it's a better family, in a way. Because we're not family because we have to be. We're family because we want to be. We chose each other.'

'Yes,' says Arthur. 'Yes, I suppose we did.'

50

While Arthur is looking around the flat, Kelly sleeps in late, and when she gets up her dad is sitting on the couch, in his dressing gown, staring at the TV. Her mum is in the kitchen, talking in a low, urgent voice. She pops her head round the door and sees it's her brother.

'Hiya, Mick.' Then she sees his black eye, and stifles a giggle.

'It's no laughing matter,' says her dad quietly behind her, and indeed she can see that Mick has his serious face on. Her mum looks at her, cheeks stained with tears.

Kelly looks at them, and back to her dad. 'What's going on? Why were you out last night? I thought you'd gone to the pub.'

Her dad barks a mirthless laugh. 'Pub? Chance'd be a fine thing. No, Kelly, we were down at the police station. Collecting your brother.'

Kelly bites her lip, remembering the wail of sirens as they ran away from the Black Diamond. 'Oh, God, did the cops turn up?'

Her mum brings in a tray of tea, pushing past Kelly in the doorway, and sets it on the little coffee table. She turns off the TV and instructs Mick to sit down. Kelly says, 'Did they do you for anything?'

Her dad gives his sneering little laugh again. 'Did they do him? Oh, they did him, all right.'

'I got charged with affray,' says Mick quietly.

Her mum is pouring the tea but the pot starts to wobble and clank against the rim of the cup, and she puts it down and puts her hand over her eyes. 'He could go to prison! For three years!'

'That won't happen,' says Mick. 'That's just the maximum sentence, and only if it goes to Crown Court. I'll probably just get a fine.'

'Oh, that's all bloody right, then!' shouts her dad. Kelly can see he's absolutely livid. He points a shaking finger at her. 'And it's all your fault. Everything is always your fault! Why does it always come back to you, Kelly?'

She blinks at him. 'What?'

Her dad rubs his forehead. 'Pissing about playing at bands. In a pub! The Black Diamond! You know Keith goes in there! What were you thinking? Trouble follows you round like a dog. If you're not starting bloody paint fights that lose me a job, you're getting a whole pub fighting and your own brother arrested. How am I going to show my face with them again?'

'It's not my fault!' screams Kelly. 'You can't blame everything on me!'

Her dad strides over to the back of the room, and snatches up Kelly's guitar. 'This what you were playing in the pub? Where did it come from?'

Kelly glares at him. 'It was a present. A Christmas present.'

'Who from?' shouts her dad, leaning into her, his teeth bared. 'Who bought it for you?'

'Arthur! All right? Arthur!'

Her dad's hand tightens around the neck of the guitar. 'Why's he buying you presents?'

Kelly's nostrils flare. She knows she's going to say it, even as she tries to stop herself. But it's as if it has to come out. 'Because you can't!' she screams. She jumps up, almost as tall as her dad, and points a finger back at him. 'Because you can't do anything! You can't get a job and you just sit around moping and when you do get a chance you blame it on me when it all goes wrong! You could have phoned Oldfield Engineering up and said you were going to be late for your interview. You could have told them what happened. But it's easier just to blame somebody else, isn't it? And you just sit there with Keith bloody Cardy saying it's his fault, or their fault, or anybody's fault! Everybody thinks what happens to them is somebody else's fault, instead of just getting off their arses and trying to make things better themselves.'

'Don't speak to me like that,' says her dad quietly.

But Kelly's blood is up. 'Why not? It's all true. You don't do anything. You never do anything. You're quite happy to sit in your dressing gown and whinge about how unfair the world is. You're happy to let Keith Cardy tell you it's immigrants who took your job away. You're happy to think everything is down to somebody else. You've been told you're worthless so many times that you've started to believe it.'

'I'm not worthless,' says her dad.

'But that's what *you* think you are!' shouts Kelly. 'People think we're all worthless on this estate. They think we're nothing. Jesus Christ, Dad, they tell me I'm worthless every day of the week and you're fine with that. When was the last time you ever asked me what I wanted to do with my life? Never. Because you don't think I want to do anything. You've had your life beaten out of you so why should I want to do anything with mine?'

Her dad stares at the guitar in his hands. 'I should have bought you this. *I* provide for my family.'

'But you fucking don't!' cries Kelly. She points at her mum. 'She's doing what she can to make ends meet, and if that means looking away when Mick stuffs a roll of fivers in her handbag, then that's all right.' Kelly slaps her head. 'And you know what? That *would* be all right. Because we're a family. We should pull together. But you've just . . . I don't know, withdrawn from us. It's not going right for you, so screw the rest of us while you just sit in there and try to find somewhere else to put the blame.' She shakes her head. 'You're pathetic.'

Her dad stares at her. 'Pathetic? I'll tell you what's pathetic.' He holds up the guitar. 'This is pathetic. Pretending to be in a band.'

'We're not pretending. We *are* in a band.'

'Playing games,' says her dad. 'You know what you need to do, Kelly? Open your eyes and see the real world. You're never going to be in a band. You're never going to be a rock star. You're never going to do anything.'

Kelly can feel hot, angry tears in her eyes. 'Don't say that.'

Her dad sneers at her, an ugly, twisted look. 'The sooner you wake up to how your life is going to be the sooner you can just knuckle down and get on with it.'

Kelly closes her eyes and feels the tears running down her face. 'You're my dad. Why would you break my heart like this?'

'You'll be happier in the long run,' he says. 'Dreams are for those who can afford them.'

'Brian,' Kelly hears her mum say warningly.

'Shit, dad,' says Mick.

When Kelly opens her eyes she shrieks. Her dad is holding the guitar by the neck, above his head, his face set in a determined grimace.

'Please, Dad,' she begs.

But he does it. He does it anyway. He brings it down on to the carpet with such force the body snaps away from the neck with a twanging of the strings. Kelly just stares in horror, rooted to the spot, as he lifts it and smashes it down again, and again, and one last time, before throwing the mangled, jagged pieces of the guitar down on to the floor.

He stands there, his eyes closed, breathing heavily as though he's just run a marathon, his shoulders slumping. Kelly waits until he opens his eyes, and his gaze – the fire gone out of it now, his eyes dead and black, like a shark's – meets hers.

'I fucking hate you,' she says.

Kelly elbows past him and goes upstairs to get changed, not even bothering with a wash or doing her hair. She gets her coat and shakes her head at them. They're all still standing in the living room, Dad and Mum and Mick, like they're a display at a waxworks museum, nobody speaking. Kelly wrenches open the door just as the postman is about to shove a sheaf of envelopes through the letter box. Kelly snatches them off him and turns back to the living room, throwing them at her dad.

'There you go,' she says. 'Overdue, overdue, overdue. Provide for your family, why don't you?'

She casts one more look to the wreckage of the guitar, then walks out and slams the door behind her, off to bury what's left of her dreams.

51

'You're kidding me,' says Gemma. 'He smashed it? To pieces?'

'To pieces,' says Kelly. She rifles through the tops on the rail in the shop. 'This is all shit.'

'Sales stuff,' says Gemma, looking around the shop. 'What about those cargo pants over there? Reckon you could get your arse into them?'

They push through the shoppers and Kelly holds the camouflage trousers against her. 'Yeah, I reckon so.'

'Great.' Gemma pulls a folded carrier bag bearing the shop's logo out of her coat pocket and swiftly sticks the trousers inside. She leads Kelly over to the service desk and holds the bag out. 'I want to return these, they're too small.'

The harassed girl behind the counter peers at the receipt Gemma is holding out. 'You'll have to join the main queue.'

Gemma looks around. 'But it's massive.'

The girl shrugs. 'Sales, innit? You can always come back another day.'

'I will.' Gemma and Kelly head for the door and Gemma feels Kelly jump as the alarm sounds as they walk through. 'Stay cool,' she murmurs. A security guard comes over and asks to look in the bag.

'I just brought these in, they're too big, my mum bought them for Christmas,' says Kelly, waving a receipt at him. She points to the girl on the service desk. 'Ask her.'

The girl sees them talking and waves, and the security guard shrugs and lets them go. 'They must have left the tag on,' he says, but then is distracted by another beep and heads off to another gaggle of teenagers.

'You've got balls of steel,' says Kelly admiringly.

Gemma shrugs. She used to get a kick out of nicking stuff, but she's just a bit bored by it now. It was a bigger thrill getting one over on those coppers when they came round about the Buzz Lightyears. The look on their faces still gives her a warm glow. She spots Timmy and Nicola leaning on the window of Waterstones. 'There they are, Zig and Zag.'

She pushes the bag into Kelly's hands. 'Don't say I don't give you anything.'

When they reach the others, Nicola says, 'Been shopping?'

'Five-fingered discount,' says Gemma. 'Kelly's got something to tell you.'

They wander through the arcade while Kelly tells the story again. Gemma's always mildly surprised at how bad other people's families seem to be at just getting on. Hers might be highly dysfunctional, but at least they never trash each other's stuff like that. She wonders what it is that keeps them all on an even keel, and then she realises.

It's honesty.

She almost laughs out loud. Everybody thinks Terry Swarbrick's the biggest crook on the estate, but she's right. It's honesty that kept them all together. No secrets, no lies, no hiding things. Not from each other, at any rate. A united front against everybody else. That's what families should be about.

'So what are you going to do?' Timmy is saying. 'Get another guitar? The competition's on Saturday.'

'I'm not nicking you one of those,' mutters Gemma.

'We're not doing the competition,' says Kelly.

Gemma stops, and looks at Nicola, then Timmy, who both stand there with their mouths open. 'What did you say?'

'I said, we're not doing the competition,' says Kelly.

'What the fuck are you talking about?' says Gemma, and an old lady in a furry hat tuts at her as she shuffles past. 'It's on Saturday. It's all we've talked about and done for the past month, nearly.'

Kelly rounds on them. She points at Gemma. 'You've no drums.'

At Timmy. 'He can't sing a note in front of other people.'

At herself. 'My stupid pathetic dad smashed my guitar.'

269

She looks at them all. 'Don't you see? It's over. All we've got left is Nicola and her bass guitar. Which is exactly where we started off. We've just gone round in a circle, and what have we got to show for it? Sod all.'

Gemma frowns. 'That's not really true . . .' she says. 'I mean, we've had a laugh, haven't we?'

'And we solved the Moonflower Mystery,' adds Timmy.

Kelly shakes her head. 'And where did that get us? All we did was screw up Arthur's life. It would have been better if we'd never done any of all this.'

'Not for me,' says Nicola quietly. Gemma sees her glance at Timmy. 'Not for me. Or my mum. It's changed my life.'

'We could still do Battle of the Bands,' suggests Timmy. 'If we're borrowing somebody's drums, could we not borrow a guitar as well?'

Kelly sighs loudly. 'It's not about the guitar. It's about what the guitar . . .' She searches for the right words. 'It's about what it meant.'

'Which was?' says Gemma.

'A dream,' finishes Kelly. 'A stupid dream. We're just going to forget about it all.'

'But we're good,' says Nicola. 'We could pull it off.'

Kelly closes her eyes and just shakes her head again.

'Hang on a minute,' says Gemma. 'What about *fuck that shit*? What about all that stuff you said to Green in detention? All that stuff people expect us to do, which is nothing? Get a dead-end job, get pregnant, waste your life watching daytime TV? What about, we're The Mollies, we can do anything?'

Kelly shrugs. She nods her head towards Timmy. 'He'll probably be a doctor, like his mum wants him to be.' She points at Nicola. 'She's clever enough. She'll probably do A Levels, now her mum's on the mend. Might even go to the music college in Manchester. Get out of this shithole.'

Gemma feels angry and upset all at the same time. 'And us, Kelly? What about us?'

Kelly looks her dead in the eye. 'Leave school with no GCSEs. Get a job in the factory. Drink so many alcopops we let some scrotey boy screw us and we get pregnant. Get a council house. Rinse and repeat.'

Please say *fuck that shit*, thinks Gemma furiously. Please say it. *Fuck that shit*. Just say it.

Kelly doesn't say it.

And at that moment Heather Wilson walks past with her gang, slowing as they pass the four of them. Gemma steels herself for a fight. Heather has a mobile phone, a Nokia, with the little aerial pulled out, saying loudly, 'Yes, Mum, I'll be back for dinner. See you later.'

Heather kills the call and pushes the aerial back in with the palm of her hand, keeping the Nokia visible. 'Oh, let me see, is it Blur or Oasis? Or is it a bunch of losers with a singer who can't sing and a drummer whose dad nicked her instruments?'

Gemma looks at Kelly, waiting for her to respond, but she just looks away. Gemma says, 'News travels fast.'

Heather waves the black slab of the Nokia at her. 'Well, you've got to stay connected in the modern age . . .'

The phone trills a little tune and Heather makes a big show of answering. 'Oh, hi, Dad.' She puts her hand over the phone and wrinkles her nose at them. 'See you in school.' She nods at Kelly. 'Hope your dad finds a job soon.'

When they've drifted on Gemma glares at Kelly. 'What is the matter with you? Why are you letting her get away with speaking to you like that? The old Kelly would have—'

Kelly cuts her off. 'No. The *new* Kelly would have done something. The Kelly who had stupid dreams. I'm the old Kelly again, the one who knows that dreams are only for those who can afford them.'

They stand in silence for a moment, then Nicola says quietly, 'I'd have thought dreams are for those who *can't* afford them. That's why they're dreams. People who can afford dreams don't need them, because they can just do what they want.'

'Dreams can come true, though,' says Timmy. 'Can't they? Didn't we nearly make one come true?'

'It's over,' says Kelly. 'I don't want to do this any more. It was stupid and childish. We've got to live in the real world now.'

'What happens at school?' says Timmy. 'Are we all still friends?'

Gemma raises an eyebrow at Kelly. 'Well?' she says.

Kelly looks back at her. 'What, you going to hang around with Nicola now? Am I going to have my dinner with Timmy?' She looks each one in the eye. 'We had the band. That's all. Now it's over. We should just forget everything. Move on.'

Timmy and Nicola look at each other. They'll still be together, thinks Gemma. What about me and Kelly? We knew each other before, enough to say hello to. Do we just go back to that? After everything that's happened?

'I'm going home,' decides Kelly. She smiles tightly. 'We'll still go to the march though, yeah? For Arthur?'

Gemma watches her go. She looks at Nicola, who says. 'I have to go, too.'

'And I've an errand to run for my mum,' says Timmy.

They both walk off in opposite directions, leaving Gemma alone.

And is that it? she thinks. Do I just go back to being Terry Swarbrick's daughter, the apple who never fell far from the tree? Being in the band has unlocked something in her, something she can't quite put a name to or identify properly. It's like a desire for more, for something other than people say she's meant to do, for a fresh hand of cards to play with instead of the one she's been dealt.

And Kelly Derricott wants to take it all away from her, wants her to go back to how things were, just because her dad smashed her guitar and trampled on her dreams. Does Kelly not realise it wasn't just *her* dream? It belonged to all of them. They're The Mollies. How dare Kelly just decide that it's over. It's not her decision. It's bigger than her. It's bigger than all of them.

Gemma is not going back to a life of no hope.

If Kelly isn't going to say it, then she will.

'Fuck that shit,' she breathes, and hurries in the direction that Nicola walked.

* 52 *

On New Year's Day her mum cooks a roast dinner, and Kelly eats it in silence while mum and dad chat. She's furious that they seem to be pretending nothing has happened. Kelly glares at her mum, hating her for siding with her dad. Mick and Jane are here, talking like nothing's happened. Only Mick's black eye to show for it. Plus, he probably paid for the food anyway.

On New Year's Eve her mum and dad had stayed in, as usual, because they didn't have any money. Her mum had opened a cheap bottle of white wine and her dad had had a four-pack of beer, and they'd watched Jools Holland's *Hootenanny* in strained silence. Kelly could feel a row brewing as her mum got to the bottom of the bottle, so had taken herself off to bed before midnight. The pieces of the guitar have been put in a black bin liner and dumped in the hall by the coats, like they want to rub her nose in it, remind her every time she leaves the house or goes upstairs that right there, in a bin bag, are the pieces of her dreams.

After the Angel Delight Kelly stands up and announces she's going out. She's planning to go to Arthur's to break the news to him about the guitar. She hasn't felt up to doing it since Saturday. It feels like that will make it all final, and irreversible. She knows he's going to be upset. He'll think that Kelly and her family and the rest of them are what everybody says they are, just scum.

'Where are you going?' her dad says.

'To Arthur's. Tell him what you did.'

'Sit down,' he says quietly.

'Fuck you.'

He slams his knife and fork down and says, 'Kelly!' She ignores him and gets her coat, noticing her mum waggling her eyebrows at Mick, who sighs and stands up as well.

'I'll walk with you,' says Mick.

She stares at him. 'Why?'

'I want to.'

'I don't want you to.'

Jane says, 'He needs to go and, uh, get something for me.'

Kelly shrugs and puts her coat on. 'Whatever.'

Kelly strides off up the Avenues, Mick hurrying behind her, zipping up his jacket. He catches her up at the top of the road and she turns off along the patch of spare land, intending to climb over the cemetery wall and cut through the old part of the graveyard to the chapel. 'Wait,' he says. Let's walk over here for a minute.'

He's pointing to the landscaped dirt dunes of the old mine site. Kelly shrugs and follows him through the spindly, leafless trees and on to the wide expanse of flattened land, bordered by the graveyard and the intercity train route. Kelly wonders if she'll ever take a train to London, and perhaps never come back. If she had the money she'd do it right now.

The site is scrubland, patches of tall grass and little hillocks of muddy earth, rainwater pooling in the divots carved out by motorbike scramblers. Half of it is going to be used for the proposed housing site for asylum seekers and refugees, which is going to spill over into the graveyard and result in the demolition of Arthur's chapel, unless the protest on Saturday changes things. Kelly follows Mick to the middle of the site, where there's a small pyramid made of stone. He taps it with his foot.

'This is where the main mine shaft was,' he says.

Kelly glances it and looks away, bored. Where is he going with this?

Mick looks around the site. He says, 'Dad started here straight from school. Marigold Brook. Half of his class did. They were told they had a job for life. It was dirty, and it was dangerous. But it what they did, Kelly. They dug the coal that powered the entire country.'

Kelly says, despite herself, 'I didn't know he actually worked down the pit.'

Mick nods. 'For a few years, I think. Then he got bumped up to supervisor, then manager. By the time you were born he was wearing a suit and tie and working in the office buildings. It was good money, and he was good at his job.'

Mick digs in his pockets and finds a cigarette, and lights it, shielding it from the cold wind with his hand. 'Then Thatcher started to close down the pits. The big strike happened in 1984, when you were two. I was seven. I remember it dead clearly.'

Kelly has seen pictures on the telly, and in books. 'Was he on strike?'

Mick shakes his head. 'I think he was on this team of managers and engineers who had to keep the mines maintained while they weren't being worked in. People were worried they might collapse or there could be a build up of gas. They had these special passes to get past the pickets. Arthur Scargill came down once to support the strikers. You know who he is? Boss of the National Union of Mineworkers. King Arthur, they called him. Dad said he shook his hand said to him, "I know you'd be out with us if you could. You're doing an important job".'

Kelly doesn't really remember her dad working at the pit at all, just flashes of him coming in at teatime and the first thing he always did was take off his tie, undo his top button, and sit down on the couch. But she remembers something else, from that haze of early childhood. The fact that he used to smile, and laugh, and play with her. Why did I never notice that man disappeared, she wonders?

'The strike fizzled out and men started drifting back,' he says. 'She'd beaten them. Thatcher had won. And she made the miners pay for what they'd done. They closed this place down ten years ago.' Mick takes a long drag of his fag. 'So much for his job for life, eh?'

'I was four,' says Kelly. 'I think that was when I remember him being at home all the time.'

Mick nods. 'He thought he'd walk into another job. He was a good worker, he'd had a lot of promotions, he was on a decent wage. But he'd been out of the job market for a long time. The pit was his first job and he'd never had to look for another. By the time it closed unemployment was over three million. There weren't any jobs.'

Kelly looks at Mick curiously. She didn't know he knew so much about stuff. She thinks what he might have done, if he'd been given a chance, an opportunity. But now he's just another Marigold Brook cast-off.

He says, 'The longer he was out of work, the harder it seemed to get. Even when he did get an interview in some place, they wanted to know why he hadn't had a job for three years, or five years. Suddenly everything was computers. Times had changed, things had moved on. He was being left behind.'

Kelly suddenly feels bad about what she'd said to her dad on Saturday. He shouldn't have smashed her guitar, but still . . . She says quietly, 'I shouldn't have called him pathetic.'

Mick smiles and puts a hand on her shoulder. She doesn't knock it away. 'He is pathetic. But it's not all his fault. He's broken. They broke him. He just wants to work and it's like they won't let him. He wants to look after you. He really does.'

'Why doesn't he just get a job, then? Any job?'

'That's what I wanted to talk to you about, really. On Monday I went to the Job Centre with him. There's not a lot but he says he's prepared to do anything. Work in a supermarket, a warehouse, a driving job.' Mick looks at her. 'He's a tiny bit less . . . broken, Kell. And it's your doing.'

She takes the cigarette from Mick and has a drag. 'What, because I called him pathetic?'

Mick shakes his head. 'There's something else. When we were going to the Job Centre we saw Mr Oldfield in the street. The man who runs Oldfield Engineering. Where he was supposed to have the interview.'

'I've met him,' says Kelly.

'I know,' says Mick. 'He told us. He told us what you did, going into the office and asking him if Dad could have another chance.'

'He said Dad would have probably got the job,' says Kelly. 'It really was all my fault.' She starts to cry.

'Come here, you daft sod,' says Mick, and embraces her. 'You're a good person, you know. And Dad has been a bit of a twat. But just . . . try to understand how he got from there to here.'

'OK, get off, Prick,' she says after a minute, pushing him away and wiping her eyes, but laughing as well.

'You don't have to tell me twice, Smelly,' he says, punching her in the arm. 'Look, if I can get some money together, I'll see if I can get you a new guitar. It won't be for a while, though.'

Kelly shrugs. 'It doesn't matter. We're not doing the band any more.'

Mick looks shocked. 'Why not? I mean, I know the gig was an utter fucking disaster, but you at least looked the part . . .'

Kelly doesn't say anything. Why not? She doesn't really know any more. She yearns to pick up that guitar again, to make that sound, for the noise from all four of them to wind itself together into something magical and big. But it's too late for all that now.

'It was just a stupid dream,' she says. 'And I can't afford dreams, can I?'

* 53 *

'So, we're going to start at the roundabout and walk up towards the cemetery. We're going to set up there, do the speeches. I reckon we'll have a good hundred of us, maybe more. The *Observer* is sending somebody to take photos and do a write-up.' Keith Cardy peers at Arthur. 'Are you all right?'

Arthur nods, coughing violently and banging his chest. 'Just a cold. I'll be fine.'

Cardy frowns. 'Will you be up for walking with us? Or do you want to meet us at here?'

'I'll see tomorrow morning,' says Arthur, wiping his mouth with a handkerchief. 'Do you think this is going to make any difference at all?'

Cardy nods vigorously. 'Absolutely. This is going to send a message to them as is in charge what they won't be able to ignore. They've walked all over us for too long. It's time they started putting the needs of people who were born here before anybody else.'

Arthur goes to the kitchen to get a glass of water to try to clear the frog in his throat and Cardy calls, 'Another cup of tea would be lovely.'

He looks back at Cardy and Graham, poring over sheets of paper and maps and speeches. He shakes his head and puts the kettle on. This doesn't really seem to be about him any more. He read through Cardy's planned speech and it's all about foreigners and immigrants and protecting people's rights.

'Is that how you spell indigenous?' he hears Graham say.

'I don't need to fucking spell it, I'm not going on *Countdown*,' says Cardy. 'I just need to say it.'

When Arthur brings the teas back Cardy shakes his head mournfully and says, 'I heard about what happened. With that bastard leaving flowers on your wife's grave. What a liberty. Must have been a shock for you, Arthur, finding out that your Molly had been up to all sorts with a . . .' He leaves it hanging there.

'Aye, well, that's got nothing to do with this, has it?' says Arthur brusquely. 'It all happened a long time ago. He's been told what's what and he's been sent on his way, and we won't be seeing him again.'

Cardy claps a big, meaty hand on Arthur's shoulder. 'Good man. Still, if he ever shows his face round here again, you can count on us to do the right thing.' He shakes his head again. 'Cheeky bastard.' Cardy consults his list and says, 'Item five. Graham, is the band all sorted?'

'Yes,' squeaks Graham, blinking rapidly. 'We're using the drums we got back from them thieving little sods. That lass what's been using them has bashed the hell out of them, though.'

Arthur coughs. Nobody has yet made the connection between The Mollies and him, and he's happy to keep it that way as far as Keith Cardy is concerned.

'Did you go to the police?' says Arthur tentatively.

Graham shakes his head. 'No point, really. The EFAF lads were happy they got a bit of a scrap in on Friday night, and as far as we can tell one of them lasses was Terry Swarbrick's daughter. Probably him and that Crushing Ken nicked 'em, but they seem to be made by bloody Tefal. Nothing sticks to them. We're just glad to have the drums back.'

'On the subject of police,' says Cardy, 'item six. I didn't bother putting a formal application in for a road closure. I've got a couple of mates on the force and they're just going to park their car at the roundabout for half an hour, block the road off on the quiet, like. One of them'll stand at the top, just past the Old Hall, to stop traffic coming down.'

'Is that it?' says Arthur. 'Only, I was planning on having a bit of an early night, get myself fit for tomorrow.'

Cardy glances down the list. 'Nothing else to trouble you, Arthur. That's all the important stuff sorted.' He drains his tea mug and stands up. 'Don't you worry, Arthur. We'll get this on the front page on Monday. They won't be able to ignore you any longer. We'll save this place.'

'Hands! Off! Arthur's Chapel!' shouts Graham, punching the air.

'Save your voice for tomorrow,' says Cardy. 'You're going to need it. Arthur, we'll say goodnight.'

A good night is anything but what Arthur has. He wakes himself coughing several times, and lapses into short periods of sleep disturbed by dreams that make no sense. His throat is dry and he keeps having to get up for water, his bones and muscles aching. He is drenched in sweat but freezing cold, and even deep under the blankets he has feverish shivers. He wonders if he should see the doctor, after the march is over.

He has no idea what time it is when he opens his eyes but it is dark and quiet, as though the rest of the world has ebbed away. He kicks his feet to try to disentangle his twisted blankets and comes up against something solid.

There's someone sitting on the end of the bed.

At first he thinks it's a burglar, or maybe one of the kids, or Keith Cardy, or even that Leon. He fumbles for his bedside light but can't find the switch. Then a voice says, 'Hello, Arthur.'

He stops what he's doing and slumps back on to his sweat-damp pillow, the strength draining from him.

'Hello, Molly,' he says.

'I've missed you,' says Molly.

Arthur reaches for the bedside table again. 'Let me put the light on. I want to see you.'

'Just talk,' says Molly. 'You haven't talked to me for a while. At my grave. Since you met Leon.'

'I didn't know what to say.'

There's a dry pause, and then she says, 'Are you very angry with me?'

'Yes. No. I don't know.'

'It's all right to be angry with me,' says Molly softly. 'But don't be angry at Leon. None of it is his fault.'

'I'm not angry,' says Arthur, deflated. 'I'm just . . . it feels like everything was a lie. Our whole life.'

He can't see Molly, other than as a shape against the darkness on the edge of his bed, but he imagines if he could she'd be raising her eyebrow at him, like she always used to do. 'What's changed, Arthur? What is different about the forty years we spent married?'

'Forty-three years,' says Arthur.

'Forty-three happy years. Are you saying that's all gone, now? Because of a mistake I made before we were even married?'

Arthur says nothing. He wants to put a hand out to touch her, to hold her against him one more time. But he's scared to, in case she melts away at the brush of his fingers. He says, 'Am I dreaming? Or am I dead, too?'

'You're alive, Arthur,' says Molly. 'But being alive isn't enough. You've got to live, as well. I think that's what those girls have showed you, isn't it? That people need other people.' She pauses for a moment. 'You can't go on just talking to the dead for the rest of your life.'

'I want to be with you,' whispers Arthur.

'You will be. When you're ready. But that isn't yet.'

Arthur feels his face tighten, his eyes grow even hotter. He puts his hands over them, feels the wetness there. 'I love you, Molly. I loved every minute we spent together. What you did doesn't matter. I wouldn't change one day that we spent together. I just wish . . . I wish . . .'

'Yes, Arthur?'

'I wish we could have had children. Wish we could have had a family all of our own.'

Molly says nothing and for a long moment he fears she's gone, like a will o'the wisp. But then he can almost sense her smiling in the blackness. 'You have got a family, Arthur. You've said it yourself. To the girls. Your family can be as big as you want it to be. All you have to do is open your heart.'

'My heart is full,' he whispers. 'Full of you.'

'That's the funny thing about hearts,' says Molly. 'They're big. Bigger than you could ever guess. And yours is the biggest heart of all. There's plenty of room in there, Arthur. Plenty of room for whatever family you choose.'

He breathes out loudly, sinking back into the pillows. He's so, so tired. Molly murmurs, 'You should sleep. You've a big day tomorrow.'

'Don't go,' he says, but he can feel his eyelids drooping, heavy as lead.

'I'm not going anywhere,' she says softly. 'I'm in your heart, remember? I'll always be in your heart.'

'Big day, tomorrow,' he murmurs.

'Big day,' agrees Molly. 'There are people relying on you, Arthur. People waiting for you to do the right thing. People who you can help, and who can help you. People who you shouldn't let down.'

He frowns sleepily. 'Keith Cardy?'

'Open your heart,' says Molly, but she already sounds distant and faint. 'Open your heart, and then you'll know.'

✳ 54 ✳

Arthur rises early, and puts on his best suit. He fastens his shirt cuffs with the links Molly bought him for his fiftieth birthday, and he delves into a trunk to find a long, thin, polished wooden box in which he's kept his regimental tie for the past half a century. He brushes his hair down and puts a little pomade on it. He has a shave and polishes his boots. And at long last he stares at himself in the cracked mirror he's hung behind the bathroom door.

Arthur Calderbank, he thinks.

He narrows his eyes. Who *are* you?

Arthur Calderbank, the war hero, figurehead of a growing movement for good, honest, hard-working British people to stand up and say, no, enough is enough, we will not be treated like this any more. We will not have the country we were born in overrun and the things we worked hard for taken away from us. And Arthur has worked hard, all his life. He turned this chapel from a shell to a home with his bare hands. And they do want to take it away from him.

Arthur Calderbank, the doting husband of a beloved wife taken too soon. The man who longed for children, but fate had other plans. Who instead poured all his love into his marriage, who never had a cross word for his wife, never spent a night apart from her, who loved and cherished her until she breathed her last. And even then, he couldn't bear to be parted from the place where she rested.

Arthur Calderbank, unlikely patron of a group of kids who had no hope, no opportunities, no ambitions. Until he let them into his home, taught them how to play, gave them a space for their dreams to take root and blossom and let them dare to think there was more in their futures than their lives had mapped out for them.

Arthur Calderbank, who was deceived and lied to and made a fool of. Arthur Calderbank who was betrayed by the person he held most dear in the world. Arthur Calderbank who can never trust another soul for the rest of the miserable years he has on this earth.

'Who are you?' he says. He has no idea.

He stands stiffly to attention and salutes his reflection. Today he must be Arthur Calderbank, the war hero. Even though the bottom has dropped out of his world, even though he almost doesn't care whether he stays in this drafty chapel or not, he has made a commitment. He must march for what is right. Or, at least, what people tell him is right.

Arthur Calderbank, the war hero. He stares at his reflection, and imagines he no longer wears his suit, but his uniform, and his hair is not grey, but black, and he is not here, at home, but there. It is not now, but then.

The Liberation of Paris was all but over by the time Arthur's unit marched into the city. The Free French 2nd Armoured Division and the US 4th Infantry had done most of the donkey work. The occupying forces had surrendered and were in disarray, many of them fleeing the city. Arthur's unit crossed paths with a rag-tag bunch on the outskirts of Paris; there was an exchange of fire. Arthur remembers sheltering behind a farm building, a bullet pinging off the corner of the stonework, sending shards and dust up in a cloud that he would always remember vividly sparkling in the August sunshine.

Arthur chanced a glance around the corner. The enemy was making a run for it, only half a dozen or so of them left. Suddenly, the big corporal who Arthur didn't like was at his shoulder, saying, 'For God's sake, shoot, man!'

'They're retreating,' pointed out Arthur.

The corporal sneered at him. 'Shoot. Or I'll have you up on a charge.'

Arthur stepped around the building and raised his rifle. There was a crack from nearby and one of the men running across the field fell down. Arthur fixed his sights on one man, then moved an inch to the left. He would miss, and by the time he took another shot the men would have reached the treeline at the top of the field. Arthur squeezed the trigger, but at the last second the man veered to the left, looming large in his sights just as Arthur fired off a shot.

The man threw up his hands, arched his back, and tumbled forwards into the dry earth.

The corporal clapped Arthur on the shoulder. 'Good man, Private Calderbank. That's the bloody spirit.'

Arthur stared through the sights, at the fallen man, a dark patch spreading on the back of his uniform, where Arthur had shot him. Where Arthur had shot him in the back.

A knock at the door brings Arthur out of his memories. It is Brian Derricott, who nods and says, 'Keith sent me to pick you up.'

There's a taxi waiting for them, and he sits in the back with Brian as it takes a circuitous route to avoid the closed-off main road and get them to the start of the march. Arthur says, 'Your girl, Kelly . . .'

Brian looks at him. 'Oh, God, what's she done now?'

Arthur smiles. 'She's a good kid. Strong-willed. Clever. And talented on the guitar.'

Brian looks at his hands. 'I'm, uh, sorry that I smashed the guitar. I take it she told you.'

'Yes, she told me.'

They sit in silence for a bit, listening to the local radio station. There's an item on the news about the march. Brian coughs, and says, 'Do . . . do you hold with all this that Keith says? I mean, about the . . . the asylum seekers and the . . .'

Arthur looks at him. 'Do you? You're one of his mates, aren't you?'

'Well, not really mates, as such,' says Brian, looking out of the window. 'I mean, I just started going in the Diamond, and drifted in with that lot, and Keith . . . well, Keith was the only person who'd really put it all together, for me. Why I couldn't get a job. He was the first person who made me feel like it wasn't all just my fault.'

'Aye,' says Arthur mildly. 'He's good at that, is Keith. Telling folk what they want to hear.' He pauses, then says, 'Somebody told me something once. It was something along the lines of this. *I think people always need somebody else to blame, don't they? But they don't always blame the right people. The government tells you that these foreigners are coming over and taking benefits and houses, and people start to blame them for what they haven't got, instead of the government.'*

'Sounds like the sort of thing Keith would call lefty bollocks,' says Brian.

'What do you think of it, though?' says Arthur.

Brian shrugs. 'Well, between you and me . . . I suppose it makes a lot of sense, really. Who said it?'

'Your daughter,' says Arthur, as the car pulls up outside the Rock Ferry Inn. He looks out of the window. There's a mass of people there already, with banners and flags. 'Looks like we're here.'

Keith Cardy is there to greet him as he climbs out of the taxi, throwing his arms wide and booming, 'Here he is! The man of the moment! What do you think of this, Arthur? Have we done you proud, or what?'

There must be a hundred people milling about in the road, half of them drinking pints from the pub. There are several dozen with shaved heads and bomber jackets, the EFAF crowd, and Graham's band is tuning up on the grass verge beside the pub. It looks like half the community has turned out, and Arthur can see banners and Union Jacks proclaiming them to be groups with names such as *British Force* and *Free England* and *UK Defence League* and more that Arthur is pretty sure aren't local.

Keith forces a pint in his hand but Arthur says, 'No, it'll just make me want to go to the toilet in this cold.'

He hands it to Brian as he gets out of the taxi, but Keith says, 'Quiet word, Brian. My lad Colin told me something last night. Apparently your girl decked him in the arcade before Christmas.' Brian looks at his shoes and Keith says, 'Just keep the cocky little cow under control, yeah?'

Brian mumbles something and Keith claps a meaty paw on Arthur's shoulder. 'Right, fella, we're all set. You come and join me at the head of the march, and we'll get this show on the road.

We're going to walk up to the cemetery, set up shop near the Old Hall, do a few speeches and that. You see, my old son, nobody'll be moving you an inch after this.'

Keith and Brian lead Arthur through the throng to the front, where someone hands Keith a loudhailer. He switches it on with a squall of feedback, and bellows, 'Right, we're off! Let's have something rousing, Graham! And all together now, Hands! Off! Arthur's Chapel! Hands! Off! Arthur's Chapel! Hands! Off! Arthur's Chapel!'

* 55 *

'What a shit-show,' says Gemma. Kelly is inclined to agree. The four of them have come out to the rally to support Arthur, greeting each other awkwardly, like nobody wants to say what they're all thinking. *We were in a band. We were good. And you blew it, Kelly.* They're starting off at the roundabout, where there's a police car parked up containing the two officers Kelly recognises as the ones who went round to Gemma's before Christmas.

'Dumb and Dumber,' says Gemma, leaning on their car. 'Should have known you'd be thick with this lot.'

The copper glowers at her. 'Off the car, Swarbrick. And we heard about those drums. We're going to get your dad, you mark my words. He's going to slip up soon, and we'll be waiting.'

'Eat my shorts,' says Gemma, sticking two fingers up to them. Kelly laughs. She really is good at taunting authority. Kelly looks at the march as it sets off. Arthur's at the front, with Keith Cardy and his boys. Arthur looks very smart. Her heart sinks as she sees her dad, right at the front with Cardy.

He gives her a look she can't read, and she gives him one back, which she hopes is as plain as day. *What are you doing here with these wankers? You're better than this.* Whether he gets the message or not, she sees his brow crinkle and he turns his gaze to his feet, like he'd rather be anywhere else in the world. Good, she thinks. I hope you feel like shit.

There's a lot of them, more than she expected, and when they all start chanting it makes a hell of a noise. They sound more menacing than encouraging, especially the England First and Foremost idiots, with their shaved heads. They look dangerous in the daylight, and Kelly thinks again how brave it was of Mick to go wading in to them. For her.

At the rear there's that little Graham band, all marching in formation. They're playing 'Jerusalem'. The day has been dull and overcast, and it's already starting to descend into gloom. The weather man said it might snow again.

'I'm freezing,' says Timmy. 'They're walking so slowly. It'll take ages to get up to the cemetery.'

'Yeah, and we don't really want to march with this lot,' says Kelly as they pass by the Rock Ferry Inn at a glacial pace. 'Let's cut through and wait for them up there.'

There are a few people at their doors or garden gates along the route, one or two have draped St George cross or Union Jack flags from their windows. They take a detour through the edge of the Avenues and into the cemetery, coming out of the main gates, right where the march is going to end up.

'Look,' says Gemma. 'We haven't spoken properly since we were in town the other day. It feels weird to end everything like this.'

'I'm not changing my mind,' says Kelly, looking down the road. 'There's no point. We're not allowed to have dreams.'

'Bullshit,' says Gemma. 'And you know it. It's just that people like us can't sit around and wait for dreams to come to us. We've got to go out and get them.'

Kelly looks at her sidelong. 'I thought you were just all about fitting in and keeping your head down?'

'Yeah, well, if you weren't such a gobby cow maybe I would still be like that,' says Gemma. 'You shouldn't give people hope if you're just going to snatch it away again.'

'Try telling that to my dad,' says Kelly.

'They're coming,' says Nicola, joining them with Timmy. And Kelly can hear a low hubbub of chanting, just as the march turns the corner and comes into view. The photographer from the paper crouches in the road and starts snapping off shots. The band is playing 'Land of Hope and Glory'. The EFAF boys are all chanting 'England First and Foremost', over and over again. Some of them are punching their fists in the air. They look an awful lot like the old pictures of Nazis that Kelly's seen on telly and in the school history books.

A little further up the road they've set up two rows of upturned beer crates, near to the where the canal towpath entrance is, and it's here that Cardy and Arthur make for, flanked by Kelly's dad and a couple of men in EFAF jumpers. It's right in full view of the Old Hall, and Kelly can see faces at the windows of the old pub, watching the proceedings impassively. They move up with the head of the march, stopping to lean on the fence. Kelly's dad catches her eye then looks away.

Everyone has cans of beer and starts to gather near the make-shift stage, save for Cardy, who's swigging directly from a bottle of whisky. Someone hands him the megaphone and he climbs on to the boxes, beckoning Arthur to follow him. When the bulk of the crowd has gathered, Cardy flicks on the megaphone, which wails with a squall of feedback, then booms, 'Welcome, everybody! Welcome to the fight to save Arthur's chapel!'

A cry of 'Hands! Off! Arthur's chapel!' goes up, and the crowd picks it up, chanting it in unison, the EFAF boys punching the air. Cardy listens to it for a moment – basks in it, thinks Kelly – then calls for quiet.

'This man,' says Cardy. 'This man, Arthur Calderbank. A bloody war hero. And what are they doing? Kicking him out of his own home. It's a disgrace.'

There are shouts of agreement. Cardy points a meaty finger at the Old Hall. 'For them. For people who have no right to be in this country. An absolute bloody disgrace.'

A good portion of the crowd starts pointing at the Old Hall, chanting, 'England First and Foremost!'.

Cardy carries on, mentions of Arthur and his chapel receding as he launches into a diatribe against immigrants and foreigners and asylum seekers, swigging from his whisky bottle. Kelly glances at the others. It was never what you'd call a carnival atmosphere, but the mood is darkening along with the skies. Cardy invites somebody from EFAF to take the stage, and he spits and hisses even more venom than Cardy did. Arthur looks distinctly uncomfortable, and Kelly is now sure it's nothing to do with being ill.

Women are coming around the gathering with trays of beer, which the crowd is sloshing down. The band strikes up again, with a song Kelly thinks is called 'I Vow To Thee, My Country'.

Chants of *England First and Foremost* rise up, almost drowning out the band. The crowd edges further up the road, closer to the Old Hall, stabbing fists and pointed fingers at the building, and the faces behind the windows. The front door to the old pub is ajar, and suddenly it opens a little further.

Kelly has one eye on the Old Hall, and doesn't see that her dad has extricated himself from the crowd and appeared at her side. He says, 'You should go home.'

She looks him in the eye. 'So should you.'

'Keith says you hit his son.'

'He deserved it.' She continues to stare at him. 'You should have heard what he was saying. I thought you'd be on my side, not Keith Cardy's.'

Her dad glances back at the makeshift stage. 'I'm not . . . I'm not really . . .'

'You're standing with them,' says Kelly with a shrug. 'That says it all. You should go back before Keith wonders where you are.'

Kelly can hear Cardy talking to Arthur, telling him it's his turn for the speech when the band has finished. Kelly's not sure anyone's interested in what Arthur has to say any more. Their blood is up and they're baying at the windows of the Old Hall, chanting and shouting.

'Fucking state of it,' Cardy says. He picks up the megaphone. 'Absolute state of it,' he shouts. 'Houses, hospitals, schools, benefits . . . they just want it all.' He puts the megaphone to his mouth and spits into it, 'Be quiet, please! We're here today for one reason, and one reason only.'

'Send 'em back!' shouts somebody, and the cry is taken up until Cardy bellows for quiet. 'We're here because the council, in its infinite wisdom, is planning to tear down part of this cemetery behind us to turn it into an accommodation centre for asylum seekers.' He looks around the crowd, nodding. 'Yes, you heard me right. A cemetery. A Christian cemetery. Consecrated ground. But more than that. The chapel in the middle of that graveyard is the home of this man. His name is Arthur Calderbank, and he's a war hero.'

291

A cheer goes up from the crowd. Cardy puts his arm around Arthur's shoulders. 'A war hero! Arthur Calderbank, everybody!'

To a round of massive applause, Cardy pushes the megaphone into Arthur's hands and steps down off the crates. Kelly leans forward. Puts the loudhailer to his mouth, then down again, and looks around at the faces turned up to him, the sea of people stretching right down the street.

Then Arthur lifts the megaphone up again, and begins to speak.

✳ 56 ✳

He's never liked being the focus of attention, has Arthur. He's never been one for giving speeches. Never had much to say. But now here he is, standing on a crate, a megaphone in his hand, and all these people. Hundreds of people. He looks around at them. Somebody shouts, 'Go on, Arthur!' and there's a ripple of applause.

He takes a deep breath. His mouth his dry and he can't think of a word to say. But he remembers his feverish dream – or was it real? – from the small hours, and what Molly, or his imagination, said to him.

There are people relying on you, Arthur. People waiting for you to do the right thing. People who you can help, and who can help you. People who you shouldn't let down.

'I'd like to thank you all for coming today,' he says haltingly. 'It means a lot.'

Buoyed up by the applause, he smiles, then catches the eye of Kelly, leaning on the cemetery fence. They're all there, The Mollies. Or, he supposes, just the gang, now that they've decided not to do the band. Shame that. They had promise. He coughs. Focus, Arthur, focus.

'You might have heard I'm a war hero,' he says. They cheer and applaud again. He half suspects they'd cheer and applaud if he just read out his shopping list. 'This country,' he says. 'This country is where heroes are born.' They love that. Emboldened, he says, 'Any single one of us here could be hero, in the right circumstances.'

Keith Cardy claps his hands together, looking round and nodding approvingly. Arthur's about to speak again but something catches his eye. The Old Hall door is slightly ajar, and it opens a little wider. A battered football bounces out and rolls to the gutter on the main road. Arthur frowns as a figure appears at the door then runs out, a tiny little girl with pink ribbons in her dark hair. She seems not to see or hear the crowd at first, until she reaches her ball and looks up, and blinks.

It's that little girl, the one who was playing with her dad in the cemetery.

Arthur feels the attention of the crowd shift and move, like it's a physical thing, turning away from him and sniffing towards the little girl, who's in the middle of the road, crouched over her ball, like a rabbit in front of a pack of wolves.

'Fucking state of it,' spits Cardy. He puts his fist in the air and roars, 'England for the English!' Then the crowd is pointing at her, chanting and chanting and her face is falling, and her mouth is quivering.

Somebody throws an empty plastic glass which bounces in the road. Then another figure runs out of the Old Hall, a man with dark hair and a leather jacket, who cries in anguish, 'Ajša! Ajša!'

The man crouches by the little girl as another empty cup hits the road near him. The crowd moves further forward, towards them.

'Should burn the fucking place down,' Arthur hears Cardy say. 'That's how you deal with vermin. Smoke 'em out.'

Arthur puts the megaphone back to his mouth, trying to win back the crowd's attention. 'Heroes,' he says, but the momentum seems lost.

'These are the people who want to take your home, Arthur,' Cardy takes the megaphone roughly from Arthur and shouts. 'Are we going to let 'em do it, lads?'

'Wait a minute,' says Arthur, but no one's listening to him any more. The crowd roars and moves even further forward. Then, from the canal towpath, another figure appears, tall and lean, running across the road and putting himself between the terrified father and daughter and the advancing mob.

Arthur stares at him. He recognises him.

It's Leon.

*

Arthur stares at Leon, standing in the road. A spot of rain hits him on the shoulder, then another on the nose. He takes a deep breath, and the air hurts his chest like a knife.

'Just look at that,' says Cardy, spitting. 'Is that him, Arthur? Is that the bastard who tried to sully your memories of Molly?'

'Aye,' says Arthur slowly. 'That's him.'

'You've no more bloody right to be here than the rest of 'em!' shouts Cardy.

'Go now!' shouts Leon. 'Leave these people be. You're scaring them.' He looks down. 'You're scaring a child.'

'Piss off!' bellows Cardy. 'Who do you think you are, telling us what to do? This is our country and we'll do what we want. You're one bloody man against the will of the people! England First and Foremost! England First and Foremost.'

As the chant goes up, Cardy pushes the megaphone into Arthur's hands. 'I think you need to say something, Arthur.'

Yes, thinks Arthur. I need to say something. I need to do something. He wishes Molly was with him. Wishes he had someone he could trust. Wishes he had a real friend to guide him, wishes he had family.

'Your dad was right,' says Timmy with a little whimper. 'We should get out of here. It's getting dangerous.'

But Kelly is just staring at Leon, standing in the middle of the road, in front of the little girl and the man, crouching behind him. Leon. He didn't go away after all. He came back. She follows his gaze, straight to Arthur's, some invisible cord connecting them.

'I think I agree with Timbo,' says Gemma softly. 'This is going to get really ugly.'

'Yeah, we should make a move,' says Kelly. 'Come on.'

She pushes herself off the fence and looks at the others. 'I said, come on.'

Then she walks into the road and over to Leon.

'Kel!' hisses Gemma from behind her. 'Oh, shit.'

She stands in front of Leon, and nods. 'All right?'

'All right, Kelly,' he says, his eyes still fixed on Arthur's. 'This isn't really the smart thing to do, you know?'

She takes up a position by his side, seeing Gemma dragging Timmy across to them, Nicola taking up the rear. It's different, facing the mob rather than walking with them. It's scarier, putting yourself in front of them instead of behind them. She says to Leon, 'Didn't you hear? We're Marigold Brook kids. We're from the Avenues. Nobody ever accused us of being smart.'

Gemma stands with her, and Timmy and Nicola go to the other side of Leon. Gemma says out of the corner of her mouth. 'Hope you know what you're doing.'

Kelly gives her the ghost of a smile. 'I'm Kelly Derricott. I always know what I'm doing.'

The crowd has fallen into a kind of confused silence since they walked out there, but someone shouts, 'England First and Foremost!'

'Fuck that shit!' shouts Kelly back.

Standing by Arthur, Keith Cardy hoots with laughter.

'Is that it? One bastard and four kids? We could take that bloody place down brick by brick if we wanted, and there's not a thing you could do about it,' he shouts. 'It's time we heard from Arthur.' He turns to Brian. 'That's your daughter out there, Derricott. Didn't I tell you to take her in hand? What sort of a father are you?'

The chant *Hands! Off! Arthur's Chapel!* is taken up, and Cardy nods encouragingly at Arthur. He takes a deep, painful breath. He has to focus. Remember why he's here. This was to save his home. He has to concentrate on what's right.

There are people relying on you, Arthur. People waiting for you to do the right thing. People who you can help, and who can help you. People who you shouldn't let down.

Arthur says through the loud-hailer, 'Wait.' The crowd falls silent. He looks at Leon, at The Mollies, at the girl sheltering in her father's arms. No, not her father, Arthur remembers. The man who took her on as his own, because she needed love. Just like Keith and his gang have taken Arthur on, though they didn't have to.

He takes a deep breath, strengthening his resolve. *People who you shouldn't let down.*

He points at the Old Hall, and says into the megaphone, 'This is a disgrace.'

The crowd breaks into a huge, triumphant cheer.

57

Cardy takes a triumphant swig of the whisky as the mob starts to cheer. Arthur gingerly steps off the box stage and pushes through the crowd until he gets to the road. He can hear Cardy behind him asking what the bloody hell's going on. Arthur keeps walking until he gets to the small group. The Mollies are beaming at him. Leon looks at him impassively.

'Arthur,' he says with a nod.

Arthur inclines his head back, 'Hello, Leon.'

Then he turns to the crowd and says into the megaphone, 'I don't think you understand me. *This* is a disgrace.' He waves his arm in their direction. '*You* are a disgrace.'

There's a momentary silence, then a rumble of muttering begins. Arthur cuts them off with a dismissive flick of his hand. 'Oh, shut up, the lot of you. You keep calling me a war hero. You're wrong. I just did what I was told. I shot a man because I was told I had to. That's not what heroes do.' He looks at Leon. 'Putting yourself in front of a crowd of drunken idiots to protect an innocent little kiddie, that's what heroes do. It's the bravest thing I've ever seen since a man called Peter Bergmann saved my life. A man you'd have called the *enemy*.'

Arthur shakes his head, looks from face to face in front of him. 'And you lot, you EFAF mob. You just don't get it, do you? You just don't get it. When I went to war . . .' Arthur closes his eyes, as though their stupidity is causing him physical pain. 'When I went to war, it was against people like you.'

There is silence. Arthur points at them. 'You. And you. And you. You were the enemy. You still are the enemy. People who pick on the weak. People who are scared of what they don't understand. People who get told their troubles are the fault of other people and believe it because it's easier than the truth . . . which is that you've been battered down because you've let the people you voted in on the back of hollow promises and fear batter you down.'

'You're wrong, Arthur!' shouts Cardy. He steps forward out of the crowd. 'You're wrong.'

'I'm right!' shouts Arthur back. He casts his arm at the Old Hall. 'These people . . . they're not coming here to take your benefits off you, Keith. They don't want your jobs or your houses. They're coming because they're running away from absolute horror. And it's our job to help them.'

Cardy points at Leon and The Mollies. 'You've had your head turned, Arthur. By these stupid kids. By this bastard who's wormed his way in.'

Arthur puts down the megaphone. 'Stop calling him a bastard, Keith. He's Molly's son.' Arthur closes his eyes.

Open your heart. Open your heart and then you'll know.

Arthur says, 'That makes him my son, too.' He puts the megaphone to his lips again. 'You can all go home now. It's over. I'm not going to stand in the way of the planning application. These people need homes more than I do. Go home. It's over.'

'Bollocks,' says Cardy. His bottle of whisky is a third full. Arthur frowns as he pulls a handkerchief out of his pocket, rolls it up, and stuffs it into the head of the bottle. 'Give me a tune,' shouts Cardy.

'What are you doing?' says Arthur in horror.

Cardy holds up the bottle, sloshing it around so the alcohol soaks the handkerchief. 'Taking matters into my own hands.'

The band starts playing. 'Three Lions'. Arthur frowns as the crowd starts swaying. Cardy turns around. 'What the fuck is this? I want something rousing. Like the bloody 'Ride of the Valkyries' or something.'

'Don't do this, Keith,' says Arthur quietly. 'Whatever you're going to do, don't.'

'Smoke out the vermin, like I said,' sneers Cardy. He reaches into his pocket and pulls out a lighter. He flicks it with his thumb, once, twice and on the third go it leaps into flame.

Then Leon's pushing in front of Arthur, and pointing at Cardy. 'Put that down. Now. Put it down.'

Cardy grins and puts the lighter to the whisky-soaked rag and it wooshes up into bright yellow flame. Arthur takes a step back. He's going to do it. He's really going to do it. He's going to throw it at the Old Hall, all those people . . .

'Do something, lad,' murmurs Arthur to Leon.

He turns, and Leon's eyes are wide, reflecting the flickering flame in Cardy's hand. Then Arthur remembers. The *Sir Galahad*. The fact Leon wouldn't go too close to the wood burner. Seeing your best mate burned to a crisp, diving into the sea while everything around you is on fire. Leon is shaking, his mouth working silently. The fire. It's bringing it all back.

'It's all right, Leon,' says Arthur softly. 'I understand.'

'Yeah,' says Cardy. 'It's all right. We understand.' He waves the burning bottle in front of Leon's face. 'Another fucking coward. Now get out of my way so I can sort this once and for all.'

Leon stands up straight, his fists clenched. 'Arthur was in the army,' he says. 'And so was I. I had time to do a lot of reading. Do you know what a man called Ralph Waldo Emerson once said?'

'Sounds like a foreigner,' shrugs Cardy. 'Or a poofter.'

'He said, a hero is no braver than an ordinary man, but he is brave five minutes longer.'

Then Leon steps forward, and with one big, powerful swing, knocks the bottle out of Cardy's hand. It skitters into the gutter then explodes, just as the rain starts to fall, heavy and cold and extinguishing the flames before they even have a chance to take hold.

And that, thinks Arthur, that is a hero.

'You bastards!' shouts Cardy, the rain hammering him, plastering his hair to his face. He turns around, looking for support from the mob. Instead he finds Brian Derricott, standing right behind him.

'You stepping up at last?' says Cardy.

'Yes,' says Brian. He brings back his fist and punches Cardy hard, once in the chin. Cardy sits down stupidly, hard, on the tarmac, rubs his chin, then flops backwards, unconscious.

'To answer your question, I'm *that* sort of father,' says Brian. He looks at Kelly. 'Is that how you do it, love?'

She smiles and runs to her dad, embracing him. 'It wasn't as good as mine, but yeah, that's how you knock a Cardy down.'

Arthur picks up the megaphone and faces the crowd. 'You can all go home now,' he shouts. They stand there, unsure what exactly has gone on. 'Go!' says Arthur again.

'Give it here,' says Gemma, taking the loudhailer. 'Free beer at the Rock Ferry Inn!' she shouts, and finally the mob starts to disperse, and head back the way they came.

It's over, thinks Arthur, then feels someone tugging at his coat. It's the little girl. Ajša, he remembers.

'Hello, nice man,' she says.

He smiles at her and her uncle picks her up. 'Thank you,' he says to Arthur. 'Thank you all.'

'Don't worry about it,' says Arthur. 'And if everything goes according to plan, you're going to have brand-new homes, soon.' He points at the chapel. 'Over there.'

Kelly looks at him. 'Really, Arthur? You're really going to let the chapel go?'

He smiles. 'Yes, I think I am.'

'But why?'

He thinks about last night. Dream? Real? He doesn't know, and he doesn't much care. 'Because it's what Molly would have wanted. I'm sure of that.'

Brian is looking worriedly at Cardy. 'You don't think I killed him, do you?'

Leon kneels down and feels his neck. Cardy groans, then breaks wind. 'Doesn't look like it. But maybe we should get him an ambulance, just in case.' He stands up.

Arthur closes his eyes. They feel hot. And he's shivering and sweating all at the same time. 'Yes,' he says. 'I think an ambulance would be a good idea.'

Then he slumps into Leon's arms and everything goes black.

58

The Mollies wait a little way from the ambulance while Leon talks to the paramedics, and then comes over to see them.

'They're pretty sure it's just the flu,' he says. 'But they're going to get him to hospital. They think he'll be all right.'

'Can we see him?' says Kelly.

'They said just for a minute. They'll wave us over when they're ready to go.' Leon looks at them all in turn. 'That was a brave thing you did, coming to stand with me.'

Gemma shrugs. 'You've got to do the right thing. God knows what would have happened if you hadn't been there.'

'We thought you'd gone for good after Christmas Eve,' says Kelly.

Leon nods. 'I was going to. I got a hostel and was planning to be away on Boxing Day. But something kept me here. I don't really know what. I felt like I hadn't finished it properly with Arthur. I wanted to be close by. I felt . . .' He frowns. 'I felt he might need me, for some reason.'

Timmy's eyes widen. 'That'll be Molly. A message from beyond the grave.'

Nicola punches him in the arm. 'Shut up, stupid.'

The paramedic waves at them and they crowd round the back of the ambulance, where Arthur is strapped into a chair, a breathing mask over his face. He looks pale and old and tired. He pulls off the breathing mask says, 'Bloody pneumonia.'

'Half a minute,' says the paramedic. 'Then we're off.'

Kelly says, 'Arthur, I just wanted to say that's the best thing I've ever seen anybody do. They were right after all, in a weird way. You *are* a hero.'

'Just not a war hero,' says Arthur.

'You're a peace hero!' says Timmy brightly. 'I think that's much better.'

'What will you do?' says Kelly. 'After you're well?'

'Revd. Brown took me to see a flat. I think I'll take him up on it if it's still available.'

'Won't you miss being near Molly though?' says Gemma.

Arthur smiles. 'I can visit her grave every day if I want. Besides, that's not Molly. Not really. That's not where she is.' He puts a hand to his chest. 'This is where she is.'

'Right,' says the paramedic. 'We're going to have to leave. Arthur, do you have any family? Is anyone coming with you?'

'And I'd very much like it if Leon came with me,' says Arthur.

The paramedic looks at Leon. 'Is he a relative?'

'He's my wife's son,' says Arthur. 'So he's family.' He looks at Kelly, Gemma, Timmy and Nicola. 'They're all family.'

The paramedic puts the breathing mask back over Arthur's face and helps Leon into the ambulance, then closes the doors. A paramedic is talking to Keith Cardy, who tells him loudly to fuck off out of it. He walks past them, shrugs and climbs into the ambulance, and it drives away.

'You should get off,' says Gemma to Kelly's dad, nodding at Cardy.

'I'm not scared of him. Or impressed. Not any more.'

'Yeah, but you don't want him to press charges for assault,' says Gemma, as the sound of sirens rises in the air, the police finally on their way. 'Don't worry, we'll say you never touched him.'

Kelly embraces her dad. 'Thank you,' she says. 'For doing the right thing.'

'Finally. I'm sorry for everything,' he says. 'I'm going to try to make things right.' He smiles, and Kelly feels her heart almost bursting. It's so long since she's seen him smile. 'Like that song, eh? 'Things Can Only Get Better'.' When her dad's gone, Keith Cardy finally drags himself to his feet. He looks around the almost empty road. The protest has melted away. He glares at the group and starts to walk over to them, his finger wagging, but then a strident shout of his name causes him to stop and turn angrily.

A woman, as big as he is, wearing an apron and a face that would stop traffic, is marching up the road, her arms folded across her chest. 'Keith! Keith! Come fucking home right now!'

Cardy glares at her. 'Kathleen. I'm busy.'

'Not as busy as you're going to be. It's Colin.'

Cardy sighs. 'What's the little shit done now?'

'He's only gone and got some bird up the duff. And a posh bird as well. Her bloody mum and dad are at our house, playing merry hell. Get home now,' says Kathleen, glancing at The Mollies then staring back at Keith.

Cardy frowns. 'A posh bird? Our Colin?'

'Heather Wilson,' says Kathleen, then grabs Cardy by the collar. 'Home. Now. And sort this fucking out.'

Kelly and Gemma look at each other, mouths gaping, then high-five as Kathleen drags her husband back down the road.

And then the four of them are alone in the rain-slicked road. It's almost properly dark.

'Well,' says Kelly. 'What are we supposed to do now?'

'We can't even go to Arthur's chapel,' says Nicola.

'What did you used to do before the band?' says Timmy.

Gemma frowns. 'I can really remember there being a *before*.'

'I suppose we should probably just go home, then.' The thought of it fills Kelly with a dull ache, a widening void. Not because she doesn't want to be with her parents, but because she doesn't want to not be with her friends. 'School starts on Monday.'

They all pull faces at each other. Can they really just go back to school and settle back into their old lives, just like that? Has it really all been for nothing? She thinks about the Battle of the Bands competition. That's tonight. Was it all just a stupid dream, thinking they could even get there, never mind win? Kelly's fingers itch, like she needs to put them on a guitar fret. She glances at Gemma, who's absently drumming her fingers on her things. Timmy is tapping his foot to some unheard tune. Nicola has that look of concentration on her face she always has when she's playing the bass.

A big white van crests the hill by the Old Hall and coasts to a stop near them. The driver leans out of his window, frowning at banners and flags abandoned on the road, then leans over to the passenger side and winds down the glass.

'What's going on here?' he says. He's a lad in his twenties. Manchester accent. Quite fit, thinks Kelly.

'Long story,' says Gemma.

The driver glances down at something on the passenger seat. 'Does anybody know Marlborough Drive? Am I close?'

'That's my street,' says Kelly. 'What do you want there?'

The driver puffs his cheeks out. He looks down at the passenger seat again, and says, 'Do you know a Kelly Derricott?'

Kelly blinks. 'I'm Kelly Derricott!'

He narrows his eyes. 'Yeah, yeah, you'd say anything. What number do you live at?'

'Nineteen!'

He reads whatever's on the seat again. 'And what's your dad's name?'

'Brian!' She pauses. 'He was just here. But he didn't hit anybody.'

The driver pulls a face. 'Never said he has, did I?' He peers at the other three. 'And I suppose this is your band. Remind me what you're called again?'

Kelly is confused. 'The Mollies. But I don't understand.'

He hands something through the window. It's a letter. 'This was sent to the Creation head office. You're lucky there was some intern in over Christmas. She sent it over to us.'

'Creation?' says Kelly. 'As in Creation Records?'

'Yeah,' grins the driver. 'Are you going to read that, or what? It's Saturday night and I went to get back to Manc to have it large.'

Kelly reads the letter, then reads it again, then has to read it again, because the second time she's crying so much.

'Well?' says Gemma, irritated. 'What is it?'

Dear Mr Gallagher,

I can't say I'm a big fan of your music but I've listened to my daughter Kelly's CD and it's not bad. You've probably got a bit of a future. More of a Status Quo man myself. But Kelly's obsessed with you.

The thing is, Mr Gallagher, she formed a band. They're called The Mollies. They're very good, by all accounts. My Kelly plays the guitar, just like you. You're sort of her hero. She's not 15 yet.

But I've basically buggered it all up for her. I smashed her guitar up. I was angry and sad and I've been out of work for a bit. Now she says the band is over. I wrecked her dreams along with that guitar.

Kids like Kelly, they need dreams. They don't get much of anything else. Times have been tough for us and I can't afford to buy her a new guitar. Not yet. But I read up on you, and you seem a decent bloke, though your brother seems a bit of an arse. I know you're working class like us. You probably never had much either. I hope that means you know where she's coming from.

She's a good kid, Kelly, and so are her mates. They're trying to make something of themselves when everybody else writes them off. Everybody including me, her own dad. So I was wondering if you could do something. I was thinking if you've got time you could write her a letter, maybe tell her not to give up on her dreams.

It might go some way to making up for what I've done, until I can make it up to her properly myself. So I hope you get this letter and I hope you're able to help in some way.

Yours,

Brian Derricott.

P.S. Please don't tell your brother I said he was a bit of an arse. Kelly would kill me.

Kelly hands the letter round to the others and they all read it in silence. Gemma says, 'Do you actually know Noel Gallagher, then?'

'I'm one of his crew, yeah,' says the guy.

Kelly says impatiently, 'Did he send one, then, a note? Why didn't he just post it?'

'No note. Sorry.'

'So what are you doing here? Did you drive over from Manchester just to give my dad his letter back?'

'No.' He reaches over the passenger seat into the back of the van and hauls something out. 'I drove over to give you this.' He passes it through the open window.

Kelly forgets to breathe for longer than she can count.

'An Epiphone Sheraton,' she says, reverently taking the guitar emblazoned with a Union Jack from the driver's hands. 'Noel Gallagher's guitar.'

'Not his actual one, that's a sixties original. But one he had lying around.'

Kelly stares at him. 'And he's actually giving it to me?'

He smiles. 'He's actually giving it to you.'

She looks at the others, who are all staring at it wide-eyed, like it's the Holy Grail or something. Then she looks back to the driver. 'Did he not say anything at all?'

He screws his face up. 'Oh, yeah, he did. He said, "Tell her if she plays any fookin' Blur songs on it, I'm having it back".'

He starts up his engine. 'Going to do a three-pointer and get back to Manc.' Before he winds the window up he says, 'Good luck, The Mollies. Live forever, eh?'

They watch the van turn and disappear back over the hill, then Kelly looks down at the guitar in her hands.

'I cannot believe that just happened,' says Timmy.

'Noel Gallagher sent you a guitar,' says Nicola numbly.

'What are you going to do with it?' says Gemma.

Kelly looks at her like she's mad. 'Do with it? What do you think I'm going to do with it? Nic, what time is it?'

Nicola looks at her watch. 'Half five. Why?'

Kelly breaks out into a big grin. 'Don't just all stand there. We've got a Battle of the Bands to win.'

59

'Jesus, Nic, you're cutting it a bit fine,' says Des as they barge into Maxine's nightclub in town. 'You're on in twenty minutes.'

'Did that band say we could use their amps and drum kit?' says Nicola. 'You're really sure?'

'Yeah, I squared it with them straight after you called me,' says Des. He looks at Kelly's guitar and whistles. 'You got one, then?'

'Direct from Noel Gallagher,' says Gemma.

Des laughs. 'Yeah, right. There's a room at the back you can get ready in. One more band on before you. Tune up quick as you can, three songs, then off, right?'

'We've only got two,' Kelly says.

Des shrugs. 'Well, play one twice, then.'

In the lobby of the nightclub, the parents crowd together. Kelly's mum and dad, Nicola's mum, Gemma's dad and Crushing Ken, even Timmy's parents, dressed as though they're going to the opera and looking distastefully around.

'Crushing hell, kid, I'm proud of you,' says Crushing Ken to Gemma.

Her dad grins. 'Me too, Gem. This is brilliant. You've got a chance, you know. A chance to not just be Terry Swarbrick's daughter.'

'There's nothing wrong with being Terry Swarbrick's daughter,' she says, hugging her dad.

'Aye, well, it'll open doors if you ever find yourself in Strangeways,' says Crushing Ken. 'Not literally, like. But you know what I mean.'

∗

'Come on,' says Kelly. 'We're wasting time.'

In the room – little more than a broom cupboard – Kelly squeezes into the cargo pants Gemma nicked and her Adidas tracksuit top. '"Rock 'N' Roll Star", then "Things Can Only Get Better".' She imagines herself up on that stage in the darkened club, the lights flashing, making music.

'Does anybody else feel sick?' says Gemma.

'Pretend the audience isn't there,' says Nicola. 'Just focus on the music.'

'We can do this,' says Kelly encouragingly, though she feels as sick as anyone. 'We can. We're The Mollies. This is our big chance. We can do this.'

'I can't do this.'

They all look at Timmy. Gemma sighs. 'I knew it.'

He's sitting on the floor, cross-legged, rocking gently. 'I can't do it. I can't go out there and sing.'

'You can,' says Kelly firmly. 'You can. You're a brilliant singer. Just do what Nicola said. Pretend we're in the chapel. Close your eyes if you have to.'

He shakes his head violently. 'I can't do it.'

'Timmy,' says Gemma warningly. 'I swear to God, if you make us look—'

'Shush,' says Kelly. She squats down before Timmy. 'Why? Why can't you do it?'

He looks up at her, his eyes brimming. 'Because . . . because when I sing, in the chapel, with you, it's all right. Because of Arthur. Because he told me to focus on his face. That's why I couldn't do it at the Black Diamond. Because he wasn't there.'

'Five. Minutes,' says Gemma through gritted teeth. 'Don't blow this for us, Timmy.'

There's a knock at the door and Des pops his head round. Kelly looks at him desperately. 'Yes, we know. We're nearly ready.'

'Somebody to see you,' he says, and opens the door wider. And there, sitting in a wheelchair, Leon behind him, is Arthur.

'Thank God,' says Gemma.

'Well,' Arthur says. 'I couldn't exactly miss this, now, could I?'

*

They troop out of the dressing room, Leon pushing Arthur in front, and Kelly sees her mum and dad standing in front of the stage. She smiles and throws her arms around him. 'Thank you. Thank you so much.'

'I must say, I wasn't expecting an actual guitar,' he says. He puts his arm around Mum and they look at each other.

Her mum says, 'We've got some news. We didn't have time to tell you before, but Dad got a letter today. From Mr Oldfield. He's invited him back for an interview next week.'

'For a different job,' says Dad. He bites his lip. 'Only thing is, it might not be round here . . .'

'But we can sort that out later,' says her mum quickly. She kisses Kelly on the cheek. 'Go and enjoy yourself. We'll be cheering you on from here.'

Des is on the stage, tapping the mic and calling for order. 'Next band is on now. Give it up, Maxine's, for The Mollies!'

Kelly leads them up on to the stage, and turns around to see Arthur climbing out of the wheelchair. Leon helps him up the steps, but Des interjects, holding out his hands. 'Whoa, whoa, whoa, what's going on here, grandad?'

Arthur frowns. 'I'm getting up on stage with them. It's the lad, you see. He can't sing unless I'm there.'

Des looks at Kelly who smiles and nods. 'It's OK. It's Arthur. He's with the band.'

'Really?' says Arthur.

'Really,' says Kelly. 'We wouldn't be here without you.'

He looks at her for a long time. 'And I'm not sure I would be here without you.'

Gemma hands Arthur a pair of maracas left on the stage by the previous band. 'Just shake these. You can be our Bez.'

'I've no idea what a Bez is,' grunts Arthur. 'But I can probably do that. But first I want to say something.'

Arthur taps a finger on the mic and clears his throat. The audience quiets, more out of bemusement than respect, thinks Kelly. But they listen to Arthur as he starts to speak.

'I can't pretend to understand half of this modern music,' he says. 'And I like even less of it. But I do know one thing. These kids are bloody brilliant. And I don't just mean at being a band. I mean at being people. Human beings. Thanks to this lot, I've found the son I never knew about.' He turns around and meets Kelly's gaze. 'I've found a family, just when I'd given up on life.'

Arthur squints into the lights. 'Folks like us, we're not given much encouragement. We're told to accept our lot in life, to like it or lump it. But everybody can do something. Everybody can have a dream. And we just have to stop telling kids like this they'll never amount to anything.' Arthur trails off, and says softly, 'My Molly, she could have been a writer.' Then he coughs, and says, 'Well, that's enough from me. We hope you enjoy the concert.'

Arthur turns and pats Timmy on the shoulder. 'I'll stand over here, in the corner, shaking these maracas. You just look at me if you feel wobbly, all right?'

Timmy nods, and he looks less pale than he did before. Bloody hell, Kelly thinks, we might actually be able to pull this off.

Then she looks out at the crowd. There are hundreds of them, it seems like. Butterflies are bashing about in her stomach. There's a prolonged bout of clapping and some foot stamping. Her hands feel sweaty and she can feel a tickling at the back of her neck.

She looks at Gemma, behind the drums, at Nicola, on the bass, at Timmy, pouting and snake-hipped at the mic. Arthur, giving the maracas an experimental shake. And suddenly time seems to slow and stretch. She can hear the beating of her own heart, feel the exhalation of air from her lungs.

This is it.

This is exactly it.

She's suddenly connected to herself a month ago, sitting in Mr Green's office, being told that she was bad at this, rubbish at that, desultory at the other. Having it stuffed in her face that she was worthless, that she would amount to nothing, that she could expect only the bare minimum in life. Because of who she was, because of where she lived, because of the way she talked and the numbers on her parents' bank balance.

Fuck that shit, thinks Kelly Derricott.

I'm as good as you, she thinks. I'm as good as anyone. We all are. If only we refuse to believe them when they say we're not.

She looks out at all the people in the club, every one of them the same as her, but different in their own ways. And all it takes is for someone to believe in you, or you to believe in yourself, and things can change so much in such a little time.

Her head feels on fire, but it's a good feeling, like she's harnessed lightning. Her fingers effortlessly find their places on the fretboard. Gemma is looking at her. Nicola is looking at her. Timmy is looking at her. And Arthur, Arthur is looking at her as well. They're all there, together. Just as it's meant to be.

The Mollies, she thinks. We're The Mollies. And we can do anything.

Slowly, she nods at Gemma, who counts them in with four steady taps on the rim of the snare drum. School on Monday, she thinks. GCSEs next year. And after that? And after that? And that? Who knows. It doesn't matter. The future is there, waiting for them, and they'll make of it what they will.

But this is here. This is now.

And today, thinks Kelly Derricott, today, I'm a rock and roll star.

'Hit it!' she shouts.

Twenty-Three Years Later

We didn't win, of course.

But The Mollies put on their first, best – and last – performance of their lives. I don't count the Black Diamond debacle, obviously. We came third at Maxine's, which surprised pretty much everyone. The judges said we had a bright future. And, really, that's all that I wanted. To know we could be better than everyone who wrote us off thought we could. Even Heather Wilson had to keep her mouth shut at school on Monday. We made the local paper.

Dad's interview went well, and they offered him a job. The only thing was, it was at a factory in Herefordshire. He started the following month, and in March me and Mum moved down. By May, Tony Blair and New Labour had won the election, and that old tune, 'Things Can Only Get Better', had been used as their campaign song. It was everywhere. Mick stayed up north. Got away with a fine for the fight in the Black Diamond. Him and Jane had two kids, then they split up and he moved down near us.

I started at a new school, forgot about Marigold Brook. I began to find out I was better than people thought, especially at English. I made new friends. I lost touch with Gemma, Nicola and Timmy, and then forgot about them, other than as part of that strata of childhood that's always with you but which you rarely think about. The internet was in its infancy then, social media still a decade away. We might have kept in touch better if we'd have had Twitter and Facebook, but we had nothing other than the ties that bound us together; distance and time stretched and eventually snapped them.

I did A Levels and went to university. I got a job on my local newspaper, and then did some work for the nationals as a reporter and feature writer in London. I wrote a book, which nobody ever read, then another one, which some people did, then a third, which was quite successful.

An auntie let us know that Arthur died in 2009. I was briefly sad, but, again, it was all part of that world I'd left behind. I'd got married in 2004. I had a daughter. I got divorced.

When I heard that Leon had died last week, it brought everything flooding back, all the things that had happened that Christmas, all those people I'd moved on from. When we're young we always think those days are going to last forever, that we'll have the same friends until we die. And then, often, life happens. Life that had made me barely register Arthur's death when my mother told me in a phone call, when I was probably trying to do some work or arguing with my husband or chasing my daughter Molly around the house.

Oh, yes, I should have said. I called my daughter Molly. Perhaps some things stay with us, after all. But hearing of Leon's passing made me think of Arthur, and how there was no one to remember him now, and after everything that happened – after all he did for me– it seemed only right and proper that I should finally come home.

I admit that at first I perhaps had an inkling that it might be the start of a book or something. *The Moonflower Mysteries*, heh. I was late for the funeral, of course, stupid trains. Wrong kind of snow. By the time I got to the old place, and had secured a bunch of moonflowers – which wasn't easy, but seemed appropriate – it was dark.

I learned later, after looking at the old newspaper reports that had been put online from 1996, that after the rally, Arthur had indeed rescinded his objections to the planning application and it went ahead. They didn't demolish the old chapel, though, they turned it into a community hub for the new residents of the development. They called it Calderbank House, which was nice. Leon was given a job there, pretty much as the same thing Arthur had been, a caretaker and groundsman, and a small apartment. The plans were

314

altered slightly, so not as many graves were moved. Molly stayed where she was. Arthur moved into sheltered accommodation, but visited Molly's grave pretty much every day, as far as I knew. Leon and Arthur were inseparable.

It's only when I'm in the cemetery that it all properly hits me, as though walking those paths has unlocked the stories I'd packed away as part of a life I no longer lived or cared about. I brought two bunches of flowers; the first I place on Leon's fresh grave. The second I put down on Molly's. Or, rather, Molly and Arthur's. His name is carved beneath hers; they're together at last.

It's then I hear the fine crunch of footsteps and a lost but familiar voice says quietly, 'Gotcha.'

I almost don't recognise Gemma. She's slim and looks great, looks younger than I do. She's vaping, blowing out strawberry scented clouds. I later learn that after school she, sadly but perhaps inevitably, got into trouble and even got a three months' suspended sentence for burgling a warehouse. Then she went back to college and resat her GCSEs, then did A Levels. Then, somewhat astonishingly, took a law degree. She's a defence solicitor now, working for a big firm in Manchester. And pretty successful and well-known, by all accounts. Poacher turned gamekeeper.

I can tell Nicola straight away, still stocky, still wearing those glasses, her hair now a vibrant pink. The third figure is a man with a paunch and a bald head, wearing a dark suit. It takes me a moment before I say, 'Timmy?'

'Doctor Timothy Leigh,' he says loftily, then smiles. 'But I suppose Timmy will do.'

Then we fall together for a hug, the four of us, all knocking on forty but, in some small way, fourteen forever.

'Still got Noel's guitar?' asks Gemma. 'Still play it?'

'I've got it, but I never play. Did you keep the band going?'

'We tried, after Maxine's,' says Timmy. 'We did a couple of rehearsals. But it wasn't the same, Kelly. Not without you.'

And suddenly, surprisingly, I feel a rush in my head, and my tears come, and the last almost quarter of a century whizzes past my eyes and none of it seems as bright and as relevant as the time I spent with these three, as the things we did.

'I read your books,' says Nicola. 'They were good.' Nicola has a rainbow knitted cardigan on, festooned with badges proclaiming causes from *Reverse Brexit* to *Hope Not Hate* to *Immigration Works*. The apocalypse her mum feared never came; or at least, not the one she was expecting. Maybe we're constantly facing lots of little apocalypses, and perhaps it's people like Nicola who fight them most strongly.

'You live in London?' says Gemma to me.

I nod. 'I hate it. Too busy and expensive. But my daughter is in her last year at school and I don't want to disrupt that.' I pause. 'You all still live around here?'

'I live in Manchester,' says Gemma. 'But I come home a lot to see my family. Mainly to give free legal advice.' She rolls her eyes. 'Dad's not changed at all.'

Timmy has a GPs practice in town, Nicola did indeed go to the Royal Northern College of Music and now teaches music. At Marigold Brook. 'It's in special measures,' she says. 'It's got its challenges. But they're good kids.'

They always were, I think. They just needed someone to believe in them.

'Anybody fancy a drink?' says Gemma. The others nod. Gemma looks at me. 'My car's on the road. We can go into town.'

They begin to walk away and I watch them for a moment before following. Time and distance had brushed these people from my thoughts, left them lurking there deep in my memories, subsumed by school and work and success and marriage and divorce. But just being here, in the cemetery, back where it all began . . . I can feel those layers I'd built around the girl, who was next to useless and would never amount to anything, I can feel them cracking and falling from me like dust. Like it's not 2019, but 1996 all over again. And I look down at the old Kelly Derricott who's been hiding inside me all this time, and I think, you know what, you weren't bad. You weren't as bad as everyone wanted you to think you were.

The three of them pause a little way ahead, painted by silver moonlight, and turn back to me. Gemma says, 'Kelly? Are you all right? Are you coming?'

But I just stand there, and look at them. At us. The lawyer, the teacher, the doctor, the writer. The kids who never had a chance, and didn't know they were allowed to dream, until they met the old man who never had a family, and had forgotten how to love. Arthur Calderbank and The Mollies. So different, and yet, in some ways, so much the same. I can't stop myself breaking out into a wide grin. 'Hey,' I say slowly. 'I've just had a brilliant idea.'

Timmy blinks owlishly. Nicola frowns. Gemma puts a manicured hand to her face. 'Oh, God, Kelly. What?'

I shake my head, open my arms, and say to my friends I should never have let slip from my life, 'You know what we're going to do? We're going to get the band back together . . .'

THE END

90s playlist

The 1990s was a fluid, organic, remarkable thing that refused to be contained in anything as mundane as ordinary measurements of time. It started, probably, sometime around what we called the Second Summer of Love in 1988 or 1989, or maybe when the The Iron Curtain was parted, and it ended with the bombing of the World Trade Centre in 2001. In between, everything was an exciting, optimistic, cross-pollinated mess. But a largely good mess. The music was incredible, and bands and artists were kicking down the sides of their pigeonholes and crossing over into everyone else's. Indie bands had suddenly "always had a dance element to our music", techno bands were sampling guitar riffs and bombastic prog rock choruses, DJs became best friends with shoe gazers, everybody in the top half of England claimed to be from Manchester, and there were bands that nobody could explain, who threw everything into the mix all at once, like the Happy Mondays.

The 1990s crystallised when Tony Blair's New Labour swept to power in 1997 and the new Prime Minister invited Noel Gallagher to a party at Number 10. His brother Liam appeared with then partner Patsy Kensit on the cover of Vanity Fair, beneath a Union Jack duvet and with the legend London Swings Again. Geri Halliwell wore a Union Jack dress for the Spice Girls' performance at the 1997 Brit Awards, and suddenly it was all right to have pride in Britain again, the country's colours were seized back from the racists and fascists and meat-headed idiots and while there would never stop being wars around the world, including ones the UK were involved in, at least for a short period the biggest conflict making the evening news was whether Blur or Oasis would get to number one in the charts.

I've made a playlist of songs that would make a good accompaniment to this novel. If you're on Spotify you can listen to it here: https://sptfy.com/8S33

I'll probably keep adding to it, but in the meantime, here is an essential top ten of 90s tunes I think sum up Things Can Only Get Better; I'm including Concierto de Aranjuez which, while written in 1939, did appear in the 1996 film Brassed Off. That's the 90s all over really; we made our own rules, for one glorious decade that lasted at least 13 years.

Things Can Only Get Better - D:Ream
Rock 'n' Roll Star - Oasis
Smells Like Teen Spirit - Nirvana
Wannabe - The Spice Girls
Born Slippy (Nuxx) - Underworld
Country House - Blur
Common People - Pulp
Wrote For Luck - The Happy Mondays
Concierto de Aranjuez - Joaquin Rodrigo
All Together Now - The Farm

David Barnett, somewhere in a field in Cornwall, Summer 2019.

Acknowledgments

Authors are, by and large, awful people.

We're egotistical enough to think that anything we write needs to get out there and be read by complete strangers. We're selfish, and think – sometime secretly, sometimes not so – that our job is more interesting and worthy of talking about that anyone else's. We have such a high opinion of ourselves that, in fact, it isn't merely a job we do, it's a vocation, it's a compulsion, it's a form of magic. We expect our loved ones to indulge us, to patiently wait for their questions to be answered as we fix the wall with a thousand-word stare and ignore everything around us while we wrestle with a knotty plot problem. We want to be supported, emotionally and financially, while we lose ourselves in the made-up lives of unreal people in order to, on average, earn less than the minimum wage.

And, at the end of it all, we want our names emblazoned across the cover of our book, so we can shake it at the world and declare, this. This is what I did.

Yes, the author's name is on the cover and yes, they came up with the story and wrote all the words, eventually getting them in pretty much the right order. But making a book is very much a team effort.

Up to now, most of the people in that team haven't got much of a mention. My UK publisher Trapeze is attempting to rectify this a little, and in this book you will find a couple of pages of movie-style credits, detailing those who have done their bit to bring this book into your hands, or on to your screen. It's about time, really, and it certainly saves the writer the anxiety, when writing an acknowledgements piece like this, of missing out whole tranches of people who've helped to make the book a reality.

There are plenty of people not named in the credits, because they don't work directly for the publishers. I've been lucky enough to have a lot of foreign territory deals for my books, and at each one of those publishers in far-flung places there is a similar team, with the added wonderfulness of the translators who make the prose sing in a different tongue.

As an author my day-to-day work (when I'm not pretending to be a tortured artist, creating in my garret) mainly involves direct contact with my agent, editor and publicists. See, I say "my" as though they are minions to do my bidding; awful people, writers.

John Jarrold is my agent; and he's been a wonderful presence in both my professional and personal life for many years now. A tip of the hat to him, as ever. Editor-wise, this book started off in the hands of Sam Eades, who is brilliant, and then passed on to Katie Brown, who is also brilliant, when Sam went on maternity leave. And if you read a review of this book somewhere or saw someone talking about it in a magazine, newspaper or on social media, that was probably the doing of Alex Layt.

They, and people like them who do the same jobs, all indulge the author's general awfulness, to some extent. They are patient when we are having strops and tantrums. They don't get angry when we decide to do something that is completely different to what we said we would do. They are tactful and diplomatic when our ideas are stupid.

But we are perhaps most indulged by our loved ones (a special shout-out to my mum Muriel here, to who I owe a great debt), our family and our friends. They let us talk about ourselves and our books, and show the kind of interest that only true friends can, but are quick to bring us down to earth when we are in danger of taking off, filled with our own hot air. This is especially true of my wife, Claire, who has put up with my authorly awfulness for many, many years now, has supported me when times have been bad, and allowed me to celebrate with her when times have been good. I couldn't do this writer thing without any of the people mentioned in this book, but most especially her.

Therefore, know this about the book you're holding, and the next one you pick up, and the one after that: Authors are, by and large, awful people. So it's a very good job we're surrounded by absolute diamonds.

David Barnett
West Yorkshire
2019

CREDITS

Trapeze would like to thank everyone at Orion who worked on the publication of Things Can Only Get Better in the UK.

Editor
Katie Brown

Editorial Management
Charlie Panayiotou
Jane Hughes
Alice Davis
Shyam Kumar

Audio
Paul Stark
Amber Bates

Contracts
Anne Goddard
Paul Bulos
Jake Alderson

Design
Lucie Stericker
Joanna Ridley
Nick May
Clare Sivell

Helen Ewing

Finance
Emily-Jane Taylor
Jasdip Nandra
Afeera Ahmed
Elizabeth Beaumont
Sue Baker
Victor Falola

Marketing
Amy Davies

Production
Claire Keep
Fiona McIntosh

Publicity
Alex Layt

Sales
Jen Wilson
Victoria Laws

Esther Waters
Rachael Hum
Ellie Kyrke-Smith
Frances Doyle
Ben Goddard
Georgina Cutler
Barbara Ronan
Andrew Hally
Dominic Smith
Maggy Park
Linda McGregor
Sinead White
Jemimah James

Rachel Jones
Jack Dennison
Nigel Andrews
Ian Williamson
Julia Benson
Declan Kyle
Robert Mackenzie

Operations
Jo Jacobs
Sharon Willis
Lisa Pryde